Chasing Still Water
Naughty Book Four

Christine Young

ISBN: 978-1-62420-803-4

Credits
Cover Artist: Designs by Ms G
Editor: Sherry Derr-Wille

Printed in the United States of America

Chapter One

Missouri 1836

Still Water Runs Deep watched the wagon train move with lazy speed along the rutted-out road. They'd been on the trail five days now. The train of wagons was over fifty miles west of Independence where they began the long journey to a new life. For the benefit of the people he scouted for, he was called Stephen Wilkes. That was the name he would go by until he reached Lakota territory. He breathed in the clean prairie scented air, eager to reach Fort Laramie where he would head north into more rugged country. This would be his last trip to the lands of his people. With the help of the Earl of Blackmore, he bought property in England, land that adjoined the earl's holdings. While he was eager to see his mother, he was also excited to begin his new life.

Wiping sweat from his forehead, he thought of Chauncey. Thought of the kiss they shared behind the church the day his friend, the Earl of Blackmore, wed Lyssa Andrews for the third time. This one was their second kiss. Chauncey didn't know anything about kissing. Now, he was leaving her behind. While his friend the earl found love with a white woman, he doubted if the miracle would happen a second time. Lightning didn't strike twice in the same place. Before he left, he told her to find someone else. She argued. He stood his ground. The notion gave him reason to smile. When he cupped her breast in his hand, roamed with leisure across the hardening tip with his thumb, she gasped then jerked back, her eyes so wide they reminded him of the blue saucers the earl used with his tea cups. She was untried, innocent in every way. He wanted her.

When he absconded with an intimacy he had no right taking, she ran her sweet tongue across her bottom lip. She didn't understand the gesture was an invitation to him. The tip was an enticing pink color. He wanted to be the man to teach her how to kiss as well as how to please him. The timing was all shot to hell. Slow and measured, he'd brought his hand up to her chin. Holding it with his hand, he ran his thumb across the dewy softness he found there wishing he dared hope for more.

He didn't.

He understood the differences in their way of life. She would never fit his expectations for a wife. She was everything he wasn't. She was cultured. His life until he lived in England for several years was primitive as well as savage. She was pure white. He fought against the white settlers encroaching on land that didn't belong to them. Killed some when he had to defend himself. Took more than one scalp.

"I'm leaving tomorrow," he told her regretting his decision for an instant. He wasn't the man for her. If he stayed and courted her, she would eventually come to hate him. Still Water Runs Deep understood he needed to be harsh with her. "I'll be back when I'm good and ready. Not a minute sooner. Don't wait for me. Find a nice man who is white who lives in your way. Marry him. Have white children."

"Where are you going?"

Her query was hesitant as well as curious. She touched his thumb with her tongue. She wasn't listening to him. "I would go with you."

After that she set her small white hand on his chest. The nails were clean, manicured. If she traveled with him that would change all too soon. The nails he looked at now would become ragged, dirt would settle in the nailbeds. Where he was traveling would not suit this delicate woman.

Unable to help himself he touched her lips with his once more. Wishing this wasn't for the last time, he kissed her again, drawing her closer to him with his hand settled with possessiveness he didn't wish to acknowledge on the small of her back then sliding the palm lower to cup her adorable backside. If he took her here behind the church, she would be willing. Her father would have his head as was his right. He reminded himself he was leaving. She would find someone more suitable. At the thought deep raw pain sluiced through him.

Her fingers shaking, she touched him, responded to his ill-advised advance, meeting his tongue with hers. Rising on the tips of her toes, she wound her small hands behind his neck. She wasn't a short woman but she didn't come to his chin. He needed to find a female who was sturdier.

Deep and low in the back of his throat, he groaned his voice hoarse. She drew back, looking at him, questions in her vibrant sapphire blue eyes. Eyes that were darkening with the rising passion he seemed to be generating in her.

Once again, he cupped her small breast in his hand, smoothed the hidden tip with his finger, wishing he dared move the tiny sleeves of her gown lower so he could see her breasts, touch as well as suckle. He wanted to discover the color of the tender buds that even now were responding to him, hardening more with each pass of his finger. One more time he needed to remind himself that if he did what he was thinking, he would ruin her for another man. He had no business here. Nothing good could come from this dalliance behind the church.

When he looked at her bosom then back to her eyes, she looked embarrassed. She cleared her throat before she spoke. "They are not very big, nothing like Lyssa's. I would that I were larger...men like..."

He chuckled understanding what she spoke of. Lifting her chin, he kissed the tip of her nose, after that her forehead. Besotted with the woman, he couldn't stop the grin. "A man doesn't need more than a mouthful."

"A mouthful?" She blinked a few times as if mulling over his statement. "I don't understand what you're saying."

An innocent would never understand. She was so damn sweet, too tasty for the likes of him. "Yes. I'd like to taste you. Would you like that, Chauncey? Would you like my mouth to discover your flavor? What do you taste like? Your lips taste like mint along with the sweet red Bordeaux you drank a few minutes ago. They intoxicate me. What about the rest of you?" He fell silent watching the changing expressions on her lovely face.

"Intoxicate? The rest of me?"

Again, she blinked a few times before running one hand along his chest where she now stared.

Chuckling, he asked, "Are you a little parrot?"

He was enjoying himself the unsolicited pleasure immense. He'd never been with an innocent. Even in his formative years, the women who came to his bed were experienced.

Chauncey was delicious.

"Parrot?"

He laughed again while he ran his fingertip down her nose. He did want to kiss her again. They needed to return to the celebration before someone, her father, came to look for her. It was necessary for him to voice his thoughts. "Come along, little parrot, we need to get back to the festivity before anyone misses us."

"No." Her body tensing, she held her ground her lips formed into a thin line. Her chin tilted at an angle. He was beginning to understand that expression. "I want to know where you are going? Why are you leaving tomorrow?"

Leaning against the church, he tugged her back into his arms. Stephen spread his legs, cradling her next to his arousal, wondering if she felt how much he wanted her. He imagined it wouldn't hurt to tell her what she asked. There was nothing she could do about it. "Lakota territory. This might be my last chance to see my mother. She grows older. Don't know what I will find when I reach the home of my people. When Kane returns to England next summer, I'm hoping to be with him or close on his heels."

Once more, her hands rested on his chest then higher to wind around his neck. She ran her slender fingers through his hair. "I'd like to go with you." She stared at him as if the request was something he would agree to.

"No." Lakota territory was no place for a white woman. "No, as I said before it's too dangerous. You need to find a man to love. Someone who can return that sentiment with all his heart."

He did need her to wait for him. Wished to pursue this relationship to see where it might lead. He would never ask or hope for her to wait for his return. She was of marriageable age.

She was white. He wasn't full blooded Sioux, nor was he considered a half-breed as Kane was. There were hints of white man in his blood. He'd heard that his grandmother had been forced by a white

4

man, a trapper. His lighter skin coupled with green eyes was the result. Both his parents were Sioux. Just as Kane was a breed, so was he. Stephen imagined that was why they'd become such friends. They understood the vulnerability. Neither were accepted completely in either world.

"I would be no trouble. I can ride and shoot. Know how to use a knife. Enjoy sleeping under the stars. My biscuits are almost as tasty as Amorica's. You would never regret bringing me along with you. I would do whatever you told me." Her plea seemed heartfelt as well as sincere.

While he wanted to laugh, he also needed to make her understand the seriousness of this mission of his. He didn't even know how he'd be received at his destination. "A woman who doesn't belong is always trouble."

No, he amended to himself. All women were trouble. He didn't understand them. He smoothed hair from her face letting the tips of his fingers travel along her cheek then down her throat to her throbbing pulse at the base of her neck. He needed to kiss her there, explore and sightsee all of her.

Chauncey bristled at his words. He saw determination in the set of her jaw as well as the simmer in her eyes. "I would go with you. I'm never trouble. You should understand I'm not like most women."

No, Chauncey Lakeland was unique to herself. He should have never kissed her. "You barely know me..."

He rubbed the back of his neck. It was so true. They'd known each other for twenty-four hours. He felt an immediate connection with her he'd never known with another woman. He wondered if she could ride like Lyssa Andrews. He prayed then that she couldn't. If she could not, he wouldn't have to chastise her when she put her life in danger. "You would have to obey me. Jump when I said jump. I would never stand for a woman who would gainsay my orders and, in the process, put herself in danger."

"Enough to know, I want to be with you." She straightened her shoulders. "I would do everything you said."

Somehow, he didn't believe her words. Her entire life, he felt certain, she'd been pampered and allowed to do whatever she wished.

Life could never be that way where he was headed. "Such a determined little thing," he murmured, his words tender, staring at her stiff back as she walked away from him.

He didn't know what she was going to do. Now, she turned and was walking back to him.

"You're leaving in the morning?" she asked. "From Independence?"

"Yes, I'm the head scout for the wagon train. I've a job to do along the way. After that I'll head my own way."

Perhaps he told her too much. Bloody hell, she was a woman. She wouldn't just up and leave her home, her family to follow him.

Would she?

No. Women did stupid things, foolish things when they took a notion into their woman's brain. She was walking away from him again, her skirts swinging around her delicate ankles, her back stiff as if she was determined. He groaned again. He wanted to understand what she was thinking.

Those memories happened weeks ago. Now he was well past Independence. She didn't follow him. Thank all the different Gods ever worshipped.

"Terrell," Stephen nodded to the wagon master as he was jerked away from his musings and back to the present by the company of the other man.

He'd been lucky, he supposed. Chauncey stayed put as he told her to do. She would find a white man. She would marry then have children. It was all good. His memory would be like dust in the wind.

When he reached Independence there was no sign of her. He half expected to see her sitting on one of the wagons, guiding the oxen as well as horses down the long trail. He'd only met about half of the hundred or so people heading west on the Oregon Trail. She was not among them. Paranoid that she might have tracked him here, he'd scrutinized every woman he came across.

As a single woman she would never be allowed to be part of the wagon train. It just wasn't done. Families had to look out for their own, wives needed to be certain there were no extra women to tempt their men. Chauncey was tenacious. If it was something she wanted badly enough, she would find a way to maneuver all obstacles out of the way to get what she wanted. He grimaced uncertain once more. Something quivered deep in the pit of his stomach. Looking at the expression on Terrell's face, he felt certain trouble brewed.

"Stephen," Johnathan said as he too watched the wagons lumber past them. "So far, no problems. Though we are less than a week out. What do you think of the people? Of the progress?"

Stephen leaned on his saddle horn as he studied the landscape below him. "No problems. Don't expect too many. Unless the weather changes to something nasty. Of course, given enough time, it will. We're making good headway."

He wondered what question Terrell was asking him. His voice was vague yet imploring. There was something the man wasn't explaining.

Terrell tipped his hat back, seeming to want to say something to him. Stephen saw the tension in the set of his jaw, the weariness in his eyes when he watched him. The man looked to the end of the slow-moving train then back to him.

"Spit it out, Terrell. What's eatin' at you? If there is something you want to say, say it. I'm not a man to play guessing games." This was unusual for the wagon master. He spoke his mind with no hesitancy. The difference gave him pause.

The man stared at him hard, brought his hand up to swipe dusty hair from his forehead. He cleared his throat, his Adam's apple bobbing. "Just wonderin' why you camp down with me. Doesn't seem logical."

Stephen shook his head, raising an eyebrow to the bright blue sky. How to answer the question slammed in his head. Caution before coming to an answer seemed appropriate. "Why do you ask?"

He needed to know what else was on the tip of this man's tongue or in his mind that he wasn't telling him. Wished to know what was behind the question.

"Well, you see, that's just the thing," he paused looking down the valley then along the length of the lumbering wagons. Sweat beaded on his forehead.

"Terrell?" Stephen never appreciated solving puzzles when the answer could be spoken with no coercion. That was what this was becoming, a puzzle. "Spit it out. If it's something I've done wrong tell me. We'll correct it."

The man's eyes darkened. "If I had a pretty little wife, riding solo in this long train with every male this side of the Mississippi gaping at her, wanting to make her his, I'd be spending my nights with her all cuddled up and warm keeping her away from prying eyes. Making certain everyone knew who she belonged to. Don't understand what's gotten into you leavin' her all by herself." He held up his hands, "I know it's none of my business."

Wife?

He was shocked to the bottom of his soul. Deep in his chest his heart thundered. He approached this statement from a different vantage point. His first reaction was to deny the existence of a wife. His second was to shake her so silly that she'd never defy him again. He told her to stay put, to find a husband and have kids. She told him she wanted to go with him. He told her to find a white man and marry him. Stubborn minx.

Ah hell...

He had no idea how to answer the man. They were now too far out from Independence for him to return her. He didn't want her here. In danger. All he could do now was to acknowledge her then protect her with his life. His next instinct was to throttle her.

"Thought I should stay alert. If I cuddled up with my wife," he choked on the word, wishing he dared do that very thing, "I might be otherwise engaged if you needed me."

He thought that excuse to be a fine one. By the look on Terrell's face, it wasn't.

"You're our scout. A damn good one. You would know if danger threatened us at night. You ride the trail every day. Think you should see to that little woman before some man believes she's fair game. Every single man, young as well as attached, is talking about her, about her long legs and the curvaceous butt she shows in those britches she wears. If I were you, I'd insist she wear a dress. Get her out of men's clothing would be first on my agenda. Go on now, go spell her for a while. I bet those skinny arms of hers are sore from all the driving she's been doing. Don't want her hands calloused."

"Thank you, sir. Believe I'll do just that."

Stephen whipped his horse around then started down the hill toward the wagons. He was both eager as well as furious to see Chauncey. He wanted to yell at her then make love to her. The one he could do, the other he needed to keep in the back of his head. Taking her innocence was out of the question. He damn well wasn't going to ruin her chances of a decent marriage.

His wife.

She didn't have any idea what she'd done by proclaiming herself his. If he wished to do so, he could say the words and in the eyes of the People she would be his wife. The words would never suit her father. Nonetheless, in this situation the most fortuitous route might be to accept her as his wife, treat her as his wife. Furious emotions overrode eager ones to see her to hold her in his arms again, to kiss her, to have her in every way. She was so bloody sweet. The calm façade he was attempting to show slipped away as he drew nearer. His hands shook. His heart raced.

He galloped down the line of wagons nodding to people he didn't know, greeting the ones he did know with their name. His blood seemed to boil under the hot sun. When he reached her, he saw the look of surprise on her sweet features. After she smiled at him, he was bowled over by the sheer power of the sight. His body hardened just as it had the day of the wedding when he kissed her, touched her small breasts hidden beneath the fabric of her gown. She was lovely. Beneath his breath, he swore.

Her smile faded. "Still Water Runs Deep?" Now that she had time to register the fierce look he slanted her, she didn't seem so pleased to see him. "I can explain."

Stephen bet she could. "Call me Stephen." He paused as he searched his head for the right words. "Or husband."

His voice was harsh but not as harsh as he wished the tone to be. He was so damn pleased to see her. He took some of the sting out of his voice. It was her smile that did him in. Her smile that robbed him of his anger. Her smile that sent all his senses to a boiling point.

"Stephen. What can I do for you?" she spoke, the voice as sweet as her words, her head tilted as if flirting to one side. "I would..." She stopped, her gaze riveted on his eyes.

She was too certain of herself, too damn secure in what she was doing. He was pleased there was a moment of doubt no matter how brief that moment turned out to be. "Tonight, after we eat, I guess you'll find out."

The paleness of her face satisfied him. She ran her tongue along her lips. "I don't understand what you are implying. Are you eating with me tonight?"

"Scoot over." He tied the reins of his horse to the wagon before landing on the seat next to her. "I'm driving for the next hour or so. You need to rest. Have you been doing all the driving since we left Independence?" He took over, holding the reins with one gloved hand. "Let me see your hands."

Chauncey was sitting on them, shaking her head. "No. No, I don't think so. You don't have any right to demand anything of me."

"Don't want to have our first lover's spat over your damn hands. Let me see them."

He was seething. As her white husband, he had every right to ask her anything and expect her obedience. As her Sioux husband, she had even fewer rights. She was his to do with as he pleased.

"You can't expect me to do whatever you ask." She held them out, grimacing when he turned them over. "I can take care of myself."

He damn well could expect that of her. He cursed when he saw the broken blisters, the redness of her hands, the beginning of calluses. "As your husband, I've every right. In case you forgot, as your husband you are mine to do with as I damn well please. I should leave you at the next fort."

"You won't." Her chin was up in the air, reminding him of her spoiled upbringing. "You would never leave me to fend for myself."

"You gambled on that fact. Didn't you?" His lungs swelled with the hot air he breathed in. "I'm going to thrash your bottom until you can't sit. After that...well hell..."

He couldn't do that either. Idle threats got a man nowhere except into trouble he couldn't climb out of. What was he thinking?

"You won't," she told him again, the sweetness of her smile sending heat straight to his groin. "You would never hurt me. I know that about you. Otherwise, I wouldn't be here," she said with a certainty she couldn't possibly know.

"Five days, Chauncey. How did you keep me from seeing you for five days?"

His mind traveled over all the days searching for her. She would have been right up front and center when he traveled the lines looking over the train, assessing varying the abilities of the people. How had he missed her?

She lifted the shoulders he'd touched that night. They were covered now. They still looked fragile. He stared at her britches. Seems he should have noticed her butt in the air. Ah, but he might have thought she was a man. Shaking his head, disbelief prevalent. No, he would have never looked at her curves then believed her male. Her britches showed the flare of her hips that were not male.

"You never looked at me. When I saw you riding this way, I'd turn to find something in the wagon."

In a gesture that drove him crazy, she lifted her shoulders in a feminine gesture that left the softest parts of her moving.

"Made sure you never saw my face. What did you expect? I knew if you saw me too soon, you might find a way to send me home."

The little devil understood he would be angry with her as well as annoyed. She was right on all her assumptions. Now she flirted with him, testing him. Yes, if he'd discovered her a day or two out, he would have taken her back to Independence. Damn, but how on earth would he have gotten her home? He couldn't have left her alone to find her way back to the ranch even though it seemed she navigated her way to Independence with little to no trouble. Inside, he was both seething with fury as well as with anticipation. He understood that even with a desperate fight with himself, he would succumb to her sweet charms. He was only a man. Her body talked to him in ways no other woman had. His emotions were mixed. He both wanted her with him while he needed to send her home to protect her from himself from the elements he had no control over.

Her father would be worried sick, her mother...

His fury mounted at her selfishness. As he waited, listening to the sounds of the land, hoping to find some kind of peace within, he was too angry for words. He slapped the reins on the horses urging them forward to catch up with the wagon in front of them. To flay her with words would not be enough punishment. She sat next to him, stiff as the wooden brake next to his leg. He couldn't bear to look at her. If he saw any hint of victory in her face...he didn't know what he would do.

"Can I ride your horse?" she asked sounding innocent of all wrong doing. "You know I'm very good with them. Can ride just like Lyssa."

He turned to her, astonishment in his eyes. She must know the answer would be negative. The diversion wasn't going to work with him. "No." Breathing in as deep as he could he reached again for an inner peace that seemed to elude him the last few minutes. He needed to find a significant as well as successful way to deal with Chauncey.

"I don't see why? Give me a reason I can understand." She continued the discussion instead of taking his answer at face value. She would argue just to keep the conversation from her and this circumstance that was founded in foolishness. The smile of hers doomed him.

He stiffened, guarding his decisions. Practical actions as well as speech were the only way to proceed with her. "You don't have to understand my reasons."

He sipped in hot scorched air asking the gods above for patience as well as endurance to maintain his decisions. It would be far too easy for him to give in to her.

Terrell was riding beside the wagon, grinning as if he'd done him the greatest favor in the universe. After he tipped his hat at them, he spoke, "You two lovebirds enjoying a few moments of togetherness? It's about time Stephen here helped you with your burden."

Wouldn't say enjoying was what they were doing. She leaned into him, pressing herself against his arm. He felt her breasts. Heard the soft inhalation of air. Imagined how she would feel pressed against his length.

"Oh, yes," she purred, her words sounding so sweet as well as delicate, looking up at him that angelic smile of hers in place. "It was nice of you to tell my husband he could be with me. I so appreciate the fact. Driving the wagon can be taxing work. My delicate hands have suffered. My arms are sore." To put emphasis on her words, she rubbed her arms.

Her acting skills were fine. If she kept insisting he was her husband, he would have to show her what husbands did with their wives. No, he wouldn't do anything to hurt her, even though she deserved a good shock. Even if he scared her, she would have to stay with the train. There was nowhere for her to go. There was nowhere he could leave her and feel she would be protected until he returned. His was a stalemate of her choosing.

Damn the interfering woman.

He grinned at Terrell, dipping his head, smiling as if he meant to do just what Terrell suggested. "I intend to enjoy the next hour then the rest of the evening with my wife. If you need me, you know where to find me. I'm going to be with Chauncey until tomorrow morning."

He set his hand on her upper thigh, squeezed then moved his fingers closer to the apex.

She squirmed then tensed, her face flushing a soft pink. The color became her. He wondered what she would look like in the throes of passion when he gave her a woman's pleasure.

Terrell hooted while he grinned from one ear to the other. "See you're starting the loving early. Don't get too distracted. We've still got a few hours to go before we can rest for the evening meal. One can only do so much with his wife when he's got to keep the team of horses moving along."

He could do a great deal with his wife, including seducing her until she was panting with her need to discover what came next. "Never get too distracted now do I, sweetheart?"

He leaned closer. His hand around her neck to hold her still, he kissed her. Ran his tongue along her lips, pushing for her to open for him. He didn't know what he would do if she did what he asked. At this instant her mouth remained closed tight against him. He'd embarrassed her. She retaliated. Good, she deserved a bit of humiliation after what she did.

Stephen watched the wagon master ride down the column of wagons, holding his breath along with his raging thoughts. He had so many questions to ask, he wasn't at all certain where to begin. He needed to understand what she told her parents. He felt certain it would be one fine tale. Lyssa and the way she sought out Kane came to mind. She was audacious, bold as well as blunt. From the get go, Kane didn't stand a chance in hell against Lyssa's wiles. He groaned understanding Chauncey might be just as forward.

After several minutes ticked by, he turned to her. In a smooth drawl he learned from some of the guests at the wedding feast, he asked, "What did you tell your daddy? Did you tell him you were following me into Indian territory? He'll be mighty pleased to hear where you're headed. Do you have any idea what he'll do to me when I do bring you home? Scalping would be too good for the likes of the man who deflowered his daughter. Horse whipped might be appropriate."

He wondered what kind of an excuse she gave him for her absence.

She stiffened as she sent him a ferocious scowl. Her chin rose a notch as her breath hitched into her throat. After smoothing her hands along her pants, she began to speak. "Suppose I knew that question was coming. In truth...it's none of your concern. Didn't tell him I ran off to be with you. If you're afraid he will come for us, don't be. My daddy is expecting me to be in London with Aunt Ella, the duchess. Told him I thought I deserved a season. Wanted to find an earl to marry just as my cousin did."

"Supposed you must have told him something outrageous. He won't believe you longer than he can check out your sorry story. So, tell me. What is it you said that won't have your daddy showing up here with his shotgun? He could catch up to us without a blink. A man alone or accompanied by his son can move a hell of a log quicker than a wagon train."

"No, he won't. I promise you that."

"You're so certain. Know that I will hand you over to him as soon as he arrives. You've done this up all nice and tight. Chauncey, I don't appreciate being put in the position as your guardian or your fake husband. I won't be either."

He didn't see how he was going to get out of this conundrum she created.

She did grin then, flashed him her pretty white teeth with a broad smile. She touched his chest with the palm of her hand. "Not my guardian. My husband, yes. Since that kiss, I thought of little else besides being with you. I want adventure. I want to see other parts of the world. I want to learn what it's like to be with a man. Not just any man, you."

He gritted out trying to push down the raging anger. Where Chauncey was concerned right now, he wanted to shake her or make love to her. "I'm not your damn husband! I'm not ever going to be. Get that notion out of your pretty little head. If you can do that, we'll deal so much better together. We've a long road ahead of us. Unless Aric does show up to bring you home, I'm all you've got to depend on. You need to trust me as well as what I tell you to do. In your case, there are no decision you are allowed to make. If your father does turn up, hope he paddles your little backside until you can't sit for at least a week."

"Everyone believes you are my husband. I told the Murphys in the wagon ahead of me and the Greeleys in the one behind me. We share a campfire at night. It's obvious Mr. Terrell knows who you are. A young lady named Beth who is riding with the Greeleys knows. Soon the entire train will know who you are to me. You won't be able to deny the fact."

He groaned understanding that for the duration of this trip he was to be her husband. He remembered how her lips felt beneath his. How his fingers closed over her breast. How he felt when he slid his hand across the tightened bud. He wanted to discover how all of her would feel beneath him. How he would feel inside her. He wanted to see her naked with her legs spread wide just for him.

If he was going to return her unscathed to her parents, he would have the devil of a time. She set this in motion. To his dismay, he didn't want to find himself forced to marry the little piece of baggage. That was a lie. It was the other things that were important. Chauncey wasn't the type of woman a man dallied with. If he made love to her, he would have to marry her. A different scenario for them would never be possible.

"Want to know if your daddy is going to show up here."

The wagons were slowing now, forming a circle for the evening. He concentrated on what he was doing, still hoping for an answer. Her silence told him this wasn't a topic that left her feeling comfortable. Hell, he didn't feel comfortable with any part of this situation.

"I left daddy a message he would find at a later date, well after I'd been gone for at least a day."

She grinned at him as if that was all that was necessary.

"Yes. So, they are one day behind us?"

He needed to encourage her to tell him everything. This was something he needed to know. What she told her father could not be left to chance. It seemed to be what she hoped for.

She cocked her head to the side for a second lifting one shoulder as she did so. "Told him where he would find me."

She told him nothing more. Once again, the silence stretched long and thin around him. He felt his gut clench.

Stephen groaned again. He would be dodging bullets in a few days. He'd be a dead man. Once the story she conjured was out in the open, he didn't expect to live. "I don't believe any of this. I'm saddled with a wife I don't want. Can't even use her as a good wife should be used to slake my lust."

Inside, his gut contracting, he fumed wondering how he was meant to keep his hands from her delectable little body.

When he turned from her staring at the landscape then to her, she spoke. "You must not have heard me. Told him I went to London. That I missed my cousins. Wanted to meet an earl like Lyssa did. Everyone wants a title. You know that don't you? Of course, you don't. Thought that maybe the duchess would help me. Also told him I left with Tira and Jamie on board his ship."

He snapped his fingers. "Just like that Aric is going to believe you set sail for London without discussing the adventure with him along with your mother. How stupid do you think your daddy is?" He couldn't stop shaking his head at her foolishness. "Your father will ride as fast as possible to town where he'll discover your lies. He will find out no ship took you to England. You never went with Tira and Jamie. What then? What will he think happened to you?"

"No, I said I went with Tira to Baltimore then Uncle Jamie would find a ship for me." She insisted as if this plan was unstoppable.

"Are you truly that naïve?" he bit out, frustrated beyond belief. "I'm not going to be back to the east coast for a year, possibly more depending on what happens on this adventure as you call it. How long do you think it will take him to discover you didn't go with Tira and that Jamie didn't find you a ship? That you're not in London where he expects you to be. That Ella never received you safely so she could chaperone you for a season? Well?"

She sat back, a wilted look on her usually bright features. "They are going to worry about me. It's obvious, they will wonder where I am." She brightened, surprising him. The little minx had something up her sleeve.

"Does anyone know where you went? It would be nice if you told someone... anyone...your brother."

He was annoyed as well as frustrated beyond anything he could have ever imagined. He pinched the bridge of his nose, rubbing as if the stiff motion would soothe his battered nerves. Nothing eased the pain that was growing in his head.

"No, I guess..." she sounded meek, perhaps even defeated.

Stephen didn't think the crushed look would last long. She had this way of bouncing back despite the magnitude of her difficult situation. "You didn't think further than the end your pert little nose. Did you?"

He didn't have anything more to say. Neither did she. The wagons were circled. He hopped down, helping her, his hands around her tiny waist. He untied Spirit. Without another word to her, he mounted then raced away from the campsite, away from his supposed wife. For as many moments as he could tie together, he needed to find a bit of peace. He wished to think about what he intended to do with her. By showing up here, Chauncey became his responsibility. A responsibility he would cherish under different circumstances.

Heaving, spent, Stephen pulled up Spirit. He stopped. The cliff overlooking the wagons gave him a view he didn't care to examine. He saw the men and women going about the evening, fixing dinner, talking about the day or days so far, sharing their hopes as well as their dreams of starting a new life in the west. They were all risking their lives in hopes of a better future. All but Chauncey. She was here on a whim, treading on other's lives just for herself. He would have to figure out some way to deal with Chauncey. She didn't leave him much room to maneuver. Terrell believed them married. In front of some of these people, he would have to act the besotted newlywed. He had to do it without taking her innocence.

He dismounted. Sat cross legged as he set his mind to a new course. A place he'd not anticipated a few hours ago loomed in front of him. The difficulties of this new journey plagued him. The protection of this woman was at the forefront of his mind. He needed to return her safe to the bosom of her family. He would make her write a letter to her father and mother. Aric Lakeland deserved to know where his wayward daughter ran off to.

She was beautiful.

Full of life and love.

Her sense of humor filled him with joy.

If she continued with this tactic, she would indeed become his wife in more ways than one. He knew now he would take her with him, all the way to Lakota territory, all the way to meet his family. Once she was within the circle of his People, she would be his. They would insist. There would be no turning around, no changing of the circumstance. He would not walk in a backward path. Until then, if he could find the way, he would keep his hands to himself. He didn't want to bring a pregnant woman on this dangerous path. Wouldn't risk a child or the woman.

He needed to maintain his distance.

Stephen would make certain she understood. She would have to believe he didn't want her for his wife. That she must play make-believe until neither could pretend any longer. Until she slept with him on his furs in his lodge, he would not make love to her. Unless they were married by a priest or a man of God. He drew in a full breath of air, filling his lungs with the fragrant scent of the prairie, realizing he wasn't going to stand a chance of doing so.

Would she persevere in this scheme? He imagined that would be left up to the gods above.

He wanted her more than he'd ever wanted another woman. He closed his eyes, feeling the wind speak to him, absorbing the sounds of the ending summer fill him with hope.

This Sioux warrior couldn't take a white woman for a wife. Black Thunder took Lyssa Andrews as his. He was a damn earl. What did he, Still Water Runs Deep, have to offer a white woman? Nothing. She was used to being a pampered child of an aristocrat. Well, he did learn that Aric Lakeland was a bastard. Unlike her father, at least he knew who is parents were. Confusion swamped him. Changing emotions ruled his head. He imagined he would allow fate to take its course.

Ah, the complexities of life. His stomach rumbled with need. He hadn't eaten since this morning. He would see what his wife had in store for him for dinner. She told him she could cook. Her biscuits were the tastiest. Could she cook over an open fire? That remained to be seen.

There was much in this life of his that remained to be seen.

~ * ~

Standing beside her wagon, her hand shielding her eyes, Chauncey watched Still Water Runs Deep race away. He ran from her. Coward. Perhaps he didn't. Discovering her left no choices for him. That was a lot for a man to absorb.

Five days out she'd been discovered. Every time he rode by the wagon, she held her breath while her heart raced, ducking to hide her face, or pulling her hat down. With each new breaking of the dawn, she felt renewed hope that he would not be able to send her home.

He was angry, more than furious. Livid might describe Still Water Runs Deep. She'd understood that would be his reaction from the first moment she put her plan into motion.

She had posted a letter to her parents the day they left Independence. The letter told them in truth what happened to her as well as why. She needed to make certain both her mother and father understood this was her decision. Still Water Runs Deep had no idea what she planned. No one could have changed the fact she fell so in love with the man, her heart stopped at the thought of him going away. She couldn't allow him to leave for a year or more without her. If this decision of hers created problems, she would deal with them.

"How are you doing?" Beth asked placing a hand on her shoulder, her eyes searching. "I see he's discovered you. Mr. Wilkes doesn't seem pleased. What are you going to do now?"

"Imagine I'm relieved at the discovery. The worry along with the fear of the unearthing of my presence are gone. The weight is lifted from my shoulders. As to what I'm going to do, I don't have the foggiest notion. Suppose I should start dinner."

She imagined what she would do would depend on Still Water Runs Deep No, Stephen, he wanted her to call him Stephen. She would have to take her cues from him, one moment at a time.

"Beans and bacon and biscuits?" Beth asked with a tiny laugh as she walked with Chauncey to the campfire. "We need some meat of some kind. Rabbit would be nice. I hear rattle snake can be tasty."

"Yes," Chauncey mused, she did have bacon along with beef jerky she purchased in Independence.

She'd eaten very little of the stores, saving it for Still Water Runs Deep when he discovered her. Perhaps she would make this meal a bit more mouthwatering by adding the bacon to the beans. Suppose she should start to think of him as Stephen. She did like that name.

Stephen Wilkes was a nice name. Unofficially and without benefit of clergy, she was now Mrs. Wilkes. A small giggle of pleasure left her. She wished she could see him again as she did that first time she saw him, his chest bare while he raced beside fifty of the finest race horses money could buy toward the Andrews' ranch. Beth observed her for a moment with a strange look in her eyes but she didn't ask any questions. After a few seconds she looked away.

Entering the back of the wagon, Chauncey pulled out her apron tying the strings around her waist. Next, she gathered the other items she needed to put on the fire she shared with the Murphys and the Greeleys. Every once in a while, with her hand on the small of her back stretching to stare into the space outside the wagons she realized she was searching for him. He left almost two hours ago to race off his anger. He might not return to the wagon. Stephen could spend the night under the stars. She thought he would return. Believed he would protect her by complying with her lie. She needed to tell herself the falsehood was small. After all, the untruth only affected them.

Still Water Runs Deep was not a man who spoke untrue. She forced him to do that. It was necessary for her to get what she wanted. A pang of guilt flooded her. She brushed the sentiment aside. Was she that narrow minded and selfish? Yes, she must admit to herself.

What did she know about men? Nothing.

Now the biscuits were cooked and cooling near the fire. The beans with the added bacon were also finished. She dished up a bowl for herself before grabbing a biscuit from the pan. Disconsolate, she sat down on the hard ground, leaning against a wagon wheel. She imagined she deserved the abandonment. He would come home for food. Wouldn't he? Probably not. He spent the last five nights eating somewhere else.

At this point, he couldn't denounce her. Of course, he could. If he did, she would be set aside at the next tiny settlement or fort. She would have to wait for her father to retrieve her in disgrace. She was lost in thought, miserable notions, debilitating ideas. What would she do if he left her somewhere. She pulled in a long, deep breath of smoky air telling herself to stop feeling sorry for herself. She needed to tell him she posted a letter to her mother and father the day they left Independence.

"Got enough for me?"

She jerked to attention. Her gaze roamed up long legs ever higher up to meet his sizzling green eyes. He came back. She swallowed the surprise. Cleared her throat. "More than enough. Would you like me to dish up a bowl?" He was here, asking for dinner. That was a good sign. Wasn't it? She would proceed now as if everything was fine. She smiled at him.

Stephen didn't appear too pleased. "Don't need you to wait on me. Point me in the right direction and I'll dish myself up some of whatever it is you made. Would you like more?"

The tenderness in his voice astounded her.

"The food is by the fire, beans with a bit of added bacon and biscuits on the side. The bowl is in the back of the wagon along with a spoon I set there for you. Truly, though, I can get it for you. You must be tired. You've been at work all day."

He shook his head then nodded. Holding her breath, she watched him, his long lose strides eating up the short distance. After he dished up, he sat down beside her, their shoulders touching. In the chilling night air, his warmth penetrated through the flannel of her jacket. She held her breath waiting for his thoughts. She wasn't at all certain how to deal with the man. He was always so stoic and calm. This afternoon he showed more emotion than she ever remembered seeing before. His green eyes blazed at her, simmered then when he studied her, his gaze heated her.

After several bites, he spoke, "Either I'm famished or your biscuits are better than Amorica's. I wonder...well the beans are good too. You added bacon. Yes, you said that. Thank you, it's better than what I've been eating the last five days."

"Yes," she agreed happy to hear the words of praise not knowing what to say to him.

His compliment directed toward her food was sweet. The conversation was unimportant. He held her future in his large hands and he was speaking of biscuits. Given enough time, he would get down to specifics concerning how he felt about her behavior.

Between mouthfuls of food, he began to question her. He reached for a third biscuit. "What is in your wagon? I trust you had good advice when you went shopping for the long trip." He wiped his bowl clean of sauce with an extra biscuit. He set down the bowl, drank a long swig of his coffee. "We can save the rest of these for breakfast. We're heading out early, the break of dawn I believe. Well, as close to that time as possible. Need to make it to the river by mid-afternoon."

At his revelation, excitement ripped through her. "River? A bath?" she asked in anticipation of feeling clean again. The tiny bit of water she washed with now didn't give her that same luxurious clean feeling she so loved. She pulled her shirt away from her sweat-sticky body. "Heavenly."

Immersed in water.

He chuckled at her question along with her reaction. Stared at her breasts when she pulled the fabric away from her skin. "Only if I go with you. Heard there is a nice pool about fifty yards from where we will pull up. Everyone is going to want a bath though. We should go a bit farther for some privacy. This morning when I rode ahead, I spotted a pool with a nice little waterfall. No one will go that distance from the wagons." He stared at her with those green eyes of his that could tug every bit of truth from her.

The horrible man continued to laugh when he witnessed her surprise. "Go with me? You can't be serious."

He would see her naked. Without any clothing. You're supposed to be married, you ninny. She groped for meaningful words. Found none. Repeated herself. "You don't mean that."

One raven eyebrow arched with what seemed like speculation. "Yes, wouldn't leave you alone to bathe anywhere except your home. This isn't a place where women are safe without a man." He paused for a few seconds while he stared into the night sky that was now twinkling with stars. "Or my home."

She didn't say anything. Chauncey was mulling his words over in her head. Was he accepting the fact she called him her husband? She didn't know. It seemed he hid his emotions beneath a blank façade. She couldn't read him.

He would do as he pleased. She learned as much from talking with Lyssa. A woman had little control over her life once they wed. That wasn't something she was used to.

"Are you staying the night here? At my...our wagon?"

Her voice wobbled with the confusion and mixed feelings soaring through her head. She wanted him in her bed, holding her, kissing her, touching her as he did that day behind the church.

Silence hugged them until he spoke. "Don't have a choice," he said, taking her bowl from her. "You've taken all my choices away from me. I will sleep with my imagined wife." He rose, taking her bowl from her hands.

There was hot water simmering over the shared cook fire. He poured some in his bowl, swirled it as he walked to the wagon. "Soap?"

he asked. He didn't sound angry just calm. Resigned.

She didn't know what to think. Her heart raced. The air she tried to breathe was filled with confusion.

"In the left-hand corner."

Stephen washed and rinsed the bowls setting them in the back of the wagon. He stared inside appearing to make a mental note of what she purchased. She knew she did well. The wagon was full of supplies, mostly of the edible kind. One valise with a minimum amount of clothing sat near the front. It was just enough to fit into her saddlebags when they left the train. His silence unnerved her, rattled her to her core. She didn't dare watch him though she wanted to see what he was about. While she stared at him wondering what he was going to do, he was inside the wagon, going through her things, her purchases. A twinge of panic drowned her. She wasn't a frivolous white woman as he suggested. Nor was she delicate. All her life she worked the ranch with her parents. She didn't care about the wearing the highest fashions. Clothes were needed for work, practical clothes. Over the years she found men's clothing was easier to work in than women's clothing.

What would he think about her purchases?

When he sat down beside her again, her body shook with the tension she felt vibrating from her into him. His large hand settled on her leg, rested there while she felt heat rising to flame on her cheeks. While the slight breeze stirred the embers of the cook fire, he stroked her leg. Passion rushed through her. A different kind of trembling seized her. She swallowed hard, tried to concentrate on the blaze in front of her instead of the one within her.

He continued in this vein, his voice bland when he spoke. "You cannot wear these or any britches any longer. It's not appropriate for my wife, my woman to wear men's clothing. Did you bring a skirt or a gown?" he asked.

His hand settled at the top of her thigh. He waited for her to answer.

Chauncey didn't want to allow him to dictate to her. He didn't have the right. She felt his touch as if the contact seared her. Burned through her clothing. "I don't..." she began intending to deny him. "I can't..."

"You will obey me, your husband, in this. You cannot flaunt your delicious feminine butt nor the delightful curve of your hips to all the young bucks who are traveling with us. I won't have you showing all your curves to men, any man besides me. You are known as my wife now among all the people on the train. I've acknowledged you, accepted the lie you created. You will behave in the manner suitable to a real woman not a woman wishing to ape a man. Now, you are my woman." His voice was so calm, casual as if he spoke of what he ate for dinner.

She understood his anger, the fury he seemed to hide. Didn't agree with his demands. "That's your final command."

A slow shimmer of rage shuffled through her, eager to find a way out. She wasn't used to being told what to do, how to act, what to wear or not to wear. She wanted to toss what was left of her coffee in his face.

"You set yourself up for this," he reminded her stroking her again, now resting his hand as if he owned her on her belly.

He spread his fingers as if testing for something. He still didn't show emotion in his voice or his actions. He was cold. His words were colder.

"I did," she admitted, shivering with a rush of feelings she didn't understand.

The sensations were nice though. She wished for a kiss, after that another one. His head rested on the wheel. His breaths were slow and even. He pulled her across his thighs.

"This is for all our spectators. There are people watching us. Did you know that? We seem to be today's gossip. The couple who are married. The couple who have not been together for five days." He stroked the length of her back. His hand wrapped around her. One fingertip exploring along her side until he was close to her breast. She felt the pressure of his hand lifting her breast from beneath. She sucked in air, startled by the contact. Butterflies danced and played in her stomach.

"Wh-where are you sleeping?" She thought of the pallet inside the wagon. Most of the people slept in tents or beneath their wagons. Filled with supplies there was not enough room for families to sleep in the traveling homes. She was small. The space was just enough room for her. Not for Still Wa...Stephen. His thumb taunted her, teasing her, brushing across the hardened tip of her breast. She inhaled a stiff breath of air. This was what she wanted. Wasn't it?

"With my wife. You like this. Admit it to me. That's why you came after me. For more of this." He stood, setting her back where she'd been, holding out his hand until she placed hers in his warmth. "Come, we leave early in the morning. You will need your sleep. I won't be able to drive the wagon for most of the day. I must scout ahead then report back to Terrell."

She realized then that all the bedding was beneath the wagon; her pallet, the blankets, the pillows. He would sleep with her tonight. The realization of his words hit home.

He would sleep with his wife.

What to do?

Sleeping with him was what she wanted. Wasn't it?

This was real, very real as well as frightening. *It's what I wanted.* She didn't know how a woman slept with a man. With his big warm body beside her, she didn't think she would get a moment of rest. Her mother and father slept together. "I..."

She slid her tongue along her lower lip, holding back as he tugged on her to tag along behind him. She stumbled. He cursed then held her closer.

"This is what you wanted. Is it not? To sleep with your husband was the reason for your foolishness. Wasn't it? Am I wrong? Did you have no idea what marriage entailed when you embarked on this recklessness?" His voice was gentle, soft as well. She heard the huskiness of desire that she associated with her father when he wanted her mother in the bedroom. He wouldn't let this go.

"Yes." She could never deny the truth. "Yes, I wanted this. I just don't comprehend what this entails. I'm eager as well as frightened to learn what you expect."

Her steps still lagged though. She saw that he also set her nightdress out for her. She looked at him surprised. Her mother and father always slept naked. She knew the earl slept with Lyssa naked. She sucked in a deep breath of air, relieved for the moment. She felt as if he gave her armor to sleep in. Stephen was offering a momentary reprieve.

"Change then meet me beneath the wagon."

She watched him sit on the pallet to remove his shoes. He put them inside the wagon. After that he removed his shirt. Her gaze riveted on him. She waited for him to remove his buckskins. He unfastened them. At that instant he looked at her. He grinned showing a wealth of even white teeth. She ducked inside the wagon fumbling with the buttons on her shirt.

When she looked up, he stood at the end of the wagon watching her disrobe. Well, watching her fumble with the buttons on her shirt. "A dress would not give you so much trouble."

Nonchalantly, he leaned on the back of the wagon, still staring. "Do you need help, Chauncey? I wish to go to bed before the sun peaks itself over the horizon. If this undressing takes any longer, that won't happen."

"I...of course, I don't. I can undress," her voice wavered.

She turned her back on him. Finished with the buttons. Her shirt slipped to the floor. She felt the coolness of the night air against her skin. Heard the soft curses. In haste, she reached behind her for the nightdress. Found it then slipped the fabric over her head. Heaving a silent sigh of relief, she slid her pants down her legs.

She was brushing her hair when she heard him again.

"What is keeping you?" he asked from behind her. He sounded impatient, exasperated.

The smile on her face widened, "Getting ready for bed. What does it look like?" she asked putting as much sugar into her voice as possible. "I always brush my hair one hundred strokes before I go to bed."

Once more she heard his soft swearing. Couldn't understand all the words, only a few. She should not want to make him angry.

"Now, Chauncey! You've tried my patience to its limit. If you are not in bed in the next five seconds..." The threat was unspoken yet very real.

She didn't hear the end of the threat. Didn't want to. Dropping the brush, she was out of the wagon and beneath the covers he set out in less than five.

"That's better," he mumbled as he slipped under the covers pulling her close. "It's the way a good wife should be, compliant."

She bristled. *Compliant? I'll give him the opposite.*

The length of him was against her back. His hand rested with possession on her belly, touched her hipbones. She didn't know what he wanted of her. She whimpered when his lips brushed with tenderness against her nape. His teeth grazed where his lips had been a second before. He cupped her breast in his hand, holding the tiny mound with gentleness. Against him she trembled, heated at the magic his tender caresses brought to her.

When his hand fell away, she turned in his arms. His eyes were closed, his lips parted with the breath he inhaled and exhaled.

He was asleep.

Chauncey didn't think she would be able to sleep. For minutes-upon-minutes, she stared out at the darkness, glimmering stars, the silver moon. As the moon passed across the dark sky, the campfire died down to smoldering embers. While the sentries patrolled the area, they added wood. The moon now sat low on the horizon.

The swat to her bottom woke her. "You're lazing away the day, Mrs. Wilkes. Time to rise. I heated the coffee you made last night."

In front of her, he sat on his haunches holding two cups of coffee. She wanted to rage at his boldness. When the blanket slipped to her waist, she realized the gown was unfastened. Her eyes widened when she saw he stared at her breasts. With as much haste as she could muster, she pulled the fabric together, wondering when that happened and why she wasn't aware. Startled by the revelation, she gazed at him, questioning without speaking the words.

Touching her cheek with the back of his hand, he smiled. It was a masculine all-knowing grin, "You were sweet last night. I thank you for your first time."

His words shook her. Her eyes widened even more. She gasped in a tiny puff of air. "My first time? The first time for what?" She didn't understand what he was talking about. White-knuckled her fingers held the gown together.

"I'm going to have to scout ahead this morning. I'll return around noon so I can spell you at the reins. A woman so breakable as you should not find herself driving a wagon all day. Terrell has no problems. This land is as safe as it can be. No hostiles will attack us. If we stop for any reason, don't leave the wagon until I speak with you."

Even though she had no intention of exploring the land if they stopped for some unthought of reason, she bristled at his command. She wasn't stupid or foolish although he accused her of those traits. By coming here, she followed her heart. Despite his obvious dislike at having to acknowledge her as his wife, she would continue to do the same again.

As she watched his back, he vanished, mounted on his big stallion. She observed the tiny bits of dust the hooves raised. They would be underway soon. Still Water Runs Deep harnessed the horses for her. It was the first time she didn't have to do this herself. The night was spent in his arms. He thanked her for her first time. Confused...she would remember if he made love to her. What she did recall was that he fell asleep first. Tonight, would be another night. She could ask him.

Less than thirty minutes later the wagons started to move. Chauncey thought about the bath, the clean water along with the soap. She had trouble keeping her emotions in check as the day grew hotter. Sweat slid down her body, all of her body. Though she would not have believed the fact if Stephen told her, she was cooler in the gown. She wore no petticoats or corset. All she had on was her gown and her chemise even foregoing pantalets. When she lifted her skirt to mid-calf, the breeze caressed her legs then her thighs.

He still would not approve of her choice of clothing. She didn't care. He could rant all he wanted. She would dress as she pleased...to be comfortable. True, there were no young bucks who looked at her with lustful thoughts. Tapping her finger on her chin, she did recall Percival Mahoney stopping by each day with a word or two. Several times, he offered to drive the wagon for her. His eyes didn't roam very far. They always seemed riveted on her bosom. Her tiny bosom. Maybe Stephen had a point. A mouthful was enough to appease a man.

Beth liked the boy. She could have swooned the day Percival took off his hat then spoke to her. Chauncey chuckled to herself remembering, wishing Beth would have a young suitor.

"Can I ride with you?" Beth stood by the side of the wagon looking up. She looked wistful, as if she needed her for something. Clearing her throat, she began to speak. "Need conversation. Thought after the night with your husband, you might want to talk. I've been there before. It was your first time? Wasn't it?"

What she needed to know is if Stephen made love to her. Asking Beth wouldn't do her much good. Beth would know less than she did. Wouldn't she? Beth was only about seventeen. Not that much younger than her. Maybe younger.

"Wouldn't mind a bit of conversation. Climb up."

A few minutes later the wagons lumbered down the trail. She was exuberant they weren't going all the way to Oregon. These families all gave up so much for this journey. To her this excursion was an adventure in the making. To people like the Murphys and the Greeleys, it was a change in their lives. One they hoped would be for the better.

Beth looked at her with wide dark eyes. Gently, she touched her arm. "Was he good to you last night. I mean...he didn't hurt you, did he?" The girl was looking at her toes, her face pale. "I was afraid for you. I didn't hear anything though. No screams of pleasure or pain. That seems odd."

The girl just gave her a wealth of questions. She was more confused. "Yes, he was nice and he didn't hurt me. He ate then we went to bed. That was all." Chauncey didn't know what else to say to the girl. "Why were you afraid for me?"

"Promise you won't say anything," Beth began, her words solemn, her voice soft with a small tremble. "The Greeleys rescued me from a work home. I was sold to a man and woman who wanted me to service the husband because the wife didn't want him anywhere near her. Lived with them for three years before the Greeleys came along. They must have bought me from the other people. Though they don't demand much of anything from me. I still need to pay for my room and board."

Chauncey's blood froze. "Demand? What did they demand,

Beth? Service? I don't understand."

After shaking out her skirt, Beth began, "Sex. The men always wanted sex. After the first time I learned to stare at the ceiling and lay as still as I could unless he wanted me to touch him. Is that what you did last night? Drift off to a place where you wouldn't feel either pain or pleasure?"

Her breath stuck in her throat. "Does Mr. Greely want sex too?"

She would have to tell Stephen. She promised Beth. She couldn't tell a soul. Chauncey didn't know how she could keep this secret. Beth asked too much. Even though she sounded matter of fact, Chauncey denoted hurt in her voice.

"Yes. Most nights it's over fast. I don't feel anything anymore. The first times though, before I learned to relax and keep my mind blank, what the men did to me hurt. I always screamed. Some of the men liked me to yell. Now when it's done, I just curl up inside myself."

"Why are you telling me this?"

Overwhelmed with the information, Chauncey wished she could right this problem. Still Water Runs Deep would tell her it was not up to her to fix anything concerning Beth.

Beth touched her arm, moisture glistening in her eyes. "I want to help you if you need it. Men can be cruel and hurtful. I know how to help you get through with the sex without too much pain."

"Stephen isn't cruel. He's a very nice man."

It was not difficult to defend Stephen. He was a nice man. There is no meanness about him. She didn't believe he would ever treat her as Beth described.

"I know. I don't see any meanness in his eyes. Yesterday, he was angry with you. Everyone saw that when he raced away from the wagons. He had to be furious with you for some reason. What was it?"

Chauncey lifted her shoulders, knowing she could never tell Beth everything. "I can't say. He would be angrier if I spoke of it."

She understood he wanted to get away from all this unscathed. Forcing a marriage on him had never been her intent, though by her actions that was exactly what she was doing. The romantic that she was, she thought he was in love with her. When he kissed her the first time, she fell in love with him. He didn't reciprocate the sentiment.

One kiss means nothing to men. She recalled Jess telling her brother that very thing. Men, her brother, Kane, they all kissed many girls. They didn't love any of them. She'd been a fool. This might be the biggest mistake of her life. In this case, there was no going back.

"If you want to ask anything, my offer stands. I'll answer any questions. Just tell me when you wish to talk."

Chauncey didn't believe she'd be asking Beth anything. At the moment, all she wanted was to stay away from Stephen. She didn't think he would allow her the privilege of keeping distance between them.

~ * ~

Aric Lakeland stomped through the house. He'd ridden to Baltimore. Dust covered him. Filled his mouth as well as his nostrils. He conversed with Jamie Lundin to discover his daughter lied to him. She didn't go to London to visit cousins. She didn't even go to Baltimore. Her name didn't appear on a ship's manifest.

Where the hell was she? His fist landed hard on the wall.

"Sit down, Aric. I'm certain she is fine. We need to believe that or we'll go crazy worrying about her." Ravyn plied her needle in the new stitchery she worked on. "You will drive yourself crazy if you keep pacing. What exactly did Jamie tell you?"

"That she didn't do as she told us in her letter. She's not in Baltimore. Not in London." He rubbed the back of his neck, swearing beneath his breath. When he looked up to gaze at his wife, "Where the hell is she?"

"Lyssa believes she is with Still Water Runs Deep. It seems she was enamored of him though we didn't notice. She says they shared a kiss or perhaps more behind the church the day of her wedding." She set her work on her lap to meet his gaze. "Do you recall that I hid in a trunk so I could stay with you rather than find myself sent back to London?"

He swore again. The memory didn't ease his worries. "You think she is that in love with the man. She barely knows him. He's headed for Indian territory. She's in danger."

"The man is Sioux. A warrior. He will protect her."

Ravyn's words didn't calm him or soothe his stretched nerves. They just made him angrier. "He will try. There are no guarantees. They will come back wed in the way of the People. Do you think they will find some backwoods traveling minister to wed them? When they return next year, we will make certain they say their vows here. I won't have it any other way. If they haven't married in some way, there will be hell to pay. I'll recognize any marriage before I bring out my shotgun."

"That is quite magnanimous of you, dear."

She rose. Walked to him then wrapped her arms around him.

"You won't change my mind with a tiny bit of loving," he said even as he turned to kiss her.

"I wouldn't dream of doing so. They will not have a bastard for a child."

"No, they won't."

His fingers tightened on her shoulders. When he saw her look of pain, he let her go unable to figure out what it was he should do.

"I would not accept that either. Chauncey will do the right thing. She will insist they wed."

"He's a man, Ravyn. I doubt if he instigated this. If he doesn't want to marry her, no one will be able to force him to do so."

"No, he most likely did not instigate this. We both understand our daughter is single-minded."

"Admit it, Chauncey is willful. Just like her mother."

"Don't blame this all on me. Yes, she is used to getting her way in everything. She is spoiled. We did that to her. I regret that fact? No! Not for one minute. It's what makes her strong."

Aric pulled her closer, felt her warmth, knew what he wanted to ease his mind. "I will send Slade after her. He will find her."

She touched his jaw with her fingertip in an attempt to soothe. "We do not know where they went. We cannot send Slade into Indian territory on the off chance that he will find her. We could be sending our son to his death. Have you thought on that?" Ravyn asked gazing at him with loving eyes.

"No, don't know how they will travel or in which direction." He understood what she wanted, accepted the fact that in this situation they were helpless. There were too few choices to be made.

"We will wait."

She pulled his head closer, her mouth raised expectantly to his. Running her tongue along her bottom lip she asked for a kiss, for renewal of love.

He understood she was just as frightened as he was. He kissed her, let his lips explore the woman he loved. Tugged on her bottom lip so she would open for him to sightsee. Heat filled him. All-encompassing love touched his heart. The kiss was long and slow. When he stepped back from the deepness, from the magic, he knew his answer would not make her happy. It would have to do. They would have to find a way to come to terms with his need to run after his daughter then haul her home as if she was a recalcitrant child. "I don't believe I can."

"You have no choice," she murmured touching secret places in his heart. "You will have to trust Chauncey. She is an adult woman with needs you can't understand."

He groaned when her exploring hands dipped beneath his buckskins, held him, stroked his swelling length. The warmth of her small fingers never ceased to arouse him. He saw Still Water Runs Deep with his daughter. Imagined him making love to her. She was innocent. He was seasoned in every way a man could be. The man was older, would want her beneath him. He should understand what was right. Still Water Runs Deep was still a man, a very virile one at that.

Saw her belly swelled with Still Water Runs Deep's child. His stomach twisted with the notion he failed to protect her. "She is an innocent, romantic at heart. Chauncey has no idea what she has gotten herself into."

"I imagine she does," Ravyn whispered. "Maybe not everything," she amended her voice soft. She may be innocent but she has needs just as all other women. "Still Water Runs Deep and Chauncey...he will treat her with respect. I'm certain of that fact. He is like Kane."

He withdrew from his wife to stride around the room, stopping occasionally, to swear then to stare outside as if he would see her striding to the door. "I would know where she went. A father needs to protect his daughter. I failed."

He gripped his fists tighter, wishing to hit the man who would take advantage of his little girl.

"You understand it is our daughter who assumed he would welcome her with open arms. Still Water Runs Deep is most likely innocent in this deception of hers. He didn't want her to go with him. The man would never put her into danger. Escorting her into Indian territory would do that very thing. He is caught in a situation he no longer controls. A situation orchestrated by our daughter."

Aric turned on her, his fury simmering to the point where he thought he would burst. He wanted to ride hard. Needed to rescue his daughter. He didn't know where she was even though he was reasonably certain as to where she was headed. "Don't understand why you defend that man."

She laughed, setting her hands on his chest. "That man...reminds me of you more than twenty years ago. Of course, I'm going to defend him."

Aric snorted, displeased with her confession. "Still Water Runs Deep isn't anything like me."

"You were stubborn to a fault. Thought only you knew what was good for me. Intended to send me home even though I pleaded with you to let me stay. I wonder if Chauncey is pleading with her man even now. The similarities are interesting. Don't you think?"

Ravyn chose not to continue the argument. After the short diatribe she fell silent. To Aric, it seemed obvious she decided he was right and she was wrong. The front door opened. Booted feet that had to be his sons strode through the house.

"Father! I've news!"

When he entered the parlor, they stepped apart. Slade grinned as if he knew what they'd been doing.

His son was too observant. Hell, he was a young man now. Aric knew Slade wasn't celibate. "News?"

Awkwardly, they both stepped forward. Aric's hand was stretched out to take the paper from Slade's fingers.

He handed it over. "A letter from your lost daughter. I didn't read it," Slade said as he watched.

Aric's brows drew together. He swallowed the gut-wrenching fear ripping through him. For several seconds he held the envelope in his hand while his breath hitched. Ravyn's hand fluttered on his arm. It had been five days since they left...a lifetime.

"Would you like me to read it to you?" Ravyn asked, her voice soft. "Or Slade."

He tugged in a deep breath of air as he opened the envelope then stared at the paper in front of him. Tears filled his eyes. It was just as he feared. Aric looked up then began to read.

Dear Mother and Father,

The first bit of information that you should have, is that I'm safe. The second is that I did this on my own. Still Water Runs Deep played no part in my decision. You see, I love Still Water Runs Deep. He doesn't know my feelings yet. I didn't want him to leave me for the year he said he would be gone. Don't come after us. You might catch up to the wagon train but I won't leave. You would only embarrass yourself and me as well. If you send Slade, well, even though he's my big brother, he's too young to be traveling through Indian territory by himself, a place he knows nothing about. You wouldn't put his life at risk. I know you.

As for me, I'm a grown woman. I can make up my mind. You no longer have a say in what I do. I'm writing this from Independence Missouri. I took the train here. Now, we are going overland by wagon train. Still Water Runs Deep is a guide and a scout for the train. Here he is known as Stephen Wilkes.

No, Stephen doesn't yet know I'm here. I'm hoping he won't for a few more days. The more time we are out of Independence the less chance he has of taking me back. I've told everyone he is my husband. He will be furious with me when he finally sees me. Imagine, I deserve his anger.

I do want him as my husband.

When he discovers my ruse, he won't hurt me. I know him well enough to understand he is a kind, gentle man. You see, he has no meanness in his eyes. I've seen that meanness before. If Still Water...Stephen is my life. I love him.

Please forgive me. Please don't try to stop me in anyway. If you do, I'll never forgive you.
Love,
Chauncey

"He's a bloody Sioux warrior! Bloody everlasting hell! He's taken scalps! What does she mean there is no meanness in his eyes and that she's seen meanness," Aric asked letting the letter float to the floor. He turned to Slade in search of an answer. "What else has she told you?"

"It's Paxton," Slade said speaking what seemed to be from his heart. "He cornered her one day then tried to force her. She made me promise to remain silent. That is what she was talking about. Because I was there. He left without getting what he wanted."

Chapter Two

Stephen spent most of the morning brooding about his circumstances while riding hard. The distance he covered spanned more miles than he'd ridden any of the past days. He'd not intended to marry, at least not for another ten years. His plans in London didn't involve a wife though Chauncey was beautiful. The ideas he had to build a small empire for himself were meant to be solo.

Chauncey intrigued him though. Found a place in his heart when he least expected that to happen. The timing was bloody awful. He laughed at his use of the very English word he'd learned from his time spent in England. He looked over his shoulder at his back trail knowing he needed to start back.

The girl was a wealth of energy bubbling forth. When she smiled at him his breath hitched. Finding her on the train was unexpected. He didn't believe in her short life she'd ever been told, no. She was spoiled from the tips of her delicate little toes to the top of her dark head. He imagined if he had a little girl who could look at him with beautiful blue eyes the color of a crystal-clear lake deep in the Rocky Mountains, he would never say any word that came close to no. He would give her whatever her heart desired.

That was the crux of the problem. On this trip he would have to tell her no a time or two. Her willfulness could not be tolerated if she wanted to stay alive.

The dinner she made last night over an open fire was more than passable. The food was delicious, mouthwatering. He could grow fat on her cooking as he wondered how she would do using a stove and ingredients other than the barest necessity. Easily, she fit into this lifestyle. Was used to working all day, riding. He wondered if she could shoot straight. Undoubtedly with time, he would discover the answer to that question as well as myriad of others.

This morning when he woke with her nestled in his arms, he unfastened her night dress. He touched her breasts. Held them in his hands. He'd been unable to stop his roaming fingers from exploring her tender flesh, discovering the tips. Caressed her belly, longed to sightsee lower. She told him her breasts were tiny. They were but they were also soft and shaped to perfection

He'd wanted to suckle her, taste the velvet pink tips, inhale her woman's scent. Somehow, he didn't know where he found the restraint. He kept his exploration to his hands. Purposely, he left the gown unfastened so she would question what happened during the night. He wished he could read her mind.

Her first time, he chuckled deep in the back of his throat. She wouldn't understand what he meant. In both her innocence as well as ignorance, she thought he did more than touch her. He wasn't a saint. Resisting her sweet charms for the duration of this journey would be impossible. Somewhere along their path he would need to find a minister. The forts usually had clergy in their midst. Fort Kearney was the closest.

Could he keep his hands off the woman for a few more days? He didn't know. He imagined that his success would depend on her.

When he argued with himself about taking her, he could never come to the proper conclusion. Deep in his heart, he understood whether he consummated the fake marriage or not, her father would see them wed at the Methodist church with the good reverend Brown residing. The nuptials would be completed. For him, the loss of control came at a stark price. He had to decide if he wanted to be shackled to Chauncey for life.

He shook himself from his musings when Terrell rode up beside him, tipping his hat, grinning. "Did you have a pleasant night with your wife, Stephen? How long did you say you've been wed?"

"The evening was pleasant enough. I do enjoy my wife's company. Thank you for giving me the time."

He wasn't about to answer any more questions about his wife and their marriage as fleeting as it was. Chauncey could have told him they were newlyweds or that they'd been wed for years. He would have to discover her story.

"Unless I need you in the evening you should remain with your wife. Newlyweds you know, can't keep their hands off each other. Remember my first experience with a lady as if it happened yesterday." Terrell searched the horizon. "Never got up the nerve to marry."

A long line of green grass along with trees meandered southward. "We're about to the river. We'll camp there tonight and all of tomorrow. Give everyone time to replenish their supplies with a bit of fresh meat."

Nodding, Stephen looked at the sky. He rested an arm on his saddle horn. "Thunder storm brewin' tonight, could be a dozy. Comin' our way. Need to be certain all the horses are secured. Don't want to be chasin' after the horses or the oxen that pull the wagons."

Terrell nodded, pushing his hat back off his forehead going on to question Stephen's observation. "You see a storm in those clouds, not just a drip or two of rain? Can't say as I like the idea of a tempest brewin'."

"Looks like the clouds are building. The higher they go the more likely we got us a devil of a storm. I'll pick up my tent from the wagon hauling some our supplies before I see Chauncey. Once we get settled, I'm taking my wife up the river for a bath along with a bit of privacy. Not much of that to be had on the train."

He did want privacy with her. She would tell him the same tale she spoke to Terrell.

"Be careful. There could be bandits about. Thieves that look on unwary travelers as easy prey," Terrell advised.

Not an unwary traveler. Stephen was used to the trail, the precautions one needed to take. Though he admitted with a woman along that fact changed everything for him. He wondered why he didn't mention Indians. There were a few tribes farther north. Their road west didn't come close to those Indian populations.

"You just be wary. Don't want that pretty little filly you wed to get herself hurt. There's other dangers out there to keep in mind."

Terrell turned his horse to start back to the wagons.

Stephen did the same. He rode up beside Chauncey. Beth was with her. "Came to spell you. I'll take Beth back to the White's."

He was thinking of animals frequenting the water holes. Keeping them in mind was sage advice.

"Just put me on the ground. I'll have to walk until we stop for the afternoon."

Beth turned to Chauncey. "The conversation was nice. You just remember if you need anything or have questions you can talk to me."

"I'll remember," Chauncey said as she made room for Stephen next to her.

Once he sat on the wagon and took the reins, he looked to her. "What was that all about? Questions? What kind of questions would you have?"

If she had questions, he wanted her to talk to him.

Her breath swept into her lungs. She pursed her lips to look at him, her lovely brows creasing together. "Beth hasn't had the type of life I would have expected. She seems all serene and calm on the outside. Appears to not have a problem in the world. That's not the truth."

"What did you expect form her?" he asked, curious to discover some of the conversation between them. "Are you telling me she is not as she seems?"

Chauncey rubbed the back of her neck for a moment as she shook her head. "I can't say too much. I promised her to stay quiet. Besides it's not my story to tell. She doesn't want others to know she's been..."

Chauncey stopped, sifting a gasp of air at the realization she almost told him something she shouldn't.

"She's been what, Chauncey?" His voice was harsh. He wondered if he stared at her hard enough, she would give in and speak to him. "If it's important to the health of this wagon train, you need to speak up."

"I would tell you if you promised to keep it to yourself," she said her voice strained with tension a strange look in those mesmerizing blue eyes of hers. "I'm not one to promise something then immediately forget the vow."

"Kind of like your promise?" he teased watching her back stiffen.

Hell, a promise was sacred to him. Nonetheless, if that vow ended up hurting someone else, he would forget what he said.

"You don't have to remind me. I'll feel awful if I tell you." She turned to him, touching his arm with her hand. "It's just that she needs help but there is nothing you or I can do for her. Truly, there isn't. What is happening to her doesn't touch anyone else. We need to let it go."

"You don't say. What questions did she want to answer for you? That, perhaps, has me even more curious." He thought to change the direction of the conversation that wouldn't put Chauncey's promise at risk. "At least give me a clue. Maybe I could ask and you could nod your head if I'm close."

The girl was young. She wouldn't have any idea about the question he was certain prominent in Chauncey's mind.

"Can't talk about the one without you realizing the other. You would put two-and-two together. Seems," she paused for a moment, "she wanted to know if you hurt me last night. I told her you had no meanness in you. She agreed." The air between them during the pause seemed stagnant. "I don't even know what you did."

His brows rose as he speculated where that conversation might have ensued. "What did you tell her about last night?" Stephen knew he didn't hurt her. Hell, she didn't even wake up when he caressed her soft breasts, stroked his thumb across the tip, lazily spread his hands between her hip bones. When she inadvertently spread her legs for him, he'd been tempted to explore the soft flesh between her thighs. He didn't.

"That no, you didn't hurt me. Wanted to ask her about something you said, but I didn't." she was fluffing up her skirt, shaking the fabric so it floated around her legs lovingly caressing them.

He grinned watching her reveal long white legs, legs that wore no drawers. Lust exploded, sending aching heat straight to his groin. "Something I said?" he questioned trying to remember what they spoke of this morning that she would seek answers for. With little thought, Stephen knew exactly what she wanted to learn.

Chauncey looked sheepish. He'd never seen that expression on her face. As the wagon lumbered along, she looked back to wave at Beth then she turned her attention to him. "About my first time. I didn't know what you meant. I don't feel different. The only problem was my nightdress was unfastened. I don't recall doing that." She fluffed her skirt again. "Did you? Did you unfasten my nightgown?"

"Ah...you still don't remember what we did. How you moaned your pleasure when I caressed you. You did tell me you liked the way my hands felt along with other parts of me. We should do the same tonight. After that you'll be an experienced lady. It doesn't please me that you don't remember. What's a man to think when his wife doesn't remember the first magical night she spent in her husband's arms."

This taunting was not well done of him, though he loved the way she chewed on her bottom lip when she was deep in thought.

Eyes flashing dangerously, she punched his arm. "You're talking in circles. I don't like that. If you do something to me...with me...I want to remember every moment. Whatever it was you did, it was not well done of you."

He whistled for a few seconds, delighting in her questions. She was so very easy to provoke. Perhaps he would caress her tonight when she was awake. They would be snuggled in the tent, private to themselves. For now, he wasn't about to tell her anything. "We're almost to the river. Do you still want that bath?"

He deftly changed the subject. While he enjoyed watching her stumble around his words taxing her imagination for the images she didn't understand, he didn't have the heart to continue.

"Yes!" She brightened with the question. "You won't watch me."

He bent to whisper in her ear. "I will. You are my wife. I want to see you buck naked just as God intended with the sunlight pouring over you, the warmth caressing all the soft parts of you that I wish to discover more thoroughly."

With his words he swelled. Damn, but teasing her was wreaking havoc with his masculine parts.

"Your gods or my God?" she asked, her face turning brighter by the second.

"Both."

He was now very eager to circle the wagons get the necessary chores accomplished and ride with her to the pool well past where anyone else would go to bathe. He remembered sneaking peeks at the maidens in the Indian encampment when they bathed. They would have water fights, their laughter and chatter filling the air. Naked, their beautiful bodies tanned by the sun, he would pick out the maidens he wanted to know better. He didn't want to have a water fight with her. No, he wanted to make love to her in the serene pool while he pushed inside her, the cool liquid surrounding them. He wanted to suckle her beautiful breasts.

She was a damn virgin. Her first time, her real first time wouldn't happen the way his mind imagined this afternoon. In fact, it wasn't going to happen until he could resist her no longer. He tightened his fists as he strove for the restraint he needed.

She was his bloody wife.

He couldn't have her, not yet. Because in his mind, she wasn't truly his wife. He would have to wait until there were vows said.

Doing the chores seemed to take forever. She gathered the clothing she wished to wash, his as well as hers. When he objected, she tilted her head then smiled at him. He didn't want her doing the damn washing.

He sighed as he gave up and quit protesting. She was a stubborn little thing. Once she sat in front of him on Spirit, he urged his stallion into a gallop. She cried out laughing her delight as they raced along the trail leading north to the very private spot he picked out for them. Her fingers dug into his forearm as she hung on to him while her hair flowed behind her, whipping against his arms as well as his face. He maneuvered the horse down a small animal trail slowing them.

With his arm beneath her breasts, he felt each movement. Tiny as they were the small globes bounced against him. Beneath her gown, she wore only her chemise. Her skin was damp from the heat and perhaps the exertion of the ride. When he reached the small waterfall and pool, he stopped.

Her breath held tight in her lungs; she sat up straight. When she turned in his arms to look at him, he felt the tips of her breasts across his chest. She was so damn hard to resist. His body tightened, his member swelling again.

"This place is beautiful. I want to stand beneath the waterfall and let the cool drops play over my skin," she murmured setting her head against his chest, nestling her cheek on his shoulder. "You will allow me a few moments of privacy?"

"No, this isn't a place where a woman can be left alone. It's too isolated. Besides, I brought you here so I could look at you, every sweet, silken inch of you."

He did, he realized that fact. They could have gone to the other pool where the women would take their turn at bathing then the men. "I want my wife all to myself."

Lord, but he didn't understand why he tormented himself. This might very well become the end to the beginning.

"Alright. If that is what you want." She tugged on his arm until he loosened his hold. She eased off the horse. "Going to wash the clothing first if you'll toss me the soap." She'd brought a clean dress and chemise. In her arms, she held the pants and shirt she'd worn the first day he discovered her presence on the train. She also carried some of his shirts and buckskins. "You can help if you like."

"Here."

He tossed the soap her way then dismounted and let Spirit walk to the water for a drink.

Easily, she caught the soap. Chewing on a blade of grass he watched her scrub the clothing before laying the pieces out to dry. While she was busy, he slipped out of his shirt and pants. If she wasn't going to make use of the water first, he would. All he had to wash with was her perfumed soap. When he finished, he would smell just as sweet as Chauncey. He laughed, having never bathed with scented soap.

While he was walking into the cool liquid, he felt the heat of her gaze on his back. If he wasn't hard as steel, he would have turned to look at her, perhaps to taunt her. Had she ever seen a naked man? Her brother topped the list of possibilities. Her father was another possible candidate. He dismissed those thoughts.

When he was close to waist deep, he dove into the water. He surfaced shaking his head, water droplets flying around him. He swam close to her. "Are you going to finish that chore anytime soon? I want to play in the water with you."

"You could have helped," she said, her voice saucy, tossing her long dark hair over one shoulder. "You did get them dirty."

Women's work. His first reaction seemed petty. He was reveling in the cool water while he knew she wanted to be in here too. Maybe not with him though. They both spent the better part of the day working. He felt a moment's guilt before pushing the strange thought from his male brain.

"Didn't think of helping."

Out here there were two division, men's work then women's work. He did shoot a deer; haul as well dress the animal for the families who were close to her wagon. There would be two days of venison that he provided. "Do you want me to help now?"

He started from the water, rising slowly, giving her a chance to send him back.

Her eyes widened then darkened with emotion. She smiled at him, her thoughts her own. "Now that I'm almost done? Not on your life," she was quick to say. "You will owe me a boon. Something I need done but cannot do myself."

"Coward," he taunted her with a wide smile admitting that he was enjoying himself. "You afraid to look at me, Mrs. Wilkes? I would think a girl with as much spice as you wouldn't think twice at looking at her naked husband."

Her head jerked up to stare at him. She was now seeing all of him, her wide-blue-eyed gaze focused on his arousal. She moistened her lips just as her hand slipped from the wet mossy rock she was leaning on. The shriek he heard scared the life out of him. When he saw her sprawled unharmed in the pool, her hands resting on the shallow bottom, her hair plastered around her face, he hooted his laughter. He'd never thought for a moment she would fall into the pool at the sight of him. Was that good or bad?

"May I help you out, Mrs. Wilkes?" he asked, his voice humming with anticipation. She wouldn't be able to push herself from the water without either falling completely in or with his help. The predicament she found herself in was delightful.

"You," she sputtered her eyes now blazing blue fire. "You did this on purpose. Now I'm all wet."

"Wasn't that the purpose of our coming here? Now, do you or do you not want my help?"

"Help, please." She swallowed her pride.

With his hands under her arms, he lifted her from her precarious perch half in and half out. "No, but if I'd thought of it, I would have tried. You are quite fetching." He set her on the ground. "When you're ready come in and play with me."

Lifting her skirt, giving him an amazing few of her legs, she wiped her face. Stephen decided he'd done enough. He shouldn't have laughed at her. With lazy strokes, he swam in the pond, sat on the ledge shelf beneath the waterfall allowing the water to pour down on him. She finished setting the clothing in the sun.

Sighing he swam to the shore, dressed in clean buckskins. "Would you like me to wash the gown you're wearing while you bathe?"

He wanted to bathe with her. Wished he could soap every inch of her. Obvious, doing so was too soon for her. He would have to turn his back so she could undress and slip into the water.

She nodded yes to his question. Her hands rested on the fasteners as she seemed to be hesitating. "You won't look?" Her voice trembled.

For a woman who was so eager to be married to him, she was terribly shy. He tried to meld the two women he knew one from the past the other his present into this one. After all, if he didn't miss his guess, Chauncey was a virgin, a true innocent. He was positive she'd been protected as well as sheltered for her entire life, kept from the worst parts of human existence. Today, Beth enlightened her about one of man's perversions. Yes, he knew what happened in the young girl's life. Beth was a jaded soul with good reason. He also surmised what the girl meant when she told Chauncey she would answer any questions she had. The thing was, he didn't want Beth to inform his wife about sex. Beth's view would be jaded.

"I won't look," he told her with solemn words as he strode from the water to sit on a rock that was now bathed in sunshine.

He leaned back resting on another boulder, closing his eyes until he heard the sounds of Chauncey bathing.

When he did open his eyes to see if she was fine, he saw more than she would have appreciated. The rose tipped nipple of one small breast peeked through her long, dark hair. She turned to face away from him as if she sensed his perusal. If she'd been looking at him as hard as he was looking at her, she would have sensed the attention.

Her back was long stretching what seemed forever to a small waist that flared in a beguiling manner at her hips. She was lathering her hair. Her body moving with grace. She ducked beneath the surface to rinse. When she finished with the soap, she paddled then walked awkwardly across the pond to the waterfall, eyeing it. The longing couldn't be hidden. She didn't climb out of the water. As if hoping he wasn't watching, she dared a glance his way.

"Can I join you?"

Stephen knew what her answer would be. Still, if she kept this up, he would strip again. Before she could count to three, he'd be in the water swimming toward her.

She shook her head, watching him, studying him as if she wondered if he'd keep his word. "If you turn the other way, I'm going to get out and dry off."

He was a man of his word. Drying off without him seeing all of her would be impossible. He wasn't about to take his eyes off her for more than a second or two even though he felt certain the area was safe. A chance taken could be a life lost. "How are you going to manage that feat?" he asked in a slow drawl that seemed to anger her as he watched her eyes blaze blue heat.

"You'll have to close your eyes." She began walking toward this side of the pond, moving her arms within the water as if that would help close the distance. Her hesitant strokes were short giving him reason to believe she didn't spend much time in the water. He decided he would teach her. Teaching his wife to swim might be delightful.

"Not on your life."

He was dead serious. This was no time to take a risk.

"Well...then...look away while I get out. I'll put my dress on without drying myself. In this heat the water will evaporate faster than a body can blink." She stopped moving through the water.

He knew her knees touched the bottom of the pond. Her hair

spread out around her, swirling with the currents the slow-moving stream created. The look in her eyes was expectant. She waited for him to turn away from her.

Damn, he was going to have to shut his eyes for a few seconds, at least long enough for her to dress herself. His gut twisted. A premonition of danger shot through him. He ignored the sense as part of his imagination. Being a gentleman was not all it was cracked up to be. Kane lectured him time and time again on the merits. With this woman and in this specific location it was the last thing he wanted to be. This was different.

"Have it your way. I'll give you a minute." Nothing could happen in sixty seconds. He relaxed, closing his eyes and absorbing the heat. Counting to sixty was all the time he meant to give her. He started saying the numbers to himself. Was all most finished thinking with relief that contrary to the tingling of his nerves nothing happened. "Fifty, fifty-one, fifty-two."

"Don't move, Stephen." The command in her voice sent ice through his veins. He didn't understand... She was so calm and controlled.

Less than a second later, the shot terrified him. He bolted upright. "Chauncey!" Eyes wide open, he looked where he expected her to be as he grappled for his gun.

Stark naked, she stood a few feet from the pond. His pistol was in her hand. "A rattler," she told him, her voice smooth as silk, her breaths quivering with her emotions.

For a moment in time he froze, his heart thundering in his chest. "You should have called to me."

He sounded accusatory. She could have hurt herself. She could have missed. She didn't.

Still standing in the same place, her beautiful body bared to his gaze, she spoke to him, "Believe I did. I told you not to move."

She was still holding the gun. This time it was pointed straight at him. She looked down as if realizing she wore nothing. In the heat of the moment, it seemed she forgot her modesty. With a tone very opposite her steady gun hand, she asked, "Why don't you close your eyes again?"

Her sweet bosom was rising and falling as if she was running a race, perhaps for her life. She was delightfully rosy. Unable to help himself he stared, mouth open gaping at her. No way in hell would he close his eyes now that she willingly revealed herself to him. "I'm looking at every beautiful inch of my wife. Now, why would I close my eyes?"

"Because I'm going to shoot you if you don't?"

Her voice wavered as she let the end of the gun travel to stare at the ground. The weapon slipped from her hand to land on the mossy spot near the holster he'd taken off earlier before he bathed. It lay beside Spirit's saddle.

He didn't even need to say the words. She wasn't going to shoot him. As if hit by a furious surge of energy, she stepped to her gown then, holding it in front of her. Her eyes were simmering, darkening with each second.

~ * ~

As if taking every possible second he could manage, he lifted his large body from the boulder then walked toward her. He grinned. "Can I help you with your gown, Mrs. Wilkes?"

Chauncey struggled with her confusing thoughts. She didn't want or need his help. He taunted her, calling her Mrs. Wilkes. She wasn't, not yet. Perhaps never. Though this was what she wanted. Wasn't it? She wanted him to notice her. Now that he did, she didn't know what to do. This wasn't quite the way she imagined him noticing her. She was standing in front of him, naked, unable to form a coherent word. A raspy fluff of oxygen slipped into her lungs not doing much good.

"Yes," she said, her voice meek, unable to understand what it was she wanted from this man. "Yes, maybe I do need a bit of help."

He stood behind her. She felt his fingers brush her hair off her shoulders. His breath fluttered across her naked shoulders. *Dear God, all of me is naked.* She felt his lips where his fingers had been. So close to her ear, he cleared his throat. "You took a huge risk, Mrs. Wilkes. You're not to gamble with your life. Do you understand?" She felt his teeth rasp down her neck, his tongue touch upon those same places. She shivered with the cascading sensation. Heat flamed.

"No," she told him. "No risk at all. When it comes to shooting, I don't gamble. I'm a perfect...near perfect shot. I..." She licked dry lips, tried to swallow to gain moisture in her parched throat, "knew what I was doing. The rattler had its eye on you. He was going to strike. You...you could have died." Chauncey shuddered at the thought of a rattler bite, the venom, the pain. His large hands caressed her shoulders, kneading the overtaxed muscles. "I...I need to put my dress on now. If you don't mind." She didn't understand why she said the last.

"I mind." His knuckles ran the length of her back, seeming to touch each vertebra one-by-one until his palm settled on her buttocks. He stroked her there, seemed to explore. Her knees threatened to buckle beneath her weight. She was shaking. "I don't need a woman to protect me."

"You said what? A woman to protect you? That wasn't what I was doing. I was protecting my ride back to the wagons. Don't think your big stallion will let me ride him if you weren't sitting on him also," she told him, alarmed that he was angry with her again. Furious because she killed the serpent. "The snake would have struck you if I didn't shoot it. What did you want me to do?"

"Maybe. Maybe not. Never heard the rattle. I've terrific hearing. If the snake meant to strike, he would have let me know." When he turned her to face him, he was grinning from ear to ear as if they weren't arguing. "Suppose we will never know the truth. Will we? Don't want you to ever do something so foolish again."

She believed him angry. At this instant, he was just being stupid with his commands. Chauncey closed her eyes trying to ignore his hard body. He pressed her next to him. Her body lay flat against his strength, the rippling muscles as he moved. She gasped in air, as his hands roamed down her back. Once more, he set them upon her backside, caressing, exploring delving lower into dark secret places she didn't think anyone would want to touch let alone a man.

"You have a beautiful butt, Mrs. Wilkes," he whispered close to her ear, nipping the lobe. "Kiss me. Open your lips for me to taste." He pressed her closer, his hands roamed down her inner thighs before moving to her waist.

She felt his hardness next to her belly. Didn't know what he meant. When she looked at him his lips framed hers, touched upon her. She whimpered when she felt his tongue slide across the seam, probing, pushing her lips apart. Her hands rose to his neck as her fingers, slid through the silken length of his raven black hair, strands as black as a starless night. With his teeth, he tugged on her bottom lip. She started to speak. Wanted to tell him...

His tongue slipped inside. She didn't know what she wanted to say. She forgot every coherent thought. He explored, pushing farther into her mouth, running his tongue along her teeth then the sides of her mouth. A small broken sound centered in the back of her throat erupted as he continued to kiss her. His knee pressed between her legs, moving upward. She felt the soft fabric of his buckskins against her woman's flesh.

She moaned.

He cupped her breast in his hand, fondled the roundness, ran his thumb across the tip. She heard him groan, a sound coming from deep within his belly.

"You're a delight. Everything about you enchants me. I never expected so much raw passion. Will you come, a willing woman, to my bed tonight? I want you, Chauncey," he asked as if he didn't intend anything more. His hand beneath her chin, he lifted it again, kissed her again. "I want so much more from you. For us."

Chauncey wanted to know what he was going to do next. Wondered if he decided they would be a married couple in more than name only. "I want more too," she murmured into his open mouth. "Don't want you to be angry with me."

"You do? That surprises me. As for anger, fury has a way of changing to desire and desire to passion." He chuckled trailing kisses along the column of her throat, nipping again, soothing marks with his tongue. "A few minutes ago, you were too shy to bathe with me. Now you're in my arms, naked as the day you were born. I'd love to keep you that way."

Those words brought back a second of reality. "I..I need to dress." To no avail, she pushed on his chest.

"Perhaps we should make love here on this soft spot of green moss. Would you like that? Would you change your mind then deny me?" His hands were on her backside again.

Chauncey didn't know what to think or do. She repeated herself thinking this was what she wanted all along. Somehow this felt wrong to her. "I...I don't know what you mean? Make love here? On the ground?"

"Ah, well then...tonight, I will have to explain the way of things." He froze then. "It's your turn to hold still."

"Another snake?" Her heart throbbing, pain filling her, she buried her head against his chest, soaking up his scent.

"No. Not this time."

The sound of his voice was smooth, calm. Strange, she felt the tensing of his muscles. Something wasn't the way it should be.

She heard the hoof beats. Knew this small space, this tiny paradise was about to be invaded by a human. The whistle threw her off as did his answering call. Whoever was coming, he knew the man. Stephen didn't seem surprised.

"Who is it?" Her mind was racing as she thought about everyone and anyone who might come here.

"Terrell...hush now, let me talk and stay behind me. He's probably coming because he heard the gun shot. Placed in the same position, I would have done the same. He knew where we were going to bathe. Would not have intruded for any other reason. When I saw you naked, I forgot myself. If I shot once more, he wouldn't be here. Would know that all was well."

"I've got to get dressed." Chauncey started to struggle away from him. He held her tight against him. "Stephen..."

"Hold still. It's too late for you to put on that damn gown of yours. If you don't keep behind me, you will make this worse. I, for one, don't want other men staring at my naked wife." Now unmoving behind him, she pressed her body tight. Oh, Lord, what was she doing here? She should have never followed him. Her mixed emotions were going to be the death of her.

Doing as he bid, she constrained herself holding as still as she could. Her nails dug into the solid muscle of his arms. Peaking around him she could just make out the man sitting atop the horse. She sucked in a breath of air while she waited. This should all be over soon. The man would leave. After that she would once more be faced with the problem she created.

Terrell pushed his hat back, his forearm resting on the saddle horn. He grinned as he seemed to take in the scene in front of him. "Heard the shot. Never a second one. Everything alright here? The little miss fine?" he chuckled while it seemed he tried to see around Stephen. "Appears so. Did the little lady try to shoot you? She didn't like your love making?"

He was still laughing. Nothing here was funny. Chauncey wanted to tell him what she thought.

Her cheek pressed against his back, she heard the steady cadence of his heart, knew each breath he inhaled. At least he wasn't naked. No, he wasn't. His buckskins were unfastened though. She recalled staring at him wishing she could see more of his beautiful body. His shoulders lifted in a negligent masculine shrug. It was one of her brother's favorite movements when he wanted to let everyone know he wasn't concerned.

"My wife thought I needed protecting."

His voice was so calm so soothing. Still, she caught the underlying anger. He wasn't pleased this man was here.

Neither was she. If he hadn't come along, she wouldn't be standing naked, pressed against Stephen.

Stephen, in a blink of time, became Still Water Runs Deep. Stephen never sounded this way, so very glacial.

Terrell nodded, "She shot the snake?" he queried then tipped his hat. "Guess I'll be on my way then. You two don't stay up here too long. Someone told me earlier in the day there was a storm brewing."

Her body was vibrating as she listened to him ride away. If she came out from behind his back, he would see her naked again. Humiliated could be used to describe what she was feeling but that one word didn't reach to the depth of her emotions. Stephen turned, drawing her once more into his arms.

"I'm sorry for that," he murmured against her hair, sounding more concerned than she believed he would feel. "Suppose I should have expected company after the shot was fired. Let me help you dress. Once we're both clothed, we can be on our way. Imagine Terrell was right about the storm I told him about. We need to hurry."

Against his chest, she was shaking her head. She didn't want to try to come up for air. Didn't want to see his eyes boring into her raking over her nakedness. Gulping air, she spoke. "I...I'm still naked."

"Yes, I know," he spoke as if he was addressing a small child. "We need to do something about that state, though I'd like to keep you this way a bit longer. Your nakedness at the moment is not practical. We do need to get a move on."

She was in front of him now. He maneuvered her with ease to wherever he wanted her. He swatted her bottom, a broad grin on his handsome face.

She jerked at the contact his hand made, her breasts swaying against his chest. Her nipples hardening at the contact. When she closed her eyes, she felt her lashes move across him. Chauncey looked up. Once again, nerves stretching, she spoke the obvious truth. "I don't have anything on."

He barked, to her his voice sounded as if was trying to keep from laughing at her. She punched him. On his chest, he covered her fist with his hand.

"Come, I'll help." He set her aside then bent to retrieve the gown she'd let slip to the ground. Stepping back, "Put your arms over your head."

She balked. Knew he was looking at her, all of her again. She wanted to cover herself with her hands. As if he understood what she was thinking, "The dress will cover you more thoroughly than your tiny fingers. Though," he smiled at her, a heartwarming smile under the circumstances, "you don't have a lot to cover."

To her chagrin, she punched him again leaving herself vulnerable once more. "Ass...!"

The long sigh he let loose from his lungs made her look into his eyes, his beautiful green eyes. They were laughing at her too. "Do you like being naked? By now, with a bit of cooperation we could both be dressed. All our parts covered. Put your arms up so I can slip this over your head. While your state of dishabille is delightful, I want to get back to camp. We can pursue this penchant of yours to be naked more this evening inside our tent."

She wanted to retort that she didn't want to be naked with him now or tonight. She didn't. Resigned to do this his way or not at all, she did as he asked. When the dress was covering her, he fastened the buttons. He took his time though, caressing, touching, teasing, stimulating her more than she'd been before. By the time he finished she was vibrating, aching in places that until that first kiss behind the church, she never paid attention to.

"All done."

He stepped back looking at her as if he was admiring his handiwork.

"You should dress too." She turned from him then, collecting the clothes that were set out to dry. They were still damp. She would have to spread them out inside the wagon. With everything folded and bundled in her arms, he took them from her, securing them in the saddle bags. A few minutes later they started back.

Once more, she sat in front of him, his big arm around her, pulling her against him. Power and strength emanated from him. He was so big, so tall. She was dwarfed by him. Thinking of him holding her earlier, she was a tall woman, taller than most. She didn't even come up to his shoulders. For the few miles back, she leaned into his body. He seemed relaxed with her, easy going as they rode. They didn't talk. She found she liked the silence.

With the wagons in view, he spoke to her again, his voice close to her, sending tremors down her spine. "I'm getting my tent from another wagon. The one I thought to keep all my gear in before I discovered my marriage to you. Suppose I should bring all my things to your wagon. What do you think, Chauncey? Are we going to continue with this ruse?"

Now his voice sounded harsh. Wrapping her arms around herself, she shivered.

Sifting into her lungs a huge breath of air, she nodded, as she didn't have a choice. She would continue calling him her husband because she would be left behind if she didn't. Over then over again, she reminded herself this was what she wanted. "Imagine so if you aren't going to denounce me. Leave me alone, stranded on the trail."

He could do so at any time. It would not be difficult for him to part ways with her. She had no proof they were wed.

His glowering countenance told her he wasn't pleased with her comment. "I could," he told her, his breath whispering across her ear. "What would you do if I told the truth? Perhaps you should be as pleasant as possible."

Her back stiffened trying to come to terms with all his varying comments. She didn't understand how he created such heat in her with just a few words whispered close to her. Beth might understand the answer to that. Chauncey didn't think Beth felt any pleasure in her encounters with the men during her short life. Maybe she should ask Stephen as to why she was hot and feeling so different. Why butterflies tumbled inside her belly then suddenly turned to fire-breathing dragons.

He would laugh. She wasn't at all certain she wanted him laughing at her any more than he did today. When they reached her wagon, she slid off the horse stopping to take the washed clothing from his saddle bags. The simmer in his green eyes gave none of what he was feeling a way. For a few seconds, she watched him ride away.

To get his things. He was coming back. They would continue to pretend.

When he was far in the distance, she climbed into her wagon, spreading the clothing out again. After she finished, she sat back looking at her home away from home. She liked what she was seeing. She thought of sharing the space with Stephen. Well, the space she would share would be in his tent.

"Did you and your mister have a nice bath?" Beth stood behind her watching. "I did in a different little pond where all the women went. They are all so modest, wrapping towels around them. I've never had the chance for modesty. Suppose now pretending to cover oneself because embarrassment is not real. Those women are all married. Their men folk must look at them."

Heat flared on her cheeks. "Yes, my bath was pleasant." Chauncey saw the all-knowing look in the girl's eyes then the frown of concern.

The blurted question surprised Chauncey. "Did he hurt you? I'll tend to you if he did. If you're bleeding, it will have to be stopped."

Astonishment at Beth question coupled with her statement sent shock waves through her. Chauncey didn't know what to make of this conversation.

Bleeding?

Several seconds passed by before logic kicked in and she could think of words. The tiny breath of air she sipped did her no good. "No, Beth, Stephen didn't hurt me. He would never hurt me."

She didn't understand how she knew that fact. Without one doubt in her mind, she did. No, he would relish embarrassing her to the tips of her toes. He would continue to change his mind about what he wanted just so he could tease and taunt her. He touched her in ways that melted her, that caused heat to rush through her then leave her wondering what would come next. Her finger on her mouth, she thought on more of what he did. "He kissed me."

Beth was shaking her head, her brows creased together. "Kisses can hurt. I've had my mouth left bruised as well as bleeding by the time my master finished with me. Does he call himself your master?" She waved her hand in the air, slashing gestures. "Doesn't matter, I started a venison stew for you and your mister since he shot the deer. I found some potatoes and carrots in your wagon to add to the pot. Hope you don't mind me going through your things."

"Thank you. That was very sweet of you, Beth. Believe I've a few other vegetables I can put in the stew." She thought of the small tomato plant she brought with her. It was unusual but so far, the plant seemed to thrive. For how long, she couldn't surmise. She set the plant near the front of the wagon so it got sunlight most of the day and made certain she gave it enough water. The plant rewarded her efforts with a couple tomatoes a day.

Beth started to leave. After a few steps she turned. She stared at her hard. "You would tell me if you need help. I've a few ways to keep you from getting with child. I will help you with that, too, if it's not too late. Is it too late?" Beth stared at her hard the question reverberating through her head.

Chauncey found herself both nodding then shaking her head as a strange air of confusion assailed her. She would tell her but first she would ask Stephen what Beth was talking about. Again, she found herself moving her head in silent response. While there was quite a lot that went on between a man and a woman that she didn't understand, she did know she wasn't with child. Not yet. Was she?

"No, Beth, I'm not increasing."

Her mother made certain she would understand those things. She told her it would never do for a woman to wonder and fear. That time so long ago, not so long ago, when Paxton cornered her. His action alarmed her brother. She wouldn't have told her mother except her brother told her he would inform them as to what happened if she didn't. They'd always let her explore their land. For most of her life she roamed the territory with her brother Slade or Lyssa, her cousin. After Paxton attacked her, she always carried her gun.

In the wagon, she had a rifle along with a pistol her father gave her when she turned thirteen. She learned to shoot when she was five. They often practiced in the back of the house where her father set up targets. She was a better shot than her brother even with moving targets. That fact always pleased her.

Humming to herself she finished adding vegetables along with salt and pepper to add taste to the stew. She mixed up a double batch of biscuits to share with both the Greeleys and the Murphys.

Bent over, stirring the venison, she felt the heat of his hands on her waist, understood his tenderness. She wished this marriage of theirs wasn't a sham. She didn't know how to go about changing that. It seemed he was always the person in charge, the one making the decisions. Standing, she turned to face Stephen.

Wishing she dared touch his face, she smiled instead. In a whisper, hoarse with new found desire, she spoke, "Dinner is almost ready. Are you hungry?"

She was starving but she didn't think the sensation was for food. He was grinning at her as if he read her mind.

"You have enough biscuits?" He moved away, the distance left her without the fierce heat of his large body. "Then I'm a starving man," he said the words though he wasn't looking at the biscuits baking in the large cast iron frying pan. No, he stared at her, at her lips. "I want to kiss you again."

She wanted that too. Gathering a large breath of air laced with the courage to deny him, "You will have to wait," she told him trying to disguise the longing in her voice.

He hooted seeming to understand her ploy. "If that's the way you want to play this game of yours, I'm going to set up the tent. We'll sleep there tonight. Since we're not going anywhere tomorrow, we can sleep as long as you like." Before he left, he ran a callused fingertip down her neck. The sensation left promises of something more. The dragons inside her roared to life. Something she might like to explore.

The shiver coursing through her left her speechless. She wanted to yell at him that she wasn't going to sleep in the tent with him. Her wagon would do just fine. He didn't need to pretend when he didn't want anything to do with the lie. The words didn't come as she pressed her lips together.

Minutes later she realized the tent was pitched. He spread a blanket on the ground by the wagon wheel where they ate last night. He was stretched out, his hat covering his face. His feet were crossed at his ankles. He had very long legs. She wondered if he slept. Probably not, most likely Stephen was resting, conserving energy. He would hear everything around him. Seemed, he was always alert.

With two plates in hand, she sat down next to him. She didn't know what to expect now that he'd moved in, the act seeming official. "Dinner is served," she said wondering if she was waking him up. "Hope you're not sleeping."

"No, watching you, wife," he said his voice soft a bit throaty. He set his hat on the ground. "Is everything ready to eat?"

"Yes, hold these and I'll get the coffee." She started to hand him the plates.

His hand on her arm, he stopped her. She jumped from the contact. "Relax. You've had a hard day. I'll get the coffee." In a fluid motion, he rose. His long powerful strides took him to the campfire.

Beth was there seeming to wait for him. She spoke to him, her words not carrying to her. He looked to her then back to the girl. His brows were furrowed. They parted, Beth going back to the Greeley's wagon, Stephen striding to her.

He sat down beside her.

Chauncey let out a long slow breath of air. She didn't want to relive any conversation Beth had with him. Understood he wouldn't give her a choice. "Can we talk about whatever it was she said after we finish eating...or maybe tomorrow...even the next day. As I told you before the girl has been used and she thinks all men are the same."

"After we eat might be more pleasant. Though I doubt if anything we can say concerning Beth will be nice. You're right about attempting to have a pleasant dinner. What would you like to talk about now? How you deceived everyone into believing we were wed?"

She sipped in a quick breath. Deciding to ignore his words, she sent him what she hoped was a cheeky smile. Changing the tenor of this conversation was important to her peace of mind. "You could tell me about England. About this land you bought that is even more appealing than living in the states." To learn as much about Stephen was her goal. She'd been surprised when he wanted to follow Kane to the British Isles.

"Ah, the place I intend to live the rest of my life. It's nothing like the plains we are crossing or the Rocky Mountains where we will soon be. The scent as well as the landscape is different as are the people. The land is tame, civilized for the most part though there are still men who would take what isn't there's. No matter where a body lives, that fact never changes. Kane is the best friend I've ever had. I protect his back as he does mine. Can't imagine a life that we don't share in some respect."

Unable to figure out what to do with her hands, she twisted her hair into a bun. "Are you speaking of the man who wanted Lyssa so he could gain a title? The man who kidnapped her. Do you know what happened to him?" she asked wishing she could pry more thoroughly into his head. "If I am to go there with you, you won't have to worry about anything like that. I've no title for anyone to crave. My father is no heir to a title."

He looked into the distance giving nothing of his feelings away. "Don't know yet if you will be accompanying me across the ocean." Now, he seemed to be staring into the flames that were even now dying low. The embers burned. Someone always kept the fire going throughout the night.

Chauncey sucked in her breath at his statement. For the shortest amount of time, she forgot they weren't married. There were no vows tying this man she loved to her. Forgot he had no obligation to her past the wagon train. Even then if he chose, he could tell everyone the truth. Could reveal her lies. She should have expected something along that vein. She would be ostracized. Never meaning to do so, she forced him to a position he didn't have any intention of filling. Even if he made love to her, he wouldn't be bound to accept her as his wife. She would become his whore. Her gut clenched.

"No, I imagine you don't. I'm sorry I forced your hand." She spoke with sincerity.

She was sorry. She stared at her hands, wishing... What she didn't know was if he would believe her.

"Yes, you didn't know what you got yourself into when you in your untried innocence claimed me as your husband. Did you? You got a savage." One dark eyebrow rose a fraction. "Look at me," he touched her chin tilting her face so she would have to look at him. "I can take your virginity and still leave. It's what you want. Though you don't understand. If I did so, it would change your life forever. Are you willing to gamble your future away?"

The speculation was obvious to her. He was weighing his choices. She didn't like his threats. True, if given the chance she would gamble on him. "No, I didn't. Never thought you would see me naked as you did a few hours ago. You said we would be naked again tonight. I don't want to..." She bit her bottom lip in a desperate effort trying to understand what he wanted.

"So very innocent." He moved a wayward lock of hair to behind her ear. "I don't know yet what I want to do with you. Haven't decided. You've bedeviled and confused me. We need to have the look of a newly married couple. We need to pretend. At least Beth is convinced we are husband and wife." He finished his dinner, setting his plate aside. "I'll wash. You get ready for bed. I find that today has been trying in more ways than one."

"You don't have to wash the dishes. It's my job. You have other obligations." She rose as she needed to grab the plates from his hands.

With ease, he stopped her. "I need time to think. Washing the dishes will give me that opportunity. Go change to your night clothing. Brush your hair one hundred strokes if that is what you want. I'll be back soon."

That was what she was afraid of, nervous about. He would be back soon. After that, what would he do? The first rain drops began to fall. She heard his soft curse as he bent over to clean the dishes.

Scrambling, she raced inside the wagon to do as he asked. Dressed in the white gown that covered her from the tips of her toes to just below her chin, she climbed into the tent. She pulled the covers over her head then waited realizing she made up her mind. She wanted him more than life itself. Any gamble she made would be worthwhile. If she had him for one night, a week or a lifetime she made her decision.

~ * ~

Sipping his father-in-law's brandy, Kane waited for the explosion of anger he was certain would come soon. Aric Lakeland had been beside himself with worry for his daughter the last two days. It was only this morning that he brought his concerns to him. Kane understood what Aric would ask.

"You will go after my daughter and your friend." The statement was not broached as a question. "You're the only man I trust with this job. You're the only man I know who can travel through Indian territory unscathed."

His gut twisting, Kane twirled the glass, amber liquid sliding along the smooth crystal. When he looked at Aric, saw the concern coupled with fear in the furrow of his brows then the aging crease lines around his eyes and mouth, he was tempted to say, yes. The thing was, he wasn't about to leave his wife for another nine months or more especially when he understood Chauncey would be safe with Still Water Runs Deep or Stephen as they decided his English name would be.

Kane spoke with caution attempting to make his point. "His plan was to travel into Indian territory. By November, he will be with the tribe where we grew up. I could never catch up with them. Could not bring her back before the winter snows make anything but staying in place a necessity." He paused still twirling the liquid still wishing he could say yes. "Besides, you and I would never make it to the mountains before the snow was so deep the traveling would be impossible."

"You're not going to try?" Aric asked incredulous, his voice a mask of fury as well as desperation. "I should go then. Thought you would help."

"If you went alone, you would die," Kane said all too bluntly. "If the weather didn't kill you, the Sioux would or the Cheyenne or the Crow. They wouldn't ask questions. Wouldn't care why you were trespassing. You would lose your scalp."

"What about Still Water Runs Deep?" Aric shot back to him. "What about Chauncey? She's white. Will they kill her?"

He was up, pacing the room, distraught as to what was revealed just now. His hands ripped into his hair.

The conversation would go nowhere if Aric decided to pursue the topic. Changing his mind would not happen. He was shaking his head. Lyssa sat down beside him, her hand resting on his arm as if she tried to encourage.

"Not if she is with Still Water Runs Deep. If she does everything my friend says, she will be fine. He will take care of her. Nothing will happen to your daughter."

Aric's groan didn't surprise him. If Chauncey was as willful as well as stubborn as his wife there would be more problems that Still Water Runs Deep would need to deal with. He would have to convince the woman that she had to obey. These women were not brought up to obey.

"Just as she made the decision to follow the man, my daughter will do as she pleases," Aric said his voice furrowed with fear.

"I believe she said in the letter you allowed me to read that he is called Stephen now, Stephen Wilkes. Stephen will make sure she understands all that is at risk. If she is so foolish as to go against his wishes, he will find another way to convince her that he knows what is best."

Aric Lakeland would have to accept that notion for a fact.

"My daughter isn't stupid," Ravyn said, her voice soft as she sat beside her husband, her hand resting on his thigh. "She will understand the consequences if she goes against Stephen's wishes. I'm certain she will behave."

"What if she believes him to be wrong?" Aric asked turning to her, questioning her statement. "You know how she can be when she believes she has right on her side."

Lovingly, Kane set his gaze on his wife. She was much the same. "Lyssa listened to me, obeyed me when I was shot. If there is sound reason behind his words, Chauncey will do the same with Stephen."

He was having some trouble calling him by his new white name. Stephen Wilkes was the one they agreed on after they left London. On board the ship, they mulled over several different names that would carry him into English society. This one seemed to suit.

"So, the two of them are on the prairie. How many days from Independence?" Aric asked, as he tapped his fingers on the brandy glass he held in his hands.

Ravyn appeared alarmed at the question. Her eyes widened with fear. "If you are still thinking of taking Slade and going after our daughter, I want you to stop that nonsense right now. Have some faith in our daughter as well as the man who lived most of his life with the Sioux. Don't try to right one foolish act with one even more riddled with stupidity," Ravyn said as she grabbed his empty glass from him.

He watched with seeming curiosity as she filled the glass then brought it back. "Drink up. Maybe you will sleep away the night. Perhaps you will have nightmares of what could happen to you if you acted so foolishly. Maybe you can see yourself without your hair." She sat down with a loud hrmph.

Aric let loose the breath he'd been holding. "Sometime you could hold back your venom, wife. We both know she will lose her innocence. Is that what you want?" he retorted as if trying to justify his thoughts of rescue.

"It most likely vanished days ago. Why would he hold back when she wants to give herself to him? From all accounts, Nicki didn't hold anything back. As for Lyssa," Ravyn asked, searching Kane for a possibility that he would give in to their request despite the enormity.

What he and Lyssa did or didn't do was no one's business but theirs. Kane cleared his throat as if he might have something to add. He didn't. He felt certain Stephen would not take her innocence until they were married in at least one way. Just as he was honorable. So, Still Water Runs Deep was also honorable. He kept his mouth closed and his words behind his teeth, since he understood what he had to say would not sit well with the father or the mother.

"Needless to say, Aric, I will not leave my wife. We've been apart too long. She is with child. There is nothing you can do or say that will change my mind. Chauncey took the risk. She is a grown woman. It is not my place to charge forward in her behalf when I've no idea her wishes." With that said the discussion was terminated.

Chapter Three

Stephen watched as Chauncey crawled into the tent. Her delightful butt poked toward the sky as she tried to navigate the opening flaps. His body tightened with the need she so easily generated in him. He wanted her. He cursed himself and his unruly body. He could love her.

She offered herself to him. At the waterfall, he witnessed the doubt in her eyes, the few moments of fear. What he saw was simply a virgin's apprehension. For several minutes, he stood by the campfire, breathing hard in an attempt to soothe his rampaging arousal. He wondered how many more nights he could sleep beside her and not take what she offered. Part of his brain told him that since it would happen anyway, why prolong the agony, his agony? He supposed some of that was up to her and the way she treated him each night when he crawled under the same blankets.

He was only a man.

They should be wed before he took her innocence. His honor would stand for nothing less.

If he was a smart man, he would declare her as his in the way of the People. In his mind as well as his upbringing, that would be as binding as a ceremony spoken by a man of God. She didn't understand marriage as well as what it would entail between the two of them. Her life had been so very sheltered. She was a romantic at heart. In love with the idea of love. Innocent of men as well. He knew his touch sent flames burning inside her.

Once she left Missouri on this train, all that changed. She opened herself to him. Dear God, she was so impetuous, so very willful. He would have his hands full taming her to the way of the Sioux. Except with the Sioux, he hoped she would stay much the same as when he first encountered her. Taming a woman left him with a bitter taste in his mouth. It was her impetuous nature that first attracted him to her. The flamboyant way she conducted herself.

Tonight, he would sleep in his buckskins. Nonetheless, he meant to strip the damn virginal nightgown from her sweet, tender curves then hold her, press her against him. He needed to touch and caress her until she moaned and begged for him to finish what he started. If she was as aroused as he was, he would be pleased. He would give her a woman's pleasure, bind her to him in at least one way.

Those thoughts were wrong, all wrong. He needed to remain in control. Show her how he would love her. A few kisses, some intimate caresses would have to do until they could find a man of God. Needed her to understand what she could expect when they wed.

He recalled Beth's words to him this evening. She cautioned him not to hurt her. Chauncey would have to tell him what Beth said this afternoon. He was afraid those words from that very jaded young woman might have put more fear into her. Dear Lord, Beth couldn't be more than fifteen. What was going on in the Greeley's household?

He prayed it would not be too many more days until they reached the fort, prayed, too, that a minister, or preacher, or someone ordained would be in residence. By his calculation, it would most likely take another twenty-five days if the weather held. If he consummated the marriage before then the matter would be rectified.

She would be his.

He'd determined that Chauncey would be his but not this soon. Taking her into the mountains would task her strength, would put him in a position of vulnerability he wouldn't enjoy. He set the dishes in their assigned places. She was organized. Everything seemed to have its proper place. He saw the tomato plant sitting near the front of the wagon. Shaking his head, he looked over the rest of her belongings. She packed very little for herself. He noticed earlier that she brought only a few items of clothing, mostly pants and shirts. She had only two gowns. By the time he returned her to the ranch, they would be in tatters.

Slipping out of his shirt, he hung it on a hook next to her dress. After he pulled off his knee-high moccasins, he brought them inside the tent. He wasn't going to make love to her, not before they wed. He didn't know how he was going to keep his hands off her. The conflicting emotions confused him.

The rain was falling harder. He looked to the north inhaling the scent left by the rain. A blaze of lightening lit up the northern sky. A few seconds later, thunder rolled along the prairie. He'd been right about the storm outside. There might very well be another storm beneath the canvas.

Not quite certain what he was doing, Stephen crawled through the opening. He stared at her. She was sleeping, one hand tucked beneath her cheek. A chuckle formed in the back of his throat. Somehow, he kept the laughter from erupting. In all her virgin glory she was wrapped tight in a blanket. He would have to roll her to get her out of it then beneath the covers with him. He would figure out a way.

"You going to hog the covers?" he asked as tugged her so she faced him. "It's cold. I need some warmth."

Her eyes were closed tight. He knew she wasn't asleep. "Chauncey, open your eyes." He ran a fingertip down her cheek. She was so damn beautiful. "Sit up and talk to me. You should share the covers with me."

She turned, her eyes opening. "All right. What do you want to talk about? You did say you wanted to speak with me."

That surprised him. It seemed right. They had all day tomorrow to rest if they spent the evening in conversation. "Thought we decided that you would tell me about Beth. She's not very old to seem so wise to the ways of men." He let those statements hang in the air. "You've made implications. I would know if she needs rescuing."

Chauncey sat up, pushing her hair from her face, lowering until she clasped them together to settle on her lap. The blanket slipped to her waist. He wanted to rid her of the nightgown. Wished he was looking at her naked as he did this afternoon.

Son of a bitch, I just told myself I wasn't going to touch her until they were wed.

"Beth doesn't want to be rescued," she said as she pulled one of the blankets from beneath her to hand to him. "I shouldn't have taken them all. I'm sorry. Maybe she does want to be liberated. I wouldn't know how you could go about it. She's dependent on the Greeley's. Without them she has nothing, no food, no shelter, no clothing."

"Why did you take all the blankets?"

For the moment he thought it prudent to think on Chauncey's words about the young woman.

"Thought maybe you would sleep somewhere else," she said while two long, slender fingers toyed with the top button of her gown. "Didn't know if you would be back. You seemed...different." She lifted her slim shoulders. "I didn't know."

"You had my tent. Where else would I sleep?"

He was mesmerized. With slow movements, she unfastened that one button. He held her hand in his, rubbed the inside of her wrist. He wished he knew if she was aware of what she was doing. Looking a way for a moment then clearing his throat. "Will you share the blankets? The cold will chill my bones if you don't."

He was better off if she refused him. Just as he was a wealth of contradictions, it seemed to him she was also.

"Yes..." her voice faded. Her lashes lowered across her cheeks for a fleeting second. Blue-white light from the tempest outside lit the interior of the tent. A horse neighed. Steps, slow and measured, walked past the tent about ten feet from them. Once again, thunder followed. She wrapped her arms around herself. She was shivering. He didn't know if the shudders were from the cold or fear.

"Are you afraid of the storm?"

He pulled the cover across both of them then her into his arms. She was soft and pliant. Her scent was evocative, all woman coupled with a hint of magnolia. "Tell me about Beth."

He thought the best way to distract her was to keep her talking. Her head was nestled on his shoulder, her hand on his chest. He closed his mind against the sexual ache she created.

She spread her hand, splaying her fingers wide as if she measured the width of his chest. One finger crossed his small, male nipple. He hissed in air.

A silent curse hovered. He swore. He couldn't do this night after night. She pressed up to look at him, curiosity in her dark, blue eyes. He wanted to discover all her secrets, the darkest and deepest of all of them.

"That's two questions," she said, her words soft as she settled her head in the hollow of his shoulder continuing her ardent exploration. This time she let her hand drift to his belly just above his waistband. "I'm not afraid of storms. I love to listen to the tempest howl, the thunder boom across the land. When lightning flashes it seems to light up the world. Sometimes in the fall hurricanes pass through." She paused for a few seconds as if thinking. "As to Beth..."

"Beth is a troubled young girl. She's not a woman yet she knows more than she should," he said, running his hand along her back, pressing her so close he could feel the hardening of her nipples. He was tormenting himself. He should leave before he did something he would regret. Before he lost control.

"Yes, she's been sold to men. Has only known brutality. I think they force her to have sex with them. She told me she would help me if I ever needed help. Beth is the one who needs rescuing. Can you, do it? Rescue her?"

His mind raced with different scenarios. Perhaps he could find a way. The girl would have to accept a warrior. The man he was thinking of would treat her with respect. In the way of the People, he would take a wife then treat her with reverence. "What kind of help does she want to give you?" More talk might serve to distract him. "You've alluded to a few things."

Chauncey pushed up so she looked into his eyes. "She's told me several things that worry and confuse me. She said if I ever bled because of my husband, I needed to make certain it stopped. If I didn't know how, she could help."

With those words Stephen felt blindsided. He flinched. He would never hurt her so badly she bled. What was going on here? He had to be honest with Chauncey. She obviously didn't know what to expect. "That won't happen except once. That once is natural."

"I know," she breathed in then out as if she hoped to tell him she understood what would eventually happen between them, not tonight but soon. "Beth also said if I didn't want to get pregnant, she would give me the necessary things to keep that from happening. I don't understand." Chauncey was sitting now, cross legged beside him. "Do you?"

Once more she was playing with the buttons on her nightgown. Now there were several unfastened. She was nervous he decided. This wasn't something she planned nor was she attempting to seduce. He'd noticed one other time she played with the buttons on the shirt she wore. He would allow her to undo all of them. It would save him the trouble.

He toyed with what exactly to speak to her about contraception. If they were to become man and wife, she should have some understanding. He wasn't about to keep her with child year in and year out. She would have to know about withdrawal as well as sponges. There were other methods. That wasn't the method Beth would use. "She uses a sponge?"

Her baffled stare left him chuckling inside. He didn't want to explain the specifics. Every good prostitute used sponges. "It's something ladies of the evening use to keep from conceiving. It's nothing you need to worry about. You won't ever need to use a sponge unless we decide it's the best for your health."

"I see," she spoke, her fingers dancing over more of the front fasteners. Next when she spoke, she focused on him, on his mouth. "I like your chest, the way you feel beneath my fingertips. You don't have hair except..." she looked to where he'd undone his buckskins for more comfort. "Down there. My brother's chest is hairy. So is my father's."

Unable to help himself, he groaned thinking if he didn't do something soon this would become the longest night of his life. "The Sioux don't have chest hair." He didn't know anything else to say. He was stymied by her questions.

She tucked her bottom lip between her teeth. More of her soft white flesh was revealed by her nervous fingers. "I see."

He didn't think she saw much of anything. In time she would as would he. "Mr. Greeley uses Beth?" he asked. "I assume she isn't willing."

"Yes...he's not the first man to buy her for his personal use. She was sold to a man when she wasn't very old. Mr. Greeley bought her a year ago to help around the house. Mrs. Greeley doesn't know what he does to Beth after she goes to bed or whenever he finds her and they are alone. Don't know if the misses would care if she did know. Beth says the wife just wants him to leave her alone. I'm guessing the woman does know and approves."

"He hurts her... Chauncey, there isn't anything I can do about that unless she comes to me. Mr. Greeley believes he owns her. In a strange sort of way, he does. Where would she be if the man tossed her out?"

"I didn't tell you thinking you could help. I understand more than you know."

He thought that perhaps Chauncey did comprehend more than he thought. It was time to change the topic, past time to sleep. "You look tired. Come, now, let's get rid of your nightdress. Shall we? Seems I told you I wanted you naked tonight. Just the way you were when we bathed" He sat up then, finishing with the buttons she'd begun to take out of their holes. "Now, take it off."

Adorably, she was wide eyed, shaking her head. He saw the slight swell of her breasts through the opening. Remembered the way her breasts felt this afternoon pressed against him. "Would you like me to help?" His voice was tender, soothing he hoped. He didn't want her to run shrieking and terrified from the tent.

"I..." she swallowed. He saw her neck muscles working. "Don't want to just yet. Give me another minute."

"By your own machinations you are my wife. My wife will always sleep naked with me." He smiled at her as if that would encourage her compliance. While he wasn't going to do anything except sleep, she wasn't aware of that fact.

"Not really your wife. I thought. I thought we would get married along the way. A man and a woman shouldn't sleep together unless..." She stopped as if she realized he wasn't a virgin.

"You're right, Chauncey. I've slept with any number of women, none of who were my wife. Tonight, I'm going to sleep with a woman who will become my wife. That's all, sweetheart. That's all were going to do, sleep. You don't have to worry about anything else." He thought that even though he ached, perhaps he finally made up his mind. She was still shaking her head. Still denying him. Her denial in the face of her lies angered him.

"I don't know what I want. You wouldn't force me? Would you?"

Those words stopped him cold. All the raging desire he felt for her, simmered then died. "No, Chauncey, I would never force you to have sex. Come, let's go to sleep. Tonight, you can think about what it is you want. You best decide whether you want me as your husband or not."

With raging emotions, he pulled her against him again. The covers, he settled around them. Rain beat hard against the tent. For hours he laid awake listening to the tempest. Somewhere outside a horse nickered. There were other noises as the night progressed. The watch changed. The fires would be burning low. Someone would put more wood on them. She still wore the damn nightgown.

She cuddled against him. He ran his hand along her leg to her soft belly then back down. With calculated ease, he slipped the gown from her shoulders, pushing it to her waist. The few buttons left to undo were easy. She was soft and warm. He cupped her breast, ran a thumb across the hardened tip. She moaned pushing her hips against his sex.

He felt as if he was going crazy. He pushed the gown passed her hips down to her feet. She turned in his arms. Kissing her awake then plunging inside her would be heaven. The storm ran its course. Morning sunshine emptied its light into the tent. He moved back, far enough so he could see her. The sight wasn't enough. He wanted to taste her. He touched the tip of her breast with his tongue, curled it around the nipple.

"Stephen," she sighed. The whisper of his name caught him off guard.

Her hands ran up then down his chest then lower. Her eyes were still closed.

She had to be awake. "What game are you playing with my body, Little Minx?" he whispered as he bathed her neck in kisses stopped at her pulse as it beat hard at the base of her neck.

"I don't know...didn't know this was a game," she murmured still very much asleep. "I like the way you feel."

She lifted her face as if begging for a kiss. Her lips were dewy with moisture left behind with the passing of her tongue across them.

Fitting his mouth over hers, he accepted the offer. Her mouth was soft and sweet, warm, and damp. She tasted of the early morning sunshine. His tongue slipped deeper inside her mouth, exploring just as her hands investigated him. He sucked in air when she cupped him. Even through his buckskins he felt the heat from her as his body sprang to life.

One of her legs lay across his thighs. Every feminine inch of her was open to him, vulnerable, damp with excitement his kisses generated. If he took her now, she would be his through all eternity. She was asleep...at least half asleep.

Making a decision he regretted, he swatted her bare bottom. "Time to wake up, Chauncey."

She jerked to a sitting position; her eyes blazing. Her tiny breasts swayed delightfully. He'd tasted them. The scent of his woman was known to him. That much knowledge would have to be enough for now. She pushed hair from her face giving him an even more provocative view. She had no idea what those tiny movements did to him.

As she heaved in a big lungful of air, "You said we could sleep as long as we wanted."

Her words were accusatory. She still didn't try to cover herself. He would drool in a few more seconds if this tête-à-tête continued.

"You weren't sleeping, my dear," he said his voice husky with desire. "You were tormenting my man's body. If you aren't willing to give all of yourself to your husband, don't tease a man to the point he hurts."

Callously, he flung the words at her. It was his decision that kept her chaste. Beneath his breath he cursed.

She looked at him, her eyes narrowing. She appeared to be concentrating on his words. In seeming disbelief, she answered. "I'm hurting you? How?" She'd tilted her head a bit to the side, a provocative gesture sending her long dark hair cascading down to her hips and playing peek-a-boo with her rose-colored nipples. It wasn't a site a hurting man could handle.

"You probably don't want a detailed explanation of my actions. Given the right circumstance, you will understand."

Lifting his hand he touched her, sampled her breast for a few seconds, wishing her eyes weren't crossing with denial.

"What were you going to do?" She pulled up a cover as she brushed his hand from her breast. She growled at him. "Why am I naked. I didn't do this."

It was strange she just noticed. He grinned wickedly wondering what he should tell her about her wanton behavior last night. Well, it wasn't as much unrestrained as nervous. "I was hoping with a bit of encouragement you would be willing. As to the naked part, told you yesterday I would sleep with you...naked. I mean to do so every night for the rest of our lives. Despite what is between as well as what is not between us, I've decided that as my wife, I've rights I mean to enjoy."

If she understood those rights wouldn't be experienced until he found a minister or a preacher or a man carrying a bible and saying he could wed them, she didn't say anything.

"Thought you didn't want a wife," her retort caught him by surprise.

"I didn't."

He always wanted a wife and children, a family he could love. The timing had never been good. The moment still wasn't perfect. There was nothing he could do to change that fact. He wasn't about to tell her his thoughts.

"I see..."

"Doubt if you see much of anything, Chauncey. You're too caught up in yourself to see beyond the tip of your nose. Nevertheless, we've a long way to travel. If you are my wife, you will obey me without question. Your life might well hinge on your obedience."

He saw that she was thinking over his words. Good, she needed to put some relevant and hard thought into this. She still had time to cry off. Though if she did so her reputation would be shredded.

"I'll get your breakfast."

She rose, holding the blanket in front of her. For a moment, she looked lost. Her clothing was in the wagon. He held her nightdress. He didn't intend to give it back to her.

"Relax, sweetheart. I'll bring you a cup of coffee as well as your dress."

He was going to do something with this nightgown of hers. Taking it off her every night so he could hold her would be trying.

He strode to the campfire. Beth stood near sipping a cup of coffee. She eyed him warily. "I didn't hurt Chauncey," he said coming to his defense before the girl could question him. After clearing his throat, he continued, "I never hurt women."

"I'm guessing that is so. Didn't know there were men..." She shrugged lifting her shoulders, a small smile on her bruised lip. "Men like that. Never known one who didn't take what he wanted."

"What did the man do to you?" Stephen wondered if she would say anything. He couldn't help her if she didn't confide in him. "I might..." well hell, he couldn't do anything until he spoke with Jason Meeker.

Beth seemed to perk up a bit. "You might what? Get me out of here? No one can do that. Where would I go? Don't want to be left on the prairie to die."

He reached out a hand then pulled it back as she flinched away. "Would never let that happen. What did he do to you?"

He didn't know if he wanted to pursue this conversation though he felt obliged to do just that. Jason was a half breed. He grew up with him...Kane as well. The man understood that women were possessions to be cared for not abused. Jason lost his Sioux wife two years ago. His friend sent a letter to him when he lived in England apprising him of the changes in his life.

The glare Beth focused on him could have killed. "He stuck his fist inside me." She turned away when she saw Mister Greeley striding her way, those same burly fists clenched at his sides.

Stephen expected something horrible, not something life threatening. He thought she would tell him he forced her. With this information, he didn't know what to say. That was why she bled. She believed that type of behavior was normal. He was surprised she could walk. What could he say to her? Nothing. That was the inherent problem There was nothing he could say.

"I'm sorry," his words sounded lame. He should be able to help her. There was nothing more for it though. "If I could do anything..."

"What are you doin' girl? Idling the day takin' up this good man's time. Git back to your chores." Greeley spouted the words. "Go on with you. Go help the wife make breakfast."

He focused his attention on him. "Where's your wife? You keep her in bed until she can't walk? She's mighty fine that woman of yours. Not like this little girlie."

Stephen turned to Beth and nodded, his concern for her welfare uppermost in his mind. "Yes, Chauncey is a fine woman. I'm bringing her a cup of coffee."

He left with nothing else to say. He didn't want to be in this man's company more than necessary.

With her dress in one hand the coffee in the other, he entered the tent. Her dark blue eyes were wide, her face the color of new fallen snow. "You heard?"

She shouldn't know certain things. If she stayed at home, protected, she would not be getting an education pertaining to the worst side of life.

She nodded, a look of utter confusion on her beautiful features. "I'm not certain I understand but I heard the pain in her voice. He stuck his hand inside her?"

"It's not something you're ready to hear about. What he did is not the norm. Men don't do that to women. It unnatural."

Mr. Greeley was a sick, sick bastard! No wonder the Mrs. allowed him another woman. She wanted him as far away from her as possible.

"They stick their penis inside a woman. Does that make a woman bleed?" The curiosity he read in her eyes coupled with her blunt words made him groan. He would do that with her but it wouldn't be the way she was now thinking.

This conversation was not one he expected when he slipped inside his tent a few seconds ago. "Here, you should get dressed." He closed himself off from her questions. In doing so he also closed himself off from her. Dealing with this situation and talking with Chauncey were two very different scenarios. Before he could speak with Chauncey, he needed to see to helping Beth.

Blank eyed she looked at him, moving her head as if in confusion. "Did I say something wrong? You would tell me. Wouldn't you?"

The query was fair. It's just that he was in deep water, way over his head. "No. You didn't say anything wrong. Yes, I would tell you. This is my problem."

He raked his hands through his hair, both irritated as well as frustrated with the events he had no control over. He started to remove himself from the tent when she spoke again.

"No? No? It's your problem? Is that all the answer I'm going to get? You need to sit down. Explain a few things to me. It seems to me you're running away."

Well hell, he was running away from her. He didn't possess a reasonable answer or explanation. He recognized her burgeoning anger even though he'd only seen her fury once. That one time occurred at Kane's wedding. The event could have been humorous, but it involved a young woman who was being accosted by a boy. She chased after him her fist balled tight as she shook it at him. He recalled intercepting her before she could hurt herself.

"For now, Chauncey, you need to accept what I've told you. Rest assured I'll speak of this again when you're better able to understand."

~ * ~

She watched him toss her the dress he retrieved from the wagon. Stared at his back when he disappeared. Chauncey was damn tired of being left in the dark. She was also fed up with her indecision when it came to letting him make love to her. Never in her entire life had she been so unsure of herself.

Tonight, she would not act missive and shy. When he came through that tent this evening, she would be naked for him. Just the way he wanted her.

She thought about Lyssa, her bold and sometimes brazen daring, when she knew Kane was the right man for her. Lyssa told her about the recital, the bawdy words she inadvertently sang. She also spoke of the riding incident when Kane was furious with her for risking her life showing off the tricks she learned.

Would Stephen be as angry if she showed him what she could do on a horse. She wasn't better than Lyssa, or stronger. Her backside always touched the ground when she rode beneath the horse, her foot tucked into the surcingle that would keep her from falling.

He would see there were no maiden's fears in her head. That was a lie. She tugged in a long deep breath of early morning air, scented with coffee and bacon. Her stomach rumbled. No, she would do just as Beth told her when Stephen made love to her tonight. She would lie back and think of something very pleasant. He could do whatever it was that men did to their wives. She wouldn't argue or complain. She wouldn't shy away from him.

What did they do to their non-wives? Their mistresses? With Beth it didn't seem to make a difference. A field of flowers, that is what she would think of. Perhaps her mind could focus on riding her mare, the wind whipping through her hair.

Chauncey touched her breast, felt the hard nipple, hard because the air was chilled, hard because she thought of Stephen's mouth caressing the tip. Remembered how she felt when he touched her there, when he kissed her in the same spot. Deep in a secret place she felt something dark as well as magical stir. Unbidden the dragons came to life. She would never be able to lie still and think of some dream-like place. Reliving the few caresses along with the kisses, she understood the heat coupled with the sensations the man orchestrated. She would crush herself against him, explore him. She wanted to see him naked again. Recalled the way he looked when he rose from the pond.

What to do.

She was nervous. Her fingers winding through the fabric of the gown he tossed to her. The one she needed to put on before he showed up at the tent opening wondering where she was. She had all day to come to grips with the evening. All day to lose the newfound courage. No, she'd made up her mind. She would give him whatever it was he wanted. He would appreciate her decision. She would no longer hurt him by denying him. More than anything she needed to please him.

With her mind made up, she dressed then left the tent. She didn't see Stephen. He didn't stay to eat breakfast with her. Perhaps he was inspecting the rest of the wagon train or checking in with Terrell as to tomorrow's journey. He did have a job to do. She set out the left-over biscuits then made some porridge. She still had a cannister of honey to put in the porridge and sweeten it.

The sun seemed to be moving in the sky as the day grew warmer. After waiting an hour, she threw away the breakfast then tossed what remained of the coffee into the fire listening to the hissing, spitting noise that it made. She didn't understand why he didn't come back. Had he been so angry with her he couldn't stand to talk to her?

Where the blazes was he? She smoothed her sweaty hands down the fabric of her gown and wondered what to do. Remembering the conversation from last night, she'd thought he would spend most of the day with her. He wanted to talk to her. That's what he told her.

She was a fool, an idiot.

What did the blasted man eat for breakfast.

"You not treatin' that man of yours right?" A shadow fell across her. She looked up.

"Oh!" Her hand rested on her chest as she stared into the sunlight unable to see the man though she recognized the voice. "You frightened me." She didn't understand what Mr. Greeley was doing at her wagon. "What do you mean? Of course, I treat him right."

She made breakfast for him. She slept in the tent with him. Well, she understood she didn't give him all that he asked her for.

"'Peers you scared that man of yours right out of your tent. Didn't you give him what a man needs?" Greeley hooked his thumbs into his belt loops then rocked back on his heels staring at her, at her breasts. His off-kilter smile sent a sliver of fear ripping through her.

Why was he staring at her that way? Thought it best to ignore the man. She turned her attention to tidying up the back of the wagon, folding the blankets then putting them back inside the tent. They would sleep there again tonight. He might return from whatever errand Terrell sent him on late this evening. Answering Mr. Greeley was not worth her time or effort. If she ignored him long enough, perhaps he'd go away.

When the nasty man put his hand on her shoulder, she shrieked. "Don't touch me!" Chauncey found herself backed up against the wagon. She couldn't go anywhere. His hands were on either side of her, holding her. Moisture filled her eyes. "He will kill you if you touch me. Scalp you," she gritted down hard on each word as if she tried to convince herself. "I will kill you! Shoot you!"

He grinned. His teeth weren't all that white or straight. "Or what? You think that man of yours will hurt me? Nah, he'll applaud my efforts in teaching his woman how that half-breed expects his woman to act." He spit a wad of chew on the ground beside her. Her stomach clenched.

"I'll tell Stephen." She didn't know where he was. He would return soon. "Everything you're saying is wrong."

"He's gone."

Her heart forgot to beat. He didn't tell her he was leaving. Her lungs felt scorched. "No! No, you're wrong about that." Something inside her told her that the horrible man knew where Stephen went as well as why.

"Heard him tell Terrell that he was going to Fort Kearny. That man of yours won't be back for days. It's more than a hundred miles to the fort."

Fort Kearny?

"Without the wagons?" she asked her voice wavering as thoughts rampaged through her head. No...why would he ride off? He didn't find his actions important enough to mention anything to her? None of this made sense. She found that she was shaking her head, denying what Mr. Greeley told her.

"Guess he had some business with some guy named Jason. So, you can cook those biscuits you make for him and they can be all mine."

There was a thin line of brown drool sliding down the corner of his mouth.

She wasn't going to make anything for this horrid man.

"I'll make the biscuits." Beth stood behind Mr. Greeley. "Leave Chauncey alone. You know her man's a Sioux warrior. You do anything with his woman, he might remove that thinning white hair of yours."

The man reddened from his face down his neck. He choked,

shaking his head then inhaling deeply. Beth's threat must have affected him in some way. He stepped back removing his hands from either side of her head. The acrid scent of stale sweat was removed. She could breathe again.

Given the space, Chauncey darted away from him, needing to put as much distance between Mr. Greeley and herself as she could. She didn't know where to go or what to do. She needed to learn the truth. Had to come to a decision concerning Still Water Runs Deep...Stephen. What if he abandoned her? She took in several deep breaths hoping for an ounce of courage to seek out a few answers. Why didn't he tell her what he was doing? She deserved the truth.

Asking the wagon master what her husband was doing as well as when he would return, seemed like an idea of the first order. Figuring Terrell could tell her what was going on, she walked down the line of wagons. The man was speaking with one of his scouts. With her hands folded in front of her, she waited, watching the furious exchange. No doubt another person was angry with her husband's unexpected departure. When he finished, he motioned for her to come sit. The man seemed to understand she would have questions. She sat down on a log that had been pulled up close to the firepit for the express purpose of sitting.

"Coffee?" he offered, a pleasant smile on his face. He held up the pot along with a mug.

The man was trying to ease her, to keep her anger in check. He was a handsome man, with sandy brown hair. His eyes were a deep dark brown that seemed to twinkle when he smiled. He wasn't smiling right now. Though the man looked a bit worried. He wasn't as tall as Stephen, few men were. His body was well honed and muscled from the time spent in the saddle. He was older.

She nodded, returning his smile with a hesitant one. Discovering the truth here terrified her. Too many horrible scenarios ripped across her mind. She didn't want to be left behind to be discarded. It seemed that was what happened. *Who was this Jason?* "Yes, that would be nice. Coffee along with information."

The words, the question was difficult to ask even though Terrell seemed to know why she was visiting. Of course, he would know. He was the boss. Stephen should have told her what he was doing. He didn't.

Why you silly little twit? You're nothing to him except a thorn in his side. He doesn't want to be your husband.

"If you came about your man, I can't tell you anything except that he had something important to do at the fort. Didn't elaborate. That's the kind of man he is...quiet. Keeps his thoughts to himself. When he signed on it was with the stipulation that he wasn't bound to any set timeline or rules. He could come and go as he pleased. Implicated that it might happen more than once. As to whether he is coming back...I'm certain he will return."

"Why...?" she murmured despite the fact she knew Terrell had as much of an idea as she did. "Why was he in such a hurry to get to the fort? We'll be there in time. Couldn't he have waited?"

"When a man up and leaves for no apparent reason, nothing is set in stone. He did say he was coming back and that he couldn't wait the twenty-five more days it would take us to get there. If he waited someone might die. Didn't ask questions about that. Said he had to see this person as soon as possible. Assumed, as he mentioned, this might be a matter of life or death he was that intense. Told me he should be back here in fifteen days or less. Also told me it was of serious importance that he rush there. Oh... you weren't to worry. All would be as it should be when he returned."

She wondered about that. How was it supposed to be between them. She didn't know. "Yes, he would ride through the night. Use multiple horses. I've heard he can ride for days without sleep."

She'd heard him talking with Kane about the times they raided. The long hours they rode. Their abilities were like no others. Thinking about him, she sipped the strong, hot coffee he brewed. Except in the morning to wake her up, she wasn't a fan of coffee.

Terrell was nodding at what she told him. "He took three horses with him. They were all his. He brought them with him. Wouldn't be surprised to see him sooner than fifteen days. Did you have anything else you want to ask?"

Fifteen days...

What was she to do? She had a million questions, all for Stephen. He left her without one word. "I don't understand," she murmured speaking mainly to herself.

As she sat on the log, watching the fire crackle, she listened. Noise surrounded them. Children playing. Mothers shouting at them. Fathers sitting around the campfires speaking to each other. In the distance, she heard a banjo.

If Stephen hadn't left in such a whirlwind, what would they be doing. Probably arguing. Maybe at the swimming hole. She realized she was hot, sweaty. Going there by herself would make him furious. Perhaps she could take Beth with her along with her gun. That was a fine idea. For some reason she had the urge to do something that would make him annoyed. Going off by herself or with just Beth would do the trick. You'll carry on just as you did before he unofficially became her husband.

He seemed to understand her dilemma. "He'll be back before you know it. You won't have time to miss that very new husband of yours."

She looked at the man who was staring at her, grinning. The man who appeared to know they weren't married. She wasn't at all certain what to say. She tucked her bottom lip beneath her teeth. Wanted to ask what gave her away. Remained silent instead. Maybe he didn't know anything.

"Thank you... Stephen didn't even tell me he was leaving. Don't you think a husband should tell his wife important things like that?" she tossed the question out wondering what this man would say. "Do you have a wife somewhere?" She imagined that if he wasn't married, his answer wouldn't count for much. Of course, Stephen wasn't married either. Neither was she.

He stroked his jaw for several seconds before his gaze focused on her. "Never been married, ma'am. Suppose my answer doesn't' mean a whole lot to anyone. Don't have a clue about married life other than what goes on between a man and a woman when they are in bed."

He was just afraid to say what he believed. She understood most men assumed they were in control, that their word was final. Having not been brought up that way, she would never agree. Her father never treated her mother in that manner. Perhaps he did upon occasion. Those might be the times he ended up on the couch. She stifled a small giggle.

Aborting the laughter, she smiled at the thought, at the memories of her home, her parents. "I'll be going. Got a few things to think over. Are we leaving first thing in the morning?"

He nodded then tossed the remains of his coffee into the fire. The liquid hissed and spit when it hit the embers. He suddenly appeared concerned. "Yes, do you need help? You are a single woman now that your man has taken off."

"No, I'll be just fine. She would be too. Believe I'll have myself another bath later on this afternoon."

She stood then fluffed up her skirts. If Stephen was going to leave, she would wear her britches again. Her buckskins were more comfortable as well as more practical than the skirt. She could work better and with more efficiency when she wasn't tripping over layers of cloth.

Walking down the line of wagons to reach hers, she thought she'd never felt so at odds with herself. Her confusion about Stephen magnified. When she reached her small traveling home, Beth stood beside it. A small bruise, a new one, painted her cheek. Her lip was swollen more than usual. Blood trickled from a cut near her eye.

"Wanted to see how you were doing after...well...after Mr. Greeley accosted you. That shouldn't have happened." She looked around, seeming to search. "Where is Stephen? He should have been here."

Chauncey looked up feeling at peace with this young woman, a woman who suffered abuse then seemed to shirk it off, a woman who needed a friend. She needed a friend too. Chauncey lifted her shoulders in an indifferent shrug. "He left. Terrel say he will be back."

"Left?" Beth parroted as she looked back to the Greeley's wagon. "Is that why?" She seemed to guess the answer to her question.

Swallowing the lump in her throat Chauncey nodded. "I think so. Nothing else makes sense. Stephen would never let him that close to me."

Chauncey understood that for a fact. While she didn't know Stephen that well, she did understand his possessive as well as protective nature. For the time being, she was his wife. He owned her. He would also feel responsible. Possessive. She scoffed, not too responsible since he left her alone.

In that moment, she knew Stephen would come back for her. He told her that she was his. He married her in the way of the People. She didn't feel married. She was both angry as well as annoyed by his actions. When he returned, he wasn't going to get an amicable welcome.

"You need to be careful, very careful for the time he is not here. For some reason Rufus, Mr. Greeley, wants you. You've intrigued him. The man always takes what he wants. I will do my best to keep him away from you."

"Guess I figured that out a few hours ago when he pinned me against the wagon. It wasn't a pleasant feeling. Don't do anything that will make your life with the man worse than it is now. I'll keep my gun with me." She busied herself a few minutes rearranging the backend of the wagon. She would sleep in there tonight. Would have to pack up Stephen's tent and find a place to store it. That wouldn't be too hard.

Beth clutched her arm. Her eyes imploring. "I mean it, Chauncey. Watch your back. He's not a nice man. You must take care."

"I will. However, for now would you like to go to the pond where Stephen took me yesterday. We can bathe and there won't be a soul. You'll be free of that man for at least an hour, perhaps longer. We've nothing that needs attending to here."

"You can't possibly know that," Beth said shaking her head. "I don't think... What if someone comes."

"That's always possible. I'll stand guard when you bathe then you can do the same for me. I'll take my gun. Do you know how to use one? I'll teach you. According to my papa, every woman should know how to shoot straight and not be afraid to kill when necessary."

Chauncey saw the gun in easy reach on the side of her wagon. She found the soap along with the towels. Today she wasn't going to wash anything except the dress she wore, which she would put in the valise until Stephen returned to demand she wear the gown.

"I'm not sure. How will we get there?" Beth looked apprehensive. "Is it too far to walk?"

"I'll take one of my horses. You can ride in front of me. It will be fine."

Chauncey wondered if Beth had ever ridden a horse. Well, no matter. If one was to live in the west, one needed to learn to ride. She would teach her that too. "On our way out, I'll tell Mr. Terrell where we are going. He'll want to know."

She hoped the wagon master might stand guard as well. The possibility of anyone finding them bathing was slim. However, there was always the off chance. She didn't want to gamble yet she did. Simply because Stephen would not be pleased to learn what she was doing.

Hah! What he didn't know wouldn't hurt him. He could find out. Not if she didn't tell him. She smiled.

"I don't know," Beth said, as she looked up the river the direction they would take. "Wouldn't it be better to bathe with the rest of the women?"

"You can if you wish. I'm going up stream to the pond. It was beautiful, clean, and clear. Don't wish to share my water with so many people."

She thought of the snake. The gun would be kept close to her. She didn't believe Beth would know how to use the weapon. Ah...but she would enjoy the privacy. "Can you swim? If not, you'll have to stay where you can touch. Come on, it will be fun. Just the two of us. Don't stop to think, just say yes. It's girl time. Sometimes the best things in life are done impulsively."

With the slight smile on Beth's face, Chauncey was certain she won her over. "All right. I'll go with you. Let me get my soap and a towel."

"Bring a change of clothes so you can wash that dress."

Except for the shooting of the snake and seeing Stephen with nothing on, the day was much the same as yesterday. She lazed in the sun with only her chemise covering her. Birds flitted in the trees. When the long grass caught a breeze, it moved in undulating waves. As the day began to ebb, they decided to return to camp.

Chauncey dropped Beth off at her wagon. "If it's alright with Mr. Greeley, I would welcome the company tomorrow. You can ride with me. We can chat about anything that pleases us. What do you say?"

"I'd like that. Thank you for talking me into going with you. You were right. The privacy was much nicer than sharing water with all the women. I feel refreshed and clean. This was perhaps the best day I've had in a long time...maybe ever."

Tonight, Chauncey shared coffee and biscuits with the Murphy's. Some venison stew was left over. She wasn't hungry. One man brought out a harmonica and began to play, another fetched his banjo. The music was fast, toe-tapping tunes. Some of the couples danced. She leaned back against the wagon wheel where she shared dinner and breakfast with Stephen. Her eyes closed she tried to relive the brief moments of closeness she'd felt.

He was with her one night then a second. She needed more. Didn't care if he left with a good reason. She missed him. What made her furious was that he didn't tell her anything, not one thing. Left her to imagine.

Stephen left. He would show up when she least expected him to do so. While her eyes were closed, she pretended she saw him riding fast and hard on his horses, moving from one to the other, never stopping. It would not take him long to reach Fort Kearny then return. He wouldn't sleep. She brought in a sharp breath of air.

As before, Stephen rushed into her life. Inside the wagon was where she preferred to sleep. Before she went to bed, she shuffled the blankets on her pallet. Holding the covers to her nose, they carried his scent. Last night he removed her nightdress calling it virginal. It was. Just as she was. She did enjoy the feel of her body pressed tight against his even though she was afraid of what came after. He sensed her fear.

Dawn came too early. The sun peaked a few rays through the opening to the wagon. She stretched trying to make her stiff muscles move. She looked through eyes that didn't want to open, adjusting herself to the brightness of the morning. Only an hour later the wagon train was moving, lumbering along at the slow steady pace of every day.

Beth joined her riding beside her on the seat. After some time, Beth moved to the pallet inside to sleep. Chauncey was worried about her. Beth seemed listless as if she didn't care about anything. She told her she wasn't sick. Maybe not, but there was something dreadfully wrong.

Her pale face and haunted eyes proclaimed a different story. Mr. Greeley forced her every night. Chauncey was positive. Beth wouldn't speak of it. The man hurt her. She'd like to shoot him where it would do the most good.

On the eighth day after the wagons stopped for the night, Beth slid from the wagon seat. Her hand rested on the wheel, her eyes shimmering with unshed moisture. Looking up at her she spoke with such a soft voice Chauncey had trouble hearing her. "I'm leaving. Whatever you do, don't come after me. This is what I want. This is for the best."

Chauncey blinked a few times not certain of what Beth was trying to explain to her. "You don't have to go to Mr. Greeley so soon. From what you've told me, he won't want you until after dinner is finished. Mrs. Greeley doesn't like you to help with the cooking. Why don't you stay here? You can eat with me."

"No, you don't understand. I'm leaving here. Leaving the wagon train and Mr. Greeley behind. I can't do this again and again until eternity or he grows tired of me. Sells me to another man who might be worse." Beth's back was stiff and straight as she was shaking her head. "I'm not staying one more night."

Chauncey found herself in denial. This couldn't be right. "There is nowhere for you to go. You can't just...can't just walk away." She realized what Beth was telling her. She preferred to die. "You don't have to go to him every night. If you tell someone... Tell Mr. Terrell. He will help. Wait for Stephen to return."

Beth gripped the wood on the wagon seat until her knuckles turned white. "He owns me. I'm his slave. His sex slave as he likes to laugh. I must do what he asks. He paid for me. Bought me. There is only one way for me to be free of him."

"Beth...no!"

"I have to be free of him, Chauncey. There is nothing you can say that will change my mind. If I walk out on the prairie and just keep walking, I won't feel any more pain or humiliation. The winds will caress my face. I can enjoy the sounds of the night not his grunting and groaning when he takes me for his pleasure."

"No, that's not true. You'll be in pain there too. There will be no freedom for you."

Chauncey was frantic for an argument to keep Beth here. Nothing she thought of would convince her to change the course she plotted for herself. "Pain... your feet will hurt. You'll starve. You..."

"I've thought about those things since we embarked on this trip, even before we left Independence. My life is worse now. He sells me to other men. There is nowhere for me to hide from him. Those things you mentioned are not true pain. I'll die from lack of water before food. So, I won't ever be that hungry. Be it known that I've felt that kind of raw, deep hunger. No, Chauncey, I've made up my mind."

Beth began to walk, her chin held high, her back straight.

"No!"

Frantic, Chauncey scrambled to take care of her horses. It was all she needed to do before she could run after Beth. She had to catch up to her.

"You want some help?" Mr. Murphy asked after he appeared beside her. "I'll have more of your biscuits in payment," the man laughed as he began to take care of one of the horses.

It seemed as if he understood her desperate need.

"Yes, help, please."

She looked to see Beth walking away, her feet moving with purpose and determination. The girl wasn't in a hurry. Didn't seem to think anyone would come after her.

Appearing to sense her distraction and perhaps the urgency she felt, he said, "If you don't have time tonight to make those biscuits of yours, well then, tomorrow is just as good. Go after her. Bring her back if you can."

He couldn't know Beth was leaving for good. Could he? "I will. Thank you."

She was breathless as well as panicked. Chauncey was thankful she wasn't wearing a skirt. She darted after Beth, racing toward her. Catching up to her, she walked beside her trying to think of something she hadn't said in their first conversation. Death couldn't be the answer.

All her arguments were used up the first time they spoke. The first time Chauncey sensed what was about to happen. She put her arm around Beth hoping to give comfort. The two girls kept walking until Beth stopped. "You must go back to the wagons. It's getting dark out here. You can't walk alone in the dark. Stephen will be furious with you."

"Not without you. I'm not going back without you," Chauncey bristled knowing that wouldn't change Beth's mind. Anything could happen to her. There were bandits as well as wild animals to contend with. They both needed the protection of the wagons. Chauncey should have never left without her gun. It was too late to go back for the weapon now.

"Don't do this," Beth said in such a resigned little voice Chauncey wanted to cry. "You've got Stephen coming back for you. You've got a family who loves you. Your whole life in front of you to live. I don't. Let me die in peace. Go back."

"I don't want you to die!" Chauncey clung to Beth's hands, holding them tight, not wanting to let her go.

~ * ~

"Curse her! What the bloody hell does she think she is doing?" Stephen was beside himself with his anger as he watched Chauncey follow Beth from the wagon train.

He understood why Beth was walking away. That very action had been what sent him rushing to Fort Kearny. What he never expected was for his wife to follow her into danger. Hell, what else should he have anticipated. No one would expect him back this soon.

"Just as you are, looks to me as if she is trying to save Beth. What do you think? Do you want to be part of this war party or would you like to come at this from a different direction?" Jason asked while he leaned on his saddle horn. "She's beautiful, just as you told me. Imagine convincing her I don't mean her harm will not be an easy task."

"Not dressed to come at this from your direction. Besides, it wouldn't do for me to show up garbed as a warrior as you have planned.

Nor do I want Chauncey to guess at things that I will explain in good time. I will take my leave then come in from behind. When you take Beth, I'll follow a few moments later by confronting my wife. While her motives might be exemplary, her actions put her in danger. I cannot tolerate that."

"It is that way?" One of Jason's eyebrows was raised. "I guessed but until now you haven't shown your true colors."

"Yes," Stephen said solemnly, his gut churning as the two women continued. "In the way of the People, soon in the way of the Christian God. I mean to make certain her parents will not have us annulled. That is the second reason I visited the fort. I needed to ensure that a minister of some type would be at Fort Kearny when we arrive. We will be married then, man and wife in every way that counts to me along with her family."

"Surprises me." Jason hooted with laughter while he continued to keep his focus on Beth. "Just as it surprises me that I'm willing to wed this young woman in order to rescue her. My wife has been gone for years. My furs need a woman to warm them. I'm willing to take a chance on this girl-woman. I would like children."

"You're getting old just as I am. We are both in need of a wife to beget children," Stephen said, watching intently as the two women drew ever closer.

They were arguing, their voices carrying with the breeze. He couldn't understand the words. Body language told a tale. That must infuriate Chauncey. She is used to getting her way in most every endeavor. She would soon discover that she would not be doing so under his command. He would see that she put a dress back on. Maybe he should rip up her buckskins, take his knife to them.

"Do you ever think of our life before we left the People? The times when we were free to do whatever pleased us?" Jason asked as he seemed to be lost in thought. "I'm surprised the captain gave me the time to see to this."

"All the time. Think about those days whenever I'm in the open, sitting on my horse. Now, I will take my leave. Remember, she's been abused by more than one man. Treat her gently. Beth is sweet as well as innocent in so many ways. Once you convince her you are different from the men she has known, she will make a fine wife. Pleasure her so she screams your name."

There was more Stephen could tell his friend. He thought it best to let Jason discover Beth's truths for himself. He wondered how Chauncey was going to react to him. She would have been furious that he rode off without telling her where or what he was doing. Time had not been on his side. He'd been afraid Mr. Greeley would kill Beth or she would do this walk to die before he could return. Every moment was precious. He didn't have one doubt this was what she was doing.

He whirled his horse around. Riding swiftly, he made certain Chauncey would not notice him until he wanted her to see him. When he was behind her, he stopped, waited for Jason to swoop down on the two women. The ensuing scene was just as he might have predicted. Chauncey tried to fight Jason while Beth stood unmoving, waiting for whatever was going to happen. Jason scooped Beth into his arms then rode hard, away from the wagons. Chauncey ran after them, screaming and waving her hands before stopping to shake her fist at him. She was helpless to save the woman. He knew the moment she decided to approach Beth's rescue from a new view point. She stopped, bent over gasping for breath. A minute or so later she ran toward the wagons.

He raced his horse, cutting her off. With ease, he bent down and bundled her into his arms. She screamed then beat on his chest. Her nails raked across his face. She cursed him with words he didn't think she knew, least of all understood.

"Stop it, Chauncey! It's me," he gritted out while her fist slammed with amazing force against his jaw.

He didn't know she wielded so much power in her scrawny arm. His head jerked backward from the force of the blow. He swore. To defend himself, he captured her arms, keeping them secured behind her back as he slid from his horse. She was pressed against him. Her breasts were heaving from the effort. She was trying desperately for air, panting and gulping.

Surprising to him, she ceased to fight, her body going limp. Low in the back of her throat, she moaned, a slow keening sound filled the air, her head resting now against his shoulder. "Stephen?" she whispered his name the sound hoarse and raw. "You came back. I didn't think, well, I thought...thought you left me. Abandoned me because I didn't give you what you wanted." As soon as the words were spoken, she stiffened and her chin went into the air. Her demeanor changed. Once more, she was fighting for her friend. "You have to go after Beth. If you don't, I'll find someone who will."

He was proud of her, proud of her courage in the face of so much danger. A warrior respected courage. He was equally afraid of the recklessness she exhibited. He wanted to shake her until she understood there would be no way in hell anyone would go after Beth. He also didn't like the fact she thought he left her. "No, Chauncey. Beth will be fine. She will no longer be misused. If you go back with the intention of inciting the males to become a rescue party, Mr. Greeley might go after her. She might be back in his power. Do you want that, Chauncey? I promise you. She is safe. Jason will never hurt her. Just as I will never harm you."

Within the strong circle of his arms, she was trying to turn. She would point an accusing finger toward the fading form. "That was a warrior! You need to do something." Once again, she was frantic. "We have to look for them."

She didn't hear a word he said. He wanted to shake her. In the future she would have to learn to listen. He never spoke false. "I am also a warrior. As one, I will tell you true. We will never find them."

That was a lie. He knew precisely where Jason was taking her as well as where he would stop along the way. They were going to a Cheyenne encampment near the base of the Rockies. He was taking her to his mother, a healer. Beth would need time to recover from her ordeals before she could become a wife. Jason would see to her recuperation that would be weeks in the making.

It seemed Chauncey was looking into his eyes, reading what was in his mind. "You don't tell the truth. So be it. I'm going to assume you know much more than you're willing to say. After all, we barely know each other. Why would you confide in your wife?"

She was hurt, her pride wounded. He would have to find a means to make her trust him again.

"Chauncey, you know full well that you are not my wife."

That too, at least in his mind, she was his wife. He also understood that, in her mind, he was not her husband. That fact would change as soon as they reached the fort.

"You can't trust me. I understand. If Beth is with someone who will take care of her, I'm glad. Thank you if you arranged this. The question remains...will Beth be pleased to be with these people? She was always afraid of her shadow. How will she feel with someone... With a Cheyenne warrior?" She let the words fade into nothingness, into the wind.

He could read those emotions in the tone of her voice. In his arms, she stiffened. "He will treat her with respect. His mother will heal her. If she didn't tell you, she has an infection that if not treated will kill her."

"She was walking to her death. I saw no hope in her eyes." Chauncey's voice shook as she spoke the words. "I didn't know about the infection. She never told me."

"I could see the infection blossoming in the changing color of her face. Now, she is walking to life, a new and better life. She will not die. Let this go." He sighed then touching her chin, ran his knuckles down her neck. He understood he needed to tell her something. "Jason is a scout in the United States Army stationed at Fort Kearny. He took some time off to do this. Given the needed time, Beth will be the wife of a soldier. It will be a good life for her if she allows it. If not, Jason will set her free."

Thinking her anger ebbed, he let go of her hands. She stood toe-to-toe with him. He thought about making love to his wife.

Her eyes narrowed, her lips thinning. She punched him in the chest with a fingertip. "Don't think you get off so easy. I am furious with you."

"Are you now?" He tossed her onto his horse then mounted behind her.

"Yes, you bloody well know that I am!"

"Shall we discuss why you are angry?" he asked tightening his arm around her waist while he urged the horse to a gentle cantor.

"You know why. At least you should understand. I'm not going to say anything else. I'm not going to talk to you. You can guess for all I care."

He nipped the tip of her ear then laved the tender spot with his tongue. She shuddered at the contact. "You disobeyed me. I missed your biscuits."

How to persuade her, to convince her she was behaving irrationally without logic, he couldn't fathom.

Her fingers rested on his forearms, tightened when he kissed the back of her neck. "In more ways than just my attire," she blurted belying her vow to stay mute.

In more ways than just her clothing? How very interesting.

"Care to elaborate?" His mind splintered in to too many directions.

"No."

He could be a patient man. Ah, the truth would come out. She would tell him. After that they would discuss her stupidity. Before he joined Jason this evening, he spoke to Terrell. He told him of the swim that day he left as well as a few of the other pertinent things she'd done. Terrell also berated him for not telling her that he was leaving. In her silence, she seethed. Chauncey was a woman who would do as she pleased unless he stopped her.

"It's getting dark. Do we have anything to eat?"

He would have to see to the necessities before he saw to his wife. Discipline was necessary. He didn't know what that should be. Stephen didn't believe a good lecture would change her impulsiveness. He could not promise to be with her every second of every day. Before they broke from the wagon train, she would have to understand his word was law.

"No, nothing. You will have to beg from the Murphy's. I had to go with Beth. Couldn't let her walk to her death. There is no dinner." Her words were crisp and concise, her back stiffer than before. "I'm not hungry."

He chuckled, the sound soft, moving his arm higher so her breasts touched them. "The sun is just lying below the hills. I'll roast the rabbit I snared earlier. You sit and watch. All I need is a cup of hot coffee to go with it."

"I'm certain you are capable of boiling coffee too."

It seemed to him she wasn't going to give an inch. The night would be long and cold without her cooperation. He'd missed her. "I can. However, you will share my blankets with me no matter how furious you are. How many times you turn your back on me."

Her anger might change to passion if he could find the right triggers.

"I'm sleeping in the wagon. If you wish to pitch the tent it's packed in the back."

So, this was the way it was going to be. He wondered where the loving girl disappeared, the one he met at her parent's ranch. The one who followed him to Independence so they wouldn't be apart. Before she was always so eager to be with him, to laugh, to kiss. She said the most outrageous things. Since she became his wife, she was nothing like that girl.

He would find her again.

~ * ~

With Beth held tight and secure in his arms, Jason rode through the night. Three braves joined him, flanked him on this ride. He understood he would have to stop soon and see to this child-woman. She was burning up with her fever. He would have to halt to bring her temperature down. There was no place safe until further along this journey they were taking. Soon they would reach a spot on the river he followed. There would be a place where the men could guard him and he could find some privacy with this fragile young woman.

Beth wouldn't like the examination he needed to make. Stephen told him she was torn where old Mr. Greeley stuck himself inside her. He had laudanum to give her. Enough so she wouldn't be conscious when he administered to her. She wouldn't be awake to protest. That was good. She might not recall anything he was going to do or see.

He wondered what she was thinking. So far, her thoughts were a mystery to him. She'd not said one word. Beth sat in front of him unmoving. When he picked her up to set her on his horse, she didn't even flinch. She had every reason to believe he was a warrior, to fear him. She didn't seem to be afraid.

He brushed lose hair away from her neck then bending close to her he whispered to her. "I'm not going to hurt you, little one. I know you won't believe me but that's the truth. Still Water Runs Deep came to me, asking if I could find it in my heart to help you. You know him as Stephen. You will learn to trust this man."

He wanted to soothe her with his hands, to teach her men did not inflict pain. In her fragile state, he could not.

He hoped she would answer, would speak to him. Her head made a slight move. That was all...all the recognition she would give him. That gesture had to be enough for now. He had to remind himself the woman wanted to die. He wasn't going to let that happen.

"We will stop in an hour or so. When we do, you will let me see to you. My mother is a healer. She's taught me much about roots along with medicine that will help a person feel better. First, though, I've laudanum to give you so you will sleep. Rest is what you will need to recover. After that I'll bring your temperature down. We won't ride again until you are no longer burning with your fever."

Against his chest he felt each labored breath she forced into her lungs then the slight beat of her heart. She was giving up, letting herself drift in then out of a fitful sleep. One he knew she hoped she would never wake from. Perhaps sleep was good for her. He was afraid though; terribly afraid she would go to sleep forever. If he could change that course, he wasn't going to allow it to happen.

"Beth." He touched her cheek, stroked the softness. "Open your eyes. You will not sleep now. You will humor this man."

His tone was harsh. With his hand set close enough to her eyes he would feel the flutter of her eyelashes, he once more commanded her to wake. He was relieved when he felt her lashes move against his finger. "Good."

"You don't have to save me," she whispered. "I don't want to live. I don't want to feel any more pain. I don't wish to suffer a man's touch."

Jason heard the words, hated them. "Ah, you understand that if I do save you, why then you would owe me a boon. You would become beholdin' to me. You would have to do as I wish. Would that be so terrible?"

He chuckled when he felt the stiffening of her small form.

She closed her eyes again. He understood she wasn't sleeping. Her breathing would have changed. He also knew she was fading and the diminishing was because she lacked the will to live. That was something he couldn't change in the next hours and days. When he pulled to a stop, he felt great relief slide from him. She would have to live. He would make it so.

"We will stay here until the fever is gone."

Speaking to the men who rode beside him, "She will not have enough strength to ride by herself so I will carry her with me as I've done today." His friends would help. They were men who would ride to their death to protect him just as he would for them. Still Water Runs Deep was in that same category. Stephen had his own female troubles to contend with.

He set her down before spreading out the furs where she would sleep. Jason had every intention of sleeping beside her. The breath he sucked into his lungs was good, the air filled him. Beth curled up, bringing her knees to her chest. He assumed it was the way she tried to protect herself.

A few minutes later, holding her so she could drink, he dosed her with the laudanum he brought. Now, as soon as she slept, he would examine her. She would be unaware of what he was doing. He had sutures along with a needle ready. Stephen told him she'd been torn.

"Damn..." he breathed in then let the air sift from his lungs when he looked at her.

She was so helpless, almost lifeless. He wanted to gut Mr. Greeley then leave him for the wolves to find. How could a man do this to a woman? To another human being? He spent the night alternately wiping her with the cold cloth and sleeping. At one point, he carried her to the water then sank with her into the stream until she was covered with the coolness provided by the cool river.

They spent three days at the river before her fever broke. He was pleased even though he understood many weeks would have to pass before her body was mended. Jason knew her mind might not be so resilient. He prayed she would mend with no scars leftover.

"Why did you save me?" Beth asked as she watched him breaking camp on the fourth morning. "I wanted to die. You should have let me. I'm nothing. Nothing to you or anyone. Worthless except as a whore. Don't want to be a whore."

"A life is too precious for words like that." He couldn't bear to speak about her death. "We will ride. You will change your attitude."

Chapter Four

Several weeks passed before Fort Kearny came into view. For Stephen, he waited far too long. None of his plans to change Chauncey's sulk came to pass. She was a stubborn woman. He discovered he needed more patience than he'd ever imagined to deal with her childish tantrum. Autumn seemed to float around them, leaves on trees beginning to change color. He hoped they would be with his People before the first snow started to fall.

They followed the North Platte. The river provided water for the families along with places to bathe and wash clothing. Often, he thought of Jason and Beth as he knew Chauncey did as well. On one of his scouting missions, he found the first place his friend stopped. Several times he said silent prayers that Beth would recover.

Chauncey was implacable. She spurned him night as well as day going about her routine as if he didn't exist. When he spoke to her, she would walk away. The only relief he had was at night when he held her in his arms. He never thought she would be so furious with him that she would refuse to talk to him for weeks. She told him all he needed to do was apologize. A Sioux warrior didn't apologize to his woman. Besides, he had no tangible reason to seek forgiveness. His actions were the right ones. A man never apologized for doing the right thing.

Now that the fort was in sight, he would have to speak to her long enough to convince her to marry him. If that didn't happen, they wouldn't have another chance until they reached the next fort. Spending another celibate night wasn't tangible. He wanted her in his arms making love with him. Begging was not an acceptable means of convincing a woman. Neither was force. Both methods he was quite capable of using. A Sioux warrior did neither.

Shaking his head, he urged the oxen forward. He didn't

understand women. She followed him, named him her husband for the entire wagon train to accept. She never asked him if that was something he wanted. Since he left without giving her a reason, he was treading on shaky ground. He saved her friend from certain death.

What the hell did the woman want from him? Every time he asked that question of himself, he came full circle.

An apology.

If he swallowed his pride and apologized would that change anything? After everything that happened since that day, she would believe he did so just to get his way about the marriage. If she thought that way, she would be right. Disgusted with the scenario, he rubbed the back of his neck. When he looked back, she stared straight ahead. She was walking alongside, refusing to ride beside him. Curse her stubborn hide. For the first week, she even refused to allow him to drive the wagon. In return, he told her nothing more about Jason or his intentions where Beth was concerned. They reached a stalemate.

As the days passed, her chin tilted higher into the air. She stopped making biscuits or anything special. He didn't know how to change the tenor of their relationship. Without a doubt, he didn't care about the cooking though Mr. Murphy complained about the lack of biscuits. Several times he ate meals when he was on a scouting mission instead of returning to her silence.

Hell! They no longer had any kind of relationship.

With a chuckle in his words, Terrell never ceased giving advice. The man had no idea having never been wed.

"You don't wish to apologize. Could start by telling her the truth," Terrell rode beside the wagon, once more offering his words of wisdom. Chauncey was walking behind the wagon speaking with one of the other women.

"I'm afraid it's too late for that. She's been in a royal pique since I returned. Now... well...over time it's gotten worse." He held up his hand shaking his head when he thought Terrell was going to speak again. "I know what she wants. It's not going to happen."

"What's that?"

"Doesn't matter."

"Did you tell her yet that the traveling minister is waiting to perform the service at Fort Kearney? How long did he remain at the fort just for the two of you to say your vows?" The man was still laughing, hooting now thinking he was funny.

There was nothing the least bit humorous about any of this. "When did you realize the truth about us? When did you know we weren't married?" Stephen pushed his hat back eyeing the wagon master with a critical eye.

"When I mentioned to you that I knew your wife was in the middle of the train waiting to hear from you. The look on your face..." Terrell was still laughing, his eyes sparkling with the gest that was on Stephen. "The way your brows furrowed together. I knew then you didn't have a wife. Was damn sure you knew who was pretending to be Mrs. Wilkes. This scheme of your...er...wife's has been fun to watch."

Stephen bristled, understanding the innate truth of this man's words. "Maybe your advice is sound. Maybe it's not. Truth always heals wounds. I just don't know how I'm going to get her to listen to me. Her ears are closed to my words. She won't even look at me."

He thought he could hog-tie her then drag her to some spot far away from everyone, making her sit down and hear what he had to say. That deed would make her even less receptive to his truths. He didn't doubt the fact for an instant.

"You'll think of something. I've complete faith in your ingenuity. We're only spending tonight along with the next one here. If you act fast, you've got a bit of time to solve all your problems. Don't waist one moment. Get the deed done. Get hitched then you'll be in charge. As it is now, why, she thinks she can do whatever she pleases."

He kicked his horse before leaving him in the dust.

Terrell's laughter followed him all the way back to Chauncey's wagon where he sat dumbfounded staring into the distance. His future hinged on what he did today. She walked behind him until the wagons were circled outside the fort. Once she came to a stop, he unhitched the oxen. Grabbing her arm, he led her away from the wagons along with the prying eyes of their neighbors. He would take her with him whether she agreed or not. She tried to pull away, shooting him a furious glare. Her cooperation wasn't necessary though it would be nice.

"What are you doing? Let me go!" She stumbled into him, pushing at him. He shortened his strides to better accommodate hers. When she tried to swing at him with her free arm, he grabbed it.

"No, you don't. This time you're going to listen. You need to grow up. This man is tired of your little girl sulk! You're acting like a baby."

Damn, but those few words were the most she said to him in two days. It seemed the longer they were at odds with each other the less she said. He wanted to kiss her, to toss her skirt in the air then come inside her. He wanted to shake her until she understood how he felt. Inhaling a soothing breath of air, he rethought his alternatives.

"We need to talk," he blurted out through clenched teeth, his hand tightening on her arm when she tried to wrench away from him again. "If you fight me, I'll put you over my shoulder. See that spot up there? The one where there are a few trees. There is grass to sit on and it's nice and shady. That's where we are going. We are not coming back until we have things settled to my satisfaction. This pout of yours is going to end today."

He started walking again, grinned to himself when she raced along beside him. It would not have surprised him if she balked. The fact she hadn't pleased him. He would not have minded carrying her. This little woman was going to be the death of him. If she acted this way when they were living with his tribe, they would scorn her. Would expect him to discipline her in their way. He could never do that. To the core, he'd become English.

"Beast!"

She tripped, her arms flailing wildly so she could right herself. He gathered her in his arms. "Animal!"

"Is that the best you can do? I know first-hand you can curse as well as your brother. The words I've heard coming from your sweet lips..." Grinning and shaking his head he continued on his way. "Why don't you vent your spleen so we can have a real conversation? Unleash all your cannons. When you are sitting under that tree, I expect you to talk to me. No more silence. No, silence just won't do."

When she stumbled into him again, he lowered his shoulder then hefted her onto his shoulder. Her adorable butt pointed toward the sky. Her legs were vulnerable. If he dared, he could run his hand along her leg all the way to that sweet ass of hers. He wanted to feel her woman's flesh, caress the soft petals. Wanted to know if her passion ran as hot as her temper. He wanted to hear her moan and heave with the pleasure he wished he could give her. If he gave into his inclinations, that would become another strike against him. Couldn't afford another mark.

"Put me down!"

She reared up pushing her hands against the width of his back. She wriggled, trying to look at him.

He was so frustrated as well as furious with her, he could spit. If a slap on her backside wouldn't hurt his cause more than help, he might vent his annoyances. If anyone had the right to be furious, he did. "When I'm good and ready to put you down, I might do so. When I'm certain, you won't run in circles like a chicken with its head cut off, I might allow you an inch of freedom. I'm too damn tired of this game you've been playing with my emotions to gamble with your actions. Don't want to partake in a foot race across the prairie with you when we both know who will win."

At the trees he pointed to earlier, he set her down. He stood over her, his feet planted on either side of her legs. His arms were crossed in front of his chest. When he hunkered down so he could look into her eyes, she turned away. He brought her chin back with his hand. Stephen needed to look at her. This was too damn important to the rest of his life, to her life as well.

His voice calm and in control, he began to speak. "Talk to me, Chauncey. These last weeks, I've let you get away with your sulk. That was a mistake. Should have put an end to it that first night. You will stop acting like a child. You're a grown woman with a husband." He was at a loss for words, needing to hear from her before he could continue.

"What is going to happen to Beth. I know you know where she is. I deserve the truth that you are keeping from me." She was holding her breath now waiting for an answer.

He was shocked she spoke to him. The surprise caused him to

blink then not respond for a second or two. He'd been holding back for a reason; one she might never agree with. "It's best you don't know. Don't want you to worry about Beth. She is well taken care of." When she started to protest, he placed a finger over her lips. He tried to smile at her if for no other reason to reassure her. "Correct me if I'm wrong. Mr. Greeley has been asking about her. Hasn't he? Has the old man threatened you? Has he done or said anything I should be aware of?"

If the man had any ideas of substituting Chauncey for Beth, he'd scalp him. Either that or leave him naked and spread eagle on the prairie for any predator that might find him. From the bottom of his heart, he loathed the man.

The worthless bastard.

She turned pale. Her previous rise of color vanished with his question. When she looked at her folded hands, settled in her lap, he understood his guess was correct. As she looked up, there was moisture in her eyes. "Yes," she whispered. "He has been asking about her. He's furious he has no one to abuse and blames me."

"What?" He lifted her chin, needing to see into her eyes. "Tell me everything from the beginning. Don't leave out the smallest detail. Has the man touched you?" he blurted almost as an afterthought. "I'll kill him!"

"Yes, damn you! He asks every day whenever you are not around. Whenever you ride off to be alone or do whatever it is you do by yourself. This is your fault. That's why I'm so angry with you!" The last words had a ring of accusation to them. "He only touched me once. Beth intervened offering herself to him. That was when she was still alive. Now I have no one to protect me. You're never around."

His body shuddered at her words. He would always protect her. She made guilt swell up inside him. How many of those time he left her by herself he went off to brood. He imagined he had some growing to do also. "How did he touch you? When? Where?" He supposed she decided to be honest by the heating of her eyes.

"I told you. Only when you are gone. He's a sniffling little coward. If he wasn't afraid of you, he would have forced me days ago."

Standing, pacing, he swore with heat emanating from his words before returning to her. The air he tugged inside his lungs hung there for a few seconds, filling him. Stephen couldn't remember another time he'd been this angry. "I will speak to the man. I'll let him know in specific terms that he's not to go anywhere near you. If he does, he will regret his actions. Back to Beth. What does he want to know about her?"

"Yes, well..." She held up her hands. He believes I know what happened to her, orchestrated her abduction. He wants me to pay him for her, pay him the amount he gave to her last owner. She's not a slave. No one should be owned by another person. As you know I don't know anything. Again, this is all your doing."

Her temper was rising. She was spitting mad angry. She deserved her anger if it was directed in the right path. Anger he could deal with. Silence coupled with pouting, he could not.

How was he going to convince her to marry him if he couldn't bring this anger of hers to a head. First, he needed to tamp down his fury before he could help Chauncey. He could deal with this man after he was legally married to his woman.

Seeking another, different approach to the question at hand, he began to speak, "Do you think you would be able to keep the truth from him if you knew what happened to her? She is in good hands. Because of what I did, she will live. Though I very nearly didn't make it back in time to save her."

Damn, he wished he could pull Chauncey into his arms, hold her until she felt safe. He understood part of her anger was caused by fear. The need to tell Chauncey what happened to Beth swamped him. If she was to become his wife, he needed to learn to trust in her just as she needed to do the same for him.

"Yes." Her chin tilted up. "No...maybe. I don't think I would ever tell him anything about Beth. The fact he doesn't know seems to torment him. I like that. Imagine it depends whether I can throw the truth in his ugly face. If it would humiliate the man, I would not think more than twice about telling him what I know."

Satisfied he made his point, he sat down beside her, picking up her hand. Staring at it, at the callouses, the broken and chipped nails. It was small within his, fragile. Each day she did a man's work as well as her own. He gave thought to all his woman told him. She could be vicious in her defense of someone she cared about, this woman of his. He liked that. She would defend her friend until death. That part bothered him. He imagined he was pleased she no longer would feel the need to defend Beth. Loyalty was important to him.

"I promise you this, Chauncey. When it is safe for you to know, I will tell you everything. What I do want you to understand is that she is safe as well as protected. She will heal and hopefully marry a very nice man. Beth now has choices in her life. No man will ever force her again. Is that enough information?"

He looked skyward praying she would be satisfied with the knowledge.

Chauncey peered down at their hands then she looked at him. He saw moisture in her eyes a wistful expression on her lovely face. With a huge smile, she turned her attention to him. "Thank you. You're right. I am acting the child. When you order me around, I feel so defeated as if you don't believe I can decide for myself. I understand I put you in an untenable position by declaring you to be my husband. I'm sorry for that. I was stupid. You don't care about me. I understand. Let's just forget I ever made that outlandish statement. Can we move on?"

"No." He was firm and in control. "No, Chauncey that isn't the way this is meant to be."

"No?"

For a woman who said so little the last weeks on the trail she now seemed to want to pour her heart out to him. She made assumptions that were so far from the truth they were laughable. "When I tell you what to do, it is for your safety. No other reason. As your husband, I must protect you even if that protection is from yourself. I am your husband, Chauncey. Don't ever forget that."

He didn't want to think about what might have happened to her if she kept walking with Beth, if he hadn't been there, if Jason had taken longer to collect his friends to accompany him on this trip of his.

"As your husband?" she stared at him wide-eyed with wonder. "I don't understand. You don't want me. Never wanted me."

"Yes, as far as I am concerned, we are wed. If you agree, we will marry this evening at the fort in the way your parents would wish it. Tell me that's what you want." His heart was in his throat. Until this moment, he didn't think this marriage had one chance in hell of succeeding.

Once more, she seemed to bristle with outrage. Her eyes flashed a message he didn't think he was going to appreciate. "What have you done? You have just decided what is to happen and now you expect me to fall into your plans? You haven't bothered to ask. I would at least want..." Her voice rose with her anger. She broke off the last words.

Stephen felt blindsided. Nothing he'd thought over the past weeks prepared him for this denouncement. He cleared his throat while his mind raced with something intelligent to say. While he thought she would object, might fight the marriage, he'd not expected her to come at him in this way. "Should I ask? Put my knee to the dirt?"

"Get down on a knee and ask...yes! That would be ever so nice!" Her back stiffened while that tiny chin of hers, rose. "You won't. I understand. Doing so is beneath you." She turned a blushing shade of pink. "I'm sorry. I'm sticking my foot in my mouth."

He looked to the ground thinking the dirt was usually beneath a person, at least a living breathing person, "If you don't wish to marry me, I can send the good minister on his way. As far as I am concerned you are my wife. Personally, I don't need the vows to be said by a man of God. On the other hand, if you wish to set our failings aside and marry with me today at the fort, we can do so. This is up to you, Chauncey, your choice. What do you say? Would you like to get married in a couple of hours?"

This was becoming too much for him to process. He rose, extending his hand to her to help her to her feet. When she accepted the help, he felt relieved as well as hopeful. With a bit of leverage on his side, he tugged her into his arms. A kiss at this instant might be appropriate, a way to seal this proposal coupled with her acceptance.

She looked at him. As if anticipating the kiss he wished he could share with her, her tongue swept across her lips leaving a tempting line of moisture behind. With infinite patience, bending his head closer, he gave her ample opportunity to protest to deny him the intimacy. She stared at his lips as if she wanted this kiss as much as he did.

Her palms pressed against his chest, moved higher to circle his neck, wound into his hair, nails tingling against his scalp. His mouth surrounded hers, touched caressed, hoped she would open for him. With his tongue he urged her lips to open, warmed the line between them. She parted her mouth the tiniest amount. He'd kissed her liked this before, taught her to open for him. Her rounded breasts pushed against his chest. They were firm and soft. He wanted to hold them, test their weight as well as texture. Squeeze. Hear the sounds she would make. His hands found her backside, pulled her close. She would feel his hardness, his erection that was hard as stone pressed against her belly.

His groan of pleasure surprised him. He needed to end this so they could marry. The minister wouldn't wait forever. He couldn't toss her onto the grass and have his way with her here, where anyone could come upon them. The man of God, Reverend Plummer, had to get to his flock, had to see every one of them. There were few churches in this territory. He had a lot of work to accomplish. The man of God made it clear that he would not wait a minute longer than necessary.

With great effort, he set her away from him, needing some distance to separate their heated bodies. Her bosom heaved, her breaths were fast, her eyes dazed with passion. "Will you go with me to the fort? Will you marry me today? Say the words that will bind us together for all eternity?" This time he held his breath while he waited for the answer he sought.

She smiled a tiny bit before pushing her lips together. "I don't know. It's all too fast. Can we wait a day or two? You know, talk it over. You can tell me what you expect in a wife and I can do the same except that I would explain what I expect in a husband."

He groaned again understanding the game he believed she played. She was stalling for time they didn't have. "No, if we wait, the minister will leave. He stayed just for us with the intention of saving our immortal souls since we've been living together in sin. It's today or never. Well, we would have to wait until I return you to your home. By then you will be with child, a bastard child in your parent's eyes."

He thought the last words a fine touch. If nothing else that would convince her.

With his words, her eyes crossed. She poked him in the chest. "Neither of us believe that nonsense. At least, I don't. It doesn't have to be now."

Stephen didn't understand why she hesitated. For Christ's sakes she followed him because she didn't want him to leave without her. She initiated this ruse. "Will you marry me?" he asked again wishing she would accept him, accept his proposal.

Frustrated beyond anything he felt before. He wanted her to acknowledge him into her life.

"If you promise not to leave me without telling me why or where," she spoke with conviction. Her brows were furrowed together, a small vertical crease between them.

Now, he understood. Chauncey sought to negotiate the terms of their marriage. He didn't negotiate with a wife. "No, that is a vow I cannot make to you no matter how much I wish I could. Will you marry me?"

She turned away from him, walking toward the trees and away from the fort. Her hands were behind her back. He held his breath waiting for her answer. Stephen didn't know what he would do if she refused out of sheer perversity. He didn't think she'd changed her mind about marriage to him.

Holding his breath, after seconds that seemed like hours, she whirled, her skirts floating around her slender ankles, ankles he hoped to explore tonight along with other parts of her delectable body. "Yes. I will say vows to you. I will tell you now if you order me to do something outrageous, I won't. My promise to obey is false." She looked to the heavens before muttering, "A woman should not have to obey foolishness when she knows better."

"A man should not have to put up with stupidity when he knows what the truth is," Stephen told her even though he was relieved she agreed. They would not have to wait until the next fort or the next small settlement to try to marry. "Come along."

She held back, tilting her head to the side. "I need a bath. Won't get married with two days trail dust on me."

He'd been walking expecting her to follow behind now that she agreed. *A bath?* He didn't know about that. The only place she could bathe would be the river. "I will have to go with you. As soon as we talk to the minister and let him know what we've decided, I'll escort you to the river."

He remembered the day she'd become his wife in every way he acknowledged. They bathed at the pond. She shot a snake without a blink. Chauncey was unique.

"All right." She skipped up beside him, smiling. "I would like to be your wife. Your helpmate. I will even make you biscuits again."

Once more, she surprised him with this complete turnabout. Mercuric emotions... God help him. Were all women so damn confusing? He believed they must be as he recalled the days he spent with Kane while he tried not to court his now wife. Lyssa did everything she could to grab his attention. Stephen figured Chauncey would bedevil him for the rest of their lives together. If she ever tried to ride as Lyssa did, risking her life, he would lay down his rules.

Too bad Beth wasn't still here, she could take her to bathe. No, he would worry if that happened. He had to guard as well as protect Chauncey. Mr. Greeley was too close to ignore. Besides, he also needed to bathe.

~ * ~

After the vows were said, they were offered Jason's rooms for the night. The man overseeing the fur trading at the post was pleased to witness their vows as was Terrell along with Mister and Misses Murphy. The Greeleys were not invited. The man hoped that Jason was managing well. The service was short with only the barest words said as Stephen requested.

At the door, he swooped Chauncey into his arms, carrying her over the threshold. He didn't understand the custom but was more than willing to do just about anything to remain on her good side. She'd been sweet as well as compliant ever since she agreed to marry him. She wondered if he understood anything at all. She'd been so afraid when Beth left. After that he left her emotionally weak. This was the first day he showed interest in her.

When they entered, the room was dark. He lit several candles. The furniture was sparse. Nonetheless it appeared comfortable. She hoped the bed was restful as well as snug. A bottle of wine was set on the table in the main room. There were two glasses. A tray of chesses and meats sat next to the wine bottle. She found she was hungry. They'd had nothing to eat since an early breakfast.

When he set her down, his hands around her waist, she was shaking. He smoothed her eyebrows with his fingers. She wished he'd bedded her before this night. Wished she hadn't been so obstinate after he returned from his mission to save Beth. She still didn't know if Beth was saved. Perhaps it was for the best if she got pregnant. Though she didn't relish the idea of traveling in the wilderness in that condition. It would not be long before they left the wagon train to head north.

"Would you like wine?" he asked his voice easy. At her hesitation, he said with a wide smile she adored, "The wine might soothe those nerves of yours. You look almost ready to jump out of your skin What is it? Are you afraid of me? You shouldn't be. Know I would never hurt you." He had the grace to grimace at his suggestion.

"I'm not nervous," she shot back to him defiance in her voice before tilting her chin.

Truth be told she did feel as if she could jump out of her skin. With each touch, she jerked terrified of what would come next. "You will hold me naked and kiss me just as you did that first night we were together. I liked that. There is nothing to be frightened of."

She was trying to convince herself. Lyssa told her that it wasn't just a prick as Kane told her. She was afraid of the pain, of the lovemaking.

"No, no," his voice rumbled through her. "There isn't, except the pain of losing your innocence. I don't like that part although I'm pleased. I am your first as well as your last lover. The pain will vanish just like dust in the wind then there will be only pleasure for you. I can promise you that."

He was watching her, sliding his gaze over the length of her as if he recalled the way she looked with no clothing.

114

Men, they would end their sentence of inflicting pain with the words it would vanish. She remembered the way he looked when she was naked, standing by that pool of clear water along with the way she stared at him. She couldn't take her eyes from his body, from his most masculine part, hard with his lust. The only time she saw him that way was at the pond, the day she declared him to be her husband. That moment seemed so long ago, months. It had been two months of her stubbornness that kept them apart. He was beautiful. Clearing her throat, she looked away. "I'd like that wine now. Seems forever since I've had anything to drink except coffee and water. This is a treat…a treat on my wedding night."

He chuckled deep in his throat as he moved toward the bottle. "I'm surprised it's not rot-gut whiskey. That stuff can make a man's innards curl up and want to die. It's pretty much all a man gets around these parts."

Rot-gut whiskey?

"Not much for whiskey of any kind. It burns going down."

Chauncey made a little face to emphasize her point.

After her declaration he nodded as if in agreement though she'd seen him drink whiskey before as well as the brandy her father favored. He seemed to enjoy the liquor.

"Why don't you sit?" he asked while he poured the wine. He sat down in a nearby chair seeming oblivious to her. "We can talk if you like. I can tell you what will happen tonight if you wish to know. If you don't," he shrugged. "I…" he sipped the wine while he seemed to be thinking.

She did and she didn't. She wanted to understand what was going through his male mind. "Maybe it would be best if you just show me. I…" She touched her lips with the tip of her tongue. "I think I'd rather not know…how you… It will hurt when you come inside me. Lyssa told me."

He flinched with her words, his eyes narrowing as if he was angry. She didn't understand why he would be mad or what she said that would have caused the anger to rise. He handed her the wine. She drank deeply enjoying the warmth sliding down her throat. A glass of brandy would have been better. Might have soothed all her fears. As it stood now, she had too many fears simmering in her head. "I don't want to be afraid."

Her heart thundered. Pounded. Robbed her of breath. She inhaled a long deep draught of air, wishing she could get this over with, knowing too that he wouldn't like to hear those sentiments.

"Perhaps no pain. Some women feel little to no discomfort when the maidenhead is breached," he murmured as he watched her with those green eyes of his, seeming to impale her. He appeared to assess her, to look through her as if he understood all she thought. He couldn't. "Would you like to get more comfortable?" When he smiled at her it looked wicked. "You could remove your dress."

At his blatant suggestion, she gasped. He could remove his shirt and trousers. Stephen would probably jump at that chance if she suggested he do so. "No."

She thought that was something the groom did, undress the bride. Taking the gown off herself to get more comfortable was out of the question. "I'm fine the way I am."

She wasn't uncomfortable except when he stared her as if he wished to devour.

"You are fine, superb. However, that has nothing to do with comfort. You have shoes as well as stockings that if removed would give comfort. You don't wear a corset, so, of course, that doesn't count."

"I would not be comfortable sitting here in an almost naked state with you staring at me. As to my shoes and stockings, I don't have an issue removing them. I've always enjoyed going barefoot."

"What if I promised not to stare?" His gaze rested on her mouth, lingering for several seconds before dropping lower to her breasts.

"You could do that?" She would like to understand how he would keep from staring at her when he looked so ardently at her now.

He hooted, hearing her question. Leaning closer he touched her bottom lip with his finger. "No, you are right to question my abilities where your lovely person is concerned. I couldn't keep myself from staring at your amazing, beautiful assets. Believe a few of the wives put something in the bedroom for you. You see." He sipped then set the glass on the table. "They knew we were coming. One of the younger wives said she would make something for you for the wedding night. She owned fabric left from her dowry that would be wasted on her husband. She blushed a beautiful shade of pink before she told me the gift was more for my enjoyment than yours. I quite appreciated that and told her you would also. The woman is quite lonely. Most of the time her husband is in the mountains trapping. That's why it would be wasted. The man is seldom around."

Chauncey didn't understand any of this. It appeared he wasn't going to tell her. Stephen meant to make her guess. She could brazen this out. Her curiosity though was getting the best of her. "I'll go look." She rose to walk into the bedroom. She imagined the gift was a negligée. Stephen would appreciate her wearing the garment.

"Put it on before you return. I'd like to see what it is I'm supposed to enjoy...besides your luscious charms, of course." He sat down on a large chair that faced the fireplace. He stretched his long legs out in front of him. His glass of wine sat on his belly. His lean fingers, held the stem of the glass while he twirled the liquid.

"All right."

Chauncey did like to look at him. She wanted to see him with nothing on. She imagined that might happen tonight. As to his enjoyment...she wasn't at all certain. She hoped when she returned, he would have less on his person. Maybe he would undress. If she were almost naked, she would like it if he was in the same state of dishabille.

Inside the bedroom she saw the lavender gown and robe on the bed. She ran her fingers over the soft, silken fabric. The gown was beautiful, nothing like her white, very virginal nightdress. The fabric must have been precious. When she held it up, the candle light from the other room made the negligée shimmer in soft waves. If she put this on, he would see all of her. The robe would cover her.

With quick movements, she slipped from her dress and underthings before putting on the negligée that was left for his gratification.

Not hers.

There was a slight chill in the air. The fire would warm her. The silken fabric felt divine against the length of her body. She ran her fingers along the material. She gulped air swallowing the dose into her lungs. This was it. He would see her. Maybe he wouldn't want to talk. In truth, she did need to get this over with so she could relax.

"You about ready?" Stephen called out from the main room, his voice a low timbre, husky. "Time you ate something."

Oh, she wasn't ready. Yes, she needed to eat. No, her stomach wouldn't keep the food down. She wished there was a mirror so she could see how much of her he would be seeing. It was better if she didn't know.

"Chauncey?"

If she didn't show herself, he would come get her. They would be in the bedroom. He would tell her he wouldn't hurt her. He would. She wasn't a coward. Lyssa told her making love after the first time was wonderful. More than anything she needed to get past this first time. Her feet were growing cold on the wood floor. There was a large fur in front of the fireplace she could wiggle her toes in to make them warm. The fire would be warm...hot. She ran her hands along her arms, wishing the goose bumps would vanish.

"I'm coming," she said, her voice a thin line of fear whispering from her. Chauncey needed her glass of wine, needed two glasses of wine to bolster her courage.

When she walked into the room he was leaning on the mantle of the fireplace. His shirt was unfastened, falling open so she could see his chest. She followed the length to the top of his waistband. He unfastened them. She gulped understanding the time was almost upon her. It was what she wished for, a quick conclusion to her innocence. Just as she told him before, he was beautiful. She didn't think any man could be more handsome, more virile. He was so large, so tall, so broad of chest. The muscles of his thighs were fitted nicely to his buckskins.

Stephen's gaze raked from her eyes to the tips of her bare toes. His eyes simmered radiating heat as well as approval while his gaze stopped for a moment on her breasts. The smile she was feeling at his ardent appraisal turned to nervous energy. She squeaked when she tried to say something. Her hands moved higher to cover her breasts. He stepped forward, handing her the wine she left in the room. He did nothing more except smile at her.

"Drink," his throaty voice didn't sound normal. "You're beautiful, Chauncey." He ran his fingers through her hair, "So soft. Is the rest of you this soft, this silken? I mean to discover the truth this evening. The ladies were right. I do enjoy looking at you in this silken confection. I'd like looking at you wearing nothing at all better. You wouldn't be comfortable."

She had the same thoughts about him. "Yes," she murmured her voice tender.

She sat down in the large chair she abandoned earlier. Her stomach was churning with violence in mind. When she thought about the night to come, she thought she might be sick.

"Chauncey?" Startling her, he was beside her. "What's wrong?" He appeared concerned. The tone of his voice surprised her.

Stephen always surprised her. She looked at him, her eyes crossing for a second. He watched her as if he could read her mind. His brows furrowed together in thought. Oh, to know what was behind his eyes to understand his thinking.

"Nothing, nothing is wrong. Do you like the negligée?" she queried even though she felt certain she knew the answer.

Unable to drink, she set the glass of wine on the table. "Can we do this? Now?"

He stood in front of her, his hands touching her neck along with her shoulders. The touch was possessive. "I believe I understand the problem." He kissed her, with slowness ran his tongue along her lips. He tugged on her bottom lip, telling her what he wanted.

She reached up to hold onto his shoulders, pressing her body against his, feeling his heat, scenting the man. The muscles of his neck were corded and hard with tension as if he held himself back. After she opened for him, he touched her, explored the deep dark secrets behind her lips. She met his tongue with her own, dancing, playing, teasing. A soft sigh of pleasure or relief she wasn't certain ruffled from her lips. She liked his kisses. Would she like what would come next?

The soft masculine chuckle told her he understood her hesitancy along with the sigh of satisfaction his kiss brought forth. She wondered if he'd ever made love to a virgin, if she was his first. If not, he wouldn't know anything. All he did was spout words he'd heard other men recount. What did it matter. This would happen. She would lose her innocence tonight. She wanted to be pragmatic. Found the thought made her eyes cross again.

When he pulled her closer, his hands on her bottom, she felt the hardness of him pressed against her. The sensation sent a flaming jolt of curiosity along with fear through her. She wanted to see him. Then again, she did not. Just as he was a huge man, his sex would be huge. Would it? He would come inside her. She wasn't totally ignorant. She lived on a ranch. She'd seen animals mate. Even heard her brother talk about sex when he didn't know she was nearby.

"Stephen..." she whispered his name. The sound seemed to be right. Gave her confidence to pursue this without fear. "I'm too warm." Heat pumped through her. The inferno built with each stroke of his tongue, with each magical caress of his large hands. He explored, tempted as well.

"We should get rid of this robe if that is so. Don't want you to be too hot. Wouldn't want you to expire from the heat."

Beneath his nimble fingers, the robe was pushed from her arms then floated to swirl around her feet. She was vaguely aware of the fabric as she moved closer to him. His hands floated across the tips of her veiled breasts. His mouth touched her lips again. Framed them. Possessed them. Pushed them apart.

Chauncey wanted nothing between her and this man she fell in love with the moment she saw him. She understood somewhere deep inside her the only way she would be happy would be to feel his flesh against hers. "You have too much on." She pushed his shirt from his shoulders. It landed on the fur rug in front of the fireplace. Embers popped. Flames created orange-red shadows on the walls of the small room and atop his chest. Her fingers roamed to the opening of his buckskins. She wanted to push them from his slim hips. She needed to touch that hard part of him.

"As do you. However, I'll give the disrobing a bit more time before I look my fill on your beautiful body. Want you to beg me, to want me more than your fear of what will happen." He swept her into his arms then walked to one of the chairs sitting in front of the flames.

It always amazed her how he lifted her with no effort, how she fit into his arms as if she was made for him and him alone. Snuggling against his chest, she understood he was the right man, the only man for her. The smooth texture of his chest warmed her cheek. She placed her hand on his chest, spreading her fingers, touching each nipple as she did so. He lifted her chin. His eyes were deep shimmering pools of the darkest green. Within a moment, his lips engulfed hers, again toyed with them until she opened for him, accepting him inside.

He tasted of the wine and cheese he must have eaten while she changed into the filmy gown. She inhaled the spicey fragrance coupled with his own unique scent that seemed to be part of him. Her fingers wandered down his arms, thick with muscle. She wrapped her fingers around his wrist so large the tips of her fingers didn't meet. He was so gentle with her. He lifted her face, staring at her, looking concerned. With the tip of his finger, he touched her nose.

At a leisurely pace he slipped the small straps that were barely there from her arms. She felt the callouses on his hands as he moved the fabric lower, lower still until her breasts were bared to him. He cupped each one, moved his thumb with exactness over each swollen tip.

"Lovely," he said, his voice throaty with desire. "I'm a lucky man. You're beautiful, sweet, feisty, intelligent."

With that said, he sipped one hardened nipple into his mouth, sucked and laved until she arched closer, pushing against him, moaning. Gasping. Noises rippled. Her hips moved as if inviting him.

"Stephen, I..."

She didn't know what she wanted to say. What he was doing was magical, enchanting, captivating. Mercuric heat entered her, flamed and danced in the dark recess that was utterly feminine. He inflamed her from the inside out. The fire fueled higher by each touch, each stroke. His lips and teeth found one breast while his hand caressed and fondled the other.

"Chauncey?" He looked up as if waiting for her to say something. "Ah, nothing to say? I've rendered you speechless again. This time I'm pleased."

One of his dark eyebrows arched high, his smile wide.

All she wanted was for him to continue his tender assault on her senses. He pushed the fabric lower, so low her belly was revealed. He spread his finger from hipbone to hipbone as if measuring. He laid her back, her body arced for him. Across his arm, he curved her so he could gain easy access to more parts of her, to the tips of each breast. He kissed her, nipping kisses as he moved lower until he touched her belly button then across her stomach. Her muscles contracted. Her body quivered. Deep inside she pulsed, throbbed. She wanted something undefinable. Needed him to finish this so she would understand the mystery that no one talked about in mixed company. He wanted so much to make this right for her he shook.

One more time she found herself in his arms, cradled with tender care against his chest. As he removed the rest of her gown, the fabric fluttered to the wood floor beneath them. Once on the furs he spread her hair out sifting his fingers through it as he did so. Sitting back on his haunches he looked at her, his gaze roaming from her eyes to the tips of her toes then back.

"When we are in my village, we will sleep in my lodge on my furs. You are beautiful. Chauncey, you will have to learn to obey. It is not seemly for a warrior's wife to gainsay him. You will come to understand. When you are with my people, you cannot argue with your husband. When we return to England, you can have more say."

"I will understand."

She didn't but she would tell him anything now.

She lifted her arms, offering herself to him. He kissed her mouth again while his hands explored her legs, the inside of her thighs down to her knees. He cupped her. She felt his fingers between her thighs. Unrestrained, she opened her shaking legs for him seeking the unknown, the pleasure he spoke of.

"Pleasure first," he murmured, his lips on her neck, his breath whispering across her cheek.

"All right."

His groan of desire pleased her as tiny mewls and moans erupted from her lips, a puff of air, a throaty sigh, a broken sound followed.

Between her thighs she felt his hands gently move, felt his fingers sliding through her, touching her, stroking until she moaned again, spreading her legs even wider, sensing this was what he wanted, what she wanted. Unable to help herself, her hips jerked in response as he seemed to caress a more tender place, a more sensitive spot. His lips covered hers again. Ravaged. Pillaged. Magical enchantment. She felt him inside her, one finger then two. Pressure built as he moved, in then out, repeating and repeating until she was beside herself with the feelings overwhelming her. Her body was contracting, pulsing, fragmenting as he worked her. He continued to tantalize, to stroke, to change the tempo of his caresses. His other hand tugged on the tight bud of one breast while he continued his assault inside her.

"Stephen..." she moaned, a perceptible whisper in the fading light.

The candles were burning themselves out. The fire was now reduced to glowing embers. She felt the convulsions grow, felt her body pulse with need. She shattered, splintering into a million pieces. "Stephen!" She cried out as she spasmed, over then over again.

Her body responded to his attentions. He stopped moving, brought his hand to her cheek, touched her with the fingers that seduced and charmed her body to something she'd never known before.

"I felt your maidenhead. Was hoping it wasn't there."

He rose then stepped out of his buckskins. He stood still for several seconds, allowing her to look at him. Heavens, she could look at him for forever. She didn't want to stop staring. Unable to help herself, she lowered her eyes.

Stephen was magnificent. His arousal large and hard.

When she opened her eyes again, she felt as if they were glazed over. Wasting no time, he was on top of her, kissing her, stroking her again. Once more sending the tempest of desire into the most intimate parts of her. With his knees, he spread her legs apart. She knew this would hurt but she was still so aroused she didn't care.

Once more, after his kisses, the strokes of fire that sent infernos raging inside, her body was pulsing with need breaking apart with each stroke of his callused fingers. His touch mercuric. Restrained. Hesitant.

Now she understood what would happen, what to expect. He would orchestrate her pleasure. He told her what he'd do. That he would see to the ecstasy she deserved.

With no warning, this was different. He was pushing inside her but it wasn't with his fingers. He was stretching her. She was too small for him. There was no pain. She arched up against him, crying out as her pleasure built then exploded.

She was pulsing against him. Splintering a part with each small stroke. The next moment she felt the searing red-hot pain she'd expected from the first. He raised up on his arms to look at her. Pushed damp strands of hair from her forehead. His eyes were focused on her, waiting. He held still.

His eyes when they touched upon her held sorrow. "I'm sorry. Never again."

With his thumbs he brushed the tears from her cheeks. He kissed the corner of her mouth, her nose then her closed eyes as the pain began to fade. She was sore inside. Still, she felt the immense pleasure increase once more.

"It's fine. I'm fine. Don't worry about me. Oh..."

She was straining against him, feeling the growth once more of those sweet sensations. Of the fire. Flames spread. Heat devoured her. She hungered for him.

His face was strained, the muscles tight. His lips were pulled back from his teeth as if he was in pain. Inside her he was moving again, slow strokes at first. Her nails dug into his shoulders. She heard the small moan ripple from the back of her throat as if it was someone else. She bit his shoulder.

"Easy love," he whispered between kisses. "Relax...come to me...let it happen again. You know how it feels. You understand it will happen." His voice sounded strained as if he was trying to keep himself in check, to hold back. "Your pleasure is important."

She nodded to him, her body arching to meet his. "I," she moistened her lips. "I..." She was almost there, almost to that same devastating ecstasy he generated in her before. "Please..." This time she understood what she wanted, what she needed.

His big body began to move faster and harder, thrusting into her as if he lost control. His fingers stroked her with intimate care while his tongue moved inside her mouth with the same urgency as his member. She whimpered, heaved, and moaned as the pleasure shattered within her.

He cried out as he thrust one more time then again. He stilled then, falling on top of her, blanketing her, the weight of him pressing against her. She felt his seed inside her. For what seemed like an eternity, he didn't move. After endless seconds ticked by, he rolled to his side taking her with him. She felt him slip from inside her.

Her head was tucked into the hollow of his shoulder, her hand resting on his chest. She sighed a whisper of air, her breath fluttering across him. "Stephen..." she began unable to think of any words to finish the thought.

"Are you alright?" he asked, his hand wandering down her back to her bottom then back. "I didn't hurt you too much?"

She wanted to look at him again. "Fine...better than fine," she said wondering at the pressure deep inside her.

He broke through her maidenhead. It had been more than a prick. Nonetheless, the act had not hurt that much. She would forget the pain. It would become but a memory in her past, just as Lyssa told her.

"We should sleep," he murmured, stroking her hair. "Tomorrow...well, we don't have to leave tomorrow with the wagons. We'll be striking out on our own. Making our own path. The going will be harder. I'll expect much from you. However, you will need to tell me if you are too tired to go on. You will need to be honest. Don't try to do more than you are able.

"You never told me."

She was curious as to where they would go. From the start of this trip, she understood they would leave the wagons and set out on a journey all their own. She had not expected it to happen so soon.

"No, I didn't say anything. The wagon will be left behind. We will have to buy supplies along with a pack horse. I'm unaccustomed to sharing my thoughts. You will have to help me with that. If you have a question, ask. If you don't like my silence, tell me. I've never done this before, never traveled with a woman, with my wife, only warriors. Warriors seem to know each other's thoughts. We both will need to learn."

She pushed away, staring down at him, his expression unreadable. "Do you know where you're going?" It never occurred to her before that the wilderness beyond them was vast. There would be no trail to follow.

"Yes and no."

He touched her mouth. Ran his thumb along her lip, his eyes smiling with humor. "Hush now, do you doubt my ability to find my people?"

Her snort of disbelief didn't go unnoticed by him. She wanted to punch him. He was an arrogant man. She liked him the way he was. "I don't know how you could find anything out there. I will choose to trust in you. If I didn't have faith that you know where to go, I would stay here and wait for you."

She gave the ultimatum understanding he would never allow that, not after tonight. He would never leave her alone. She was his. The thought gave her reason to smile. This was what she'd wanted since that first kiss behind the church.

"The People winter close to the same place every year." He smiled when he saw the disbelief in her eyes. "Hush again, true, I've been away for several years. They will not have changed that much that I cannot read the signs that will lead me to them...and...they will find us before we find them."

"Then...there will be danger?"

She'd known this for a fact from the moment she set out to follow him. Until now, she hadn't been afraid.

"Only if you disobey me. You must trust in me that I know best. For you this is unfamiliar territory."

He stared at her as if he wished to say something else. He heaved in a breath of air before letting the oxygen out in a slow stream. "You will not, I pray. The wilderness is not a place for you to assume you know better than your husband."

"I will do as you say," she murmured with lowered lashes,

unwilling to look at him.

She wanted to be given credit for rational thinking.

"You best mean those words, woman." He paused one more time studying her, looking into her eyes. "I expect you to obey without argument. Funny, how I'm afraid you won't be able to do that. I've no faith in you on that score. Though I used the word funny, the fact is in no way amusing. It's terrifying."

She gathered his thoughts into her head. "Am I that difficult to deal with? I would tell you that if you order me to do things I agree with, all will work out for the best."

"Yes," he said as he rose. He padded to the wash stand in front of the one window in the bedroom. "You will be illogical and dangerous to yourself because you think you are right?"

His words bothered her. She didn't want to be considered difficult. "I will try to be more biddable. I don't understand..."

He waved a hand in the air, slashing. "That's exactly what I'm speaking about. You don't understand the way of the People. You won't understand. All of this will be new to you. My People are not anything like what you are used to dealing with. There are laws and beliefs passed down for hundreds...no thousands of years that must be adhered to. One stubborn woman cannot change their way of life."

"I will try." She felt contrite, berated for something she hadn't done.

"We need to wait and see. Perhaps once we are alone in the middle of thick trees with only animal trails to follow, you will begin to comprehend the magnitude of this adventure into wilderness."

"How long will it be until we reach your family?"

Desperate, she searched for a change of subject.

"As long as you make me biscuits..." He laughed at the look on her face. "Now, there will be blood, your blood that needs to be washed from you. It is natural."

Panic registered in her head when he sat down then spread her legs again. He looked far too determined. "Stephen..." Her hands pushed with no effect on his shoulders.

"I kissed you here." He stroked her with the damp cloth. "Now,

I'll wash away the evidence of your innocence as well as your pain."

~ * ~

Mr. Greeley swore at his wife, cursed as he drove into her body. She screamed. He laughed. He wanted his Beth back. She was pliant and soft beneath him. She never fought him. Her breasts sagged with the weight of years along with nursing babies. If he couldn't get his Beth back, maybe he could buy another girl. He liked his wife. He didn't want her to have to see to his needs since she didn't like him to make love to her. She always complained. Didn't want to have another child. She told him she was too old to have more kids. If that happened, she would probably die in childbirth. He didn't want that. She was a good wife.

Now, he wanted revenge on the girlie who helped his Beth leave. His Beth liked to have him inside her. He knew that by the way she held still for him. He heard a Sioux warrior took his little slave girl, his Beth. How dare that man! Well, that man would make her his slave. She wouldn't like to be a man's slave. He wouldn't treat her right or give her whatever she asked for. He'd share her with the other heathens. Heard they slit the nostrils of the women they took, burned them just to hear them scream.

That wasn't right. Beth was his slave girlie. That's what they always pretended. She was better off with him. He bought and paid for her a few years back. When she was younger, she was so damn sweet. He didn't get to take her virginity. Beth's maidenhead had already been broken by that man who owned her before him. If he couldn't have Beth, he would have the girl, Chauncey. He pushed into his wife thinking of Beth, recalling Chauncey's face. He didn't think he would ever get her back. When he finished, he pulled out of the woman who'd been his wife for more than twenty years. She birthed four children during that time. Two died. The other two left as soon as they were old enough to make their own way. He was pleased he didn't have to support them.

He was going west, going to find land. The ranch he wanted was in his reach, all that unclaimed land ripe for the taking. He would be rich. First, he was going to find Chauncey Wilkes and make her sorry for what she did to him. She couldn't tell him where Beth went. That didn't surprise him. Nobody would ever see his Beth again. Having been stolen by that savage warrior, she would no longer be alive.

Tomorrow after the wagons started moving, he'd give Chauncey a visit. In the interim, his wife could drive their wagon. If the scout wasn't around, it would be easy for him to get inside her. That husband of hers had a way of disappearing for days on end. He could use one of those days to his advantage. Before the wagons reached their destination, he wanted a taste of Chauncey. Needed to feel her beneath him when he rocked her. She'd be just as sweet as his Beth.

With a grunt, he pulled out of his wife, his seed left on her thigh. "Go on now. Get dinner started. I'm hungry. Hope you didn't get with child. For your sake. Don't want more kids either. Just more mouths to feed." Mr. Greeley pulled up his britches and fastened them. He adjusted himself, still thinking of the two girls that had been on his mind the last few minutes. "I'm going to have a look around. Maybe there's another woman I can buy for my use. I don't want to hurt you."

Mrs. Greeley pulled down her skirts, smoothing the fabric as she stood. She grimaced but she looked at him. With no fanfare, she spoke, "I'd like that if you found someone else to ease you. I'm not rightly fond of what you do to me. You know that." She held up her hand to stop the comment. "Yes, I understand it's your right. That's why I'm not complaining. You always do your best to make certain I'm not hurt. If you can find someone else, I'll be pleased."

"You're my wife. You've got to do what I want." He didn't want to growl at her.

Every time she protested, he felt a great deal of annoyance.

"True," she said, seeming unruffled by his words. "Five wagons down there is a young woman about sixteen. She's helping, earning her way west. Says she's going to find her brother. Her mother and father passed on, died of some disease. You might want to see if the family she is with will sell her to you. I would be fine if that's what you did. Use whatever idea comes to mind. We do need help with the chores. We're getting on in age. Nothing is as easy as it used to be."

"Why, Mrs. Greeley, I just might do that. Like the young ones much better. Maybe she's still a virgin. Beth wasn't." In anticipation, he rubbed his hands together then fondled himself, feeling the immediate surge of desire. "I'd like a virgin."

"Thought you would. Don't go off tryin' for that vengeance I know you're wantin'. That man who's scouting for the train, isn't a regular man if you get my drift. No, he's not a man you want to fool with. Don't want to be left alone here to fend for myself. You go now and find yourself that girlie. I'll put some bacon with the beans tonight. Maybe Chauncey will have some biscuits to share with us." She hummed as she left the tent.

Mr. Greeley stared after her shaking his head, wiping the sweat from his forehead. A little girlie to have the rest of the trip and maybe at that new ranch he was plannin'. Life was good. He would have to be easier on this new one. He grinned then spit a chew of tobacco on the ground. She'd probably be a virgin.

~ * ~

Beth looked up into deep dark brown eyes, eyes that seemed to care. Men didn't care. The man was smiling at her even though his face was a bit of a blur. She tried to reach out to touch his face. Her hand wouldn't move. Her lips were parched, her throat dry. She wanted to think but couldn't seem to form a coherent thought.

"Water..." she croaked.

Her voice didn't sound the least bit normal. Her body seemed to ache everywhere, mostly where Mr. Greeley abused her.

This man she didn't know smiled at her. "You're awake. That's good." He held her so she could drink. "How do you feel?"

She closed her eyes as the cool liquid slid down her throat. "Where?"

"Where are you? A very good question. We are almost to my village where my mother will finish healing you. You were very sick, hot with the fever, with infection. I had to keep you cool. Had to wait until we could travel."

He set her back on the furs.

She closed her eyes again, a million questions running through her head. When she opened them again, he was gone. She heard him beside her. When she tried to roll over to see what he was doing, the world seemed to tilt then move. She groaned, falling onto her back. Wishing everything didn't slant at strange angles.

He was beside her, watching, seeming to wait. "You are not ready to get up, Little One. Patience is what your mind needs to tell your small form. Your body must heal before I can allow you to move around. You grow weary with doing nothing. I understand." He sat down crossing his legs. He drank from a large mug. "Would you like to ask more questions. I wouldn't object if you kept your eyes closed. Since I know the world is spinning for you."

"Who are you?" She murmured, feeling the dryness in her throat ebbing. "Do you have a name?"

He laughed. She liked the sound of his laughter. The men she'd known her short life rarely laughed. When they did, the sound was never pleasant.

"Another fine question from the Woman Who Stands Alone. My name is Jason Meeker. I made that name up for use in the white world. The name I was given when I became an adult was White Feather. What do you think? You can call me either name. I answer to both." His husky laughter echoed within her.

She smiled feeling at ease with this man who laughed with ease. She'd never been with a man who laughed. Beth discovered she liked this man. "Just like Stephen Wilkes who also goes by Still Water Runs Deep. I will call you Jason."

"Fine choice, then I will call you Beth except when we reach my tribe. We will go by our Indian names there. Believe me when I tell you that I will protect you. No one will hurt you." He tucked the blankets around her, smoothing out the covers. "You are warm enough?"

His tribe? Panic laced with a goodly amount of fear lanced through her. She heard too many stories to feel at ease, to relax. "What are you going to do with me? Are you going to hurt me? Make me your slave?"

"If you'll have me, I'm going to marry you. I want you for my woman as for hurting you...once you are healed you will know only pleasure at my hands. I will strive to protect you, keep your belly full as well as always satisfied, give you children if you would like them. This man hopes you do. I wish to have children."

The long sigh emanating from him surprised her but not as much as his answer. "You're wife?" After the last years and the men she accommodated she didn't expect to be any man's wife. "I," she cleared her throat, "don't believe you. I've been used. I'm not a virgin. No man wishes to take a whore for a wife."

"This man wants you virgin or not. Believe me when I tell you that you are no whore. You've been a victim." He paused, caressing her cheek. "Ah, then you will have to wait for time to tell the full tale. Now, won't you? I would that you sleep again but after I feed you some of this fine broth that will help you grow stronger. Tomorrow morning, we will have to move on."

"Eat," she parroted him. "Sleep, grow stronger. Yes, I suppose those are all good ideas. How long before we are with your people?"

"Another week or possibly two. It all depends on you and how fast you can travel. I won't push you past your limits."

Her mind went back to being his wife. She couldn't allow him to think she was something she wasn't. Repeating herself, "You understand I'm not a virgin. I've been with more than one man."

Not by choice though. She despised the men she'd been forced to service.

"Still Water Runs Deep told me so. Explained to me how you'd been abused. I need a wife. Would like to have children. If I help you, perhaps you can help me. What do you think? We can work together to please each other."

With those words she panicked. Her mind could not help but linger on the things Mr. Greeley did to her. She didn't want that for herself. Not if she had a choice. "You need...why?" Her terror spiraled out of control.

It seemed he witnessed the fear she was feeling. "Hush now, I need a wife because mine died. This man will treat you with gentle care. He will give you pleasure. You will see. All your bad memories will fade into the back recesses of your mind. They will vanish like dust in the wind."

She closed her eyes, struggling to inhale, willing the beat of her heart to slow. "Pleasure between a man and a woman doesn't exist."

"When you are healed, I will show you. Yes, I will show you much. Remember, you will always be able to tell me no. When you do, I will stop."

Chapter Five

Stephen woke her with a slap to her little butt. He chuckled when she jerked up glowering at him, her eyes shooting sparks. Her passion was unmistakable. Spending more time in bed with her would be pleasant. The time for frolicking wasn't in the cards for them. They needed to make it into the high country before the first snow began to fall. When they reached the encampment, perhaps then they could wallow in his furs. Take time to learn every part of each other.

She pulled the blankets around her to cover her breasts. The action amused him. If he hadn't spent the better part of the evening exploring and caressing her, he might feel different. As it was, he could see the lush curves with his eyes closed. He could taste her, remember the scent of her. She was all silk and satin, white and soft to his every caress. Chauncy, the essence of Chauncey was embedded in his mind.

"It's time to move out," he pulled on his buckskins. "You've got five minutes to dress. If you're not in the sitting room by then, I'll come get you."

Hell, he knew that would be a mistake. He didn't dare see her undressed. Right now, it was all he could do to walk from this room without tasting her once more.

Chauncey watched him with wide eyes. "So early? You kept me up most of the night."

Her tone held a wealth of sarcasm, which Stephen wondered about. She told him so little about her life on the ranch. During their journey he hoped he would gain fresh insight.

"The next weeks are going to be hard on you. We'll leave at the crack of dawn then ride until dark. I hope you'll be able to keep up."

He didn't want to frighten her or give her self-doubts. He knew the first couple of days would be the hardest for her since she would have

134

to adjust to the grueling hours. Nevertheless, she needed to understand what he would expect of her. There would be no surprises. He focused on her still sitting in the bed, the covers pulled to her chin. "What are you waiting for?"

When she nodded her understanding, he wondered what she was thinking. She was brave, courageous as well. By the time they reached his village, she'd be ready to stop riding. Would not wish to ride a horse again. She shouldn't have come. Her life was in danger.

After she ran her tongue across her bottom lip, she slanted her gaze toward the door then back to him. He understood what she wanted. She was going to have to ask him to leave. He sat down on the chair facing the bed, stretched out as if he wasn't in a hurry to get on the road. His gaze riveted on his wife, on his beautiful wife.

She wanted some privacy to dress for the day. Looking at her clothes spread out for her on the chair next to the one where he sat then back to his face, she sighed, flirted. Her lashes lowered. Her head tilted. When she opened them again, he imagined she was hoping he would be gone. He wasn't going to leave. No, he was enjoying himself too much teasing her.

Deciding two could play this game, she stiffened needing the courage, perhaps also a touch of bravado. Defiance written on the set features of her lovely face, she tossed the covers back then rose. Pretending he wasn't watching, she strode to her gown. Her small breast swayed provocatively while the cool air in the room hardened the tips. He set what he thought was a practical gown out for her to wear. Naked, she studied him. Her beathing was labored, the only indication she was anxious.

Pulling in a long drought of air, Chauncey addressed him, "Pants would be much more practical for riding. If you insist, I'll wear this." Chauncey watched him shift his position as if he was suddenly uncomfortable.

He was.

Her blatant display of her body provoked all his masculine instincts. She won this round hands down. Curse her. He would win the next. He was irritated by her idea that she could wear britches, further displaying herself.

"No!" His voice husky with the passion she awakened.

He jerked to his feet staring at her, knowing he needed to leave her presence. The beat of his heart quickened, pulsing through him. He slashed his hand through the air. "Wear whatever you think is best!" he growled out before marching from the room, his fists tight balls at his sides.

Once outside the room, he shut the door as quietly as he could, holding in the frustrations that ate at him. Stephen never expected her to step from their bed, naked. Never lost his temper. She surprised him with her audacity. The bold way she maneuvered him.

She stood in front of him naked! Daring him to make love to her. He ran his hand behind his neck in an attempt to ease the tension that built the moment he watched her move with such grace across the room, her beautiful breasts swaying with each step. He muttered a few more curse words. At the sight of her, lust swept to his groin. He swelled and now ached. He'd have the devil of a time riding. This was hell of his making. He shouldn't have taunted her by not leaving the room and giving her what she hoped for...a spot of privacy. She was new to sexual games. Even so, he felt certain she understood what she did to him.

Her eyes had been the deepest darkest blue when he cursed then strode from the torture chamber he created and she presented him with. How was he going to survive day in and day out on the trail with her? She would always be within arm's reach. He could have her anytime he wanted her. He could even take her while they rode as Kane took Lyssa that day he brought fifty horses to her father's ranch. The bride price, ah, he would have to figure out a suitable bride price for his woman. It would need to exceed fifty horses.

His thoughts weren't helping alleviate his arousal. He was rock hard and growing harder with each thought, each image he recreated from his memory. He kept his eyes wide open. If he stared at the fire in the sitting room long enough, maybe the ache between his legs would ease. Perhaps it wouldn't. This journey was going to be hell.

He pushed away from the wall he'd been leaning against. Someone left a pot of coffee along with thick slices of bread on a tray.

He sat down at the table. He poured mugs of coffee for both of them, then slathered a huge slice of bread with the butter and honey that was also left. Surprised, he should have heard someone come into the room. Well, it must have been the nice Mrs. Treats. She was a wonderful woman. If he had the time, he would thank her for the negligée. She was right. He did enjoy that piece of clothing. The soft filmy gown was perfect for the evening. She would take it with her in the valise she packed. At least he hoped she would. On the trail, there would be no use for the gown. When they returned to England, if she wore it for him, the sight would bring back fond memories of their wedding night.

"Stephen?" Chauncey stepped through the door into the room. "What's wrong? You're glowering. You did tell me to wear what I thought best. I did. You'll be happy for me that I don't have skirts to hinder my riding. No one else will be around to see me. Just you."

She tilted her head to the side, staring at him as if she didn't know.

He didn't intend to give her an answer to something she knew. "Have something to eat, Chauncey. This is all you'll get until we stop at dusk."

His voice was raw, husky with the desire she evoked. He didn't enjoy this feeling. She aroused him before. Never to this intensity. He supposed it happened that way because he tasted her, held her, stroked her. He heard the soft female sounds of pleasure when she shattered to tiny pieces in his arms. He would never forget.

She nodded, stepping into the room. She wore pants and a shirt. He didn't like the attire. She knew what he thought. The pants were more practical. She still looked like a woman. He knew what was beneath the clothing she wore. Didn't like the fact anyone could see her sweet curves. Damn it, she was his.

"Why Mr. Wilkes, I believe you've got a bee in your bonnet, well perhaps it's not exactly a bonnet. If you stay that way, the bee might sting you. Are you going to be irritable for the rest of the day?" She drank the coffee, ate a huge bite of the bread then chewed as if she was immersed in thought.

"You havin' second thoughts about coming with me. While I

wasn't planning on returning this way, if you wanted to stay here, I would change my plans."

It seemed to him that he lost control.

"Should I?" she queried, her voice soft, slowly walking to him.

She ran a fingertip along his jawline then smiled with seduction her intent. She touched his rapid beating pulse at the base of his neck. After that she shifted her tongue across the swell of her bottom lip leaving a path of moisture behind.

It was one hell of a calculating smile, too many damn gestures that an innocent maiden, fresh from her wedding night shouldn't know. He'd give just about anything to understand what she was thinking.

"No, no, second thoughts about a trip with you. In fact, I'm going back to the original plan. You don't have a choice. I wouldn't leave you here by yourself under any circumstances. You would just get into a pack of trouble I would have to sort out next spring. If you are going to find misfortune, I want that calamity to be seen to by me before the disaster can escalate."

"Good, we agree on something. I'm coming with you. As you well know by now, I can get into trouble whether you are with me to oversee my activities or not." She picked up the valise she packed the night before. "Are you ready? Times wasting away. How many miles are you planning to cover before dusk? Do I have more than one horse to ride? You should understand that I don't have to stop to switch horses. I can keep up with you." She wrapped up the bread that was left then downed the rest of her coffee.

Chauncey walked ahead of him, her hips swaying for the first few seconds. By the time they were a few feet from the house, he strode beside her, anger bubbling up one more time. He thought about how she annoyed him with her independence. She would have to get used to his ways. Either that or he needed to get use to her ways. That thought sifted through his thoroughly man's brain. He would have to think about that.

Stephen wrapped his arm around her shoulders, tugging her closer. He felt her curves against him. He groaned even though he wasn't going to let her go just yet. Bending close to her, he whispered. "You recall your promise to me?"

"Promise?" she smiled coyly fluttering her lashes while she stared at him a blank look on her face. "What was that?"

"The one to obey. I plan on holdin' you to that pledge. If you forget that sweet vow, you'll regret your error."

Stephen knew his words irritated her. She was not a woman used to blindly obeying. He already established in his mind that her father allowed her to do anything she wished. He marched away, headed for the stable where their gear was stored. He whistled a bawdy tune her cousin Lyssa taught him. It was all good. At least the life would be, once she learned his word was law. He wondered how long it would take her to appreciate the truth for what it was. Two days at the most, he decided. Of course, it depended on what dangers waited for them. Anything could happen.

Once they set out, she rode behind him. He knew she was finishing the bread she brought with her. She wouldn't make it very far this first day. He would have to be patient with her. She couldn't be used to riding the long hours he intended to put in so he could reach the village before winter blocked their way.

His first surprise came when she rode up next to him an hour or so after leaving. He expected her to ask him to stop, to give some excuse. An excuse wasn't needed. After last night she would have to be sore. Leeway needed to be granted for her delicate condition. She smiled that sweet siren's smile that always left him aroused and in need of oxygen. "Tell me about your people. I know you grew up with Kane but I don't know much about him. Guess I also would like to understand why you plan to go back to England."

"Several questions, where should I begin?"

"With your people, who are you, Stephen Wilkes, besides an incredibly attractive man who is now my husband. You understand that's what I wanted from the first moment I set eyes on you. When you kissed me behind the church your lips on mine served to strengthen as well as reinforce my desire. You have green eyes. Does that make you a half breed?"

Was he a half breed? Yes and no. "They winter where the aspens grow thick and dense. There is a clear and very sweet spring that flows down from the Rocky Mountains. In the summer there is a pond that we swim in. Do you swim? In the pond that day all you did was stumble around, As to my being a half breed, both my parents were Sioux. I was never considered a breed though I must have some white blood in me somewhere since my eyes are green."

"My swimming skills, I'm certain are better than yours. There were other factors at play that day," she bragged with a feminine giggle to follow. "I see. Not that it matters to me. You are who you are. Your mother?"

"She grows old as we speak. Which is why I need to make this trip. She's seen many winters. Her hair was graying when I left. My father died in a raid when I was only a lad. Maybe that is why I left with Kane or Black Thunder. He was and is my best friend. The first time when his grandfather hauled him off to London, I came with them. The grandfather allowed me to do so because he was afraid Black Thunder might have left him at the first opportunity. I gave my promise that I would stick with him no matter what. Did not need to vow anything. I imagine that I could have been more of a risk to the old man. I could have helped Kane return. I did not. At that time, I didn't understand. Now, I do."

Those long-ago memories faded even though everything he saw now remained vivid in his mind. He'd not wanted to bring Chauncey here, into this wild, savage land. Fear for her safety rivaled anything he'd ever felt before.

"You must love him a lot." Chauncey sighed, the air barely making a sound. She stared into the forest then back to him. Her eyes were wide with a depth of emotion Stephen didn't understand.

Of course, he loved Kane. He didn't recall a time he didn't love the man as his brother. Stephen heard the wistfulness in her voice. Wasn't at all certain how to interpret the sound. While she amused him with her antics, he didn't think he loved her. Chauncey was also incredibly beautiful. Last night he enjoyed her body. Meant to do so every time he could. Deep in his heart, he understood she would carry his child before they returned to her home. Her parents would wish to scalp him or perhaps hang him by his thumbs. They were wed. He had every right to possess her beautiful body.

"I love Kane like a brother. I also enjoyed London. There was so much to do. When Kane decided to stay, I bought land near his. Don't think I could ever go back to living on the prairie. I like the comforts civilization provides. That way of life is in my past along with the hardships. Suppose I've grown soft in my old age. What about you? Will you be happy living in England? Away from your family?"

He didn't want her to be homesick. He hoped that with her cousin living nearby she would be happy. If not happy, content.

"Did you have a lot of...well...did you see a lot of women when you were in England?" She looked away for a moment, her beautiful face flushing with the embarrassment of asking the question.

He didn't miss the rise of color to her face. He wanted to ask her what she meant by see a lot of women. Even before he left for London, he enjoyed women and what they offered with their bodies. Lifting his shoulders, he focused his attention on her expressions. "Not that many. Women in the bars who flaunted themselves. Who needed extra coin to survive. I never went to the balls that were given for the debutantes if that's what you're asking. While Kane was invited and chose to ignore their existence, I was not acceptable to the aristocracy to mingle with their daughters. I had neither the required wealth or the title to garner an invitation."

"Oh..." she said as she nudged her horse to move faster. He saw her back, stiff, regal in her demeanor. If she'd lived in England she would have been among the debutantes. He also didn't have one doubt her parents would have sent her there in the spring. Her hair was coming loose from its pins, flowing unrestrained down her slim back. He didn't like the notion that she was forging a trail. She didn't know where she was going. Dangers lurked in the forest, unforeseen and unexpected. Anger built within, fear for her fueling the emotion. She should know better.

Intercepting her before she could put distance between them, he caught the reins of her horse, stopping her flight. His words turned into a low growl. His annoyance rising as he thought about all the possible scenarios if she got too far in front of him. He could never allow her to be so careless with her life. "Your first lesson, Chauncey. Never ride in front of me. You can ride beside me or behind. You will not forge the trail we take. Not over some ill-conceived embarrassment. If you ask a question that will discomfit you perhaps you should think twice before blurting what is in your head. That might be your second lesson. Do you understand?"

Chauncey had to comprehend his meaning.

It was obvious, he was wrong. She didn't understand his reasoning. She scowled at him, her eyes darkening. He understood she was about to deny what he put forth. "I'm not discomfited. I was just thinking about what we did. After that, I thought about you doing that to another woman. I don't like that, Stephen. Don't want to think about you with other women."

She tilted her chin into the air. She was fascinating to watch. So young and naïve she thought she could maneuver him with falsehoods.

He held his laughter in check. "You are embarrassed. I find that delightful. Rest assured there will be no other woman in my bed except you. Tonight. What do you think about sharing our blankets tonight beneath the stars? This is our first night from the trading post, our second as husband and wife."

He would share her blankets. Would make certain she understood how much she wanted him too.

She stared at him, lifting her chin as if she wished to convince herself she wasn't uneasy with the conversation. Either that or she would refuse him their pleasures this evening. "Did you have women in the village where you are taking me?" she asked the question because curiosity seemed to be eating at her.

She would continue in this vein until she felt satisfied with all his answers. With each passing second, he was beginning to understand his woman better. Her curiosity would always get the best of her.

"I had women, older women who lost husbands for various reasons. They taught me how to make love and give pleasure. Did I not pleasure you last night? Did you like what we did, Chauncey? What do you say? Shall we be together again tonight?" He did chuckle then as he watched the changing expressions on her face. "I won't have anyone else now that we are wed."

The look of relief that swept over her had him laughing again. His Chauncey was so very easy to read. She wore her emotions in her expressions, in the way her eyes changed color.

"Good because I would have to kill you if you took another woman." Her back was stiff, her chin tilted high. "You are mine, Stephen Wilkes. You cannot have another woman. I won't allow you to do so."

Once more it seemed to him she started to move past him. This time she held back. "You're learning," he spoke with concern, pleased with her actions.

In time she would learn obedience. He would see to the teaching. Once they were back in London, he could allow her more freedom. Here, freedom could prove deadly.

"What about you? How many boys or men have you kissed behind the church or in the hayloft? What liberties have you allowed. You're a passionate woman."

He grinned at her scowl. She would lie to him. He didn't have one doubt. How outrageous the fib would be was the question.

"Only two dozen," she replied with a sugary smile that didn't provoke him in the least. "Maybe it was three dozen." She touched her lips with a fingertip. "You are by far the best kisser I've had though. As you know, I've done nothing but kiss."

The statement about dozens of men kissing her brought forth his irritation. The truth here was what he sought not some outlandish story that couldn't hold any truth. He wished he could strangle her, wished he could shake her. He needed to preserve his dignity and not show his annoyance with her. He understood why she spoke outrageously. He didn't like it. He needed to temper his touchiness. When he kissed her, she had no idea what to do. She'd never been kissed before, at least not by a man. "That many? I don't believe you, sweetheart."

"Now I'm your sweetheart? It's the truth. So many men I lost count. What do you think? Should I kiss someone else so I have more men to compare you with? After all, how many women are you comparing me with?"

"Those dozens of men didn't kiss you very well," he told her mockingly watching for her reaction.

She learned nothing from all these men she dallied with. He had her now. There was no way to refute his statement.

She shot a bewildered look at him, playing into his plans as if he'd written the script. Her eyes seemed to cross with her question. "Why do you say that?"

Hurting her was not part of his plans. He reached over to smooth his hand down her cheek. "Isn't it obvious? I had to teach you what to do. Taught you everything you know. Were the other kisses mere pecks on the forehead or your cheek. Obviously, you never let the men inside you. I'm pleased with that."

She didn't answer. That was just as well. This wasn't going anywhere. All this conversation was doing was continuing to keep him as hard as a rock. He could not wait for dusk to arrive so he could make camp. So, he could set up their tent then spread out his blankets. He thought they would make love first then eat. After their stomachs were satisfied, they could make love again. It would be a long time before he got his fill of his wife...if ever.

"Will you make love to me tonight...in your tent?" Once again, she smiled at him, moving her head just to the right. "Maybe I can show you how much I've learned?" she shot back at him. "Maybe you will be the one to learn a few tricks."

"Yes."

Yes, he would make love to her if she wasn't too tired. He didn't believe this innocent woman could teach him anything. She would be sore. Her legs would ache. He needed to think of something besides thrusting into her and hearing the vibrant pleasing female sounds he was coming to adore. "We're stopping here for a short time."

He pulled up. She did the same.

"Why? Do you need to rest? I can keep going. Don't stop for me," she told him with a puzzled look on her face he thought was contrived.

He didn't need to rest. She did. Why couldn't she give an inch and admit she couldn't stay on the horse all day. He wasn't going to drive her until she couldn't walk let alone sit a horse. "It will take you some

144

time to get used to riding me as well as the horse. I mean to allow you the time to adjust. This is just a time for you to stretch your legs." Stephen hoped he shocked her. "If we're going to do both, I'll have to keep you in the best shape possible. What do you think? Do you need to relieve yourself?" If she was going to try to shock him, he would also be blunt with her. The beautiful crimson shade covering her face along with her neck was delightful. "Do your breasts turn that fetching shade of red when you're embarrassed?"

Stephen didn't think it possible but her color deepened. He'd like to unfasten her shirt so he could explore the possibility.

Mute for the next few seconds, Chauncey dismounted. For a moment, she looked around then marched toward some bushes that would hide her from his view. She should get over her shyness by the time they reached London. He would enjoy her bashfulness now. Watching her was like a breath of fresh air. After all, this was all new to her. He would know every aspect of his wife. Not too much longer, she would be comfortable with him.

When she returned, he handed her a piece of jerky. He was chewing on one. Lunch on the trail would never be more than this unless the day proved to be so horrible, they couldn't travel. "How sore are you?"

Sitting the horse couldn't be comfortable. Perhaps they should stop sooner than he planned.

It seemed she prevaricated. She looked away, studied the tree closest to her. "What do you mean by you riding me? I would know. You can't just talk in riddles. I deserve to understand."

She smoothed the fabric of her shirt, flattening it along pert well shaped breasts. Her breasts were small. They were enough for his needs. Her nipples velvet to his lips.

He kept the threatening groan in the back of his throat. A newly married man should get at least a week to discover all his wife's secrets. He'd had one night. It wasn't enough time. He wasn't going to share his thoughts now. If he did, he might have to show her. That would waste valuable daylight.

"We should pursue that topic tonight beneath our blankets. I'll teach you how to ride me. You'll love it, as will I. You will have all the control. I'm certain that will delight you, a woman who despises orders." He pointed to the horses. "We've got miles to ride before we can set up camp." He wasn't at all certain they would be able to travel those miles. He had a place in mind, if they needed to stop before dusk. When he studied the sky, felt the wind on his face gusting down from the mountains, stopping sooner would not surprise him.

The weather worried him. Not getting drenched in a downpour before he could build shelter, was a top priority. Even now, the sky darkened. The time was only an hour past noon. A brisk wind cantered down the mountain. He couldn't see enough of the sky but he wouldn't be surprised if a storm was brewing in the hills.

"I'll be an eager student. This riding business sounds fascinating. I can hardly wait for you to show me."

She tossed him a saucy wink. She mounted with the same ease as she did this morning. Chauncey didn't appear tired or sore. She looked fresh and vibrant. What was she hiding?

If she was sore from the hours on her horse or from their exertions of last night, she wasn't showing the pain. "How much did you ride when you were home?" He supposed he should have asked the question sooner. He never thought she rode expect for pleasure. He recalled Lyssa's antics on her horse, the trick riding, the danger she placed herself in by her stupidity. He groaned and prayed his Chauncey would never do something so foolish. That was something else he needed to do tonight. Ask her if she could do dangerous tricks on the horse. If she could that would be another part of her life, he needed to forbid. That dictate would hold when they were in England as well.

She pushed the broad brimmed hat she wore back a mite on her forehead. She studied him with narrowed eyes. When she sipped in a large dose of air, the hardened tips of her breasts pushed against her shirt. "That depends on the day. There were some days I rode eight to ten hours, others I didn't ride at all. If you're worried about me keeping up, you don't need to fret. I can sit a horse for at least eight hours. Probably can't ride through the night though. That is something that would be difficult for me. If you asked it of me, I would try."

Chauncey understood, if necessary, she could do anything he needed from her. "I'm not fretting about anything. I was worried though. Fretting is something the simpering debutantes would do when they waited for a man to notice them then ask for a dance."

He didn't like the insinuation he fretted. He was glad though. She wouldn't be in pain at the end of the day. A change of subject might be in order to get his mind off sex with his new wife, his delicious new wife. "How much do you know about finding your way in the wilderness? If you get yourself lost, what will you do?" The question pertinent, her answer was something he needed to know.

Her sigh of what sounded like displeasure left him wondering what she would reveal next. She looked at him, her voice soft, "Not much. Never had a reason to learn. Always knew where the ranch house was located. Can find the North Star if there are no clouds in the sky. I understand that if I'm looking at it and walking, I'd be marching north. Imagine a person has got to know where they are going to be able to use the heavenly guides. As for now, I suppose we are headed north because you told me that's the direction we would take. Also suppose that we're also going to head west which is that way." She nodded to the west. "The rest is simple logic. I also understand how to use the sun. Of course, on a cloudy day that won't help much."

He laughed softly, eyeing her carefully. "If you get lost from me, I want you to set that pretty little backside of yours down on the ground. After that is done, you're to stay put until I find you. I promise you I will always find you."

"I love it when you say something outrageous. My brother would have told me to set my butt down. You're very polite. What if you get lost? Will you set your well-muscled posterior on the ground then wait for me to find you? I will find you. Don't want my man to lose himself in the wilderness. He might get lonely without me."

He wanted to strangle her or kiss her breathless as well as speechless. She was a spicey little thing. He enjoyed her immensely. "I'll never get lost. Believe we need to stop sooner than later. The weather is changing. Have a place in mind. It's not too much farther from here."

"Don't stop on my account. I can ride much longer than you

think. Now, if you're sore from my attention last night, that's a different story. I'll sacrifice so you can rest."

At this point, she sounded both indignant as well as challenging his male prowess.

Shaking off the retort that would leave her in a state of confusion, he said instead, "Need to set up camp before the storm hits. Don't want to get myself drenched while I'm putting together a shelter."

"You don't have to do everything. I'm not a debutante or fragile. Used to hard work." She paused a moment seeming to drag in a breath of air. "The tent isn't enough?" she asked seeming curious now. "I've always enjoyed a good storm as long as I can stay dry. You'll have to tell me what I can do to help. I can be quite handy to have around," she repeated as if he didn't hear her the first time.

Yes, she was proving herself to be good at a lot of things. She made the journey so far interesting as well as enjoyable. Fielding her questions kept him on his toes. His woman wasn't boring. If he could get her to wear a dress, he might let her ride him during the day. One didn't have to get off his horse to enjoy pleasures of the flesh. After he watched Lyssa and Kane, he wanted to give this way of making love a try. He wondered if she would protest. Perhaps he should wait until they knew each other better.

The next hour was spent in retrospection as he tried to decide the best ways to reign in her impulsive behavior. He watched her as she fell behind him. They no longer sparred with words. He studied the darkening sky. When they came to the perfect place to camp for the night, he called a halt to the day's journey.

"We'll stop here," he told her, still watching her for signs of fatigue. She showed nothing that would alert him.

When she turned to look his way, her head tilted to a pretty angle. He smiled at her. She asked, her voice soft, enticing, yet also mocking. "You too tired to go on?"

"Something like that," he told her chuckling despite himself. He would never grow tired of this other side of her sweet nature. She would never allow him to forget his condescending words. He imagined he deserved the mockery.

"You going to tell me what you need?" He turned her words back to her. "I would see to all your comforts. A man cannot be expected to travel this far without a few aches as well as pains," she queried then turned away as if she wasn't certain what his answer would be.

There was not a single doubt in his mind that she laughed at his earlier words. While he was heartily pleased that she would not prove to be needy, he also wished she would allow him a bit of his masculine pride. He would have to ignore and counter. "Every step of the way you'll know my every desire," he murmured.

He grimaced when she stumbled after dismounting. She might be sorer than she wished to admit. He wished she didn't feel as if she had to best him at everything or prove herself. The farther they got into Indian territory, the more important it would be for her to tell him how she was doing. From all she did, he understood she was more competent than most women. Watching her, he wanted to take her into his arms, kiss her and hold her. Instead, he would have to prepare the campsite for their evening stay. She told him she would help.

Without being told along with a slight limp, she took care of her horse. He didn't dare tell her to sit and let him do everything. He understood because of her pride she would protest. After she finished with the horse, she looked through the supplies that were packed on the animals, stopping only once to stretch her back. The site of her breasts pushed forward was enchanting, magical. He sipped air. She took out the coffee as well as the beans along with the ingredients she would need for biscuits. When she looked at him, she smiled, a very racy smile. He wondered what her lively brain was thinking.

"I'll start a fire. You can take care of the shelter. I wouldn't know how to go about doing that. Do you want the fire close enough to the shelter so we can keep it going if the storm hits?" she asked looking at the sky which had turned from light gray to dark pewter.

After she turned her attention back to him, she waited with a half-smile on her lips. A smile he'd like to stop everything he was doing so he could taste as well as savor.

Stephen was both pleased and shocked with her. Chauncey's ability was more than he expected. She asked him questions as she went about performing tasks he would have assigned to her. He liked the fact she took the initiative. With every turn of events Chauncey surprised him. He showed her where he wanted the fire. They were close to a creek. She brought a pail of water to the campfire. There was a huge boulder behind them. He wanted to gather enough pine boughs to weave them together so they would shield them from any downpour. If the tempest hit too hard, he didn't expect they would be able to keep the small campfire burning. Though it was a good idea to build it close to the shelter.

It pleased him she was so competent. He didn't marry a city girl. He wed a woman who would complement him on whatever endeavor he chose to do. Stephen imagined she would do quite well on his arm in London. Her manners were honed by an aristocrat, born, and bred...two aristocrats. Though she told him that her father was born on the wrong side of the sheets. What did that matter?

By the time he was finished with his chores, she had the fire burning. The coffee was sizzling. Biscuits were baking over the open fire. She just stirred the beans into the pot she placed on a hot flat stone within the flames. His stomach grumbled. He was ravenous. With little to eat throughout the day, he heard no complaints from his wife. She wouldn't tell him if something was wrong. He needed to change that notion. He knew she would never whine.

Sitting on his haunches, he stirred the fire with a long stick. Embers drifted upward into the sky before the wind caught them. Tonight would be dark, black as pitch. There would be no seeable stars. He held out his hands for the warmth the fire put forth. Already the day was growing chill. They wouldn't be cold in the little nest beneath the shelter within his tent. He felt pleasure stir while he thought about her lying next to him through the night.

"Are you hungry?" she asked, laughing when she turned to face him her hands on her hips. "I am. That piece of jerky earlier did little to assuage my stomach."

She turned to stir the beans again, her sweet fanny sticking into the air. He tamped down the lust building within. Before he took Chauncey to his blankets, he needed to feed her.

Unable to decide which answer to give her since he was hungry for both food as well as her body, he tipped his hat back. "Might say so."

~ * ~

She stood. Stretching, her hands on her back, her small breasts pushed out in front of her. She wondered what he was thinking when he stared at her. Didn't dare ask him. "Well, the food will be ready in about ten minutes. What do you want to do in the interim?" She didn't give him a chance to answer as she handed him a freshly poured cup of coffee.

He found a patch of grass to sit on before leaning back on a log she pulled close to the fire. He seemed content at the moment.

"What do you want to do?" he parroted while he waggled his eyebrows at her. "I've lots of things in mind." He patted the spot beside him. "You could come sit down next to your husband. Seems since we stopped you've been busy."

"As have you," she reminded him as she cast a wistful look at the pot of beans. "I want to eat. As I just told you, that piece of jerky around mid-day didn't make much of an impression on my stomach. My belly has been rumbling as well as grumbling for the last hour."

She was laughing as she sipped on her coffee, her eyes focused on his mouth. There were a lot of things she'd like to do. For starters, she'd like to kiss him or have him kiss her. Either way worked. Where kissing came into play, she didn't care. She wanted to discomfit him as he did to her earlier in the day. He was always staring at her breasts then her mouth. She wondered if she should stare at his crotch and what type of reaction that would garner.

Taking the spot next to him, Chauncey sat back, relaxing, her eyes closed while she decided what to say to him. She wanted to tell him that she was no debutante. Her experiences went beyond dancing and singing though she could do both.

"I remember a day when the snow hit hard." While she put the events in order, she allowed a deep breath of air to sift from her lungs. "The sky was black, darker than ours is now. We had to round up all the horses before the drifts grew too large. The cattle would do fine, at least

151

that's what dad told us. The horses needed to be corralled. We all had to ride out in the snow. I found a mother giving birth in the middle of the storm. Had to stay with her. Couldn't leave her alone what with the wolves and other possible predators. Finally, when it was just about to get dark, father rode up, yelling at me to get myself home before I froze. I think he was proud of me even though he was also furious." She grinned at him, at his scowl of displeasure. "I went all day without even a piece of jerky to eat."

Only one expression showed on his handsome face. If she didn't miss the guess in her head, she was in for a lecture. Before he began, he cleared his throat, his gaze roaming the dark sky. He started, "You should not have been in the snowstorm." His voice was harsh. His grip on his mug tightened. "What the hell was your father thinking letting you go out in the tempest?"

Even though she understood these words were coming, Chauncey flinched when she heard the tenor of his voice. She shouldn't have told him that story. If she was going to tell him things about herself, she would have to leave bits as well as pieces he would object to out of the equation. This was a lesson learned. Stephen was too sheltering of her. If he wished for a helpless woman, she wasn't for him. While she enjoyed to some degree being coddled, she didn't need to be pampered every minute of every day.

Feeling indignant, she set her empty mug on the grass. She wished he would understand this one thing about her. "You are overprotective. I don't need to be shielded from everything. You don't need...," she murmured, grimacing at the words she blurted.

She didn't know how to convince him she was a capable woman. He would have an argument about that too. Something that would spout the fact that men must protect their woman, keep them safe from harm. He would also tell her she didn't have the strength of a man so she must rely on him.

She smiled too herself. There were parts of that she liked.

"I will always protect my woman," he growled as he stood, his body tense with the emotions that seemed to be stretching themselves through him. "You will do what women are meant to do."

"What is that?" she asked though she understood what his reply would entail. "I won't be put in a stereotype. Our lives will change. What I do today will be different from what is expected of me when we live in London."

Her confusion and frustration with the man simmered threatening to splatter out just as the coffee was bubbling over. She reached for the pot to move it from the heat.

"Stop." He wrapped his hand in the cloth that sat nearby. "You would have burned yourself," he muttered eyeing her critically.

She would have done just that. "Thank you." He got her so rattled she forgot what she was about. She walked back to the spot where she'd been sitting. Picking up her mug, she sipped. Why did she always do foolish irresponsible things around the man? He got her so angry. She forgot what she was about. Forgot to think. It was his fault. Not hers.

Stephen strode into the woods, leaving her to stew and think about herself. He returned with another load of wood in his arms

In a matter of time, the beans simmered. Stephen grunted in response as he dished up a huge plate of food for her before handing it to her. The biscuits were done. They ate in silence. Chauncey, contemplating what she could as well as could not tell him about herself, began, "I don't think that once we are in civilization again, I will ever eat another bean. I might not even cook biscuits."

She was laughing at the look on his face. She did enjoy the way he frowned when she said something he wanted to disagree with. Unless the topic was about danger to herself, he kept his thoughts to himself.

"Woman, you will cook biscuits."

He wiped his plate clean with the last biscuit. After that, he leaned back, his cup resting on his hard belly and smiled a smile of a satisfied man. This time before he spoke, his attention was directed to her mouth. Her nerves skittered to a halt then her blood pounded, thrummed in her ears. His smile was lazy as he watched her. "What else are you hungry for, Chauncey? While my stomach is content there are parts of me that wish to taste something else. Something I could label as desert. Are you sweet enough to be my dessert? Are you?"

She wanted that too but she was sore. Earlier, she had not told him the truth. Telling him would only make him solicitous. That was something she didn't want. She needed to prove just how competent she was. On this journey, she wished to be treated as an equal or as close to an equal he could go. Extra favors were not something she bargained for when she began this adventure. She meant to hold her own. Those first days she'd been so afraid she would lose him. She had to stay far enough back he wouldn't notice her. With a great deal of questioning when she road on the train, she learned that most people heading west started from Independence. She remembered he told her he was leaving from Independence. Knowing that, he was much easier to follow. She could stay farther back and remain unnoticed. Pleased with herself, she bought all the necessary equipment for her march west. She joined the train, lying that Stephen Wilkes, the scout, was her husband. The ploy was easy.

"What are you thinking about?" he asked as he tossed the bottom of his coffee into the fire. "You finished with this?" he asked as he held up her plate.

Tucking her bottom lip beneath her teeth, she nodded. Unsure of herself along with what he wanted to know; she slanted him a hesitant smile. Telling him she was too sore to perform her marital duties would only cause him to think less of her. She wasn't going to tell him. Besides, what he was going to do might not hurt.

"Good, we can move on to some more pleasant activities after I take care of the dishes. Thank you, Chauncey, the meal was fine. Didn't expect you to...I didn't ask for anything. I was surprised. This was one surprise I could appreciate." She watched him, his muscles rippling with every movement. The compliment left her feeling giddy and even more resolved not to tell him she hurt.

He gathered the dishes then without waiting for her answer, he started for the river with all the plates as well as the silverware. She followed unwilling to let him think she was a slacker, more determined than ever that she would hold her own during this trip. They cleaned out the pans that held the beans and the pan with biscuits. She dried everything. He moved into the woods to gather more wood for the fire.

When all was put to rights for the evening, Chauncey leaned

against the log, closing her eyes. She waited for him to return. *What was she thinking about?* It was something that might make him angry once again if she recounted the story to him. She'd been accosted. It happened in Baltimore near the house Amorica and Damian owned. The man was about fifty years old and drunk. She wouldn't tell him about that either. She didn't understand why she thought of that horrible time two years ago. She could tell him how much she enjoyed their visits to London.

Amazing how light his footfalls were. She barely heard him when he returned, placing the gathered firewood beneath the shelter he constructed. They would need the coffee pot for breakfast. In the morning, he might want her to make biscuits. If they hadn't eaten them all there would be some leftover for the start of that day's journey. She hoped to get more to eat in the morning than she did this morning. This morning he'd been in a rush. It seemed to her that now they were on their way, he wasn't going to be so demanding. After all, he stopped early today, not by choice though.

It was the storm brewing that caused the abrupt halt to the journey. A big fat rain drop hit her on the cheek then another on her nose. She looked to him to see if he felt the beginning of the rain. He finished tending to the horses as well as their supplies making certain all was protected for the night.

Now he was looking at her. She wished she could see his eyes. The sky was too dark. She gulped down a bit of air. "Time to bed down, sweetheart," he said, his words soft, looking at the sky then the tent, which was beneath the shelter he built. He held out his hand to her, beckoning her to come to him. "We will be nice and cozy beneath the canvas. Will you keep me warm tonight?" Instead of taking her hand, he strode to her, scooped her up then made it the rest of the distance to the tent.

"Will you keep me warm?" she countered her voice thinning as she thought of all the delicious things he would do.

Her head rested against his chest. The beat of his heart was loud. She thought it must beat at the same tempo as hers. He was warm. Feeling protected by him was something she cherished. She wished she could give him everything he needed. In time she would learn.

It did not take him long to devest her of her clothing. Beneath the blankets she was naked. She watched as he removed his clothing. His large body was corded with muscles. His belly taunt, his legs long, his shoulders were so very broad. Next to him he had this way of making her feel delicate. She wasn't fragile. The ranch life made her strong. He called her arms scrawny. Compared to his they were. She shivered as he moved the covers so he could slip beneath. He pulled her into his arms with a harsh masculine groan. For a few seconds he explored the length of her back, her breasts nestled against the great expanse of his chest.

"I want you. You know that. Don't you?" His lips touched upon her with passion, soft as well as warm. She opened for him. His foot ran the length of her leg, pressed against her then slipping beneath one of hers.

Heat flowed from his large body into hers. He created enchantment everywhere he touched her. She wanted to tell him the truth she denied him earlier. "Stephen," she began, hesitating, unsure of what he would think. She never lied. This was the first time. After that she compounded the lie with another one. He would be angry, furiously so. Still, she needed to set this to rights. "I've never been kissed by dozens of men," Chauncey whispered to him, hoping he didn't believe her when she spoke so outrageously. "I wanted to get back at you for something you said or implied about me."

Not waiting for a reply, she wrapped her arms around him. The tips of her breasts pushed against his smooth chest. When she moved, the friction caused a tiny mewl of pleasure to ripple from her. This was what she wanted since the first kiss behind the church.

"I know..." he murmured his voice husky. He ran his hand through her hair, brought it to his face as if he wished to savor the scent. She washed it yesterday with her favorite soap. "Magnolia."

She hit his shoulder as hard as she could manage. "How?" She didn't want to think he would believe her about so many men in her life. Nonetheless, he went along with the words she spoke.

"Your kisses are innocent. As innocent as my woman." He nipped her ear then raked his teeth along the column of her neck. He found the sensitive softness behind her ear. "As is everything else about you. Innocent. I'm pleased. Would not want you to be so very experienced when it comes to sex."

"Oh..." she murmured, no longer caring what his answer would be.

His thigh touched upon her intimately. She moaned. A sigh of pleasure followed. He rained kisses along her collarbone then lower. A sound of pleasure caught in the back of her throat.

A bolt of lightning lit up the darkness of the tent. She quivered as the following thunder rolled through the electrified air. The tempest above them pelted them with rain along with wind. Here in his arms, she felt safe and warm. The tent was small, cozy. She wasn't afraid of the thunder or the lightning.

His hands ran along her back, cupped her backside, bringing her so close she felt his steel hard erection pressing against her belly. Her body heated then burst into life. Beneath the strokes of his long fingers, she trembled. Flamed. Felt the magic. His touch was mercuric.

With just the thought of his hands in all the places she recalled, she moaned again. Could not keep the sounds of her pleasure to herself. His lips closed over her nipple, his teeth grazing while his tongue curled around the tight hardened tip. Her pleasure rumbled in a broken sound from the back of her throat. He kissed his way down her torso, butterflies leaping within her stomach then lower just as he moved lower to taunt and tease. He was laving kisses on the insides of her thighs. Her hips arched with the pleasure. He continued his exploration lower until he reached her toes. Butterflies changed to dragons.

He sat back on his haunches seeming to study her. Her legs were draped over his spread thighs. She was open to him, vulnerable. He was staring at her. She understood in the darkness there was little to see. He would not be able to see the redness there where he looked. He would not know she was hurting. She didn't want to tell him.

"I would have light to see you," he murmured as his finger caressed and stroked her so very warmly.

She cried out, tried to keep the sound of the pain behind her teeth. Her eyes closed as he spread her legs wider. She heard the curse. Knew this was one more lie he would question her about.

"Chauncey..." His use of her name was accusatory. "What is it? I didn't hurt you." The silence seemed to last forever. "Did I?" There was question in his voice then a sharp pause. "Little liar...?" This time the accusation held a bit of irony as well as question. With indignation in his harsh voice. "You told me you weren't sore."

She didn't want to tell him anything now. All she wanted was to will the pain from his caress away. In her most intimate parts, she throbbed, the ache refusing to fade. Truth be told she was raw between her legs. She wasn't used to even this short time in the saddle. It had been well over a year since she spent any time riding the range. She implied to him she rode most every day. She didn't. His voice startled, sounded angry to her.

Countering that anger with her personal need she spoke to him, trying to explain. "I wanted you tonight." The lie seemed reasonable to her. "I thought that...well...I guess I didn't think too far in the future."

"You wanted me to hurt you?" he asked, his fury diminishing a tiny bit.

With his knuckles he stroked her cheek.

The tenderness sent a jolt of guilt into her. "No...but..." she didn't know how to tell him how much she wanted him.

"Woman, I don't understand. You've a great deal of explaining to do for this man. Don't ever lie to me again. Do you understand me? Promise me." He rolled onto his back, bringing her with him as he cradled her face in the hollow of his shoulder.

"Promise..." She would try to keep that vow.

Remorse hit her hard then faded into nothingness. She didn't like it at all when he called her woman. She found herself bristling with her anger. He wanted to dictate everything. She could think as well as reason for herself. She didn't need a man to make decisions for her. "I have a name, man," she bit out, anger in her voice.

How dare he belittle the fact she wanted him. In the future she would not give over to him so easily. She wanted to make him regret what he said here.

He growled, displeased with the words she uttered. It seemed to her he would have his way in everything.

"Enough nonsense! I would that I had light so I could see the damage. Tomorrow morning, I will know the extent of your untruth. Rest assured; I will not touch you until you are healed. Your miscommunication could cost us time."

She whimpered when he left her to cover her with the blankets. She was nothing to him. What he cared about was the time lost, not her wellbeing. Still, after he returned, he pulled her into his arms, holding her tight against him. His large hand stroked her back, cupped her bottom keeping her close.

Chauncey didn't know what to think. She wanted him to care for her other than as a possession. She wondered if that was possible. The air she inhaled held the scent of him. She had to ask. Needed to know. "What would you have done if I told you I hurt? Tell me. You would believe I was complaining. I didn't want you to think less of me. I'm not a whiner. I don't complain." She blanched at the thought of talking so openly about herself.

"I would have looked at you, assessed the damage." His deep growl turned into more soothing words. His anger was not so intense. "Whether you believe it or not, we would not have traveled so far if I'd known."

"That's what I was afraid of. Stephen, I'm new to this, both being your wife along with riding in the wilderness. I don't want you spreading my legs to see how bad I was hurt. I don't want you blaming me for time lost on the trail. I have my pride."

"That's nonsense. I'm your husband. I would understand what you need as I would see to those needs. A woman's pride be damned."

"Of one day...wife of twenty-four hours," she reminded him. "Your logic does not ease my humiliation at the thought of you tending to me...there."

He grunted then tugged her close. "Don't be ridiculous."

Nothing more was said. It seemed Stephen decided not to pursue the topic any further. She wasn't going to do so. If he wanted to lay the conversation to rest, she would follow suit. The storm ragged outside their cocoon of contentment. Lightning ripped through the sky. Thunder boomed all around them. Rain fell in torrents beating a rapid staccato on the canvas above them until everything vanished into the distance. What was once above them now found other prey.

Lying next to him sent torrents of desire through her. Despite the soreness between her thighs, she wanted him. The fact she was too sore for him to touch her did not ease the frustration she felt. So aroused, she couldn't sleep. It seemed he couldn't either. The question came out of the blue.

"Do you do tricks on your horse as Lyssa does. If so, doing so is forbidden." His words were high-handed, his voice commanding.

After he spoke, she was shocked to her core. It seemed the heat he generated with so much ease vanished with the tempest that raged only minutes before. The anger she felt could not be contained. Once more he was ordering her. Expecting her to do as he said without asking about her opinions or her feelings. Well...he did ask something. She wasn't about to tell him she never got the hang of the tricks Lyssa performed. When she tried to stand, she inevitably fell off. The other things were impossible for her. Once she almost caught a hoof in her face when she tried to ride beneath her horse. At that point she decided attempting something so difficult a task she didn't have the strength for was preposterous.

In this instance she let her frustration with him turn into bravado. She knew she shouldn't. "Better than Lyssa," she proclaimed with too much sauce in her voice.

She told him the blatant untruth even though she understood he would be furious with her lie when he discovered the truth. She would have to keep him from the discovery. "There is no reason for me to cease. Don't understand this strange dictate of yours. You'll have to explain it to me."

Guilt simmered in the back of her mind. Didn't he just vent his displeasure at her lies. She almost reneged then told him she was inept when it came to daredevil tricks that frightened her. Instead, she held to her story, stiffened her backbone. She would ride this out. If she told him she lied now, he would never believe her. If she obeyed his command, he wouldn't know the lie.

"Did you hear what I told you?" His hands on her waist tightened.

"You are not to perform any type of trick that would put your life in danger!" His fury escalated as his hand tightened where it rested on her hip.

Her backbone went limp. All her daring vanished. She felt meek. Defeated. "Y-yes. I heard. You don't have to sound so angry. What on earth is wrong with performing a few tricks?" If she could understand his anger this would all be so much easier. She did not understand. Lyssa did it with so much ease.

"A woman could be trampled," he growled, his voice heated. "She could lose her life."

"So could a man," she countered in a weak voice.

She didn't have the stamina or the wish to fight him. This was not the way to find a means to fall asleep.

She felt the slow breath he took as if he searched for patience. "Don't care about a man. Care about you, my woman, my wife. You will not do tricks on a horse. Do you understand? Tell me you understand."

Once again, she almost announced her failures. Tonight, she failed him as his wife. She didn't want to fail herself. "No!" she blurted before she could confess further sins. "No, I don't understand anything, least of all this marriage business. The commands. The dictates. You order me this way then that."

His hands tightened on her. She understood the fact he was angry. There was nothing she could do short of confessing her lies. She was afraid to do that. There was so much she didn't know about this man she married. He was most often quiet, holding his feelings inside until they concerned her. Until they exploded. She wished she understood what made him so angry about riding tricks.

"Go to sleep, Chauncey. Tomorrow I'll discover the truth about one lie. Given enough time, I will learn the truth about all your lies. A wife should never lie to her husband. Don't understand why but something about the sound of your voice, tells me you are telling an untruth about performing tricks. I will wait and see. In all honesty, I pray you just lied to me about your abilities on a horse."

Chauncey didn't want to feel inadequate or inept. She wanted to change the mood from the anger he felt to pleasure. She settled her hand on his chest, brushing her fingers across the hardened male nipple. She was delighted to hear his groan of pleasure. The change of subject seemed to be good.

She pushed up to look down upon him. Her naked beasts swept across his chest. "Can I touch you?" She thought perhaps she could give him something that might be nice since she was so lacking in everything else. "Would my stroking your body give you pleasure?"

"Touch me?" he questioned, curiosity in his voice. He sounded as if he didn't believe her. "You want to touch me? Pleasure me? I'm surprised."

Her kisses followed the path of her fingers. "If it's alright with you. Yes. I'd like to touch that part of you. Down there. You know."

Chauncey tried for boldness. At the sound of his voice, she knew she needed to change this course to something else. Once again, she was humiliating herself in his eyes. Her voice cracked. "Never mind. If you don't want me to..."

His hand covered hers. With exquisite precision, he brought her fingers to him, to his sex. "Yes, touch me, stroke me, wherever you would like. I would enjoy that." As her fingers touched upon him, his erection swelled.

With a great deal of hesitation, she wrapped her fingers around his length. Heard his groan as it rumbled from deep in his belly. "I don't want to hurt you. You will tell me if I do something wrong." She was a bundle of nerves, terrified of being stupid. She didn't want him to think of her as a silly twit with no *savoir fare*.

"You can't hurt me." He jerked when her lips traveled the length of his torso to caress him. She stopped for a moment at his belly button before traveling lower. She liked the way he moaned, the way his body seemed to activate with each small caress. His belly contracted at her touch, muscles rippling.

Chauncey didn't know if she was doing this right. He sounded strained, his voice raw and husky. She swirled her tongue around the tip of his sex. His body jolted. His hand touched the back of her head as if he meant to keep her there.

Despite his hand pressing her down, she looked up. Tried to see into his deep green eyes. In the darkness of the night, they appeared as glittering black diamonds. "Am I doing this right? Can I give you pleasure this way? Will you...can you climax this way? Will you shatter into thousands of pieces as I do?"

She hoped so. She remembered the word as one he used last night. It was her fault he was in a state of arousal. Her fault he could not make love to her.

"You couldn't do it any better," he gritted out as she covered him with her mouth, sucked on him. He pulled her up the length of him.

She felt his sex on her belly. "I'm almost..."

"Yes, I am. I'm almost where you want me."

Taking her hand in his, he showed her how to move on him. She did as he suggested, watching the way his hips lurched, how his stomach and thighs tightened. Stiffened. Finally, he cried out. His seed burst from him as he covered her hand with his so she would continue stroking him.

She watched amazed as well as delighted as she viewed the milky liquid leave his body. He seemed to relax. After a few seconds he rolled over, reaching into a pocket of his buckskins he brought out a handkerchief. Before he could wipe his seed from his belly, she touched it. Brought it to her nose to smell then to taste. She was so very curious.

"This is what makes a baby?" she asked feeling as innocent as she must sound to him.

"Yes." He stroked her head letting her hair fall in strands around her face.

"You emptied yourself inside me last night. Do I carry your child?" She would like nothing more.

"You might."

~ * ~

Beth didn't understand anything that went on around her. Jason tried to explain to her what was happening in the village. She felt as if she was a foreigner in a country she should understand, but didn't. They'd been gone more than a week. He left her in his mother's teepee while he went hunting. He had many furs. He would make money at the trading post. His mother tended to her. Day by day she grew stronger.

She learned that Jason wanted her to marry him. Beth didn't understand why. The man wouldn't, couldn't love her. He knew who she was as well as what she did with Mr. Greeley. It seemed Stephen told him everything he knew as truth before Jason came to her rescue. If not for this man, she would be dead now. Beth owed Jason her life. She would marry him if that was something he wanted.

Jason sat down beside her. He smiled. They sat in front of the fire. His words were soft, his voice husky. "You are ready to become my wife. I would like that to happen today. We can travel to my home in a few days. You'll be strong enough by then."

When she started to protest, he held up a finger to stop her. She looked at her hands that rested in her lap. "Why? Why would you want me for a wife?" she asked despite his urgency for her to listen to him. "You don't love me. I owe you but I don't love you either."

She didn't want to admit to him or even to herself that she was beginning to feel more than the word care denoted for this man. He'd been so nice to her, caring for her.

He smiled at her again as if his boyish grin would change her mind. She liked his smile. It was warm as well as comforting. She liked the way he treated her though she understood as soon as he had her alone far from his mother's home, if she agreed to marriage, he could do anything with her he wished. Marriage was just another way a woman became a man's slave.

"No, I don't love you but I care for you. Care about what happens to you." He moved away from her, an arm's length as if he wished to give her room. "I want a family with children. I've given up on finding a woman in the village who will travel the white world with me. I'm Cheyenne, Indian. Most women don't want to be dirtied by an Indian's touch. I'm hoping you will not be so afraid of me that you tell me no to this proposal."

After she looked away from him remembering what men did to her, he touched her chin. With a gentleness she never experienced before, he brought her gaze back to settle upon him. "I promise you, Beth, I will never hurt you. I'm not like the men you've known. All men are not cut from the same cloth as your Mister Greeley."

She bit a small amount of air uncertain of how to reply. He could say anything to her. "Other men have said the same to me. They all lied. They expect me to do things to them. I never liked doing those things. They made me feel dirty."

Jason cursed. For a few seconds, he stared at the fire. With his thumb, he pointed to his chest. "This man has honor. He will not tell you falsehoods. Do you think you could say the words to become my wife?" For the first time Jason looked unsure of himself. "Rest assured, I will continue to ask until I get the answer I seek."

Beth found herself shaking her head, confusion rippling through her brain. "I don't know. What I do know is that I cannot stay here without you or even with you. I know that I have no skills to go out into the other world I once knew. If I try, I'll become just what I was before. A whore."

Tears fell. With the backs of her hands, she wiped them away. "I'm lost and alone. I never wanted to be that type of woman."

He wiped away one of the tears that was slipping down her cheek. "As soon as you say the words you have me. You will no longer be lost or alone. I will stand by you the rest of your life. Provide for you."

He smiled at her. His fingers held her chin. His gaze blazed with heat into her eyes.

Slow as well as hesitant, he lowered his mouth to touch upon hers. He kissed the corners of her mouth then the middle. She felt his tongue brush along the center of her lips, questing, exploring, urging her to something she didn't understand. Her lips were damp from the moisture of his tongue. She'd never been kissed like this before. There was no pain. The sensation was sweet. Intriguing. Mercuric heat blossomed within her, opening her to a myriad of possibilities with this man. As a rosebud opens to the sunlight of a new day, she felt as if her life was on the verge of change.

Curiosity brought her to touch her tongue to his. Flames exploded. Her heart raced. Her body jolted at the rush of heat that swept within. "Oh!" she cried out, stunned by the enchanting impact his kiss had upon her.

His laughter was gentle as well as encouraging. He ran his thumb along her damp bottom lip. "You surprised yourself. Should we try that again? Another kiss? Would you like that, Beth? I would."

"Was that a kiss? If so, it's my first real one." Breathless as well as terrified of her reaction, she wasn't at all certain of anything except the butterflies flittering around in her belly. "I don't feel right. Feel strange. My body is..."

She brought a gulp of oxygen into her lungs as she reached out to touch the small dimple beside his mouth.

"How so?" he asked as if he would wait forever for her response.

By the look she saw simmering in his deep brown eyes, he knew what she was feeling.

"Should a kiss make me so hot that I'm quivering? Should it make my heart thunder in my ears and my breath short little pants. I don't know anything about this. I feel as if I need something else. Is that how I should feel?"

"If the kiss is done right. Shall we try again?"

He didn't give her a chance to answer. Leaning into her, he framed her mouth with his.

His tongue ran across her lips, inviting her to open herself to him to make herself vulnerable. For a few seconds while she listened to the embers in the firepit pop, she thought to tell him no.

The touch was once again mercuric. When she opened for him sensing that was what he wanted, he delved inside her secret darkness. Touched her everywhere. Explored to his heart's content. She wanted to feel his tongue mate with hers. Needed his warmth. This was heaven to her. A place she never knew existed before this day. At the hands of men, she'd known only cruelty. She rested her hand on his shoulder then around his neck clinging to him as if she never wanted him to leave her.

His kiss was hard then soft, sweet and warm, intense as well as light strokes. He delved deep inside before retreating so she could follow his tongue into his mouth. He sucked, tempting her. Inviting her to something she never knew before. Heat flamed. An inferno ignited within her and between her thighs. A magical enchantment danced deep in her body swelled. Sensations rushed through her in waves of fire, exploding. She liked all that he did. When he pulled away to look at her, she gave a tiny start of dismay. "Jason?" she whispered his name, liking the way it sounded.

"There is more of that if you say the words. All you need to tell me is that I'm your husband. Can you do that? Can you claim me for the rest of your life? I will be yours and only yours. You can do with this man's body all that you wish," he encouraged.

She felt fear resurface, the same terror that haunted her nights along with her days for the last four years. Inwardly, she cringed. *For the rest of her life?* While she liked his tongue inside her she didn't like that other part of him to poke inside her. When that happened, he would cause excruciating pain. She would have to send herself to that place where she knew nothing, saw nothing, felt nothing. "If I do you will stick that part of you inside me that will hurt. No," she was shaking her head. "No...no...I can't do that. I can't say the words you wish to hear."

"What will you do if you don't agree to my proposition of marriage? I can guarantee you your prospects from my way of thinking are not good." His voice was no longer the gentle timbre that coaxed her to that kiss. "If that's your desire, I can take you back to the trading post. How will you survive? Where will you live? Will you have to sell yourself to some other old man who will abuse you?" Now, his voice was harsh to her ears.

"I—I don't know."

She felt as if he pummeled her with his questions. Questions she didn't want to think about. Questions she didn't have the answers for. Tears clogged her throat, filled her eyes. She didn't want anything to change.

"I won't hurt you, Beth. Yes, I will put my rod inside you but only to give you pleasure as well as generate a family for both of us. Do you want children, Beth? I do. Do you want to hold your baby in your arms? Feed the little one at your breast?" He paused giving her time to think, perhaps to adjust to his words. "I will always listen to your needs. In this man's life, you will always come first. If I hurt you, tell me to stop and I will."

"I don't know," she murmured again not liking the lingering

hesitancy.

Having never been a person to easily make up her mind, not that she'd been given an opportunity to sport an opinion, she continued to hesitate. Logic told her she should jump at the chance to become this man's wife. She felt certain if she agreed, she would never regret her decision. "You've always been kind to me. Stephen is also a kind man." She imagined that all men were not like Mr. Greeley or the others she'd known.

"Beth?" The brown of his eyes darkened, glittering with emotions she wanted to understand. She saw passion along with lust in the way he looked at her. She understood all too well both emotions. Jason was different. "Make me the happiest man alive. Be my woman."

Considering all her problems, how could she refuse a plea such as this one. Biting her bottom lip then praying that she wasn't making the biggest mistake of her life, a life that had been filled with mistakes, she nodded her head. The first time a man offered to buy her, just like this she agreed. She'd no idea what he wanted to do with her. Her father told her she would have new clothes, food, as well as other nice things. He'd been wrong. Many times, she wondered if her father understood what that man wanted.

Jason's laughter was soft almost musical. He brushed wispy ticklish strands of hair from her face. "You need to do more than nod your pretty little head for this agreement to be solidified. You have to say the words, sweet Beth. It doesn't count unless you say the words. Tell me what's in your heart."

She turned away as she gathered her courage, the strength needed to commit herself. Nodding was far different from talking as he just explained to her. With a great tug of air that seemed to sear her lungs with an explosion of heat, she began, barely able to speak the words for fear this would all go terribly awry. "You, Jason are my husband."

Was that all it took? Once spoken the deed seemed far too easy.

His whoop of delight told her she most likely said the right words. "You, Beth are my wife from this moment on." He took her mouth in his for another long drugging kiss. A kiss that sent shock waves of pleasure into every fragment of her female body.

With slowness that made her need more, he drew away. "Is that all there is?" she asked wondering when he meant to claim his husbandly rights.

Her body shook with the very real possibility he might do so this instant.

He tapped her on the nose. "For now, that is all there is. Later when you are healed, I will show you the delights you can find in the marriage bed with me. I promise you, Beth. I will please all of you."

"I hope I never heal," she murmured with a soft voice.

With the drawing together of his brows she understood he heard.

Chapter Six

Stephen woke with a start. Chauncey was missing. Panic raced through him. He swept his hand across the place beneath his covers where she should be. He sucked in a cold breath of air. Fear rushed into his lungs. A second later the scent of wood smoke coupled with baking crammed the air. In quick jerky movements he found his buckskins. He pulled them to his hips. His moccasins were next. Without donning a shirt, he barreled from the tent, searching for her. He pulled up to a brisk stop when he caught sight of her slender form. She looked at him. Questioned.

She was sitting by the freshly started fire, sipping a mug of coffee. When he started toward her, she smiled at him. Her smile always sent lust swirling straight to his groin. She left him on purpose. He smelled the coffee, the biscuits along with bacon that was now cooked and waiting for them to share. His stomach was delighted even while he wanted to shake her. She should be in the tent beneath his blankets resting. She was hiding from him. No way in hell was she going to elude him. He needed to see to her injuries.

He understood what she was about, her motivation this morning. He would give her time to think she won the game she played. She would not. He would have the correct facts from her. Nothing, no protest of any sort would dissuade him.

Stretching, then rubbing his belly, he accepted the coffee she offered. He didn't look at her when he spoke. He stared into the woods, focusing on the nearby stream. Aspen leaves rustled with the slight breeze. High above an eagle soared on the wind currents. "You've been busy this morning. A fire started and breakfast before I rose. Why? One would think, you didn't want to stay in my bed."

The blush staining her cheeks was adorable. He liked the way she played with her fingers when she was nervous. This morning, she had a lot to account for. She should be anxious. When he sat beside her on the log, let his leg touch hers, she scooted away from him. If she was going to use this ploy to keep him from looking at her, from touching her, she was going about it the wrong way.

She lifted her slender shoulders, the ones that could stiffen with contempt when she wasn't pleased. "Wanted to prove I'm a good wife," she said tilting her chin into the air. "Didn't want you to have more reasons to lecture me."

"So, we get to the heart of the matter. There are other qualities in a woman that make her a good wife. Don't care if my woman can cook. Although that is a benefit of choosing the right woman."

Most likely she didn't want him to pursue her lies. The topic could wait until they both had a full belly. A wife should not lie to her man. He would have to make sure she understood then obeyed.

Her eyes were wide, questioning. "What are you talking about? All I did here was seek to please my husband. Now you cast my work in mocking tones." She sniffed, feigning her anger. "I won't cook you breakfast again if that's the way you plan on treating me."

Chauncey did please him in so many ways. What did not please him was her need to embellish or ignore the truth. It also didn't please him that she thought him so stupid as to not know when she lied. "I will still look at you. A hearty breakfast will never dissuade me from my purpose. Later, when you are healed, you can show me your riding skills so I can ascertain the lecture to be given. If you are indeed a better horsewoman than Lyssa, I'm terrified."

He recalled that first time he watched Lyssa riding beneath the Appaloosa Kane gave her to ride while she was in London. Her saucy butt hit the dirt so many times he was certain she wouldn't be able to sit for a week.

"There were no ulterior motives in this." She waved her hand to encompass the fire along with the meal. "We need to eat. I did my woman's part. So, I would please you. If you were not happy then I'm sorry. Tomorrow I'll lie abed." There was a pause between, "Don't lecture me again. I had quite enough of your heated words last night."

Another pause followed. "You will not examine me to assess the damage! I'm quite capable of riding. I will not hold you back. We will proceed as you planned."

Her determination in light of such foolishness frustrated him beyond a level he understood. Her taking charge right out from under him pleased him less than her bravado. What could he do? He couldn't haul her inside the tent then shuck down those damn breeches she wore. After that spread her legs so he could look at her. She would never forgive him. He needed to find another way.

Gritting his teeth, "You must allow me to see you. You're my wife. I've every reason as well as right to look at any part of you I so wish!"

Those were not the right words. They were foolish words formed by both frustration as well as fury at her position. Ones coming from an exasperated man.

"No!"

Suddenly, he found himself in a yelling match with her. He rarely, if ever, yelled. Calm would describe him. She had this way of pushing on every male part of him he possessed. She was not acting the obedient wife he needed. Inhaling then exhaling deep breaths of air, he rearranged his anger as well as his annoyance. He understood if he bided his time with her, he would win. She was a novice in dealing with a man.

After he smiled at her, her eyes seemed to cross. Her fingers played with her long silken hair. Seemingly unable to meet his direct gaze, she looked away. He was pleased with her reaction. She was all boldness and brass until he confused her. "Finish eating. You can take care of the dishes. I'll get the horses ready to go if this is what you want."

He would play her game until she could speak no more falsehoods.

While he'd rather stay here at least another day, once she sat the horse for an hour or so, he would be able to assess her state without spreading her legs. Doing more damage to her already raw parts was not something he wished to do. If she was going to be so insistent, he didn't have a rational choice except to give into her will. At least for a short time, he would allow her the control. Once she pushed herself too hard, all would be finished.

He imagined doing dishes was something she expected to do. Once they were on the trail again, he would address her other lies. Three lies by count at this point needed to be talked about; the men she kissed, her riding abilities along with her injury. He wondered how long it would take for her to give into her pain.

Less than an hour later, they were headed northeast, headed toward the base of the mountains. Watching her mount the horse left him sweating then swearing beneath his breath. After she settled on the animal, it seemed she tried to stand in the stirrups to ease the pressure riding in the normal way would put on her injured parts. This might be the second longest hour of her life. Stephen didn't have any doubts the ride yesterday was the longest. All he wanted from her was honesty. Was that so hard? He was bedeviled by her.

This time he wanted her to ride in front of him so he could watch her back, the slumping of her shoulders when exhaustion took over. He didn't dare change his dictates now. He remained in front. If he did, she would challenge him at every bend in their journey. When he heard the tiny whimper, his gut curdled. It was time for her confession. He hoped she would tell him that she couldn't ride. The truth from her sweetly kissable lips would be music to his ears. When he turned to look at her, her truth was in the rigid set of her shoulders coupled with the strain lines around her mouth and eyes after she looked over her shoulder. The woman would not give in anytime soon. What the devil would it take for her to admit to him she couldn't ride any longer?

Her stubbornness didn't suit him. His stubbornness wouldn't help her walk when she dismounted. He would have to carry her. If he did so, he would examine her. There was no other way for him to proceed then get his point across to the foolish stubborn woman. They could take a break every ten minutes or so. That wouldn't ease her problem. Stopping, resting, healing time would be all that would put her back in the saddle. Healing would take at least a day...possibly more. Her obstinance was making everything worse.

Well hell! He didn't know what to do. Confrontation, at least from experience with her would only serve to stiffen her already rigid backbone. This was quickly becoming a nightmare. A wobbly uncertain breath of air entered his lungs. Frustrated beyond measure he rubbed the back of his neck.

He turned needing to speak with her, needing to make some headway in the game she played. They would have a conversation. "Come ride beside me," he called out.

He didn't wait for her to reach him. With a slight tug on the reins, he slowed the pace. It wasn't much. Nothing she could call him on. Still the constant tempo would put increased pressure on her injuries. He needed this situation to come to a head so he could put an end to her foolishness.

By the time she reached him, he understood her ploy was almost over. The way she bounced on the saddle made him ache. If he could, without her protest, he would call a halt to the day. Somehow Chauncey needed to figure out how to admit she shouldn't remain in the saddle. A lesson needed to be taught as well as learned. He would push her until she could be pushed no longer.

She was riding beside him now. He would continue with the previous conversations. "Tell me about the men you've kissed, the dozens. A husband needs to learn about these things." He needed the conversation to take a new angle. Knew she confessed. Would rather learn about her riding skills. "No, forget the men. Tell me about your riding skills."

He smiled at her, tipping his hat as he watched her. He wondered if she could talk and if her pain would be reflected in the manner of her speech. He needed to be attuned to any subtle nuance. If she was foolish enough to continue this charade, he would call a halt. He just didn't know how much more time she needed. With each desperate breath of air she inhaled, his resolve lessened. Every time she tilted her chin in the air as if to defy him, he changed his mind. He couldn't allow her to have her way since it might do major harm to her.

"Why? I don't see that you should care at all about my past. You are not an open book about yours," she seemed to grit out the words between each bounce. She hurt so bad she could not ride the horse. She was not an inexperienced horsewoman. "What if I don't want to talk about all my various beaus or my riding skills? Didn't I explain last night that I've no beaus? Besides, you already knew I lied."

"Just curious. Keeping hard facts to yourself is no way to treat a husband. Has any man besides me touched your breasts? Other parts we explored on our wedding night? If you've ridden as Lyssa does, does your butt hit the ground? Can you stand on the back of your horse without toppling or pick up something from the ground as you ride by?" he queried in an innocent manner, his gaze roaming to the delightful swell of her small, pert breasts. A glimmer of unshed moisture clouded her eyes. She fought to keep a whimper of pain behind her teeth.

He cursed. Swore.

What she was thinking illuded him. He wished he would understand what prompted her to brazen this out. All she had need to do was admit the truth about any number of things. Damn, he wanted to love her tonight as well as this afternoon. She was in so much pain that wouldn't happen until he could convince her getting to the village as fast as possible wasn't necessary. His only concern was for her health along with her safety. She was defying him in both.

"I'm sorry if I displease you," she said the words with a distinct pause between each one. "I will try to be more straightforward...won't lie to you again. I will fulfill your every wish. I will be the woman you wish for me to be if that is what you want. Did you wish to marry a hussy? You should have told me."

She misconstrued his words. If the situation wasn't so serious, he might have laughed. His every wish was for her to speak only truth. "You should do that. Last night you were a bit shameless when you saw to my pleasure. I enjoyed your fingers on my sex. You surprised me. Not entirely sure why you asked for my permission. A woman with so much self-confidence would proceed without consent. Would know a man would want her attention in just that manner."

If she wasn't in so much pain the discussion might be amusing. Damn, he wished she would tell him she could no longer ride.

Her face blossomed with color even while tears of agony began to slip down her reddened cheeks. When the hell was she going to admit she was hurting. He found himself shaking his head with confusion as well as irritation even while he admired her courage and determination. She should learn that it didn't please him when she put his wishes over her health.

This madness had to come to an end. Another few minutes in the saddle she would be unable to walk. All he wanted was to hold her in his arms. He needed to tell her...tell her what? That she could lie to him and he wouldn't hold her accountable. He stiffened his resolve. As to her lies, he would have to see this to the end no matter the cost.

"Stephen..."

His whispered name surprised him as much as the fact she dropped behind him. When he turned, he saw her slumped over her horse, her small slender fingers wound into the animal's mane. She was holding on for dear life. If he didn't act with haste, she would topple to the ground. She swayed in her saddle.

In an instant he was beside her, scooping her into his arms. Damn, he couldn't stop now to set up camp. There was a place he remembered about two miles ahead. He would carry her across his thighs until they reached the small clearing. If the horses didn't follow, he would have to come back for them. He should have thought of this earlier when she insisted they continue to the village.

Her body was limp against him. Sliver tears now streamed down her cheeks leaving tracks he wished he could kiss away. He was a bastard for continuing this so long. His emotions along with his instincts were torn into two pieces, his nerves stretched to the limits. She tested him in ways he didn't understand. With any other woman he would have insisted on his way despite the protests. With every turn of events, she confused him, making him delve into the darkest aspects of his behavior.

With Chauncey...damnation she had him twisting and turning uncertain of how to proceed with her. Damn her sweet little hide.

He held the reins of her horse in one hand. All the others followed. It was apparent they didn't wish to be left behind. They knew who fed them.

They rode. He cradled her, trying to ease what discomfort she felt. Her pale face terrified him. No amount of protest on her part would stop him from seeing to all her needs. He knew of herbs that would ease her pain as well as heal. Kept many in his saddle bag. He would have to search the contents to see if he had what he needed. This was something he should have insisted on this morning. He was too much the coward to do so. If her injury increased, became rawer and more swollen, serious complications could ensue. More time would be lost. Not that he cared about lost time when the hours were weighed against her life along with her comfort. He would find the village, reunite with his people. Chauncey was what mattered now. She was his only concern. She would do as he said.

"You're not a silly twit without sense, Chauncey. Why did you persist in this game? You knew you should not be riding," he whispered the words not expecting her to hear them or reply. "I would not have thought less of you if you told me the truth. I'm responsible for part of your distress."

With a tear-stained face, her fingers wound into his shirt, "I didn't want to let you down. I know you would have thought me weak. In your eyes I would seem less than I am. I never wanted to hold you back."

At least she didn't deny the fact it was a game she played. Maybe she didn't have the strength to digest all his words. Hell, she was weak. She was half his size. Possessed half his strength. She needed to learn to depend on him. More than that she needed to trust his instincts, trust in his knowledge.

I didn't want to let you down.
She could never let me down.

That was something else he needed to impress upon his wife. She could never let him down. He could see through her lies. Needed only to understand why she couldn't speak true to him. He would have to teach her. It was something he thought she understood. She possessed more courage and strength than any woman he knew. It wasn't her fault he couldn't get enough of her female charms on their wedding night that he made it near impossible for her to ride the long hours he insisted upon. Bloody everlasting hell! He wasn't used to being a husband.

Hanging on to her as she adjusted her position, he caught the sweet scent of his woman. "I'm the one responsible for your condition. Don't blame yourself except for the fact you should have never ridden today. I allowed you to have your way. That was also my decision. My mistake. It doesn't matter if we spend a few days in one place so we can recuperate. We will reach the village before the snow starts falling. You need to heal. I need time alone with you."

He spurred his horse forward, wanting to get to the campsite he had in mind as soon as possible. Yes, if the snows didn't start early this fall, they would have plenty of time. Weather just as wives was always so uncertain.

She clung to him. His shirt was wet from her tears. The only other person he'd ever put before his own welfare was Kane, the Earl of Blackmore. They lived together as warriors. After that he followed him to London. This was different. This precious woman needed him. She wouldn't allow him the pleasure of taking care of her. She gave him pleasure last night. That wasn't the same.

"You're not going to look at me."

Her voice was the thinnest of whispers yet he caught the determination that told him she would fight him. He smoothed his hands along her back while she cried silent tears of agony.

Stephen didn't wish for another argument. He wasn't intending to counter her statement with one of his own. When the time was right, he would proceed without her permission. What he did or did not do would never be dictated to him by this woman, only by common sense coupled with rational logic as well as necessity. Telling her he would do whatever was necessary could wait.

"After we eat lunch and you nap for a while, I would like the information I requested. We will sit together, you and me. I'll hold you in my arms and kiss you if you like while you tell me the truths that I should learn about from you. I don't want to think a moment longer about this. It will be done. If you do this minor inconvenience on your part and humble yourself to me, I'll forgive all the lies. Perhaps then we can start over. What do you think? Would you like to be forgiven? Would you appreciate a new beginning? Will you be nothing but honest with me?"

When she gasped then pushed away from him indignation written on her lovely features, he understood he said too much. Pushed her farther than he should have. He was condescending when he should be empathetic. He commanded when he should have given her a few choices.

His slow breath of air didn't instill confidence in him about the next few days. She was hurting to such an extent she couldn't waylay the tears. His gut churned. She wouldn't be able to sit a horse. He felt certain she could barely walk.

"Perhaps you need to be forgiven," she shot out, her anger evident despite her pain. "Don't know if I can do that. Forgive you."

He liked what she told him despite the fact she defied him. He liked the hint of spice in her character. "I will ask your forgiveness when it is warranted."

Unable to help the smile that came to him, he grinned at her.

Ahead of him, Stephen saw the little clearing he set his sights on earlier. It appeared just the way he recalled. This place would do for the next few days. The small waterfall behind the pond sent sprays of water crashing into the air. A bath would be nice even if the water would be chilled. Maybe they would visit this spot on their way home in the summer. They could swim, could frolic in the warmer water. He assumed she could swim, not well though. At the place where they bathed, her strokes were awkward. Asking her would need to wait until some of the issues between them were cleared up. He didn't want another mistruth to cloud his decisions. She might tell him she could swim like a fish when all she could do was paddle from one point to the other. Another mistruth was not tenable. He wasn't going to give her the chance.

"Thank you for taking me off the horse. If it's any conciliation, I was stupid. I would have fallen. You rescued me. I apologize for my lies."

"Yes."

He wasn't going to compound the guilt he heard in her voice with more recriminations. If she didn't learn this lesson, there would be more times in their future she would be tested. It was unfortunate, her stubborn insecurities caused this. He needed to figure out a way to convince her she was welcome to speak her mind, especially if it was about her health.

She looked up, her beautiful azure eyes searing into his. She seemed to have a moment's indecision. "You're not going to lecture me?

Tell me how stupid I've been. Oh, but you've already done just that. Haven't you?"

"No."

If he said too much, he would end up telling her his views on all that she did to hurt herself. How did a man protect a woman who didn't listen to common sense? In the future this would have to change.

"No?" she asked sounding as surprised as he felt at his decision. "You don't have words for me to muddle over?"

Still unwilling to answer, he dismounted. "Can you walk? I'm going to set you on your feet. Hang onto my arm if you need to steady yourself."

She nodded as if she thought what he asked was possible. When her knees began to buckle, he held her again, lifted her so he could carry her. With her in his arms, he strode to a grassy spot and set her down. She curled her legs beneath her before leaning against a large rock. "I'm sorry." The strain in her face was more prevalent than before. "I never meant for any of this to happen. Thought I could be stronger. Didn't want to complain. Needed to be everything you would want me to be."

Stephen pinched the bridge of his nose before he turned to take care of the animals. If he tried to speak with her, he would not speak to her with the calmness he needed. She confused him. Annoyed him. Enchanted him. He admired her courage while he also condemned the bravery as illogical. She was already everything he wanted her to be.

When she stared at him with wide uncertain eyes, he cursed. He brought her a blanket to cover her legs then went about securing the campsite. The next time he looked at her, Chauncey's eyes were closed. She was curled on the ground, one hand beneath her cheek while she lay on top of the blanket. He covered her with a second blanket. A rush of tenderness he'd never felt before swept through him.

An hour passed. A fire flamed heating the coffee he made. Tonight, he would make their dinner. He supposed her sleep was a healing sleep. She would teach him how to make her biscuits. All would be good. Tonight, they would have some leftover from this morning. She also cooked more bacon than they could eat. He added the left-over crumbled bits to the beans. When he got a chance, he'd go hunting. Some fresh meat would be nice for a change. They would stay here for at least three days, more if need be.

Sitting on his haunches with a mug of hot coffee for her, he nudged her gently hoping she would wake up. His heart lurched for her when she moaned, the sound touching his heart. She adjusted herself, pulling the blanket higher in an attempt to get more comfortable. For this woman, his feelings were tender, all-encompassing. In such a short time, he felt as if she'd become a part of him.

After setting the mugs on a boulder, he touched her shoulder. "Chauncey...time to wake up and eat something. Chauncey...I need to feed you."

She brushed his hands aside, turning again appearing to refuse his entreaty.

"No, you don't. There will be plenty of time for you to sleep after you eat. I'm not going to ask anything of you tonight. We will enjoy the moments you can stay awake. Come on, now," he tugged her to a sitting position.

Her lips were pouty, damp with moisture. Her eyes were wide, softly blue. Silken hair flowed across his hands while he held her. She blinked a few times, her eyes dazed, groggy from an afternoon's sleep. "I don't want to eat," she sounded petulant.

Her stomach rumbled its discomfort.

Appreciating the moment, he laughed. "Your stomach is telling a different story. You can eat. Afterward, if you wish to go back to sleep, you will have to wait until I've pitched the tent. While it's not going to rain tonight, the evening will be chilly, perhaps even a frost in the morning. Together beneath the canvass we'll stay warmer."

"You will interrogate me," she accused. "Don't want that. Don't want to listen to you tell me how stupid I am."

Well, he didn't want to say those words either. He touched the tip of her nose with his finger, "No questions tonight. I promise. This evening is for rest. Tomorrow you will not rise early to cook a meal. You will remain in bed and allow your husband to cook."

At her look of defiance, he wished he could shake her until she agreed. Wished she would tell him what he wanted to know without him asking questions. "You are so exhausted you fell asleep the moment you sat down." When it seemed she was about to argue with him, he pressed his finger to her lips. "No, it's true as well you know. You're going to follow this man's dictates and eat. You are going to sleep as long as you wish. After that, you will eat again."

The cup was in her hands. She appeared to trace his movements through the camp as she sipped on the liquid he brewed for her. When he stopped his chores to make sure she wasn't asleep again, her eyes were wide pools of vivid blue. She looked as if she wanted to bare her soul. He could only hope.

"I never kissed anyone except you," she spoke to him.

As seconds passed, her voice grew stronger as she confessed again. Her nerves would be stretched with the apprehension she must harbor. He felt certain she didn't know how he would react. "You were the first man to kiss me other than father. Of course, those kisses were much different. When you kissed me the first time, I thought I would swoon."

She lifted shoulders that were carrying too much burden. Chauncey wouldn't understand why this was so important to him. He failed to impress upon her how he lived his life. In time, she would learn.

"Thought so," he told her again with the merest hint of a chuckle as he didn't mean to laugh at her distress.

The clarity he read in her eyes told him she was distressed. She appeared wounded. Truth was what he wanted. She was giving the truth to him. The sooner they cleared the air the sooner they could move on in their marriage.

She blinked a few times seeming to push away the moisture that threatened to fall. "Don't know why I would lie about something like that. Just did. Seemed I wanted you to be jealous. You've had so many lovers. You've experience where I have none. You've been to London, lived with the aristocracy. I was feeling the green-eyed bite of jealousy."

That emotion never crossed his mind. For some reason her concession satisfied. "Not so many lovers. That fact pleases me. Correct me if I'm wrong but your mother has aristocratic ties. Isn't she related to a duchess, The Duchess. Wasn't that woman her aunt. I can claim nothing like that," he told her but he couldn't keep count of his lovers on two hands.

Over his lifetime it didn't seem to be so many. He liked women. They liked him. He indulged a need. The women reciprocated.

"Furthermore..." She set her hands on his shoulders seeming to be prepared to rid herself of the burdens she orchestrated. "I can't do tricks on a horse. Never could. Lyssa was always so good. When I tried, I failed miserably."

"Thank all the gods above," he told her as he rolled his eyes.

He wasn't going to laugh at her. The relief he felt seared him soul deep. He wouldn't need to keep a wary eye turned her way.

The stunned expression on her face gave him pause. She pushed her lips together as if she didn't understand. Once again, he would have to clarify. There was obviously more to this than she was letting on. Prudence would dictate he let her finish her story. Still, he could not stop himself. "You say she is good at her tricks? So good her little butt hit the ground when she tried to ride beneath the horse. If she persevered much longer that day, she would not have been able to sit."

He did laugh then as he recalled that time when Kane first discovered her unique riding abilities. The anger. The fear. Sheer terror was what he saw in Kane's eyes as he held his breath waiting for her to stop and unable to react to the horror he watched.

Clearing her throat, she stared at him for the longest time. He held his breath, his gut telling him he wasn't going to like what she told him next. "That isn't all of it. Is it? You know that for a fact. I imagine I should explain just how horrible I was...am."

She gulped air before she could speak again. "I...almost...well...let's just say my face barely missed the hoof of my horse when I fell once. I might have been trampl—"

"Chauncey!"

His heart stopped for a few hair-raising seconds as he envisioned the scene she mentioned. He stuffed his lungs with a gulp. The need to lecture drowned him. He started to say more. Caught himself when he focused on her. She seemed frantic to him. This man would give her a chance to explain if that was what she wanted.

Her hands were clasped beneath her chin, expectancy in her eyes. "Stephen, let me finish. After that I decided I should be better served to ride in the normal fashion. I didn't understand why anyone would want to ride under the belly of a horse. To me there was no reason to stand on the animal's back. I found no need to pick things up off the ground while riding as fast as I could. I've no clue why I told you I was better than my cousin. It's not true. Neither is the fact I might like to be better. Lyssa and I are very different people. While Lyssa basks in doing the most audacious things, I would rather let others standout in the limelight." She let her hands fall to her lap. "I don't like to be the center of attention. Lyssa does."

Unable to help himself he pulled her into his arms, pressed her face against the expanse of his chest. Her small hand rested on his shoulder. She understood. Now, there was only the issue of her discomfort that remained. For some reason he didn't think she would tell him how she felt or allow him to look at her.

He would. There was laudanum in her coffee. She would sleep soon.

~ * ~

Chauncey understood she addressed all but one issue between them. She would need to say something to him. Would devise a way to convince him she was quite able to take care of herself, her needs. He didn't need to interfere. She'd been doing so for many years. The prospect he put forth embarrassed her to the tips of her toes. A glass of wine at this moment would ease her mind. Out here, she didn't have that glass of wine. This was the first time she had second thoughts about her impulsive behavior this morning. She'd been so eager to prove herself as well as satisfy this man. His anger with her was reasonable even to her.

If she didn't tell Stephen about herself, he would do just as he told her. She had no doubts. Curse him. His doing so would humiliate her. She would not be able to look at him again. Ninny, he saw all of you on your wedding night. That was different. It wasn't clinical.

She could only answer her thoughts by admitting that night was very different. On the night of her wedding, she was overcome with passion. The strokes of his hands along with his mouth made her writhe with need. He composed undeniable magic, creating a song in her heart. She wasn't thinking. All she did was feel the amazing sensations he orchestrated within her.

If she didn't admit to the pain, the soreness, the rawness between her legs, he would look. She was damned if she did as well as if she didn't. If he was going to look no matter the path she chose, she might as well give him what he wished for. She would prove herself to him, would get everything out in the open.

Maybe later.

He handed her a plate of food. His voice was stern. "Eat it all."

Perhaps she was disillusioned. Her thoughts were a muddle in her head. If he didn't confuse as well as frustrate her with his dictates, she would deal better with him. If he gave her choices, she wouldn't react. Something in the back of her mind told her he wouldn't be dealt with by a woman. His gruff voice didn't give her more confidence.

He sat down beside her. The closeness was nice. His big body next to hers was something she could get used to with no effort. Unhurried, she chewed. She thought about all she said this afternoon. The wind seemed to shift directions. Chauncey wondered if that meant anything. Stephen always seemed to be testing the wind. He could teach her a lot. He knew things she never dreamed of.

With his fork left on his plate, he asked, his voice soft, a whisper in the air, "Do you hear that?" He pointed into the woods before he looked at her as if expecting an answer.

Her attention was on her troubles not on the conversation. She had to think about his question as she cocked her head to the side, listening to the silence of the ending day. "No, hear what?" She was shaking her head, puzzled. Turning toward him, she stared into his fathomless dark green eyes, eyes that were the color of the darkest green one could imagine. "I don't hear anything different or significant. Should I?" Chauncey was not certain of what he was asking or the direction of his thoughts.

"Listen...concentrate...tell me what sounds come to you. It's important to hear, to listen to what the forest is telling you." He waved his fork in the air pointing toward the wealth of trees surrounding them, toward the stream that swept so close to their camp in the direction of the small animal trail that visited the pond. "I want you to still your heartbeat so you can hear. Hold your breath for a moment. Close your eyes if that will help. The land always speaks to a person who is willing to listen."

"Don't understand what you want."

Though she did close her eyes, held her breath until her lungs burned. Did try to do what he asked. She heard little. His large hand rested on her shoulder massaging tired muscles, relaxing her, lulling her in too many ways. Bringing in a deep breath of air, resting as he suggested, she began to listen more thoroughly. "I hear the stream in the distance. The wind sighing through the aspen leaves...the waterfall plays on the rocks." She paused as another sound came to her. "The scurrying of small feet. The swish of wings as if a large bird sought its dinner."

"What do you think those small scurrying feet belong to? Where do you suppose they are going?"

He settled next to her. His arm wrapping around her, he drew her against him. She let her head rest on the broadness of his chest, finding the hollow by his shoulder. He was warm. His muscles rippled with each movement he made. Within the circle of his embrace, she felt safe. He would protect her with his life. She understood that. By keeping things from him she didn't help. She was little-by-little beginning to understand his way of thinking.

When she looked at him his eyes showed humor. "A mouse? Maybe a squirrel," she guessed wondering if she guessed correctly.

Pleasing him seemed important to her.

"Do you hear the frog now? He's singing to his mate, coaxing her to come to him. Would you be more willing to come to me if I made croaking noises?"

His voice was low vibrating as if he saw something humorous in his words.

Unable to stop herself, she giggled, enjoying the sound of his amusement. "I don't believe you would ever croak. Perhaps you would make other froggish noises."

This was more like the man she fell in love with. Oh, he told her when she embarked on this trip into the wilderness, she would have to do everything he commanded. Said those words more than once. She ignored the warning thinking he was just asserting his will. He was not.

Perhaps that was what he did. His commands now that they were a day and a half out from the trading post seemed different. He had not been this autocratic when they were with the wagon train.

"Was it a mouse or a squirrel?" She wanted the answers to his questions, all of them. "Something else?"

"Rabbit. Running from a bird of prey. Most likely an owl or a hawk looking for its dinner tonight. Out here the scenario reads as survival of the fittest. If the rabbit found shelter before the hawk could grab him, he would survive another day. The hawk of course, can find other prey. In the end though, the hawk must eat."

The forced air she made go into her lungs brought forth the words she would rather not say. "I was wrong, Stephen. Was wrong when I didn't tell you about my pain. When I didn't tell you, the last thing I wanted was to ride all day. When I didn't listen to you, I found that it wasn't that. I was too embarrassed. From the very start, I understood how my body was feeling." She was wringing her hands that were settled on her lap. "Won't ever do that again. I promise."

"I know you were wrong. What matters now is that you appear to have learned from that mistake. I'm glad. Now we can move on to the next hurdle."

Of course, he knew she was at fault here. The mistake was hers to make. He didn't have to lay his feelings on the line so blatantly. "You could be a little more solicitous. Perhaps excuse me for my *faux pas*." She didn't know what she wanted. Having put her heart on the line, she needed something in return for her efforts.

"Don't want another argument, shouting or silent. You do understand that I will have to look at you. Seems I cannot count on your word of honor. I'm not stupid, Chauncey. Won't be wrapped around your little finger. You will never command me to your whim. You need to get used to that idea." His voice sounded strained as if he didn't want to say the words. "Didn't mean to bring the tiny fact up so soon. I've given you laudanum. I'll wait until you sleep. You won't even know what I'm about. Will that make you feel better? It's the only concession I can give."

"I understand that's what you believe you must do. Can't you just take my word that I will be fine in the morning. I will be. There is nothing wrong with me that a small amount of time won't heal."

She didn't understand his obstinacy. Mayhap if she'd been truthful from the beginning, he would take her word now. The past could never be retrieved. She needed to move forward in the manner he expected.

"No, Chauncey. In this I cannot do what you wish. For me to understand your reluctance to allow me to look at you so I know when you are healed is impossible. In this, we will do as I say. You've no words in your head that could sway me."

He pulled her into his arms, holding her close, rocking her.

She'd done this to herself. Given him no recourse except to continue as if she lied. His hands settled beneath her breasts. She sat between his legs. Felt the bulge at his crotch grow. "If I promise never to lie to you again?" she asked trying to keep the yawn from growing. "Will you leave me to my word."

This was her last argument. She spoke even though she understood Stephen would never change his mind. She also comprehended that she wouldn't know.

"Chauncey, my sweet Chauncey." He ran his fingers through her long hair, letting the strands fall across his arms. "I'm not a fool you can wrap around your little finger. I'm a man. You're my wife. I'll never let anything take you from me. You will have to prove yourself before I can accept your word as true."

She'd been afraid he would say that very thing. She imagined the sooner she got this over with the better. Her body slowly relaxed against his. She would accept his words. "How long before I sleep?" she asked still feeling the rush of embarrassment, the heat of his questing gaze.

She didn't understand how he could so casually do something of that nature to her. Didn't understand why he believed his word was law.

"I didn't give you much. Just enough to relax you so you wouldn't care what I did. You will sleep. I'm hoping you will sleep through the night."

"I'm hungry, Stephen." That wasn't a ploy to prolong anything. "Truly."

"Then you must eat more food." She shivered when the heat of his body left her. She watched him take two long strides to the campfire where the beans still simmered.

He dished up a huge plate of food for her, filled it until there was no room left on it for anything more. "Whatever you don't eat, I'll finish. When we are done, I'll take care of the dishes. You will relax and wait for me in the tent." After he handed her the plate, he settled her against him again.

Her nerves stretched to thin wires while he watched her eat. The food took away some of the sleepiness she felt. The beans set heavy in her stomach. She nodded, her hands slipping from the plate. He set it aside. She heard the soft chuckle. She thought she would have been able to keep from falling asleep after eating the food. She could not.

"Get on with it," she whispered as her eyes shut. She floated in a dream world as the blackness behind her lids seemed to take on colors of their choosing.

"Not so fast, love. Only when you are soundly sleeping. You won't even know what I'm doing." His soft chuckle unnerved her, touched a part of her that wanted to yell at him. Her lashes fluttered.

"You shouldn't have told me."

He planned this to perfection. Orchestrated everything in the exact manner he wished the events to transpire. Until she drank the coffee, she didn't know he drugged her. She imagined the plan was a good one. Still, when she woke, she doubted if she could look at him as she would continue to know what he'd done. When he picked her up, she felt weightless. She sensed the movement as he set her upon the bedding inside the tent. After he stripped her of her clothing, cool air washed over her then the blanket. What surprised her was that he left her. She thought that he would spread her legs then humiliate her.

The tiny moan left her lips. He wasn't there to hear her. He was walking toward her with long fast competent strides. He knew what he wanted. She saw him coming to her across the lawn at Lyssa's wedding. His body so large it would dwarf hers. He was larger than her brother, larger than Kane. He was so tall. Without straining, he could reach the ceiling with his fingers. Each time she looked at the man, he stole breath from her lungs.

After he took her hand in his, he asked her if she would come with him. Even though she didn't know where he meant to take her, she nodded. Going with him wherever he wished was her plan. She would follow him to London if need be. They walked behind the church where Lyssa was married. She hoped someday to marry him in that same church. Perhaps she was getting a bit ahead of the situation. She didn't know if he liked her. Thinking about marriage to the man was a ridiculous notion.

She leaned against the wall, bracing herself. One of his hands was next to her face, the other one stroked her cheek then her neck. The caress sent heated shivers throughout her body, sent butterflies to dance deep in her belly. He stopped where her heart thundered at the base of her neck. She wished he would kiss her. She ran her tongue along her parched lips. Didn't think she could be so bold as to ask him. She didn't understand but felt shyness bubble up inside. To hide the emotion, she closed her eyes for a moment. With this man she didn't want to be shy. She wanted to be daring, to go after all she wished for. He would leave her without the kiss if she acted a virgin.

She was a virgin.

His smile warmed her, heated her almost as much as the gentle stroking of his fingers exploring a path across her collarbone, to dip lower to the valley between her breasts. "May I kiss you, Chauncey? Would you like my mouth on yours? It's your choice." His rough voice tumbled from him. He sounded uncertain, almost undecided when he asked. Sounded as if he questioned himself or perhaps her. Unlike what she thought of his personality, he was hesitant when she believed he would be audacious. He touched the tip of her nose. "Have I misread the signs? I thought perhaps that was what you wanted...a kiss."

He smoothed a long bronze finger along her eyebrows, watching as well as waiting for her to give her consent. She didn't want him to have so much patience. She wanted him to sweep her off her feet then carry her to his teepee just as Kane did to her cousin Lyssa. She wished he would set her upon his furs. She would give him whatever he asked for.

"Chauncey...?"

Her name said in such a questioning manner surprised her. Lost in her dreams, she blinked a few times. He wanted an answer. Well, yes, when asked if she wanted him to kiss her. "Yes, please." Once more, she swept her tongue across her lips. With the gesture the green of his eyes darkened too nearly black. "A kiss would be nice." Her heart quickened just as her breath caught in the back of her throat.

His grin of what looked like pleasure flashed across straight white teeth. She scented mint on his breath. She thought that was nice. If a girl was going to be kissed, the man should smell sweet. His large hand was beneath her chin. He tilted her head, allowed his thumb to travel across her bottom lip.

"Are you certain? I wouldn't want to take advantage of you."

No matter how hard he tried he would never be able to take advantage of her. Chauncey did want him to do whatever he wished. Telling him no would never happen. She wanted to learn everything she could from this man. He fascinated her. She found she couldn't speak. Words seemed to stick in the back of her throat. Instead, she nodded her head, a slight smile curving her lips.

After his hand settled where her shoulders met her neck, he lowered his head. Her pulse beat frantically. His lips were a hair's width away from hers. His other hand wrapped around her waist, tugging her close to his body, so hard and strong. She was pressed against him. She felt him flush next to her, the steel hardness of him.

When his lips framed hers, touched their enchantment upon her, she fought the moan that wanted to break from her. Found she could not stop the sound from reverberating from her into him. He groaned. She whimpered. The heat was magical, the sensations mercuric. Her body flamed to life, became an inferno of throbbing need. His tongue slid across her lips leaving moisture behind. She wanted to reciprocate, to create the same passions within him. He ran his hand along her back then lower to cup her buttocks holding her close.

After his teeth tugged on her bottom lip, she gasped opening for him as she sought air to fill her lungs. His tongue explored inside her mouth, caressing deeply, stoking more fires. She didn't understand. Had not thought a kiss would be like this, so hot, so dark and secret. The sensations were powerful, penetrating every pore, her knees seemed to weaken as she stood pressed against the wall of the church. She was thankful for the building for holding her upright. Without the wall's support she would collapse in a mindless puddle at his feet.

"Touch me with your tongue, little one," he murmured as he swept his across her teeth then farther into her, exploring the depth, touching her as if he'd known her forever. "I like being inside you, love. Do you like me there?"

Nodding for him, she liked that too. Somehow, she thought there was another meaning in his words. She would have to ask him about that. Hesitating a moment, with her tongue she touched his mouth, then his teeth. After that she pushed her tongue into the potent depth of him. His hard body encapsulated hers. He was hot, sultry. Tasted of the sweet wine he must have consumed earlier when he toasted Lyssa and Kane's marriage. Chauncey liked the way he tasted, his scent, the feel of him pressed so near to her, loved everything.

He deepened the kiss, pulling her closer, so close she felt his body changing next to her belly. She didn't know what it was or what it meant. His hand slid up her ribcage. He cupped her breast in his hand, toyed with the hardening bud. Another sound of need broke from her.

She gasped, pushing away distancing herself, confused as well as eager for whatever would come next. He looked down on her, his eyes dark, inquisitive. She touched her lips with her finger. "I shouldn't have. Sweet God, Chauncey, I have to touch you. Didn't mean to surprise you. If you don't want me to touch you, tell me no. I'll stop if you say the word. For now, I need more of you if you'll have me."

"Yes...I like what you are doing. Touch me. Set me on fire. It's just that what you do surprises me. Never..." She struggled for air along with rational thought. Never been kissed, not like that. No one has ever...done what you did...I, well...Jeoffrey once... then..."

His pleased smile pleased her before it turned to a frown. "Jeoffrey?"

"He never meant anything. I, well, I slapped him."

"Good, I'm glad. A man likes to know he's the first man to truly kiss his woman. You're telling me the others don't count? You didn't like the kiss?"

"Would it matter if you weren't the first?" she asked with sauce in her voice, feeling as if she might understand some of the sensations rushing through her, drowning her in need she didn't comprehend as she watched the furrowing of his dark brows. Chauncey didn't understand why she teased him.

After a long pause he spoke again. His fingers stroking her body, exploring new territory tugging on her skirt to feel the length of her leg. She shuddered with the vibrations ripping through her.

"Yes and no." His lips found hers again, touching. Caressing. Caressing more boldly with each passing second. He didn't hold back. His lips were hard, his tongue deep. Over then over again, he stroked her, bringing her to a point where tiny sounds slipped form her. He brought his hand back to her breast, his thumb rubbing across her nipple.

She needed him more than ever. "Don't stop," she pleaded. "Please don't stop."

Her hands sifted through the strands of his black hair. It was so soft, so cool to her touch, satin, and silk. She ran her hands down his back, tugged at his shirttails wishing she could feel the smoothness of his hard body enjoy the rippling of his muscles beneath her fingers.

The deep groan then his words followed as if her pleading brought him back to reality, he spoke, straightening her gown. "We need to get back to the festivities," he told her as he lifted his head from hers. "If we don't, I might not stop what my body wants."

"What if I want you to do all you're thinking of?" she asked certain that she wished he would never stop kissing.

What he was thinking couldn't be that wrong if he gave her this much pleasure. At least in her mind, they were meant to be together.

"My sweet, you have no idea what you are saying. I would teach you all you wish to learn but today is not the day. We will wait until the time is appropriate."

He continued to adjust her gown where his questing fingers dallied. With the backs of his hands, he touched her breasts. As if he didn't want to leave her, she heard the long-drawn-out breath of air rippling from his lips.

She found that her breasts hardened even more with the last fleeting caress. The need to know more swirled within her. Her body ached in secret places. Dark places that his kisses seemed to bring to life. To understand more was at the forefront of her mind. "When I return from the west, we can pursue this further. If we did what I wanted..." he broke off seeming unwilling to tell her his thoughts.

"What? What are you talking about?"

He coughed then ran his hand across his face, "You are an innocent, Chauncey. I'm not going to... Let's go join the celebrations. You can dance with the beaus who might wish to see your favors bestowed upon them. Or...you can save all your dances for me. What will it be, Chauncey? Me or all your favorite men, the ones who have kissed you. How many?"

"Not many..."

True she'd been kissed a few times. The sensations were nothing like what she experienced in this man's arms. She told him as much. Those kisses didn't stir her or cause parts of her to ache with desire she didn't understand.

"That is good."

It seemed to her his words caught in his throat when she mentioned others kissing her. To make him understand she spoke again. "Don't want to dance with anyone except you. Do you dance? I want to be in your arms. Want you to kiss me again. Need for you to do other things."

She shouldn't be so forward. He would think her brazen.

He shifted hair from her face. "I dance. Something the earl made certain I learned when we were in London. I would not embarrass you. Nor would I step on your delicate toes. Would you like this next dance?"

She snorted then was embarrassed by the unladylike noise. He laughed with clear amusement by the sound. "Would you dance with me? I do want to be in your arms. It seems dancing is the only way that is going to happen tonight."

"I will dance with you, Chauncey. Do you promise not to step on my toes?" he asked her smiling at her.

"I won't step on any part of you," she retorted.

He hooted with his laughter. "Good. It is settled then." He clasped her hand in his. After that he pulled her along, tugging on her appearing very eager to dance. "Let's dance this second dance. If we stayed behind the church any longer, your father would come looking for us with his shotgun. I've the feeling he wouldn't appreciate what we were doing. Don't want you to feel embarrassment. Nor do I wish to explain myself or my intentions where you are concerned."

She found they were running. She was breathless trying to keep up with his swift pace. Once they reached the rest of the merrymakers, he swept her into his arms. A waltz played. He held her close, too close. Her father would have something to say about that. She thought she would swoon. He was so strong, so masterful.

They danced and danced beneath the moonlight. The day had been hot. Now, the night was sultry. He walked with her to the guest house where her family was staying, kissed her next to the large oak tree near the house. She leaned on him. He spoke of his journey which would begin in a few days. She told him she wished to go with him. His words were harsh when he told her no. She didn't like being told what she could or could not do.

At that very moment, she decided she would find a way to follow him. She shifted in an attempt to find comfort. Her head pounded. The dream faded. Sunlight filled the tent where she slept. She was no longer home. It took her a few moments to recall where she was. Chauncey leaned back on her elbows. Stephen wasn't sleeping beside her. He told her to sleep as long as she wished. She'd been exhausted. He gave her laudanum. She wondered if he gave her anything else.

Falling back, she closed her eyes. Heat washed over her face and neck as she remembered his intentions of the night before. He would have looked at her. She couldn't recall him doing so. Perhaps what he did was for the best. She no longer hurt. Once more she sat up searching for her clothing.

"Good morning to you." He poked his head inside the tent grinning. "I see you are awake. How are you?" His gaze was focused on her breasts. She heated more. The way he could do that to her, unnerved her.

With a quick movement, she pulled the blanket to her neck. He hooted with his laughter as he watched her. She shot him a scathing glance. At least she hoped it was scathing. By the look in his eyes, she didn't believe there was anything scornful about it or he was too dense to understand. "Go away. I'll be out in a minute, in less than a minute."

The man was still laughing. "Have it your way." He vanished, the flap of the tent following over the opening.

Chauncey didn't understand why she was so petulant with him. He'd done nothing wrong. Nothing except see her naked. She hadn't been ready for that.

~ * ~

Slade Lakeland along with Jess Andrews watched the older man blunder through the forest. He made enough noise to scare all the animals he was trying to hunt for food. The two men followed Greeley from the trading post where they learned Chauncey married Stephen Wilkes. Both young men wanted to travel west. Adventure called to them. They wished to purchase land then build an empire in the Rockies. Chasing after Chauncey seemed to give them both an excuse to follow their dreams.

Slade was surprised when they caught up with the old coot who made no bones about wanting to take Chauncey away from Stephen. The man, Mr. Greeley, blamed Chauncey for the loss of his girl, Beth. With Beth he could do whatever he wanted. He bought her from an old man who'd been using her for years. Beth never blinked or moved a muscle when he took what he wanted from her. Beneath him she didn't move. That was the way he liked his women.

Scouting ahead, Jess learned that Chauncey and Stephen were

only a few miles northwest of them. Neither brother or cousin understood why Stephen was taking so long. Why he didn't seem to care if they traveled very far. It appeared today he wasn't going anywhere. The first surveillance of the pair told them that Chauncey was still abed. They would make their appearance known to them by nightfall.

What Slade didn't understand was why the two weren't moving at all. When he voiced his concern to Jess there was no answer. Winter snow would come to this part of the country at any time. They needed to be some place secure when that happened. Alone in a tent in the middle of nowhere was far from secure.

Their furious father finally gave permission for Slade to go after Chauncey. At first Aric thought it would not be wise to travel so far west. Nonetheless, he, with Jess' help, convinced both Aric along with Damian this was something they intended to do with or without parental permission. They were both of an age to make decisions for themselves. They would locate Chauncey then make certain she returned home unhurt.

"Should we send Mr. Greeley on his way or let Stephen do the honors?" Jess asked as he looked in the direction they headed.

"Believe he will not survive unless he returns to the settlement. He's starving and has no idea how to forage for food. He didn't bother with a packhorse. Now, he's scaring all the animals into hiding. After all we've heard about him do we care if he lives?"

"So, you're telling me we should let nature take its course," Jess hooted. "I'm afraid that would be tantamount to murder. If we leave him alone, he might discover Chauncey's whereabouts. Even though he's starving, he can still do mischief."

"Though that does seem to have some merit and it's logical, I won't be party to murder despite his intentions toward my sister," Slade said as he chewed a piece of jerky.

He was thinking of many punishments. Nothing he came up with was suitable for this situation.

"You're saying that allowing the vile man to waste away in his self-imposed journey is murder? That's a bit harsh don't you think?" Jess asked as he put in a verbal contribution. "We could always visit him.

Give the old man a few pointers in survival. In the process, we can discover if what his wife told us was true. Just because a bitter wife cannot keep her mouth closed, doesn't mean what she says is true."

"Why would she lie?" Slade asked with the lift of his shoulders. "She appeared pleased to be rid of the old man. Didn't expect him to return with Chauncey or even without her. She seemed to have settled into the trading post quite nicely. One of the trappers seemed interested in her."

"Do you think Stephen needs to be informed of the man baring down on him?" Jess asked directing the conversation back to the pair they came to find.

"We might interrupt something."

Slade thought of his sister. Wondered why she took off without telling anyone. Neither his mother or father gave him a reason. He imagined it was possible neither knew. Kane told him that Lyssa saw Stephen take Chauncey behind the church on the day of the wedding.

"You can't be angry with Stephen," Jess said thoughtfully as their gazes clashed. "We both understand how impulsive our sisters are. Just as Lyssa did just as she pleased with the man of her choice, Chauncey is following in her footsteps. A man can only deal with so much. Chauncey, when she wants something is a force to be reckoned with."

"Heard Nickie ran off with this McInnis fellow. She was increasing by the time her father caught up with her."

"Don't want an impulsive woman for my wife," Jess mused as he tossed a pinecone toward the fire. "Want a woman who is biddable. Who will pander to my every whim. Who will do as I tell her."

"No, you don't," Slade said with a soft chuckle, calling him out. "That would be far too boring. Just as I would lose interest, so would you. However, marriage for me is years from now. Don't have any interest in the institution."

"Let's catch up with your sister and her husband. What do you say? Should be interesting to see the looks on their faces when they find out who is following them. What do you think they'll do?"

Chapter Seven

Stephen felt her presence behind him before she spoke. He heard the swish of her skirt when she walked toward the fire. Caught the scent of magnolia on the slight breeze. She would have questions for him. Questions about last night. As far as he was concerned, none of her queries were answerable.

"How do you feel?" he asked as he poked the fire with a long stick. She would have to see to her needs. He set out a basin of water along with soap for her to wash. The stream was freezing.

"Coffee...?" she asked as she stepped up beside him. Her hands were clasped in front of her as she stared at him waiting, he imagined, for him to speak. "Is it hot?"

"Very, take a small drink first."

The conversation was bland. Just the way he wished the tête-à-tête to go.

He handed her the mug he filled when he first heard her dressing inside the tent. "I need to wash some clothes today. Assume we aren't' going to travel." She sipped gingerly, eyeing him over the rim of the cup. "The coffee is good."

"Not as good as yours."

He turned to her, smiling at her. Her eyes were focused on him, on his hands then back to his eyes. There was nothing flirtatious about her actions. He knew what she was thinking. Wondered how long it would take her to ask. If she didn't broach the question on her mind, he wasn't going to do so.

"Take care of your needs." He nodded toward the stream. "You can take a bath if you wish."

Fondly, he remembered the bath she took that day after he discovered she was on the wagon train. The day after he learned he was her husband. It was the first time he saw her naked. Today, he wouldn't join her in the water. "You need to make it quick, the water is freezing. Later on in the day, you can wash your britches and shirts if you've the stamina. Prefer you wear your gown. Once we reach my village, you will be expected to wear the clothing I provide. You will not gainsay me in this. Until then, wear what you would feel the most comfortable in."

"Thank you, I do understand. It is the way of your people to make a woman plead for her man's permission."

She walked away from him without argument. Her back was straight, her chin tilted into the air.

He felt the subtle slap to the face. Even though the blow wasn't physical it stung. Somehow, he understood she would walk upstream where he couldn't see her. One day she wouldn't be so shy around him. While today wasn't that day, there was danger in going too far away. "Don't go far. I want to be able to hear you. Would rather be able to see you," the last he whispered beneath his breath.

"Oh! Why?"

She whirled staring at him, her lips parted, her eyes questioning what he told her. The tilt of her head told him she was curious. With her lips pressed together, he comprehended she would argue.

She needed to cease her questioning. Needed to do as he told her. There might come a time where a question could cost her her safety, even her life. They were closing in on Sioux territory. They could have visitors at any time. The warriors who would join them would expect complete compliance.

"In case you didn't notice, love, we're in the wilderness. I'd prefer you bathed in my line of sight. Not that I intend to watch you bathe. It's just a precaution I wish for you to observe. There are all types of wild animals that could do you harm, including the male variety. Would that be too much to ask?" He tempered his voice, moderated it so she would not think of his words as a command. "At this moment, it is your choice."

"Yes, sir," she told him, dipping her head as if she agreed. "I'm not a silly twit. What you say has meaning."

Her answer shocked him. He turned his attention from the

cooking biscuits to watch her. She walked with fluid grace, her hips moving from side to side with each step. While she could do many things a man could, she was fragile, her bone structure delicate. True to her word she stopped where he could see her. He watched as she stripped, her clothing falling to the ground. When she was bare, she folded the pieces before setting them on a boulder. All the while she kept her back to him. Her back was beautiful, the line of her spine straight. Two dimples at the base beckoned for his kiss. He sucked in air while he gazed at her lovely features. Was she tempting him on purpose? She must know what the site of her would do to him. Most likely, she didn't. Chauncey was new to the sexual games men and women played together.

All he could see was her back as he wished for an unhindered view of her front. It wouldn't happen. Her small, nicely rounded butt was charming, the sway of her hips enticing as she walked into the water. When her feet touched the liquid, he watched her stiffen. Her long auburn hair fell to her waist. He grinned at her gasp when that beautiful butt of hers touched the liquid. The water was unpardonably cold. He knew because he bathed earlier. He couldn't get his fill of the sight of her. He hoped she would turn toward him so he could see her breasts, the hardened rosy tips made that way by the chill of the stream coupled with the morning air. She would not stay long. He watched her lather herself then sink below the surface. She was out in five minutes tops.

When she sat beside him near the fire she was shivering. She held her hands out to the fire for the heat the flames offered. To warm her, he wrapped her in his arms. "You never told me how you were feeling."

He thought she would tell him she was cold, freezing in fact. Didn't expect her to speak the silent question between them.

"Did you look at me last night?"

She turned wounded eyes to him.

His gut churned. He thought it best to proceed as he intended for the rest of his life. He wasn't going to pretend with her. "Spread your legs wide this morning. Don't you remember?" Stephen had to shake his head. He'd not meant to speak quite so bluntly. "Yes, I looked at you, Chauncey. Sorry, if I...well hell!"

He stood, leaving her to shiver then walked around the fire

several times. He stopped, staring off into the trees as if they would give him the needed words.

She fiddled with the hem of her shirt while her gaze remained focused on him. "You're my husband. I've wanted to be with you since Lyssa's wedding when you kissed me. Eventually, I'll get used to you looking at me. Not certain I will ever get used to vulgarity. Maybe I'm too finicky."

She picked up the mug of coffee, looked into the mug. "I know you are teasing with your words or maybe taunting. In any case, I don't understand the game. Perhaps you are attempting to provoke a response. I hope you are. I would like to be able to speak so bluntly to you. Would love to tell you my thoughts as soon as they burst into my head. If I did so, I'm afraid you'd be angry with me more often than not." Now she lifted the fragile shoulders that he loved to kiss. "I don't understand the words you use or why when it comes to some of your plain speaking. It would be nice if you would explain."

Once more she stunned him. She told him more about her feelings than he expected. He did enjoy the curious look in her eyes when he said something outrageous. Wasn't positive he wished for her to understand the double meanings. "We won't travel today. You are still a bit raw. I applied a healing cream to the area while you were still asleep. Another day of rest will do you good. After that, I'll expect you to tell me how you're feeling when I ask. I will push us hard. You understand this." He waited for her to recognize the fact she evaded his question twice.

She flashed a smile at him as if she knew the tenor of his thoughts. "I feel wonderful actually. The night of sleep seemed to erase the exhaustion I felt."

He studied her for a few seconds, assessing the truth of her words. He rubbed the back of his neck. Leaving her now left her vulnerable to any stranger or beast. The damage was done. It would be a while before he trusted her. "I'm going to hunt. Assume you can use the pistol I have. I'll leave you with both. That will give you a total of four shots if you need to use the weapon."

Tapping her finger to her chin, her look mischievous, "I'm a fairly good shot. When I'm lucky, I can hit the broadside of a barn," she told him smiling once more, leaving him breathless, nearly panting for air. Her's was a brilliant smile. The sight knocked him off his thoughts. Hit him hard between the eyes.

"Hitting the broadside of a barn might not be helpful in a dangerous situation. You would have to strive for better aim. One cannot just point and expect to hit something."

His stomach flipped over. He imagined he shouldn't leave her. Remembered the snake. He paused.

She seemed to notice his frustration then changed her story. Before she proceeded, she sipped air, pressing her lips tight together in the aftermath. She slanted him a pointed look. "I lied. Sorry. In fact, I excel with a rifle when I can brace the barrel on something. I shoot a pistol with deadly accuracy. You must recall the snake. That was no accident."

She smiled at him again as if she understood his reluctance to believe her then sipped her coffee. Pointing to the pan, she said with a touch of humor in her voice, "The biscuits are going to burn."

Stephen reached for the pan. Yelped when the heat seared his fingers. He grabbed the cloth he set aside then pulled them from the flames with little damage done to either his hand or the biscuits. Embarrassment flooded him with heat. He cursed long and fluid as he realized his face was red.

"Thank you, you can understand why I'm loath to take your word for anything." he murmured when he managed his emotions. He dished up the breakfast he made. Earlier he found eggs, pheasant eggs. He scrambled them. Along with the bacon this was a treat from their usual fare. If his hunt this morning was successful, they would have a special dinner this evening. While Chauncey was still sleeping, he had set snares as he hoped for fresh game without having to shoot.

"I couldn't help myself. If you are going to be rude about my person then I reserve the right to tease when it feels right. I did correct the lie almost before it left my lips."

He acknowledged the truth of her words by nodding. "Very well, I'll think on what you've just said. In the meantime, I'll be gone around an hour before I check back on you, less if the fruits of my labor are successful. You will take care. Don't wander from this site." He hoped she wouldn't fall asleep. Instinctively, he believed she was still tired. There were shadows beneath the magnificent blue of her eyes. She needed to remain awake as well as ever watchful.

Chauncey nodded her understanding. Looking over the rim of her mug, she asked, "How are you feeling today? Not to sore from riding? Are you? I could...well...I could spread your legs and take a look. What do you think? Would you like that?" The half-smile that always intrigued him flashed for his view. Her eyes twinkled with merriment. She had no idea what those words did to his body.

Little devil.

With the advent of her teasing challenge, he burned. Stephen understood he could get used to life with her. Her disposition was sweet as well as saucy. If she stuck to the straight and narrow, he didn't mind the heat she could dish out without blinking. He imagined he would have to since they were wed. Thought that if he expected truth from his wife, he should give her the same consideration. "Apparently not as well as you. Sharing a chaste bed with one's wife doesn't always have the desired effect on a man's body. Spreading my legs to stare at me is a novel idea. I will consider your notion."

The wedding night, her raw passion so readily given, sprinted through his mind. He needed to relive that night. The evening before when she stroked his sex was magical. She brought him to a shattering climax, marveled at the sight of his seed on his belly. "Last night...well...perhaps tonight will be a bit easier on my man's body."

He didn't think she was ready for him yet. Didn't want to increase the damage. He wasn't a man with no control over his body. He could wait until she was healed. Perhaps by the morning.

She flushed the most becoming shade of pink. He hoped she would be ready for him by morning. They didn't have to start their journey at the crack of dawn. Comprehended the fact he had no business making love to her tonight while she was still sore.

This behavior around one's wife was not a characteristic he wanted to cultivate. He wanted her healthy so they could take pleasure in each other.

"I would like that, Stephen. Would like for you to make love to me another time. I'm sorry I failed you." Her soft voice vibrated in his heart.

He needed to change the conception that she somehow failed him. "You didn't fail or disappoint me. All of this can be set at my feet." That was the truth of the matter. "Do not blame yourself. I knew better than to push too hard. Understood a virgin shouldn't be taken several times in one night."

"All right."

He would like to make love to her too. "If you see anyone, shoot first," he warned. "I'll hear the shot then come running." He bent to kiss her on the cheek when he wished he dared bring her into his arms then kiss her hot and deep. If he did, that might well lead to other things, an intimacy they shouldn't share.

With quick strides, he headed in the direction of the first trap he set. He looked for small game, thought of his talk about survival with her last night. He hoped she would relax in the sunshine while he was gone. She meant to wash her britches. He'd much prefer she wear skirts. When he reached his family, she would have a leather gown fashioned for her. He would insist she wear the dress.

Once there, they would wed in the way of the People. He would have to hunt horses to bring to her father, Aric Lakeland. The bride price was important to his ways just as her customs were important to her. He would need fifty horses as he didn't wish for Kane to outshine him. Kane's endeavor was easier. The earl bought the horses. He would need to hunt for them.

Cold wind blew down from the mountain peaks that were far to the west of them. The chill brought on thoughts of snow. Restless energy assailed him. Needs he didn't understand filled his soul. He wished Chauncey waited for him where it was safe at her parent's ranch. Fear for her played a major part of the restlessness he felt. Late last night his gut instincts stabbed at him. The feeling that someone followed them possessed a very real place in his mind. The signs were subtle, nevertheless very real.

He left her with pistols to defend herself. She told him she was an excellent shot. What if she lied to him again? What if she didn't even understand the concept of firing a weapon. He imagined that if she could hold it up and point the pistol, she might be able to hold off a person who meant her harm. That ploy would never work with an animal. *She shot the snake without a blink. She didn't flinch. That could not have been blind luck.*

The fresh meat was not a necessity. With the packhorse, they carried plenty of food. He checked the first trap. It was empty. Saw rabbit signs around it but nothing in the snare. Rabbits weren't supposed to be that smart they would avoid the trap. He thought maybe the hawk he heard last might have beat him to this animal.

Trees rose up around him as he strode deeper into the forest. He followed the stream, watching for tracks. Three deer drank at the small pool as well as a large cat. The tracks were visible. He couldn't shoot a deer. He wouldn't be able to use the meat. He should have tried his hand at fishing. With patience, he used to be able to snare a trout with his bare hand. He was long out of practice.

The next trap held the game he sought. He had one more to check then he'd turn back to camp. The hair stood up on the back of his neck, telling him he best hurry. Luck was with him. The third trap also snared a rabbit. He put them inside the bag he brought. His mouth watered with the prospect of a different meal tonight as well as tomorrow. He would roast both. They could eat the second one in the morning.

The shot he heard shook him to his core. No! Racing through the woods, hurdling over fallen logs, he thought he would never reach camp. Brambles tore at his face and clothes. He'd wandered too far from the site. It would take forever to reach her.

Chauncey was alone and vulnerable. He prayed that whatever or whoever she shot at she hit. His heart lurched when he heard the reverberations of a second shot. His body tensed. Fear for her sliced through him. His heart thundered beneath his chest.

Minutes that seemed like hours ticked by with maddening slowness. He reached the stream leading to the camp. Plowing through the water, heedless of the liquid soaking his moccasins, he raced forward.

Whoever was at his camp was shouting. The words were lost to him, thundering in his head an incoherent jumble.

It was then he heard Chauncey's voice. She was yelling. Venting her ire. He was pleased with her.

"How dare you!" He heard her scream. "You stupid old man. I won't go with you! Just forget what you're thinking. Go back to your wife. You married her. You can't have me!"

Who the hell was at his camp? Greeley? From his stand point he thought she might know whoever was there. The first site of her stole his breath from his lungs. She stood, her feet braced apart, the pistol unwavering in her hands.

Chauncey held the gun, pointed direct at a person, several persons to be concise. Her hands were moving back and forth, aiming at three men. One pistol was on the ground. She held the second one with both hands.

"Sit down," she said, her voice calmer than he expected. "Stay put so I can figure out what to do with the lot of you."

He was too far away to do any good. As he watched her, a grin spread across his face. Now he didn't dare yell her name or distract her. Stephen slowed his reckless pace, tugging in oxygen, examining the scene. His Chauncey had everything under control. He was proud of his woman. It seemed she could shoot as well as she bragged.

Three men.

His woman held them all at gunpoint. She was remarkable. Taking as much time as possible, he walked into the area. He picked up the pistol she'd dropped. He loaded it then slipped it into his belt.

"Mr. Greeley," he said, his voice thick with emotion. "What the hell are you doing here?" He turned his attention to the other two men. "Slade? Jess? I could ask the two of you the same question. Your baby sister got the best of you. Didn't she, Slade?"

The pair looked relieved that he was here. Their hands that were behind their heads began to lower.

"Wouldn't do that if I were you," Chauncey told her brother and cousin with a syrupy voice that the two men seemed to understand since they stopped moving. "I could shoot the two of you for just being here.

You've no business following me. Did daddy put you up to this?"

Slade wore a wicked smile as did Jess. They seemed patiently waiting for something else to transpire. Slade looked to him, expectation in the shimmer of his eyes. He shook his head as he wasn't about to interfere in a squabble between siblings along with cousins.

Her brother spoke first. "We came to rescue my sister from the likes of you, Still Water Runs Deep. Understand we were too late when we heard you married her. Offered to take her home with us. She refused." Slade shrugged his shoulder, his grin one of wicked amusement. "The two of you are traveling awfully slow."

Stephen didn't miss the implication slick in the youngun's voice. The boy made assumptions.

"What he said," Jess told them, the smirk so obvious Stephen wished he dared strangle him.

Having Chauncey's brother and cousin with them would make his life more difficult.

"If the facts are spoken true, we wanted an adventure more than anything. Used Slade's sister for an excuse to head west. Since the two of you are married, all right and tight, why then, we'll just go with you wherever it is you are going. You don't have to..." Jess cleared his throat a few times then ran his finger around his collar seeming unwilling to finish the statement.

Stephen nodded to Greeley. "You?" he questioned, thoroughly disgusted with all that was going on. "Don't suppose you were trying to rescue my wife too. What were you planning?"

Greeley paled, his eyes narrowing as if he sought the right words. "Rescue her from the likes of an injun, that's what I was doing alright. A white woman has no business laying beneath...beneath scum of the earth." The man rubbed his graying whiskers.

The words didn't flay any skin off his hide. It wasn't the worst he'd been called or the first time. "I see." Stephen turned to Chauncey who surprised him by saying nothing.

She darted a furious glare in the direction of Greeley. She looked as if she wanted to shoot him. "How dare you call Stephen scum. He's a good kind man," she rallied to his defense.

Pleased, Stephen continued. "Do you want to be rescued by any of these men?" After sending Chauncey an approving smile, he lifted an eyebrow in speculation. After their last two grueling days, Stephen didn't have any idea how she would respond. What he did know was that they would work out their differences if left alone. He didn't need her brother or cousin tagging along, listening to them, their arguments as well as their lovemaking. He didn't doubt there would be a few disagreements.

"Only want to be rescued by one man, my husband," she told him with so much sugar coating her voice he grimaced then she lowered her lashes for a soft enticing flutter.

The answer was to his liking. "Come here." He held out his hand. She walked to him, her gun never wavering from its targets. He wrapped his arm around her. "Can we let your brother and cousin go now? You don't truly want to hold them at gunpoint now, do you?"

The ensuing smile told him she was enjoying this power over her brother and cousin. "Never got the best of my brother before. Are you going to take away all my fun? Seems like another few minutes in my power wouldn't hurt. He might learn a valuable lesson."

Stephen wondered what lesson she was trying to teach Slade. "Good God, no! I'd never take away your fun." He chortled with the pleasure of his woman. "Think you should do whatever suits your fancy. Sometimes brothers need to be taught a lesson in decorum. Is that what you're doing? Trying to refine Slade's manners?"

"I'm not certain. I'll need time to think about that. Let's take this man's fate into consideration." She pointed the gun directly at the man Stephen knew she despised. "Greeley here has been following us with the intention of kidnapping me. I don't like the idea of letting him go even if he promises to leave us alone. The man can't be trusted to do what he says. Blames me for the fact he lost Beth to your friend. Don't see how I'm accountable for that."

"The man looks as if he hasn't eaten since he left the trading post," Stephen said still wondering what he would do with Greeley. "Should we feed him before we see to his punishment."

"If left to his own devices, he'll starve to death," Slade spoke up with a chuckle despite his sister's earlier words. "Say, little sis, can I take my hands down from behind my head? My arms are getting tired." There was a hint of contrition in the man's voice. "Don't know why you pointed that gun our way. You know we don't mean you and your husband harm."

"You could have killed one of us. The damn bullet whizzed by my ear," Jess said with a hint of admiration for her shooting skills. "Though I understand if you meant to kill, I wouldn't be sittin' here talkin' to you."

"Yeah, we both know if she wanted to put that bullet in the middle of your forehead she would have. That shot was a warning shot, nothing more," Slade spoke a few admiring words of compliment for his sister. "She's the best damn marksman I've ever seen."

"Put your hands down," Chauncey said, her voice soft. "Someday I'll get even."

When Greeley started to follow suit. She shot him a furious word. "Not you. Not ever you. Not until someone ties you up." Her gun riveted on the old man.

Stephen decided he would let this play out the way Chauncey would like. She was in control. He stoked the fire then went about getting the rabbits ready for roasting. Once that chore was complete, he made coffee and set the beans to simmering. His stomach spoke up. It was past time for a meal. Someone still had to make the biscuits.

~ * ~

Stephen left about fifteen minutes ago. She felt at a loss, as if she was missing someone, him. Being left alone was not her first choice. She imagined she needed to get used to the notion. He was checking traps. She could have gone with him. Now, the hair on the back of her neck stood up, chilling her body. She felt as if someone watched her.

Chauncey, with a strange sense of *deja vous,* watched Mr. Greeley stagger into the clearing where Stephen had made camp. Her gut twisted while her mind went to Beth. Beth, who almost took her life to escape this man. He was a horrible, horrible blood thirsty, dirty old man who was also selfish and cruel.

What the devil did he want? There was only one logical answer. She shivered with dread. Her heart lurched while she tried to sip smoke scented air into her lungs. While the breeze hummed in the trees rattling the leaves, she froze. As she sucked in each breath of air, she regained her ability to move.

"Well, lookee here. It's the little missy who thinks she's better than everyone else. Thinks she can dictate other people's lives. You can't." His words slurred as he stumbled forward. He meant to take her. "Well, I came here to claim what's mine. You're going to be mine, little gal. You see, I don't lose what is mine."

Chauncey held the distinct impression the man was drunk. Inebriated, he would be more dangerous than when he was coherent. With caution, she stood. Held the gun in front of her, the barrel pointing his way. She was glad her hand didn't shake. "I'm not yours," she told him with a clear distinct voice. "Never will be. You go on. Get out of here with your life. Won't hesitate to shoot you straight through your cold heart." She moved the barrel in the direction of the trading post. "Go back to the wagon train if they'll have you. There's nothing here for you, especially not me."

"Missy, I see things different, way different. You caused me to lose my Bethy. You owe me." He moved forward reaching out for her.

"Don't take another step!" Her words were filled with emotion as well as the command she sought. "I'll fire. Don't doubt that for a second. Best you not move a muscle." She aimed at his ear. If he moved, she would take it off his head.

When he grinned, his stained teeth showed. He licked his lips as he slobbered. "Ah, sweetheart, women don't know how to use firearms. Now, just put that there weapon on the ground before you hurt yerself. You could shoot your big toe off."

The placating was more irritating than her brother's teasing. She would shoot his big toe before she shot hers. She would have to give him a lesson it would be wise for him to remember. "I told you. Stay where you are!" She thought if she fired a warning shot into the air, he would understand.

The shot she fired ricocheted off a nearby rock. Shards pelted his skin. "Curse you!"

He shook his fist at her. Seemed to get control of himself, realizing she missed him. Greeley stepped forward one more time then smirked. The next step he took toward her brought another shot. This time the bullet grazed his right ear. He yelped. Blood spurted from his ear, ran down his neck to pool in the collar of his shirt.

She was content with the new lesson she taught him. Chauncey thought she should hear Stephen's footsteps. That was two shots fired. He told her he would come for her if she shot the pistol. For a miniscule of time, she searched the forest in the direction Stephen left.

Greeley's hand was on his ear. "Hey, what do you think you're doin'? You little hellcat. Put that pistol down." His voice held a dash of panic. His eyes showed his fear after that the expression changed to placating.

He still didn't believe. She did put the gun on a boulder near her then picked up the second one. Two bullets remained. If she could keep the pistol directed his way, she could reload. Noticed that his ear was still bleeding, running, blood dribbling on the ground.

"Mr. Greely, that shot was not a mistake. The bullet hit you just where I planned. Does your ear burn? The next one will go in the middle of your forehead where you won't feel anything...forever."

Her voice should be shaking as should her hands. She'd never fired at a person before, game and targets had been the only recipients of her marksmanship. If she killed the man, it would be murder. After what he did to Beth he deserved to die. "Sit down, Mr. Greeley. You're not going anywhere. Stephen will be back soon. He heard the shots. Sound carries for a long way around here." She wondered who else might have heard.

When he seemed to think twice about obeying her, she pointed to the rock that she shot first. "Sit there."

"I'd do what the lady says," the voice came out of what seemed like nowhere to her. "She's wicked when she's mad. At this time, she doesn't look mad. She appears angry as a little hell cat. Don't think I've ever seen my little sis with rage splintering from her eyes."

The voice was familiar to her. "Slade? Slade!" She whirled,

turning to the right, astonished that she would find her brother here.

Her brother and her cousin stepped from the protective sheltering of the trees. Her breath caught in the back of her throat. She was both angry and pleased to see them. There was only one reason they could be here.

To check up on her.

She wouldn't go home. She was a married woman now. Following her husband was what she was meant to do. Slade flashed her a smile. He was so confident and sure of himself, so much like Jess as well as Stephen. She would have to stand strong in her convictions. He would have to drag her out of here.

"I'm not going home."

Chauncey thought it best to make her position clear. She wouldn't be bullied by her brother. Stephen would never allow her to leave.

Would he?

She didn't think so. Recalling that he didn't want her to follow him west, she shuddered. Things changed. She was married now. He would want her close. Maybe not if he had a way to send her home where he wouldn't have to worry about her. She would still be his wife.

For that matter where was her husband? He told her he would be here if he heard a shot. Oh God, what if Greeley found him first. The man could have shot Stephen. Whirling, turning in circles she searched for Stephen. Her heart pounded. Her breath hitched. She thought her stomach would never stop tumbling. She knew she had to keep her sibling and cousin at bay too.

"Put your hands up. I've got two shots. One for each of you."

"Chauncey," her brother said.

He must have seen the look in her eye. His hands shot into the air. Jess followed suit.

"Keep them there." Her voice was calm even with the fluttering of her stomach.

Relief flooded her when Stephen strolled into the clearing. His grin pleased her. He wouldn't yell at her. At least she didn't think he would. Stephen would convince her to let her brother and cousin go. He told her he wouldn't deprive her of her fun. She'd never bested Slade. She had to allow him to go. She couldn't keep holding him at gun point. Slade wasn't the enemy.

He rested his hands on her shoulders. Kissed the nape of her neck. Ran his hands down her arms. "How are you, love? No one hurt you?" he whispered so close to her the vibrations sent shivers down her spine. "Have Jess and Slade put their hands down." She did because she didn't want them to see her with her husband.

Slade and Jess were taking care of their horses, seeming to realize they needed a few seconds together with no one watching. He squeezed her. "You were wonderful. Did you know you scared me out of a year of life. I heard those two shots. I was so far away. I was afraid I wouldn't make it back in time to rescue you."

"When I saw Slade, I was relieved, knew all would be fine." She pointed at her brother and cousin. "I don't want them here. They need to go home." She was thinking of the nights, of Stephen making love to her. They would hear. Turning in his arms, giving him warning of her feelings. "I won't go home with them. Please don't send me."

"Unfortunately, they are with us. They will probably stay the winter in the village. You will have to put up with the two of them. Will it be so terribly hard?" He touched the back of her neck with his lips. "I wish..." He brought a huge breath of air into his lungs then let the oxygen vanish into the waning light.

She shivered, her body vibrating from the brief contact. With the slightest touch of his lips, he could do that to her. He could make her passion race. She wanted him. "Yes, it will be horrible. I want you all to myself."

"Those words make me a contented man. Have no fear, we will find our privacy. Not tonight though. Perhaps in the morning we will play before we resume our journey."

He ran his large warm hands down her ribcage then back up until her unfettered breasts rested against the backs.

When she looked to see her brother and Jess, they were tying Greeley. "Does that mean what I think it does? We're going to keep Greeley here?"

"Believe so." With a smirk on his too handsome face, he swatted her on the bottom.

"Stephen!"

"Would you like to make the coffee? Do you want me to do the job?" he asked as if there was nothing wrong with his behavior.

She jerked at the contact between them before glowering at him, sticking her chin in the air while she tried to ignore the pleased expression on his face. "I'll make the biscuits. Though I would think you would be growing tired of them."

"Never," Slade said as he strode up to her, reaching out his arms. "Give me a hug, Sis. Being held at gunpoint for hours does little for my disposition. Would think you would like to make it up to me."

"You do mean minutes. I don't have anything to make up to you." She opened her arms for a hug. "You will contribute something for dinner. What have you got packed away? Something sweet perhaps. You do know I've a sweet tooth."

"You're always thinking with your stomach, little Sis. I've got a bottle of wine you might enjoy. It's not a bottle. The wine is in the canteen. Filled several before we left home. Do you want Chianti or Bordeaux? Thought I might have to do some making up of my own once I caught up to you and Stephen. Comprehended the fact you wouldn't be pleased with our appearance."

She sniffed, her nose in the air. "Chianti. Pour me a big mug. Hope there is enough to keep us in wine for more than a day. I'm dreadfully tired of coffee. Never cared for tea or milk." After he poured and handed it to her, she drank deep. The wine was delicious, a Chianti, if she wasn't mistaken, from her uncle's winery in Italy. The Bordeaux would have come from France. "Thank you." She stirred the batter before pouring the contents of the bowl into the sizzling frying pan.

"You are very welcome. I could eat an entire pan myself." He snacked on a handful of nuts and dried fruit. "Know it would be difficult to make more than one batch." His sigh was heavy as he stared at the pan where the biscuits were baking.

"Did father send you to drag me home? If he did, you can turn around and leave without me. I'm not going," she told her brother as she sat on a rock near the fireplace, enjoying the wine.

The rabbit turned on the spit, juicy drips sizzling in the flames. The sight was mouthwatering. Her stomach shouted out to her.

"Yes and no, mother wouldn't let him. If she knew he was behind this adventure of ours, father would be sleeping on the couch until we return." Slade laughed as he stared at Jess. "Damian, too, if Amorica got wind of what we were doing.

"Yes, that would be the way of it if mother was against the two of you following me. She understood I had to do what was in my heart. Of course, I had no idea Stephen would marry me."

"Don't get me wrong. She was dreadfully worried about you. When all was said and done though, she was certain Stephen would take care of you. Seems he did just that." Slade slanted Stephen a glare. His voice turned into a low growl when he asked the next question. "Did he bed you before he married you?"

Chauncey bristled at the irreverent question that was so inappropriate. She didn't intend to answer. Her brother could be rude beyond anyone she knew. "I told everyone on the wagon train Stephen was my husband. He had to acknowledge the fact or I would have been kicked off. As to when we slept together, that is none of your brotherly business."

As usual, Slade was making her angry. He had this knack of doing so, having honed it since she could walk. More than not, she would be blamed for something he did. Sometimes he would trick her into hitting him then claim all innocence. No longer. He wasn't going to provoke her.

She thought of that first night when Stephen was incensed with what she did. He made her sleep next to him with nothing on. She'd been so embarrassed she couldn't think straight. He thought to teach her a lesson. There was nothing learned. Given the chance she would have done it all a second or even a third time.

"You two going to keep arguing? Perhaps the discussion is so you can make up." Jess asked as he looked to Stephen. "Where do you want us to bed down? We can pitch the tents anywhere you like. No, you must want privacy." His smirk didn't go unnoticed.

"As far from this tent as you can get." Stephen stirred the beans that were simmering on the fire. "Want a small mug of wine too. Just as Chauncey said, it will be a welcome reprieve from the coffee. Are you going to journey with us? If so, we need to set down a few rules."

Light from the fire played across the chiseled angles of Stephen's face. He was so handsome and strong. She admired him in so many ways. His green eyes flashed dangerously when he spoke to her family. Even when he was angry with her, they never sent that message her way. She thought to change the subject. "The rabbit is about roasted? I'm starving. Seems it's been ages since breakfast."

What she wanted was to be alone with her husband. While the added company was nice in some ways, she already missed the privacy they had the last few nights. She looked longingly at the tent then back to Stephen.

"Imagine so," he said staring at her as if he guessed her thoughts. "Not tonight," he whispered for her ears only. "Maybe in the morning. We'll see how you're doing."

"Can I see to your needs?" Chauncey blurted with an effort to keep her voice low before she could think better of the words.

She meant to be flirtatious. The words didn't sound that way. She watched as his face grew taunt; his expression unreadable. Though his eyes...his eyes shimmered with what she read as desire. He wanted her to touch him again. This waiting was just as hard for him as it was for her. After he introduced her to the delights in a marriage bed, she wanted him every time she looked at him. Every time her gaze traced his broad shoulders, so strong she was certain he could do anything. Every time she stared at his trim hips and flat belly. Before he could answer, she heard the clearing of a throat. The sound came from her brother. He stood within a few feet of them. She prayed he didn't hear the brazen question she asked Stephen.

Slade cleared his throat a second time, his expression all-knowing and masculine. "Seems I'm interrupting. Carry on," he said, his voice bland.

"Appears you are," Stephen said, his voice harsh seeming to resent the intrusion to their private conversation. He waved his knife through the air before pointing to the finished meal. "Doesn't matter. Dinner is ready. If you would fill Chauncey's mug again, I'm certain she would appreciate the wine. Help yourself to the food. There's plenty for everyone." He stared at Greeley as if he didn't want to feed the man.

While they ate the meal there was little conversation. The silence seemed to encompass her thoughts. Chauncey was grateful for the meal, something besides the norm. She would also be pleased in the morning to enjoy a second round. She noticed that her brother and cousin pitched their tent a goodly way away from theirs. The distance made her happy. She didn't want them to hear anything that might be said between her and Stephen.

"You are leaving in the morning?" Slade asked as it was just as much a statement as a question. "We would like to travel with the two of you. Jess and I won't get in the way. We've both been out to Colorado before. Want to get the lay of the land. Meet a few of the indigenous people. Make some plans for our future."

Her brother leaned back in his usual manner, stretching his long legs in front of him. The mug he held on his lean belly.

He was so much like Stephen except in appearance. They were both large men, tall and broad of shoulder. It seemed to her Stephen dwarfed her brother.

"If we mean to keep him alive, Greeley will have to pledge to leave Chauncey alone. Don't know if we can trust the man," Stephen said, his eyes focused in Greeley's direction. "Perhaps we should leave him without a horse. By foot it would take him several days to reach the trading post."

"He would die without a horse. Might anyway. This meal has given him a few more days," Jess gave his opinion. "Just as the rest of you feel, I can't, will not trust the man. He would sell his mother if the opportunity arose."

"I'll get up early. Take him as far as I can get by midafternoon. Should make it about halfway to the trading post. After I deposit him with enough food to make it back to the settlement, I'll catch up to you," Slade volunteered as his gaze drifted between Greeley and her. "Don't want to murder the man. He was doing such a fine job of trying to kill himself before we caught up to him. Why should we bother?" he queried as his gaze was too focused on the man tied to the tree.

"I can do that. You stay with your sister," Jess said as he looked from Chauncey to Stephen. "Wouldn't want to break up the family. Besides, I can ride faster than Slade."

Slade grunted as if in disagreement but said nothing. Chauncey felt certain there would be an argument to Jess's outrageous claim. Nothing seemed forthcoming. Stephen slipped his hand in hers then winked. "I'll wash the dishes. You look exhausted. A long night's sleep seems to be in order. Go get ready for bed. Dawn will come before we know it. Tomorrow we will travel with as much speed as possible. Want to make up for lost ground."

She was loath to sleep. The dreams she had the previous evening stirred her body in so many ways. His kisses, just imagining them, did things to her she wished she could deny. They set an inferno within, raging heat, an ache she was loathe to acknowledge. When he looked at her his smile seemed to say he understood her discomfort. She also understood he would do nothing to compromise her healing.

"Jess and I will take care of the dishes. You two fixed the dinner. Least we can do." Slade gathered the dishes, taking the plates from both her and Stephen. "We'll bed down as soon as the dishes are put away. Will stoke the fire."

Jess refilled her mug.

"I'll go as soon as I finish this treat." She sat back, closing her eyes enjoying the sounds of the night even though nothing was quiet as it was the night before. The calm serenity was gone. Jess and Slade moved with little sound around the campfire but they weren't silent. Greeley had fallen asleep after he'd been fed. He was snoring, his head lolling on his chest. After the past two nights of silence, she now felt as if an entire village was here.

Stephen wrapped his arm around her letting her snuggle against his chest while she finished her drink. She wondered what he would do when he came to bed tonight. The evening would be too dark for him to look at her. He told her already he would not make love to her. The thought of Stephen kissing and touching her in all those places with her brother only a few feet away, heated her with embarrassment until she knew her face would be beet red. She would have to get used to his presence. As it seemed they intended to travel with them.

The clang of the dishes drowned out the more natural sounds. Soon there was nothing to hear except the crackle of the fire as the embers hissed and spit as well as the breeze rustling through the trees. She rose to take care of her needs.

He stood beside her, his hands encircling her waist. "I'll meet you in the tent," he whispered close to her ear, his tongue touching with tenderness on the lobe. He teased her with sensual pleasure that would be withheld tonight.

When she walked to the stream, she felt his gaze on her back. She walked by Slade's tent. He was inside sleeping possibly. It wasn't that late. Trying for speed, she washed then returned to their tent. Inside, she disrobed down to her chemise. Stephen wouldn't be pleased if she wore it. With her brother so close, she couldn't bring herself to take it off. She rubbed her arms, shivering.

Beneath the blankets she waited for her husband. Soon he crawled into bed beside her, pulling her into his arms. The heat of his body warmed her in so many ways. With the gentleness she was getting used to, he kissed her forehead, ran his finger along the line of her brows. She heard the soft rasp of his breath. Felt his heartbeat against her breasts. Felt his swollen rod against her belly. He wanted her.

"You would like to caress me?" he laughed his voice a whisper in the night, stroking her along the ladder of her ribs. "Is that what you told me? I would like that if the offer is still valid."

"You remembered my question. I thought you might wish to ignore what I said."

Chauncey wasn't at all certain she wanted to touch him intimately. The other night caressing him inflamed her to a point where she could barely sleep. She'd wanted him as much then as she had the night before when he kissed her.

"Yes, I recall everything you say." His voice was soft now, cajoling, mesmerizing. His charisma was overwhelming. Soon he would have her under his spell. "Well...do you want to touch me. If you do, you will have to allow me to give you a woman's pleasure. Do you remember how you responded so very wildly in my embrace? If you don't hurt when I stroke you, I would be happy to finish what you might begin with my man's body."

"I...I c...cannot."

She had misgivings on every possible level. Insecurities swept through her. Terror that her brother would hear what they did. Slade wouldn't like to think of his little sister in the arms of any man.

Beside her she felt him stiffen. Understood he would want to know why the change of heart. "I understand," he murmured his voice held a hint of anger. "Close your eyes, love. Morning will come soon enough."

She couldn't let him believe she didn't want him. "It's my brother..." her voice trailed off as she tried to figure out what else to say to him. "He might hear what we are doing."

"Your brother will be with us for months on end. He will have to get used to the notion his sister is married. I don't plan to remain celibate past tonight." His voice was harsh, grating in her ear. "In the morning, despite what we do or don't do at this moment, I will make love to my wife. I don't care what anyone hears."

"I know. Can you humor me for one night? This is all new to me. When Slade showed up, his presence put a new twist to something that was..." she didn't know how to finish her thoughts. No matter what she said, Stephen would have an argument. He would try to dissuade her.

"They would not hear you unless you scream your pleasure," he told her pushing strands of hair from her face, touching her with gentle strokes, sliding his finger along the column of her neck then across her collarbone. The mercuric touch was evocative. Sent her body spinning. She gasped as he ran the palm of his hand across her nipple, once then twice. Heat flamed.

"That was blunt," she told him, gasping again as his mouth latched on to the nipple he played with, sucking hard. Seems he wasn't about to take no for an answer. He would do what he would do. "Would they hear if you yelled out as you emptied yourself inside me. You did yell that first time." She wasn't going to allow him *carte blanch* in embarrassing her.

It seemed he read her thoughts. "If you think to embarrass me, it would take more than that for heat to rise to my face or for me to have second thoughts about the way I mean to treat my wife this evening. Don't understand why you left this on. You know how I feel about sleeping together." His fingers were on the ribbons to her chemise, pulling each one through the eyelet with evocative slowness. The fabric fell away from her breasts. Soon, he pushed the thin straps from her shoulders. His mouth closed over hers when his fingers touched upon the hardened tips of her breasts.

The soft moan from the action he generated floated up from the back of her throat. She whimpered when his hand rested on the flesh of her belly then explored lower spreading her, slipping between damp folds. He pushed the chemise down her body, following the path with soft tender kisses.

"Lift your hips, love. I don't want anything between us."

His skin brushed against her as he moved up her body to capture her lips. He reversed his haunting path. She moved, coiled to his ardent touch.

She did as he said, lifting her body. "Stephen..." she sighed, felt the touch of his teeth upon tender flesh. Her hips rose when he caressed the inside of her thighs. She jerked when he bit and nipped.

Once more he moved back to her mouth. "Open for me," he whispered into her parted lips as his tongue delved, sweeping into tender places, sensitive spots. He seemed to know where and how to stroke her. "Open yourself to me, heart, and soul. Don't hold anything back. I want all of you, Chauncey. That's it, sweetheart. I want your passion to rage out of control."

She knew he wanted her to spread her legs for him, give him room to sightsee on the most secret parts of her. She wanted that too. Needed to feel those intense sensation he orchestrated. Remembered all the magical feelings he imparted to her. As one thumb journeyed back and forth across her nipple, he explored her feminine parts. She allowed him intimate access. Entry only a cherished lover should receive. A purr rippled from deep within her. He absorbed the sound into his mouth.

"You are dripping with your sweet honey. Wet. Sultry. Dark. Your body rains moisture at my caress. Does this hurt?" he murmured as he touched upon sensitive parts of her as he thrust his finger inside her then another. Her hips moved, jerked. Wave after wave of pleasure rocked her. She arched. Heaved and moaned as he brought her to that point where she cared about nothing save the ecstasy, the scorching pleasure.

"No, nothing hurts," her words sounded as a thin wail in the darkness of the night.

She heard the fire pop. She ran her tongue along her swollen mouth wishing for one more kiss then another after that one. Tonight, she was certain he would deliver all she wished for.

"Touch me." He guided her hand to his sex. Groaned when her fingers closed around him. She was pleased. He was hot and hard, satin to the touch. She ran her hand along his length then back to the base.

Unlike the first evening they'd been together, tonight, she understood what he wanted, how he needed her to move her fingers on his hard length. Beneath her fingers, he swelled. This time he didn't have to show her what he wanted. She began to move, up and down until he stilled her hand.

"No, more," his breathing was harsh, labored. "At least not yet."

Turning his attention to her needs, he thrust his fingers into her slow then fast, deep then hardly at all teasing her. Pulses licked her core. Blinding ecstasy rippled through her. She lost all ability to think. She reacted as he sent her to a dazzling place of intense delight. When she cried out her pleasure, his mouth closed over hers while he continued moving her hand, showing her that he still needed her attention. With a final stroke he erupted, his seed falling on his belly as well as hers. He groaned then pulled her to him. His hand soothed her back while he whispered soft words.

"That was nice, Chauncey, more than nice. Did you like that as much as I did? In the morning before we leave the tent, I'll be deep inside you. My seed will find your womb. Perhaps a child will be created. Would you like a baby?" He reared up looking down on her. In the dark he would not see her. "I did not hurt you in any way?" His hands settled on her bottom, caressing her as he spoke.

"I would be more than happy to have you do as you say. Though I'm not happy that my brother will know what we do here."

"Even if we make no sound, he will guess what is going on in our tent. It is what he would do if he was wed to a beautiful woman."

~ * ~

Greeley heard the muffled sounds of two lovers reverberating from the tent. He gritted his teeth wishing he could yank the woman away. She should not be lying beneath that man who didn't deserve a white woman. Where was Beth? He'd still rather have his little Bethy. She wouldn't fight him. She always laid very still, her eyes dazed as if she was in a different world. He liked that. He could please himself without having to do much with the woman. Chauncey would fight hard. A spitting clawing little hell cat was that one. All he wanted from a woman was to be inside her soft body.

Tomorrow, if he didn't do something to change the fact, he would lose this woman forever. He knew better than to try for her again. Back at the trading post, he had his wife waiting for him. She was his for all eternity and she pleased him. After all, he taught her how he liked his women, docile as well as biddable. He was a man who needed more than one woman. If he wanted to live to buy a new woman to have as his sex slave, maybe he should comply to the wishes of the people who had him tied. He could go on his way. Could resume the life he intended when he started west.

A part of him cried out that he didn't want to give up Chauncey before he had her at least once. Just thinking of her soft creamy body, his sex swelled and ached. At least once in his life, he deserved to feel her woman's flesh. He wanted to fight his restraints with his whole being. God, the woman shot his ear. It bled like crazy and burned. She needed to be punished for her audacity. He needed revenge more now than when he came after her, following her to this forsaken place.

Dawn arrived. He heard the injun making love to Chauncey again. His gut lurched. His body heaved with sexual need. The tiny sounds of her pleasure filled the clearing, hardening him further. With his eyes closed he could imagine pumping into her. Could feel his release. He groaned.

Her brother should be there to stop them. Instead, Slade was stoking the fire, seeming to be oblivious to what was going on in the tent behind him. Jess was saddling his horse to take him God knew where? Not for one instant did he think the plan was to return him to the settlement, to his wife. He felt certain, sure, this Jess would take him deeper into the forest where he wouldn't know one end of this earth from the other then leave him alone to find his way to civilization.

He would die. Sioux or the Cheyenne injuns would find him. They would kill him, torture him. He'd heard stories. Stories that weren't very nice.

"You ready to leave?" Jess stood in front of him, hands placed on his narrow hips, feet braced apart as if he owned the world. His eyes blazed into him with hatred. "I'm in a hurry. Suppose the question is redundant. We're heading out. Not taking any stops on our way."

"You plannin' on leaving me somewhere then skedaddling away so's I get lost? Not goin' anywhere with you. Gonna stay right here." Greeley was putting up his last chance at resistance. With his luck, they'd probably take him for his word and leave him tied to this tree. "Never mind."

Jess hooted. "Tied to the tree? A bear would get you or a wolf. Rats would nibble at your toes. What was left of you the vultures would pick you clean." He studied him for a few seconds. His hands made a steeple beneath his chin. "Now, the way I see this, I can drag you behind my horse or you can ride. One way is dignified, the other..."

The man lifted broad shoulders, his grin never leaving his arrogant face.

It was just like youngun's to think they could have their way no matter how it hurt someone else. These pups were far too sure of themselves. He looked to the rising sun then the campfire. Slade was bent over heating the coffee. His mouth watered in anticipation of food and drink. He could almost taste the coffee warmin' his gullet. He needed something to go on. He needed to relieve himself. "You gonna let me have something to eat?"

Jess handed him a piece of jerky. "There will be another one for you when I leave you on the trail. What did you decide? Ride? Walk behind me with a rope tied to your waist?"

Jess looked amused when he watched him.

Greeley wasn't going to be anyone's amusement. Choking out the words, he spoke. "I'll ride." He mounted, chewing on the dried meat thinking he would find some means to backtrack the trail. He would get Chauncey yet. When he did...

"If you're thinking about deceiving us, best you think again. You come back for Chauncey, you're a dead man. That's a fact you best not forget. We won't be giving your life a second thought. Keep up now. Don't wish to waste any more time on the likes of you. If you can't keep up or don't want to, we can do this a different way."

With the reigns of Greeley's mount in one hand, Jess urged his horse to a trot. Greeley found himself jerked forward, clinging to the saddle horn as his horse followed the fast pace Jess set. The man did seem in a shameful hurry to leave him behind.

It was just past midday when Jess slowed to a stop. He turned to stare at Greeley. "Here we are. You're safe and sound, not a worry in the world. All you need to do now is find the fort." Jess pushed his hat up, his gaze blistering into him. "Best you get on to the settlement before dark. Never know what can happen after night falls. The wolves come out. Sometimes the bears. If you hurry, you can be there for dinner and not become some wild animal's evening meal. I'm certain your wife won't be pleased to see you though. She thought you were long gone. Never coming back. She thought she was free of the likes of you. She was quite pleased you left her at the trading post."

Greely stiffened. He didn't like what the pup was tellin' him. He needed to make sure that the boy didn't believe him concerned by the spoken words. "She'll be happy to see me," he gritted out furious with the whippersnapper for insinuating his wife would be less than pleased to see him.

The first thing he would do after he ate would be plow her belly. If she felt the way Jess implied, she would need to be taught a lesson.

Women needed to be put in their place. They needed to know who buttered their bread. He needed relief. Thought he would get that from Chauncey.

"Is that the way?" He looked down the trail. Interesting that they didn't follow anything expect animal trails to this point. "What's down that way?"

"You've plans of reneging on your word? Down that way leads to a Cheyenne encampment. If you go the other direction, you might run into a Crow village. Course, it would take you at least a week to get to either place. With your innumerable talents, you would starve by then. Starvation would be better for you than what the natives would dole out. That Cheyenne village doesn't cotton to ugly, old white men."

A prickle of unease shimmied up Greeley's back. He wasn't about to tempt fate again. Unless he could purchase a guide, he'd best leave this endeavor in the back of his mind. There were other women available to ease his lust. For now, until he found a new woman to purchase for his pleasure, his wife would have to fill the void.

"Not reneging on anything. My word is good. Don't plan on doing something stupid," he spat, his palms damp his forehead dripping with sweat despite the chill in the air.

"Glad to hear that. Catch." Jess tossed him another piece of jerky. He fumbled, the food dropping to the ground in front of him. "It will keep your belly full until you find the trading post. Enjoy the ride home. Hope you are resigned to your less than welcome home coming." With that said, Jess whirled his mount back the direction they came from.

A few moments later he vanished from sight. Greeley heard his departing laughter.

Curse the man. Curse Chauncey. Curse the injun. Somehow, sometime he would seek his revenge on all of them.

Greeley stared at the piece of jerky lying on the ground then swore again. He slid from his mount to pick the meat up. He brushed it several times across his pant leg. Damn, but his britches were dirtier than the ground. Picking off a pine needle, he decided he didn't care. He was too famished to take fault with a bit of dirt.

The sky was black when he rode, tired and hungry, into the

trading post. Thick dense clouds covered what might have been a moon. At the home he rented for his wife, he slid from his horse tying the reins on the hitching post. He'd see to the horse after he ate and had his woman. Stepping a bit crooked up the porch, his swollen member anticipating warm female heaven, he stopped dead still.

Laughter came from the main room. Girlish giggles rang out. A man chatted with Mrs. Greeley. That was all wrong. Lights blazed from the main room. He stepped cautiously as he wanted to understand. When he peeked through the stained dirty window, he could see nothing. His woman should be by herself, pining away for him. When he stepped inside, he caught the whiff of baked bread. Saw the stew made for dinner simmering over the fireplace. A table was set for two. His blood boiled when he caught a man backing his wife into the bedroom, his lips on hers. His hands places that belonged to him.

"Hold it right there. I oughta' kill both of you!" Greeley shouted, incensed that his wife dared cuckhold him.

The man's hand rested on the pistol that was still tucked into his pants. Greeley wanted to kill the stranger first. After he showed his woman who her man was, he'd kill her too. He didn't need a woman that bad that he would covet another man's leavings.

"Who the hell are you?" the man asked, his stubby fingers twitching on the pistol.

"The lady's husband," Greeley growled as he moved forward, his hands fisted tight in front of him. He was ready for a fight. Needed to show this interloper who was boss. "I'm going to kill you then I'm going to kill my wife."

The blast hit him in the chest. Greeley jerked backward. He looked at the blood. There was a hell of a lot of blood. This wasn't at all like the bullet that whizzed by his ear yesterday. He felt nothing. His body was numb. The room swirled in a red haze. He looked at his wife. She grinned at him, an all-knowing smile he wanted to wipe off her face. He looked at the man. The pistol was still smoking. The couple were laughing and pointing at him even though his wife appeared shocked.

The floor met his face.

Was this how it felt to die?

Chapter Eight

Two weeks passed before Stephen read the signs left on the ground that would lead him to the village. The first snow fell the night before. Wind whistled down from the mountains. The weather was every bit as bad as he thought it would be. Chauncey spent the evening curled up next to him watching the embers sizzle in the campfire. When they went to bed, she kept some of her clothes on. He made no objection. The extra furs he packed coupled with the body heat they generated kept them both warm. They made love. If she didn't already, she would carry his child soon.

He wasn't certain how he felt about that. He feared that very scenario when he first realized she followed him west. From the first second he saw her driving the wagon, he understood he would not be able to keep his hands to himself. She stirred every masculine part of him, a fever to his body. She would be more vulnerable as the baby grew.

He would expect company soon. A few men from his tribe would follow then make contact. With two white men along with a white woman, the reception would be different than if he rode into this territory alone.

Men would come to see who dared travel into their territory, who dared set foot on this ground. A week earlier he changed to fringed buckskins. Made certain Chauncey wore a dress each day. Jess and Slade stayed close though neither man thought they were in danger. They both spoke a few words of Sioux. By the time they left here, they would be fluent. He would see to that. As to Chauncey, he hoped she would also learn the language of his youth. He hoped his mother would approve.

By day, he taught her words that she would need. By night, she learned love words he wished to hear her speak to him. Another day passed before they encountered anyone he knew. When he looked up from the breakfast fire, he saw two old friends. Men now, young adults when he left with Kane. They both nodded as they approached carrying bow and arrow. Rifles were carried. Their black hair braided and long. In unison, the two men stopped. Their feet were braced apart, their expressions unreadable.

Holding his cup of coffee, he waited for them to make the first move forward. He left his guns alone, the rifle leaning against the boulder near the fire, his pistol in the belt of his buckskins. He held up his hand, a smile on his face. In greeting, he began, *"Hau."* Stephen hoped at least one of the men would recognize him.

"Hau, Still Water Runs Deep."

The man they called White Pony stood in front of him, relaxed, seeming at ease. "Many winters have passed since you left. Why do you come home? Your mother has shed many tears waiting for your return."

The ploy worked, as guilt swamped him. His mother would have to rely on others to keep her fed as well as clothed. "I wish to see my mother as well as my sisters and brothers before I return to London. I fear I might not come to this part of the country again. This might well be the last time I'm in this territory."

"You come with a woman and two men. What should we think? Do you come in peace?" Red Feather asked as he focused his attention on the woman. "They are *wasichu*, white. They have no rights here. We cannot welcome them. There will be those in the village who will take umbrage that you bring a white woman into their midst."

"They come in peace, with me. You will allow them safe passage. The white woman is my wife. She will honor our ways." He motioned to Chauncey then Slade and Jess. "They wish to learn your traditions, to speak the language. I will be responsible for all of them." Stephen held his breath as he waited for an answer. He never expected this to be easy. The silence grated and stretched every nerve he possessed.

White Pony nodded, "Come," he said then turned to his horse.

He headed down a small animal trail toward the west.

The silence seemed oppressive. Stephen thought they had been dogging his trail now for three days. He figured they must be close to the village. What he didn't understand was why they didn't introduce themselves sooner.

They scrambled to put all their gear together then douse the fire. He didn't bother to wash the dishes. That could be taken care of later. By the time they were ready the men were waiting for them farther down the trail.

He smelled the smoke from the lodges long before they reached the outer rim of the encampment. As they passed by trees, warriors fell in behind them. A few who recognized him called out his name. When he looked at Chauncey, her face was drained of color. Her hands holding the reins shook. It was obvious she was terrified. Stephen didn't blame her the fear. He could remember feeling much the same the first time he rode into a white village. People stared at him. Thought less of him because of his heritage.

As they came closer to the center of the village more people fell in behind them. Children raced ahead to spread the news that Still Water Runs Deep had returned to his people. Excitement grew with each passing second. More people milled around them. Some of the children reached up to touch Chauncey. She gasped in air yet tried valiantly not to jerk away from the curiosity of the children.

Chauncey rode closer to him, seeming to feel more reassured by his nearness. He whispered to her, encouraging her. She was doing well. There would be a time when the warriors separated them. He prayed his mother would take charge, would control the people when it came to Chauncey's wellbeing.

His friends stopped in front of the main fire in the center of the encampment. More people congregated. Women began to surround Chauncey, seeming to swarm as they poked and prodded. A lurch of concern swept through him. The chief stood by distracting him, his face devoid of emotion. The chatter of the women grew. He heard a tiny cry. A shrill cry. Excitement escalated. Drums beating reverberated in the smoky air. The pace quickened. He held his breath looking for her. He couldn't see her. The crowd parted. She was on the ground shielding her head with her hands. The women were circling her. One dragged her to her feet, shaking her. Others pulled at her hair.

"Chauncey! Stop!" He cried out. No one heeded him.

More women separated him from Chauncey. They gathered around her, chanting. She shrieked loud and clear. He heard the terror in her voice. His horse was led away from her. He tried to get to her. Women pushed her toward the river. She stumbled. On her hands and knees, her hair spilled around her. He understood all too well what they assumed. *"No!"* No one would hurt his woman. He tried to explain. No one listened or heard as he cried out. The women believed her to be his slave, captured from some white family.

Chauncey was shoved hard again, her arms flailing as she tried for balance. Her face scraped on the ground. "Stephen!" His name so frantically cried by her swept him into a whirlwind of danger. He had to protect. She should have called him by his Sioux name. He never told her to do so. The women could not mean her harm. She was his wife. They didn't know that for a fact. What Sioux warrior would wed a white woman? He recalled other similar incidents when the *wasichu* woman was not a wife. The woman was tortured in front of everyone. His heart thundered. If not put to an immediate halt, the women would brutalize Chauncey.

She yelled out again. The terrified scream wrenched his heart. Now she was fighting and clawing at the women who surrounded her. Hands were everywhere, hitting her, tearing at her. The clothing she wore was ripped, torn from her small body, shredded. All she could manage now was to defend herself. She covered her head with her hands as the women were tearing at her scalp, ripping at the fabric that kept her covered. She was almost naked. Her breasts fell free. Nothing, not even a scrap covered her back.

"Slave!" the women chanted. "Slave..."

The word slave was cried out more than once. Her bodice hung below her waist; the skirt torn baring her legs. She was trying to cover herself with her hands. She was sobbing. He could hear her terrified cries. They were taking her away from him. Slade and Jess both tried to get to her. Men held their horses, kept them from interfering.

"No!" he bellowed pointing toward Chauncey. "No!" He pointed to his chest several times. "My *win*! Leave her be."

He spurred his horse, challenging those who kept him away from his wife. The stallion reared on its hindlegs keeping the men around him from stopping him. Not heeding who he knocked over, he raced to her. He swept her off the ground then onto his horse. Fisted hands rose in the air. The women were angry with him. Her bared breasts pushed against him. The naked length of her leg fell across his thighs. Except for a few scraps of material, she was exposed, so very vulnerable. He covered her with the coat he wore.

At his direction his stallion danced in one direction then the other. Whirling around and around the People scattered away from the life-threatening hooves. He shouted into the crowd. Yelling in the language of his people. Cursing in the language of his adopted people.

Bloody, bloody hell! Why hadn't he foreseen something of this scope? He was a fool. All the precautions he took were for naught. All needed correcting.

From the corner of his eye, he saw his mother walk from her lodge. Her back was straight, her chin held high. The nod she gave him brought comfort to his heart. His mother understood his anguish. Understood what this woman meant to him. She was making an appearance when he needed her the most. His mother would take care of his woman. Would see to Chauncey's needs. He directed his horse toward her, toward her lodge. He would not be allowed to stay with her until he explained that Chauncey was his wife.

Within the steel embrace of his arms, she trembled clinging to the torn fabric. He saw the tear streaks down her cheeks that slid through the dirt and grime acquired from the attack. Of all he imagined, this had never been a part of the scenario.

"Don't leave me alone," she whimpered, pressing her small face close to his chest, her body shaking against him. Her body trembled as much from the cold as it did the terror inflicted upon her. "Please..."

When she turned her face his way, he watched more silver tears slide down her face.

"I will leave you with my mother. She will take care of you while I'm gone. Be brave. I know you can."

"Please, Stephen, don't leave me," her voice broke on another sob. "Please..." she was begging, clinging to him. Her small fingers holding onto his clothes.

His stomach churned. His nerves stretched. If he could, he would remain with her. He could not. "I'm sorry, so very sorry. I've no choice. If we are to stay here, I have to meet with the chief. Must explain my actions in rescuing you. All here thought you were my slave. In that case all they did was justified, expected. If you were my slave, I would not protest. It is the way of the People. If you were my slave, there would be little I could do to protect you from the women, at least not this first night. After that, I could do what I pleased with you. Do you understand?"

Chauncey shook her head.

"Trust me in this. I will do what is necessary for your protection." He held up his hand, halting the further chatter, the anger coming from the people surrounding him. *"Win!* Mine! Chauncey is no slave. She is my wife! Mine! My woman!" He yelled the words in the language of the Sioux.

Seeming to sense his fury, the group of people fell silent when the chief stepped forward. "She is your woman not your slave?" he questioned his gaze running over her naked flesh. "You should have made that clear from the beginning. The woman cannot be faulted for their deeds. They do not like white women with good reason. Nor do they appreciate white men."

He stared pointedly at Slade and Jess.

"Chauncey is my wife. The men with me are her brother and cousin. You will treat them as *koda*. They are my friends as well as family and will be the tribes as well. Slade is my brother by my marriage. He and his cousin will honor all our laws. If you still take exception, we will leave. All I ask is for safe passage from your lands."

"We will see what happens. You will speak with me of your plans. Your brother will come too, as well as his cousin. We will talk."

"Yes, we will honor you," Stephen said as he watched his mother approach. "I would see to my wife first. She is terrified."

The chief waved his hand in the air stopping Stephen. "No, you will come with me. Your mother appears to have this in hand. We've much to speak about before we can make plans for you and your woman."

The chief turned stepping quickly toward his lodge, expecting the men to follow.

Stephen nodded at Slade and Jess. "Go, I'll be right behind you."

He was still determined to see to his wife. Her eyes were huge blue circles of fear. He needed to hold her, to touch every part of her to make sure she was not harmed.

His mother stepped forward, her hands stretched out. He hugged her. "It has been long years waiting for you."

She looked to Chauncey. "I will take your woman, your wife, to my lodge. She will stay there until the two of you are wed in the way of the People. Do not expect to sleep with her tonight. You will not share your furs with her. Come." She motioned to Chauncey who was pushing back against his chest, gripping him. Her fingers biting into his shoulders. She was shaking her head, burying her face against his chest.

"I don't want you to leave me," she sobbed. "Please Stephen."

Her tears brought moisture to the back of his throat. "We have no choice in this," he said prying her icy fingers away from his shoulders. Stephen set her away from him on the ground. She clung to his coat. "Go with Little Flower, my mother. No harm will come to you. Here, in this village you must call me Still Water Runs Deep. You must do everything my mother says. She will not lead you astray." His voice was harsh. He hoped and prayed she would remember she needed to obey his every command.

"I don't understand what she says."

"The two of you will figure out a way. She will be patient. You will be obedient. Little Flower speaks for me."

Chauncey was looking at him with huge blue eyes, her back stiff, her small chin in the air. In this instance, her stubborn nature would serve her well. Eyes that were still filled with moisture cried out to him. She stood her ground, small hands fisted tight at her sides. "I don't want you to leave me."

She seemed to gulp air as he stared at her. With no warning, she nodded. Stephen thought she might argue. An argument now would not suit well for her. He wished he could go with her. Not only did he hope to reassure Chauncey but he wanted to hug his mother again. Too many years passed since he walked in the same path as his mother.

Age was not taking its toll on her face though her hair was gray around the edges. A few lines spread out from the corners of her eyes as well as laugh lines around her mouth. Her vibrant green eyes, the color of green moss in the glade where he and Kane used to swim still seemed to see everything. She nodded then smiled at him when she took Chauncey's hand in hers. With slow steps, they walked toward the lodge where his mother lived. He would be there as soon as he could.

Chauncey didn't fight his mother. To Stephen she appeared to be walking in a daze. He was terrified for her. Still, she was with his mother. Little Flower would see through her fears, would ease her way. Feeling some reassurance where Chauncey's fate was concerned, he handed the reigns of his horse to a young man. The horse would be taken care of then left to pasture.

"Bring our belongings to my mother's lodge," he told the boys taking care of the mounts. Both Slade and Jess dismounted. They were cautious but didn't seem fearful. Slade's gaze didn't waver from his sister until the two women disappeared from view.

"Chauncey will be well taken care of," Slade said as if he hoped his words were not brokered in the form of a question. "She didn't look well. I've never seen her in such a state."

What did her brother expect? He doubted if Chauncey ever found herself stripped by women who meant her harm, by women she couldn't understand. To Chauncey this would be akin to being thrust into a foreign country. He nodded to Slade. "With my mother, yes. The other was a simple misunderstanding. We will be given a different lodge to sleep. My wife will be kept with mother until the ceremony of the People is performed. She knew to expect that but not the other. That was my fault. When we rode in together, I never thought the People would see her as my slave. It should not have been unexpected."

He'd been away from the People far too long. Away from their customs. He forgot. He understood most if not all white women who came to an Indian village had been captured. Their fate always rested in the hands of the women first, the men later when they wanted to make

236

use of them or claim them.

Stephen spoke with the chief for several minutes. The men sat in the chief's lodge. They smoked. Stephen was told they would be given a lodge where they could sleep, furs to keep them warm, a female slave to see to their needs. He was to keep his woman hidden away. The women were not going to accept her until they had no choice. If she dared show her face, it would go badly for her.

"When will you claim your woman? The sooner the better."

"Tonight, if Little Flower will allow her out of the shelter of her protection. She can be very possessive. She will not believe her son took proper care of his woman. She will want to chastise me until she sees my remorse," Stephen said thinking he didn't wish to spend a night by himself.

He'd grown used to her warm body lying next to his. His mother would scold him, tell him that he failed her. If she had her wooden cooking spoon, she would beat him on the head just as she used to do when she thought he misbehaved.

"You will pay a bride price to me before you wed your woman. She deserves your respect. By doing this you will earn the admiration of the tribe. The more horses I'm given, the greater the People's respect for her will be. There is a heard of horses near the canyon. Take your *Koda,* bring them to me and all will be well. Until then you will have to spend your nights alone. Your woman will sleep in your mother's lodge. While you are gone, I hope she can protect the woman you call your wife."

"She will."

"Your woman must understand our laws. As we speak here, until you wed her, she has no rights in this village. If she is left outside the lodge, the women have every right to chastise her in the way they see fit."

Stephen understood all too well something he'd previously taken for granted. "I have to speak with her tonight."

Fear for her rushed through him. He would be gone for several days. Anything could happen in his absence. He had to explain to her that Little Flower could only help her if she obeyed. She had to learn that she would not leave the confines of Little Flower's lodge unless she accompanied her.

"No. That would not be wise. Tomorrow I'll visit Little Flower along with your wife. I'll explain to her what you, her brother and cousin are doing. She will understand. She will learn and accept our ways while she is here." The chief let out a long slow puff of smoke.

The chief's English was limited. His mother's less than that. Chauncey would never understand what the man was trying to tell her. When he rode out without a word to her, she would feel abandoned, left alone and forsaken. If he told the chief what he thought about his lack of English words, he would be insulted. Just because he once lived among these people didn't make him one of them now. He'd lived as many years in the white world as he had in the Sioux.

"Just give me five minutes."

If he could beg and gain what he wanted, he would do so. He could not.

"No. I have spoken. It will be the way I say it is to be."

The next morning as Still Water Runs Deep rode toward the canyon flanked by Chauncey's brother and cousin, he was filled with dread. She would do something impulsive. The women would never allow her freedom to come and go. Even if all she did was look outside the lodge, that would be enough to condemn her. Chauncey was a prisoner. The chief would never tell her the exact words that would explain to her how she was being treated. He didn't have the English words to do so. He would never be able to lay down all the rules so she would understand.

"What will happen to Chauncey while we are away?" Slade asked as he rode beside him, his expression grim. "Is the situation dangerous for her? I fear she is too spontaneous to survive here by herself."

More life-threatening than he wanted to tell her brother. The women didn't like her. They especially didn't like the fact their play was brought to a very sudden halt last night. Pearl was among the women tormenting his wife. When they were younger the woman slept with both him as well as Kane. At one time, she hoped to wed Kane. Stephen had no idea if she harbored expectations toward him. One never knew. Pearl would seek revenge of some sort. He understood the fact by the way she looked at him.

"Yes, it could be very dangerous. She is not as impulsive as Lyssa. Still, she has a mind of her own. Has a set of values that cannot be compromised. If she believes she's been wronged, she might do anything."

Stephen looked to Jess for a reaction. There was only the slight nod of his head. "Chauncey is still willful and doesn't appreciate being told what to do. Mother can only protect her so far. If she chooses to break any rules set forth, she will be disciplined by the women of the village. While I could have explained these rules, there is no one else living in the encampment who has the words." Stephen realized that life would not go well for his wife while they were gone.

"If that is the case, we best hurry to this canyon for the horses."

Jess urged his mount to a faster pace. The others followed.

When they reached the canyon three days later well over fifty horses milled in the narrow ravine. They would be easy to catch. Corralling them for the long ride back to the village was a different issue. Some of these he meant to take back with him to the Lakeland ranch. He would gift the chief with ten of the best.

"Are all these meant for the chief? For the bride price?" Jess asked amazed that anyone would give so many horses to one man.

"He told me he would take five horses. I will give him ten. After that I spoke to him about more for Chauncey's father, Aric. It is all good. Whatever he doesn't take, I'll find some means to get them back to Maryland."

"That won't be easy," Jess said with a whistle. "A challenge I will look forward to. Best we get on with this."

"No, it won't be easy," Stephen agreed. "It will be well worth the effort when I best Kane though he most likely won't be there to see it. Do you suppose I should race them into the coral as Kane did then take Chauncey up on my steed to make love to her."

That sight would forever be etched in his mind. He meant to have Chauncey that way, sooner or later.

~ * ~

That night then into the next day, Chauncey waited for Stephen. He didn't come. No one could explain to her where he was. Buffalo Stalker, the chief of this tribe, sat down the morning before to talk to her. All she understood was that she was to stay inside Little Flower's lodge. She was to do whatever task Stephen's mother asked of her. That wasn't too difficult. She also understood that Stephen along with her brother and cousin left. Where or for what purpose, she didn't know. Sioux words eluded her.

She didn't understand why they left her alone here in this strange, foreign world. Over the morning she ground meal of some sort. She filled leather pouches with dried fruits and nuts. Little Flower showed her how to weave a basket. She kept busy. This wasn't the active life she was accustomed to. When it was time for the meal, she made biscuits with the grain she ground.

"Good!" Little Flower told her nodding and grinning at her as if surprised. "Still Water Runs Deep pleased with his wife?" she asked of her. "Make good wife. Feed husband's belly with biscuits."

It seemed Little Flower learned the English word for biscuit. While she learned the words for stay in the teepee. Hearing Little Flower say biscuit made Chauncey smile. She was also picking up a few words.

Chauncey nodded wishing the woman spoke a little more English. They communicated with their hands, pointing at things and either shaking the head for no or nodding for yes. "Still Water Runs Deep likes my biscuits. When will he come back here? When will he come for me? I don't like being left alone in this strange place."

She tried to speak with her hands. She wanted to leave the village. Understood they could not depart until the spring. She certainly couldn't leave on her own.

Little Flower frowned, her brows drawing together, her lips pressed close together as if in concentration. "Come back," she told her then held up four fingers. "Soon."

Chauncey guessed she meant four days would pass before Still

Water Runs Deep returned. She didn't think she could stand being cooped up in this lodge for four more days. Little Flower went with her when she needed to relieve herself. She accompanied her to the stream where they bathed. Other than those few times each day, Chauncey remained in the lodge. Buffalo Stalker brought venison on the third day. He came to dinner that night. To the approval of Buffalo Stalker, she made biscuits again.

There was a small pond where the water was still rippling around a few boulders. One couldn't stay in very long. The water was frigid. It reminded her of the quick bath she took in the pond one of the first nights they were traveling. She spent no more than five minutes in the water there as well as here. Haste mingled with fear, she ducked underwater to lather her hair with the soap she brought with her, using as little as possible in hopes the bar would last until they returned home.

The packs were taken off the pack horse and brought into Little Flower's lodge. She found her magnolia scented soap. Buffalo Stalker visited every day. He sat cross legged by the fire, speaking and gesturing with his hands. She understood Stephen left to hunt horses. He would gift Buffalo Stalker with five of the horses when he returned. The rest would go to her father. Her father didn't need a bride price for her. Chauncey would rather have his warm body next to hers, would rather here his laughter.

"Bride price?" she asked him, lifting her shoulders. "Why would you receive horses? You're not my father."

Chauncey had no idea if he understood. Between the words coupled with the hand gestures the man was as confused as she was.

He grinned, beaming his pleasure that she understood. "Bride price, has to pay a man to marry you. I will be your father since you have no one else." he said mimicking her words. "A good thing for woman. Show respect." He spoke in broken English coupled with the Sioux words she didn't understand. "Good for father if husband respects him." He waved his hands in the air gesturing toward himself as her father.

Well, she couldn't argue with his reasoning. Would he pay her father a bride price? He would have to be gone longer to find more horses, fifty of them if she remembered correctly was the number he would aim for. Still Water Runs Deep would never allow Kane to best him. She wasn't there the day Still Water Runs Deep and Kane rode into the Andrew's ranch though she heard numerous renditions of the tale. Kane was bold as well as audacious. He scooped his wife right off the ground wearing only his breechcloth. She wished she'd been there.

The third day, by midafternoon, Chauncey was restless again. Pacing the small circle that was the lodge, she wished for sunshine. She needed fresh air, at least a whiff. The smoke from the wood fire in the lodge settled in her lungs making her cough. Cooking smells clung to the buckskin dress she wore. The walls were beginning to close in around her. Her head pounded. She tugged in air that didn't want to obey, wrapping her arms around her. What little air she did manage fell in a lead weight into her lungs. Unable to stop herself, she moaned. Whimpered. Distressed by the confines.

Without thinking she rushed to the opening of the lodge. The need to run fiercely assailed her, seeping into her to torment. It was all she could manage to keep her feet planted in the lodge. Over and over again she heard Still Water Runs Deep's words coupled with the warnings from Little Flower. *Don't leave the lodge.* She wouldn't put one step outside but she had to see something besides the four walls surrounding her. She pulled the flaps apart, staring out into the sun kissed sky a few white clouds appeared. It was clear and cold as the very pits of hell but the fresh air filled her lungs. Relishing the moment, she closed her eyes. Two times she breathed deeply of the pine scented air. Two times she wished she was free to walk in the sunshine.

The shriek of fury sent her lashes flying upward, her body trembling. Ice chilled her spine. She was so shocked as well as confused she didn't withdraw into the tent. Instead, she looked around to see to the discomfort she felt.

Pearl stood in front of her, yelling at her, speaking to her in words she didn't understand, shaking her fists at her. Without further provocation, she found herself yanked from the lodge by her hair. As she dug in her heels, other women joined Pearl, all talking at once. For an instant her arms were pinned behind her back. A woman held a length of her hair in her hand and was pulling her in one direction. Another woman tugged her in a different direction. Her arms waved to keep her balance. Chauncey thought she would lose the hair the woman gripped so tight. She stumbled. They jerked her back to her feet. Cruel fingers dug into her arm. Chauncey thought for sure the women would drag her if she could not keep her balance.

She couldn't go with these women. They would hurt her. "No!" she cried out trying to resist, tugging backward. She needed Still Water Runs Deep. Needed Buffalo Stalker. "Little Flower! Little Flower! Buffalo...!" She could not see, the pain forcing her eyes closed. She had to open her eyes. Had to fight with all her strength. Her breaths were ragged excruciating gulps. Her scalp was on fire.

By now other women joined Pearl. They were pushing her and tugging her, talking about her. She heard her name, heard Still Water Runs Deep's name. Two women held her upper arms, keeping her upright. She fought hard, used all her strength against the women. Even with her resistance, they drug her through the camp. Buffalo Stalker stood at his teepee, his arms crossed over his chest. While his feet were braced apart, his expression was grim. He looked her over sending another wave of icy chills down her spine. He wasn't going to help.

He nodded to the women as if giving them approval for whatever they planned. "You should not have left your lodge, Still Water Runs Deep's woman. This is out of my hands." He held his hands palms open. "You disobeyed the rules." Once more he looked at her, his gaze roaming the length of her. "Still Water Runs Deep did not teach you your place. You show no respect."

She didn't understand any of his words. Knew though by the reaction of the women, the chief would not stop them. She stumbled again, down to her hands and knees. She sucked air. Her hands were scraped. Pearl jerked her to her feet, her hair ripping from her scalp. Tears slid down her cheeks. She tried to stop them.

The river loomed in front of her. Did they mean to drown her? Dear God, if she got away, she would swim. She would flee run as fast as she could. Where would she go in the middle of winter. The men of the village would hunt her down. Somehow, she would find Stephen. He would save her.

Now, the women were tearing at her doeskin dress. She tried to fight their hands. They jeered and held her arms behind her back. Just as the first time they meant to strip her of her clothes. Desperate to stop them, she shrieked at them to cease. Crying out to them to stop. It wasn't to be. Pearl jerked hard. She cackled her delight when the fabric ripped at one of the seams. The doeskin fell away from her. She tried to cover her breasts with her hands. They pulled them away then yanked until the dress pooled around her feet.

She was naked, bared to their gaze, to whatever horrible torture they planned. They circled her. There was nowhere for her to run. They jeered as if daring her to try to break through the solid circle of women. Stories she heard swept through her head. The brisk wind chilled her bone deep.

Suddenly, she found her wrists bound together then lifted high over her head.

Stephen, dear God where are you? Help me.

They tied her to a tree, her arms in the air, her back to them. A woman took her moccasins from her feet.

"What are you doing! Stop!"

She cried out when a lash whipped her back; another then another. Her back stung. Pain knifed through her. They were hitting her, flaying the skin from her back. Taking turns. Heat along with raging agony soared through her. She whimpered. Moisture stung the back of her throat. Tears slid down her cheeks. For as long as she could, she held herself rigid, fighting the searing pain, fighting to stay alert. The world spun. The earth moved. She jerked herself back to reality. She didn't want to faint. Didn't want the blackness to engulf her.

The beating went on and on. To keep from crying out in pain she clamped down hard on her jaw. She would not give them this win. She kept her eyes open. Someone would come for her. Buffalo Stalker saw the women take her. Little Flower would worry about her. Stephen's mother would look for her. With the slow passage of time, her body became limp as her mind ceased to focus. She hung by her hands, her knees on the ground, her body bent forward. Each breath she inhaled was a struggle.

For a time, she counted the lashes. One...two...three...twenty-four...thirty-nine...forty... At forty she lost count, her eyes dazed over with pain. She heard animal's scurrying beneath the bushes somewhere in the forest. Water rippled around the boulders in the small pool. A fish jumped. Wind dashed down from the snow-covered mountains.

Water was splashed into her face. Jerking awake, she heard the laughter of the women, the chatter as if they were deciding what else to do with her. After that the lash came down one more time. Pearl walked around her. With a length of her hair, she jerked her head up. The woman held a burning stick to her face. She spoke words that Chauncey didn't understand. The evil laughter, she comprehended. Pearl ran a nail down the side of her face, drawing blood.

Some woman told her no to the firestick. She heard her husband's name. Knew then that the only thing keeping the women from scaring her or branding her with the fire was the name of her husband. The lashes on her back were deep. They would brand her for all time.

"Let me go..." she breathed knowing the women would do what they pleased when they pleased. "I've done nothing to you. Deep Water Runs Deep will seek revenge."

When the lash hit her again, she lurched, arching her back so surprised they resumed the torture. How much longer would this go on. The women must be getting tired. They were taking turns wielding the whip. Every time she closed her eyes, frigid water was tossed into her face to keep her awake, to keep her feeling the pain. All she wanted was to fall into oblivion, to sleep, to die. She didn't care if she ever woke.

Burning heat assailed her. A woman ran her hand down her back then over her buttocks. Another spread her legs then ran her hand down her flesh to her feet. *What in God's name did they have in store for her now?* The women were beating her lower down her back, down her body where their hands explored. A fleeting thought flashed through her that she wouldn't be able to sit. If she survived, all she would be able to do would be to lie on her stomach. Her legs were not left untouched nor were feet. She wouldn't be able to walk.

Dear God, she didn't think she could live through much more of this. Still the beating went on and on.

Stephen, I'm sorry I never told you I love you. We never said those words. I was always afraid that you would reject my love. That you didn't love me. I did deceive you by following you when you told me to remain at home. You told me this would be dangerous. I should have listened. You were wise. I was foolish.

Oh, I know you care about me. I've always wanted a man to love me. Now, if I don't live through this, I'll never get the chance to tell you how much I love you. It was stupid of me to go against your wishes and follow you here. I guess I never believed a life with your family in the village could be this dangerous. I thought you would always be with me. Where are you? I need you. Little Flower said four more days. I don't even recall how many days ago she told me that. You went for horses, for my bride price. When you return you won't have a bride.

The women stopped. Frigid air caressed the wounds. They were talking, chanting then it seemed they ate and drank. What were they planning now? She didn't know. She wasn't even certain she cared any longer. Her arms, still held above her head, ached. Sleep seemed to take her despite the pain burning down her back all the way to the souls of her feet. The world turned dark then black.

More water spilled across her face. No! They were hitting her again. She felt as if lash marks were biting into wounds already inflicted. More attention was given to her feet. The soles burned, felt as if they were on fire. She felt blood trickle down her legs. Pain cramped her stomach. She writhed, crying out, shrieking. Oh God, she was losing the baby, Stephen's child. No...no...no!

Pearl hauled her to her feet after cutting the bonds that tied her to the tree. Her knees gave out. She slipped to the ground then was hauled once more to her feet. Water from the river was poured over her head. The cold night breeze whipped around her. Even though her body was on fire she was chilled to the bone. Her body continued to cramp, wave after wave rolling through her frame.

She was pushed and shoved, kicked in the stomach and ribs. She crawled trying to keep away from the feet. Pearl grabbed her by the arm, jerking her forward. Rocks cut into her battered feet. They walked and walked. It seemed as if she hobbled alongside the women for hours. After what seemed an eternity, she was thrust to the ground. Her face in the dirt, she breathed in the scent of the forest floor. She didn't know where she was. Couldn't hear the sound of the river. Lights from the village could not be seen. She stared into black darkness. Mercifully, her eyes closed. She tried to think of anything but the pain, the heat, and the cold the despair, her child was gone.

The women left.

Snow began to fall, light flakes at first. She always loved snow. Hugging her arms around herself, she tried for warmth. She had to leave. Had to get back to the village. Alone in the blackness, Chauncey didn't know if she should be thankful or terrified of this new situation. They left her in the forest, bleeding and alone. Horrified and freezing. Her wet doeskin dress was tossed on her. She tried to slip it over her head. It wasn't to be. The dress was cut, shredded into thin strips. The best she could, she wrapped the fabric around her, hoping that even as wet as it was it would keep her warm through the night.

If she stayed the night in the open, unprotected, she would die. She didn't want to die. She was blessedly numb. Couldn't feel her fingers or her toes. Perhaps that was good. Not being able to feel was good. Somehow, she needed to get back to the village to Stephen's mother. Looking to the sky, she found Polaris. The village was east of the river. That didn't mean she was east of the village. Though she didn't think she'd gone very far. They made her walk. Each step shot pain through her legs, tore more flesh from her feet.

Heading east, crawling on her hands and knees she moved. What seemed like an eternity passed before she saw the village, smelled the smoke from the cooking fires, saw the lights within the lodges. Her hair hung around her face. She tried to keep it from her eyes and from dragging on the ground.

Strong arms picked her up, cradled her. She cried out when those same arms touched her back. He moved her so he carried her as he might carry a sack of grain. She found herself tossed over his shoulder.

"You break rules."

It was Buffalo Stalker reprimanding her. Yes, she looked outside the lodge. She didn't deserve to be beaten and left to die alone in the woods. Chauncey found she was shivering hard, her teeth chattering.

"Little Flower!" he called out. "Little Flower! Come!"

She wondered if the man would have looked for her or if he would have left her all night in the forest. The man must have known what the women did to her. Little Flower must have wondered where she went.

You break rules.

The words reverberated in her head. Rules. Damnation, all she did was look outside. It wasn't as if she meant anyone harm. Little Flower was beside her now, chattering. The room swirled in an orange, red haze.

Buffalo Stalker must be explaining what he knew. Little Flower replied. She wanted to scream, to understand what was being said between the two of them. Telling them both this was a vendetta inspired by Pearl wouldn't help her situation. For some reason unknown to her the woman despised her.

She was both burning up as well as chilled bone deep, her body still cramping. Fire churned within her, threatening to scorch her, all of her even while her teeth were chattering. The chief lowered her to the furs. Little Flower removed what was left of the dress she wore.

Little Flower's wail of despair ripped through the lodge. She heard Still Water Runs Deep's name. For the longest time, she heard nothing more. Little Flower was rocking on her knees, her arms clasped to her breasts. Buffalo Stalker soothed her.

When she next opened her eyes, light shone into the lodge. She tried to sit. Fell back in blinding pain. Little Flower's voice reprimanding her filtered through to her mind. Everything seemed to swirl around her in a daze. All of her body ached. She tried to remember what happened. She didn't want to remember.

The women.

The lashes.

The frigid water.

"Stephen," she whispered wishing he was here that somehow, he returned. She didn't want to open her eyes. Didn't want to feel any more pain.

Her head pounded. She needed to rub her temples.

"Hush, now..."

Stephen. It was Stephen. He was here.

"You shouldn't move. How do you feel?" He ran a cold cloth along her back then down her legs. "I was terrified something like this would happen in my absence. You broke a rule, I've heard tell," the last was gritted out in a quiet angry voice. "Unfortunately, there is nothing I can do. You defied what we deem sacred. You were disobedient."

How did she tell him she did nothing wrong. It was Pearl who held the vendetta against her. She was guilty of nothing. Nevertheless, Stephen had preconceived notions about her.

"How long? How long have you been here? How long have I been asleep." She ran her tongue across her dry, cracked lips. Her mouth and throat were parched. She didn't think it was the next morning. Chauncey recalled Little Flower bathing her wounds, clucking over her injuries, spreading the healing salve. She remembered his mother trying to feed her broth until she finally kept the liquid in her stomach.

"I've been back three days. You were attacked two days before that as my mother tells me. I'm sorry. If we were to stay in the village for the winter, I had no choice. I had to seek out the horses. I will also have to go on hunting parties."

Closing her eyes, she wondered about choices. Over the last few months, she made a lot of terrible decisions. There was so much to consider. She didn't know if she regretted any of the decisions she made.

"When will we go home?" she blurted unthinking.

Chauncey didn't mean to bring this up so soon. They'd not been here very long. She wanted to leave. He wouldn't blame her for all that happened. At least she didn't think he would. He told her she broke the rules.

"When the winter snow thaws," he told her. "I'm going to put more of this healing ointment on you. Mother tells me it will leave no scars." He touched every part of her; her back, her bottom, her legs as well as her feet. When he finished, he wrapped her feet in soft cloth. "Don't walk. Not yet. You are not healed. If you need to go outside, I will carry you."

"So soon," she said weakly wondering if she would live that long.

Stephen was back. He would protect her. He told her he would leave on hunting parties. Who would keep her safe from Pearl then?

She heard his soft chuckle. "That soon, is as soon as it will be safe. I must go on a hunting party this afternoon. Little Flower will stay with you. The village needs meat. Don't think I'll be very long." He soothed her, the ointment was cooling on her heated skin.

"Not to worry," she told him. "Doesn't seem I can walk. Besides, you gave me the command not to walk. I will obey your every word."

He chuckled again then touched the tip of her nose. "I do like your spirit, love. After the hunters return, we will wed. As my wife, you will be safe then."

"Can't we do it before you leave?" her question sounded petulant. She understood all too well she wouldn't be safe from the women until they saw them as married. Even then she would have to stay clear of Pearl.

"As you say, you can't walk. Don't believe you can even stand."

She jerked when he kissed her on the bottom then her shoulders. "Stephen..." her voice wavered on a thin wail.

"Still Water Runs Deep," he corrected.

"That's hardly fair of you to...to..."

"Do my lips on your sweet little butt arouse you?" he asked as he kissed her again. "It arouses me. I can barely wait to make love to you. Little Flower tells me it will have to wait. "I'm sorry about the child."

At the thought, pain ripped through her. Until he reminded her, she forgot about the loss. "I feel so empty. I didn't even know I carried the babe." She breathed in deep then letting the events sift through her brain. For this moment she wanted to put all the sadness aside. "No, not today. Everything still burns. The stuff you are putting on me helps though. What do we have to do to be considered wed? I would try to stand. Mayhap you could keep me off my feet for long enough to convince everyone."

"No, we will wait until the time is right. Until you are whole again." He set his hand on her bottom, kissed her again. After that he drew the furs over her.

"If you leave me alone again, Pearl will kill me or she will scar me with a burning stick. She threatened me."

She heard the grimace in his voice, the hesitancy when he spoke. "What happened? I've heard very little of that night. None of the women are talking. No one else besides you understand what went on. While it's obvious they lashed you. All that happened after that until Buffalo Stalker found you on your hands and knees, naked except for a few scraps of fabric, is unknown. Except by you. None of the women will talk. I think some are embarrassed about what happened. They are still responsible."

"They made me walk into the woods. I couldn't. Most of the time they prodded me while I was on my hands and knees. Pearl yelled at me. Don't know what she said. They all left me in the forest. The night was pitch black. I didn't know where I was. I think they believed I would die. Every one of the women wanted me to die."

She told him the rest of the story. Told him about her guess as to where the village was. "I don't want to stay here without you."

"We've no choice but to remain here until the winter snows are no longer a threat. Even if the weather becomes unseasonably warm in late March or April there can still be a blizzard," he murmured, bending low to kiss her cheek.

"Will Jess and Slade go with the hunters?"

He didn't like the idea she had to live in fear. This was his village, his people. He grew up with them. They all, including the women, should respect his choice of a wife. "Jess is going. Slade will stay here to look after you. We will never leave you alone again. He and Little Flower are your only protection from the women. It seems Pearl has rallied most of them against you. Take all the rules with the seriousness they deserve. Please. You are no longer confined to the lodge. Still, you must take care. Don't go out without mother."

Oh, she would take every conceivable care. She would do nothing, not even glance out between the flaps of the lodge. Today, the vow would not be difficult to keep. Tomorrow, she might have more trouble.

"You coming?" Jess hollered. "The hunting party is ready."

"Take care."

Chauncey didn't understand what would happen next but she knew this wasn't over. Pearl hated her.

~ * ~

"What do you think will happen while we are gone?" Jess asked as they rode behind White Pony and Red Feather. "Will Chauncey be safe? Will we return home to find her beaten again?"

"I pray that she will remain safe. I didn't want to leave her alone. Buffalo Stalker insisted I go with the hunters. Next time, I will stay with her. He said that nothing would happen to my woman since she could not rise from the pallet of furs for days. She was too hurt to do so. There would be no disobedience."

"All that is true," Jess chortled. "I've known the girl her entire life. If there was trouble to be found, she and Lyssa found it. Chauncey is not so forward as my sister. Most likely for the afternoon, there will be little she will do besides sleep."

"Today, my wife cannot rise off the pallet. Tomorrow?" He lifted his shoulders, his brows furrowing together. We will be here for more months than I care to count. She will be well enough in a week or so." Stephen thought about all that transpired so far on this journey west. He was horrified she lost their child. A child he'd only guessed at its existence. He missed the babe even before he could get to know his child.

"In the eyes of this village you will be man and wife soon. That fact should protect her from Pearl along with the other women."

They rode in silence. It wasn't deer they found that day but three beautiful elk. The men returned to the village in triumph just before dark. Still Water Runs Deep would not be called upon to hunt for another week or two. He would spend the time with Chauncey.

Before he could reach the lodge, Pearl stopped him, drew him away from the other lodges. "I have to speak with you."

Her eyes were wide, dark brown. She rubbed her hand along his arm.

Stephen yanked his arm away from her. He didn't like to think he'd made love to her not once but multiple times. That was a long time ago. Life was different now. He growled, his voice harsh. "Because you are my wife's enemy, you are also my enemy. What have you to say for yourself, woman? You almost killed her, murdered the woman I love. She lost our child!"

He spoke severely understanding the woman would continue in her ways if she wasn't put in her place. Even then Stephen wasn't certain he could do anything to stop her.

"She broke the rule. There was only one," Pearl said, her voice cracking with her anger. Her face was a mottled red, her eyes dark pools of hatred. "I didn't want to talk about your wife."

"You tried to kill her." Stephen wondered if she would have the audacity to try to deny that fact. "She almost didn't survive. You knew she was important to me. Why would you do such a thing?"

Her chin tilted up. Her dark eyes blazed with her fury. "She is *wasichu*. She is not good enough for you, Still Water Runs Deep." She leaned into him, rubbing her breasts against his arm. "I would make you a much better wife. I understand the way of the People. I would never humiliate you."

Revulsion centered in the pit of his stomach. He pushed her away. She stumbled then righted herself. His hand slashed through the air. "You, woman, are not good enough for me? Don't ever speak ill of my wife. No, you would never survive in the English world I plan on returning to. While no one would try to murder you, you would be ostracized. What you don't know is that I've come to love my wife. She means everything to me. By your actions our child died."

"She is not your wife!" Her hands were tiny fists at her sides.

He tried to calm his raging emotions. Her stiff shoulders and proud jutting chin made it difficult. "In the way of the world I plan to live in for the rest of my life, she is my wife. Soon, as soon as she can stand long enough to wrap her in my furs, she will be my wife in the way of the People. I've delivered the bride price to Buffalo Stalker who is acting as her father. You will do nothing more to harm Chauncey. If something happens to her, you and only you will suffer the consequences."

"You will regret what you do."

Stephen found himself shaking his head at the woman's audacity. "Never. Chauncey is everything I've ever wanted in a woman. There are no regrets nor will there ever be."

"You used to want me," she said peevish, moving so her breasts swayed. "I was the woman you took into the bushes. I was the woman you eased yourself with."

"I wasn't your first or even your fifth lover. You were the woman all the young bucks eased themselves with. You're a whore, Pearl." When she started to protest, he placed a finger to her lips. "You cannot refute that you slept with Black Thunder or White Feather as well as Red Pony. I know there were others. Don't lie to me. No one wanted you for a wife because you slept with any man who looked at you with lust in his eyes."

She turned away from him before turning back. With a lift of her shoulders, she stared at him, "You don't know if it is true."

He tossed his head back to yowl with the humor of it all. "I saw you with Kane, Black Thunder to you. I saw you in the bushes with White Pony, your legs spread while he pumped his seed into you. I heard you moan with your pleasure. The men bragged when they had you. Talked about your breasts as well as other part of you. A man doesn't want a woman such as you for a wife. He would never know whose child you carried."

Disgusted, Stephen walked away from her. Heard her curses. When he stepped inside his mother's lodge, he inhaled a large draft of air. Chauncey was right. Pearl hated her. He was afraid the winter would be very long.

~ * ~

Pearl lay back on the furs while the man thrust himself inside her body. She didn't like this man. He was old. He smelled. His teeth were yellowed, some rotten. Nonetheless, he promised to give her what she wanted for the use of her body. She enjoyed sex even with a man such as this one. There was always the second man. The one with the broader shoulders and leaner hips. She would give herself to him too.

The two men might need her help. That was easy also. She knew men who would do anything for the right price. The man he came with was stronger more virile. He was a trapper, knew the wilderness. She would give herself to him for a price they would both appreciate. Perhaps these two men wouldn't need additional help.

She smiled when she thought of what would await the *wasichu* woman. Still Water Runs Deep would come to her for solace when his woman was gone. He would think she abandoned him for the men she was going to hire. All the signs would indicate she left with these two men willingly. Still Water Runs Deep would never come after her. Having betrayed him, she would no longer be his woman.

While she didn't have the coin to pay the men, she didn't mind using her body to purchase what she wanted. A woman had to use whatever means she could to get what she wanted. All men wanted and needed was sex.

"What are you smiling about?" The man asked as he rolled onto his back, pulling her with him. She lay on top of him, straddling him. "You look all sweet and soft but that smile tells me something different. What are you plotting?"

"Revenge. I'm thinking about revenge and just how sweet it can be."

She purred when the man touched her nipple with his thumb, running it back and forth across the tip. Pearl learned to speak passable English years ago. She loved the fact she heard and understood all Chauncey's pleas. That night she understood all she said, all she cried out.

"You should take care. If you reach for the stars all can backfire," His lips possessed her breast sucked until she moaned with her pleasure. "We will do what is necessary. I will have that woman as my slave."

His tongue, licked, flirted, then took possession of her other breast. She arched into him. Stephen was right. She was a whore. She loved men and the way they made her feel. Her fingers wound into his hair as she whimpered at the onslaught.

"Lie still, sweetheart. I don't want you to move. Just open your legs for me. Want to see you," his voice was harsh, grating against her ear. He spread her legs again. Thrust into her. He pumped and heaved until he spilled his seed one more time inside her body.

"I would that you gave me pleasure too," she told him as her hands ran down the length of his back squeezing his butt.

He wasn't her first choice for a paramour. In fact, at this moment she believed this would be the last time she let him take her. The man was a selfish lover. He only thought about his pleasure.

He was too old, too wrinkled. His breath too fetid for her liking. She could do better than this man. Indeed, she would when Chauncey was no longer part of Still Water Runs Deep's life.

"Pleasure is for men, not women. It is your job to be subservient, to open your lovely thighs for me. To touch yourself if I tell you to." He rolled over. In a few seconds he was snoring.

"You satisfied?"

The second man stood above her. He watched them. She liked that also. "Would you like a real man to take you now?"

She sat up. Pearl smiled then reached her arms into the air. "Will you give me pleasure?"

"If you are good, really good, sweetheart, I will give you the moon as well as the stars."

"Yes."

"In that case I'll consider it."

Chapter Nine

The winter was mild. Spring came with the melting of the snows and the blossoming of the first wildflowers to burst forth from beneath the canopy of white. Stephen stood near the river that ran through camp. His arm was wrapped around Chauncey's waist. She leaned into him, her body pressing against his. She healed well. They were married in the way of the People. He was pleased most of the village accepted her.

"Are you happy that it's spring?" he asked giving her increasing waist a little squeeze before running his hand higher to cup one swollen breast.

He smiled down at her. She wouldn't be able to see the pleased grin that was meant for her. She was staring east in the direction they would travel soon. He understood more than anything she wanted to leave the village. Leaving, for Stephen, was bittersweet as he understood he would never return. He would never again hug his mother.

"Yes, it's confusing though that Pearl disappeared. Where do you think she went? I can't imagine why." After voicing her question, Chauncey shuddered.

Stephen understood Chauncey's fears. She still woke in the middle of the night screaming for him. Her fears were real and they stayed with her. His thumb grazed the covered nipple. She inhaled a sharp breath.

"We should not think about Pearl. She is a woman who will always manage to land on her feet. I've not dismissed the fact she might return at any time. Neither should you."

Stephen didn't want to admit to Chauncey that he was also worried. Pearl was not the type of woman who would give up, who would fade into the past. She told him she did everything she did to Chauncey for revenge. That motive wouldn't just go away. What she planned though mystified him.

"As you say," Chauncey said, her head pressed against the breadth of his chest. "I will constantly watch over my shoulder."

Stephen didn't have any reason to believe those were words his wife meant. She said them with a note to her voice. "I'm serious. Where Pearl is concerned, you should take care. I don't want you to go to the stream or anywhere else alone. Preferably you should only go with me."

"Is that a command?"

She turned in his arms slanting him a saucy look. His fingertips trailed across her collarbone.

He appreciated the way she shivered at his caress. At this instant, he had ideas. "You are not as afraid as you once were. That is good. Don't get over confident. That would be bad."

His questing fingers found their way beneath the top she wore. He encountered soft silken flesh. He wanted to rid her of the blouse, suck her breasts in his mouth so deep she would cry out with the pleasure.

"No...should I be?"

She touched his lips with a finger as if asking for a kiss. His tongue darted out to meet her finger tip.

He wasn't going to kiss her until she understood the danger he felt. She wasn't to take this calm for granted as if it would last forever. "I feel it deep in my bones. Don't know if you can understand. You should not be afraid. You should be very careful. There is something brewing. It's as if I can smell it on the wind, taste the danger to you."

"The weather is wonderful."

Her eyes flashed with wicked intent.

He understood what she was about. Perhaps she wished to think of something more pleasant than Pearl. "Weather in the Rockies can turn in the blink of an eye."

"Pearl is gone."

"She can come home. The other women..."

"Their leader is gone. A few of the ladies I've become quite fond of. Believe they might defend me this time around."

The sensitive hollow behind her ear beckoned to him. "There cannot be a second time. Dear God, I almost lost you. Did lose our child.

258

This can never happen a second time."

Once more he felt the terror of that night. Felt the despair when he learned the baby was gone. The child he would never get to know. The child that was never named. They didn't know if the babe was a boy or a girl.

Chauncey set her hand on his chest. "You are frightened? That surprises me." Her eyes were wide, concern so very evident. "I've done nothing to make her so angry. She should not feel as she does."

"Apparently, you are the victim. From what I've garnered from the other ladies, it is Kane along with myself who she is angry with. Pearl is taking her fury out on you. We left her when she thought she was special to us. God, how can a woman who gives herself with no thought to any man who comes her way be special to anyone?"

That was something he didn't understand. Didn't know if he ever would.

"So, it is your fault!" She laughed dancing away from him.

He watched her move. She was graceful, her second pregnancy just beginning to show. Her lovely breasts so tender and sensitive, he wanted to howl his delight. He figured she was about three months along. She didn't have trouble conceiving. He supposed they should talk about how many children she would like. At some point, they would need to take precautions.

Stephen followed. He wished he dared make love to her here on the green grass near the river. Anyone could venture into their private world. He wished he didn't fear for her life. If he didn't tumble her to the ground right here, he could take her farther into the forest. Beneath the shaded canopy of trees, he would make love to his wife.

She'd taken her shoes off. Her feet were healed though there were still a few scars on the soles. Stephen knelt beside her, taking her small feet in his hands. With his fingers he massaged the tender flesh.

She pulled back resisting the attention. "You're tickling me..." She laughed, giggling as he continued.

His sigh was one of loss. It wouldn't do for him to let down his guard. When they returned to his home outside London there were several places where he would make love to his wife. "We should get back to the lodge before mother sends out search parties. She is wary about your health as well as mine," he murmured, his voice soft.

Her feet were small. They fit nicely into the palms of his hands. He wanted to kiss her delectable toes then suck on each one until she squirmed. Later tonight in his lodge he would do whatever he wished. He would kiss her everywhere. He would open her legs. Kiss her soft petals. They would be safe from any intruder. He could strip her of all her clothing with no fear of the chill she might take.

"It's still early," she murmured as she leaned back on her elbows, thrusting her breasts toward him.

Little minx. She knew what she did to him.

"Not too early for this."

He ran his hands the length of her legs reaching beneath the doeskin dress she wore. His mother made it for her during her convalescence. It was adorned with beads. Both the shirt as well as the skirt were fringed. The gown was white. He insisted she wear it during the ceremony when he would claim her as his wife. Since then, her mother fashioned two more dresses for her. He liked the gowns. It was easy for him to find her tender, sensitive places, to touch her in the heat of her sex. He loved the fact her unfettered breasts always moved with her. To watch her was heaven to his soul. His hands found the sensitive places on the insides of her thighs. "Part your legs wider for me."

She shivered with the contact that was arousing him as much or more than it was Chauncey. Her body lurched. He continued his wicked assault, touching, flirting with secret dark places meant for him alone. "Stephen, you cannot do this here."

She was telling him this when her body was responding as well as encouraging him. Her hips arched. She did as he asked.

"Why not?" His questing fingers came between her legs as he worked her dress higher on her thighs, sightseeing tender territory. One hand rested on her belly while the other stroked her, found her slick, damp with her arousal. "You're wet. Hot. Soft."

"People..." she gasped for air as he boldly thrust two fingers then three within her satin core. He moved slowly watching her eyes darken with her passion.

"People?"

He cocked an eyebrow upward speculating what she would tell him next. Encouraging him, she moved her thighs farther away from each other, giving him more opportunity to explore, to seduce. He wished he could put his mouth there where his fingers were. "You want your pleasure. I think you like this. You are so damp and hot. Nod if I'm right."

Her eyes assumed a dreamy appearance. She moved her head for him a small hiss of air into her lungs followed. "You know I do. Stephen..." She drank in another deep breath of air as his questing fingers found more erotic places to caress. She arched bringing him more pleasure. "That doesn't mean...oh!" She moaned. Her body bucked.

"You are always ready for me," he spoke softly, smoothly. "You want me inside you, all of me so deep I'll touch your womb."

"Always," she panted, her fingers curling into his shoulders then traveling higher to wind into the length of his hair. Her head tilted back. The pulse at the base of her neck thundered delightfully. He touched the spot with his lips, sucked and nibbled. Caressed more until the sensitive spot reddened.

He flashed a grin her way while he thought again of burying himself deep inside her. As he looked around the small clearing, he understood his pleasure would have to wait. He didn't want to be surprised with his buckskins at his knees. The climax quickly coming her way was close. He could tell by her eyes the mercuric sensations were building. It would not be long before she cried out her frenzy, the unrelenting explosion of feelings.

"Doesn't mean what?" he queried as he watched her moisten her lips with her sweet pink tongue.

He wanted to taste her, every part of her, plunder the sweet essence of her. The tiny jewel that brought her to ecstasy was damp and swollen with anticipation of what was to come. He wanted to use his tongue on that very place, suck so hard that the contact would send her flying toward the heavens. Feel her body rippling in waves. Splintering. Wished he dared. Instead, he stroked, flirted, touched upon her sweetness until her whimpers and mewls of pleasure grew and grew.

"That..." She swept her lips again with her tongue leaving a trail of moistness in its wake, a path he could not ignore. "I...that...you should...Stephen," she cried out as he continued the assault on her person.

"Yes, call out my name love. Now open your beautiful eyes for me. I want to watch you shatter into a million pieces of delight. It's about to happen. I can tell. Let it go. Trust me."

Her hands were still braced on his shoulders. She was panting with her need. He had her exactly where he wanted her. "Oh...God...oh! Stephen!"

The pleasure detonated in her lithe body, sending her to unparalleled heights. Her body clenched around his fingers. She closed her eyes. Her forehead now resting on his chest as she was nearly there, nearly consumed with the glorious need, nearly at that point where she would lose all control of her body.

"Look at me, Chauncey."

He was staring at her. He wanted to control when she came. Needed to prolong this sweet ecstasy she was experiencing. He pulled his fingers nearly out of her. He saw the dismay in her eyes. With slow strokes, he moved his fingers in then out, in then out. He felt her core clamping around him, kissing him, pulsing her woman's pleasure telling him she loved what he did. He felt the tremors grow, faster, harder, higher. That was how he moved his fingers inside her. God, he wanted his sex to be deep in her core.

He could resist the sirens call of her lips no longer. His mouth molded on hers, framed her lips with his, while he continued his onslaught of her senses. He pillaged and raided the depth of her core. Inside her lips, his tongue moved in the same ardent pattern as his fingers. She was beside herself with the raw vibrant passion he orchestrated.

Good Lord, he needed his member to be inside her, buried deep, feeling the exotic strength of her passion, of the magic that was Chauncey. He saw the strained expression on her beautiful face. Saw the lines of tension that always formed just before she reached the peak just before the explosion of her beautiful body. Her head was thrown back.

Knew when she arched and her body stiffened, she would soon reach that climax he was sending her to.

"Let it go, sweetheart. Don't hold anything back."

She cried out again and again as it seemed she did as he said. Until her supple young body slowed, the tremors diminishing, he continued a gentle assault inside her. When she collapsed against him, he held her close. Listened to the raspy breaths she inhaled then exhaled.

"Stephen..."

"Yes?"

"You did it to me again."

He pushed back sweaty, damp hair from her face. Watched her eyes, beautifully dazed by the moment of raw passion she experienced in his arms. "You were marvelous, sweetheart. Should we try this again in our lodge after our evening meal with mother? I want to taste all of you. Want you to taste all of me. Wish to suck on that tiny jewel that is buried deep in your woman's petals until you scream. Will you do that, Chauncey? Put your mouth, your lips on my sex?"

"I don't think I can look at your mother. I'm certain she will know what we've been doing."

She was scarcely breathing, hardly able to open her eyes. She thought of his mother's reaction if she knew what they just shared.

He hooted. His mother would be delighted. "Because that dreamy expression in your eyes will always give you away, love? Because you are embarrassed by the wonderful pleasures we share? You will have to look at her if you wish to eat. We have nothing, no food in our lodge."

She could hide nothing. He wanted naught more than to forget the meal they were obligated to attend. Spiriting her to their lodge and burying himself inside her hot, satin depth was his soul intent. His breath heaved. He would be thinking about that for the duration of his dinner.

"This is all your fault."

She sat up straight now, trying to adjust her skirt. His hands were in her way.

He needed to gaze on for a few more minutes before he allowed her to cover herself. The skirt was above her thighs. He could see her, her secret places that he just caressed. The dampness between her legs from her nectar, glistened in the remaining light. "True." He was running his hands along the inside of her thighs again, knowing he could bring her more pleasure.

There was no time. They were expected.

"You are wicked, a very wicked man, Stephen Wilkes. What should I do with you?"

She tried to bring her legs together. His hands and forearms were keeping her from doing so. Even now, he touched her belly, believing she carried his child. Their second child. He vowed nothing would happen to her, or their babe; never again. He would keep her close. If all went as planned, they would be home before the birth.

"I want to taste your budding, pink nipples. Wish to hold them within the depth of my mouth. Suck. Nibble. What do you say? Would you like me to do so?"

He told her, staring at her breasts that were even now rising and falling with each harsh breath she inhaled. While he touched them earlier, he couldn't see them behind the doeskin.

"Well..." she paused for air, staring at his crotch, smiling a siren's smile as she ran her sweet pink tongue along her soft lips.

The dampness left behind beckoned to him. "I want to lick and nibble then flirt with your shaft until your eyes cross. I want to suck your member deep into my mouth until you moan and heave with all the pleasure I give to you. Would you enjoy the moments of gratification from having your cock in my mouth?"

He sucked air.

She smiled when his breath caught in the back of his throat. His woman knew what she was about. With words she seduced him. Understood all that would please him. He taught her very well. Though at the moment he was in deep pain. He ached. Throbbed. Blood pounded. "I promise. When we are alone, you will be able to do what you wish. You will have me tonight. After dinner you can have *carte blanch* with my man's body. I'll allow you to do whatever strikes your fancy. Kiss me. Flirt with me, caress all of me, dally wherever pleases you, especially the most sensitive places on my man's body." Again, his voice cracked.

"What are we waiting for?" she asked as she tried to stand, his hands on her knees stopping her from rising.

He didn't want to stand. He was as hard as the boulder she sat on. Dear God, he wanted her to sit on him, to ease him. It would take only a moment for him to send his seed pulsing and writhing into her body. He swallowed, the sensations rising to the forefront of his head. There would be time for that later. He inhaled several hard-earned breaths of air, trying to calm his raging manhood. Nothing seemed to work.

"For me to put your moccasins on your tiny feet, unless you wish for me to carry you through the village."

He would like nothing better than to carry his woman. It would show sign of possession. To any one questioning her status it would help the women's refusal to acknowledge his true relationship with her. She was his wife.

"Do what you must."

She held each foot out after he removed his hands then pulled her dress down so it hung below her knees.

For a few seconds, he stared wistfully at her. Trying for a lighter mood, "I will."

He winked at her, grinning, thinking of the night to come, the two of them both naked beneath his furs, the light of the cook fire casting a warm glow.

When he carried her into the lodge, Jess and Slade were there. Once the meal was served the discussion became one of their return to civilization. Many things were decided that night. Stephen was relieved to be leaving the village behind. His sojourn here had been tumultuous. He'd feel better if he knew where Pearl was as well as what the woman was up to. She'd been gone two weeks tomorrow.

"We will leave in one month," Stephen said drawing a path they would take in the ground. I want to stay clear of most of the villages. With our pack horses, we won't have need to stop at trading posts. The fifty-five horses we are traveling with will prove a temptation to thieves. Red Feather and White Pony will go with us. I'm not certain why but they are eager to see more of the country. I feel as if they see an end to the life they know and understand. Red Feather once spoke of traveling with me to England. We will see," he murmured while he looked to Jess and Slade for an opinion.

"It will be good for them to see how white people live," Jess said thoughtfully as he sipped a cup of coffee. "Just as it was good for me to see how they live. Sometime we will all have to live in peace. At least I pray that it is so."

His mother didn't seem at all pleased at the topic of her son leaving the village. She'd known from the start he wouldn't stay. This was merely a visit before he made his home in England. She seemed to understand they were organizing his departure. When it came time to retire for the night, she hugged him fiercely. She spoke to him. He told her yes, they would leave soon.

Stephen thought that perhaps they should speak of Pearl though the thought left a rancid taste in his mouth. "Do you have any idea where Pearl has gotten herself off too?" He looked directly at Red Feather and White Pony. "She is a danger to my wife. I would know where to look for her. Don't want any surprises."

White Pony cleared his throat speaking in the Sioux language. "I was told she travelled with two men. One was older, one a trapper who seemed to be in control of the situation, the leader. He told the others what to do as well as when."

"Did she go willingly? I would not have any woman forced." *Even Pearl.*

When it was mentioned that one was older, Stephen's gut tightened. No, Greeley wouldn't have the audacity or the knowledge to travel this far north. The man had been warned, threatened to stay away from Chauncey. Greely would never be able to find his way through the forest or live doing so. Though Stephen understood the man would still want revenge. If he found a way, or someone who knew the way, he might try anything despite the threat to his life.

"Seemed so," Red Feather told him. "She was laughing and talking in English. I did not comprehend Pearl could speak English so well. She sells herself to the men. Spreads her legs for what they will give her. It is something she has done before. The woman has no shame."

"What did they look like?" Stephen asked, needing to set his fears to the back of his mind. "Would help me sort this out if I knew."

"The older man was thin except for a paunch, white bushy eyebrows, white hair. The other was broad of shoulder, lean of hip. He had light hair the color of sand. His eyes were steel-gray...hard. Pearl sat in front of the younger man, her thighs spread for any exploration he might want, her dress around her hips. While he fondled her, she laughed, encouraging him. He took what she offered."

"She is bartering herself to these men for some reason. To what purpose remains to be seen. Nonetheless, I've a bad feeling."

Stephen stared at Chauncey. She didn't know what was said. He would have to tell her tonight when they were gorged with their pleasure. The fact that the fear would increase didn't sit well with him. "All we have are guesses. Pearl might have decided there was nothing for her at the village."

"We will have to wait and see what transpires," Jess said speaking in a whisper, his gaze fastened on his cousin. "Pearl does not need rescuing. I'm certain she is more than happy with the attention of two men heaped upon her. From what I understand she is voracious. Her sexual desires unquenchable."

"She might have decided she was tired of life here," Slade said. He too seemed worried about Chauncey. "She might need to move on. This could all be innocent. Perhaps we are making more of this situation than we should."

Stephen waved a hand in the air, slashing it as the anger as well as terror grew. "None of you believe that. The vendetta she has against Chauncey is strong. She will return to get her vengeance. I'm certain of that fact."

"She would not let fer feelings go so easily," Jess said as he shifted his gaze from Stephen to Chauncey. "A woman who acted with such malice would not give up. We need to stand guard. Someone needs to be with Chauncey at all times."

"You're right. It's obvious. Pearl is selling herself so she can hire these men to hurt Chauncey," Red Feather said. "She has given her favors away before though she's never sought to have another person hurt by her actions. Pearl has always sought something for herself, a pretty bauble, a new dress, shoes. What would we find if we searched her lodge, I wonder?"

Stephen heard enough guesses. He stood holding his hand out to his wife. He needed to hold her in his arms, to reassure her that all would be well. He wasn't at all certain how to make everything right in her mind, "Come. We've things to speak of in private." Things to do. She had a promise to fulfill before the night was finished. His thoughts turned to the intimacies they would share soon.

Chauncey rose. Dusting off her skirts she slipped her hand into his. She had more calluses now than she did when he first met her. Even though she would soon be increasing, expanding, and swelling in many intriguing places, she was thinner. Pearl stripped her of her spontaneous courage. At one point, he was so afraid for her he'd wanted that to happen. Now that it was gone, he wished for a place and time when he could have all of her back. This place stripped so much life from her. He could not have foreseen that happening. Though when he told her no, she could not travel with him, he'd been afraid for her. All his fears came to fruition. Though he never expected another woman to be the seat of her terror.

During the short walk to their lodge, they moved in silence. Darkness descended early in the mountains. The air was chilled with a brisk wind. "There will be snow on the ground tomorrow. We will be cozy beneath our furs."

She turned to him, placed a finger to his lips. She was smiling at him. It was the first smile since he brought her pleasure this afternoon. Now, she flirted with him, teased him with his words. "You know this how?"

She was grinning as if she understood some private joke. He expected she understood more than she let on.

"Are you mocking me? My knowledge of the mountains?" He asked knowing that if she ever told him she wished she had not followed him, he would never say 'I told you so.'

"No...yes...maybe a little. You say things sometimes. You have this way of making them sound as if the words are gospel. Why I always believe you, I don't understand. I wonder how you know these things."

He lifted his shoulders a small movement, wishing he were

wrong. He was afraid they were in for more than one night of the white stuff. The wind smelled cold, the scent one of a blizzard that would keep them secluded for a long time. Blizzards would often cover the plains and mountains in snow. He meant to make his intuition clear to Chauncey. "The scent of moisture is in the air. It is too cold for that moisture to come down from the heavens as rain. So...it must be snow or sleet. Either way we will lie abed tomorrow in my furs. I can make love to you all morning or until mother taps on the flaps of our lodge and wants us to come for breakfast."

Stephen opened the flaps of their lodge, letting her lead the way. Inside, he pulled her into his arms, kissing her soundly, deeply wishing for more than just the kiss. They would need to speak first of Pearl. The one man's description spoke of Greeley. The other man resembled a trapper Jason told him about who wandered through these parts from time to time. The man was tenacious. He knew the woods along with many of the tribes. He spoke several languages. He traveled through Indian territory with freedom. Was respected as well as trusted as a man of his word. Pearl might have known him before this. Perhaps she sold herself to the man at other times.

"Sit down while I stoke the fire. If I'm right about the change in weather, we will need a warm fire through the night."

He wasn't worried about staying warm. What he thought constantly about was Pearl coupled with what she was planning. "You understand we have many things to talk about. I don't know how much you understood..."

"Not much," she said. "Yes, I know you spoke of Pearl and that she was gone from the camp. I've noticed her absence for quite some time. What is she doing? It cannot bode well for me. Can it?"

Stephen wished to get back to the topic of the fire and staying warm. He would rather they could talk about Pearl later. He smiled at her wishing they were in his home near London. The fact she was in constant danger was not something he liked to explore. There was no other choice.

She didn't wait for him to speak of Pearl. It seemed now that the name was mentioned, she didn't want to talk about the woman either.

"You will keep me warm tonight." She smiled at him though she appeared wistful. "If it is snowing the day we are to leave, we won't leave."

He thought she might be questioning. She was not. Her words were as much a statement of fact as anything. "We won't. We will have to wait until the weather clears. Though, as far as the weather is concerned, there will be no guarantees. We will travel as the tribe does. Instead of our lodges, we will have tents to sleep within."

"How long? We will have to wait until the snow melts," her voice wavered as she parroted his words. She looked toward the flaps.

Stephen understood all the reasons why Chauncey didn't want to wait. "What is wrong?" He sat down next to her, pulling her onto his thighs. Stephen was certain this had something to do with Pearl.

"I don't like to say the words when this was your home. When you love these people, for me to think unkind thoughts is reprehensible. I would have you know that if not for..."

"Pearl." He spoke the hated name for her.

"Yes, Pearl, the other women also. Pearl could have never done the things she did to me without their help, their approval. When I was naked and hurting their laughter reverberated in my soul. I heard what you said, what you and my brother's talked about. It's Greeley, isn't it? He's come for me. With Pearl's help, he will find a way to take me from you. I will kill myself before I let him touch me." Her hands fisted on his chest, her lips a thin ferocious line.

"You speak our language better than I thought." He paused for a few seconds stroking her hair. "You will not think thoughts of killing yourself. You hear me? I won't have it. I will keep you safe."

"Your mother taught me to understand what she was saying and in return I taught her. You have no idea what it would do to me if he forced me. Don't make promises to me you might not be able to keep."

He smoothed hair from her face, ran his knuckles down her cheek then down the long column of her neck. His hands lingered on the pulse point, delighted with the frantic beat. "I want you, now."

He didn't want to speak of these ugly men, men who took whatever they pleased believing it to be their right.

"Not until you tell me if what I heard is correct."

"Your guesses are the same as ours. We cannot be certain and neither can you. We must proceed one small step at a time."

~ * ~

Chauncey shuddered at the thought that Greeley came for her. Cringed that his grudge went so deep he would risk his life. She recalled the one time he touched her, the shudders of revulsion that coursed through her. He was a mad man, crazy. For the sport of it, he enjoyed hurting women. Even with this trapper helping him, she didn't think they would find her without Pearl's help. Pearl would lead them straight to her. The woman would laugh when they captured her, forced her to their will. She would laugh even harder when the men hurt her. She couldn't let that happen. She would fight with everything inside her.

"What does she want with me? I've naught done anything to her. She's hated me from the first moment she set eyes on me."

Chauncey wished she'd never met Pearl. While she understood jealousy, Pearl would never mean anything to Stephen. Wasn't this carrying rejection too far? In the distant past, Stephen only used her as other men in the tribe used her. She was a whore.

"That is a guess. From what you've told me about the man, Greeley wanted you for his sex slave. He needed for you to take Beth's place. He blamed you for her departure. I believe that is Pearl's intent, to see you as his slave, with no options. The woman would take great joy in watching you humbled. That is what she did to you that night. She shamed you. Brought you to a level below her. How the two of them met then came together, is strange. They are kindred spirits where you are concerned. Was all this a terrible coincidence? We believe Pearl is selling herself to them so those men will help her get what she wants, revenge against you. She wants you to vanish."

"What she probably doesn't understand is that all she needed to do was lead Greeley my way. As to the other man, what would he think to gain?" she gritted the words out, both furious as well as terrified. Deep in her heart, she also understood what the man must have been promised

271

by Greeley. They would both force her.

"That won't happen." Stephen said with strength in his words. "I won't let anything happen to you, love. You're mine. You belong to no one else." His beautiful green eyes, darkened with passion as he touched her, caressed her, sifted his long lean fingers through her hair. "Lift your arms," he spoke his words tender in the night air. It seemed he wanted to do the things he talked about earlier. "I want to get this off you. Need to see you wearing nothing at all. Wish to feel you naked and pressed against me."

Earlier, she taunted him with suggestive words. She could recite every one as she memorized the sculpted lines of his dear face. Words that seduced and charmed him. Chauncey didn't know if she could do all the shivery things she told him she wanted to do. She didn't know if she could be so brazen, even though he wanted her to caress him every way she spoke of. She never sucked on his shaft, touched the tip with her mouth. Her body heated just thinking about doing so. Butterflies danced around deep in her belly. When she closed her eyes, she saw him hard and throbbing with need for her. Watched her fingertips sliding along his length. She didn't know if the heat on her face was generated from embarrassment or her arousal, maybe a little of both.

The blouse was on the floor beside them. Her breasts thrusting forward to tempt him, the rosy tipped crests hard from the chill in the lodge. She played with the laces holding his shirt together. Taking infinite care, she loosened them, pulling each lace through a hole. Without being asked he lifted his arms over his head. The grin on his face was wicked. She tugged the shirt free of his body. She ran her hands along the broad expanse of his chest feeling his muscles ripple against the leisurely glide of her fingertips. With the shirt gone, her rounded globes pushed against his skin tantalizing her, hardening the rosy hued tips of her breasts even more than the cold night air. He was so strong and smooth, his corded muscles undulating beneath her fingers. He was so handsome. She wanted him naked and vulnerable to her.

Intrigued with his body, she bent over to lick and nip at his small male nipple. His husky groan delighted her, tempted her to more brazen behavior. More than anything, she wanted to do what she said. She pressed her fingers on his nipple, squeezed, watching his eyes darken with the raging passion that grew within him.

Obliging her wishes, he moaned his pleasure, a husky sound coming from deep in the back of his throat. His hand rested with heated possession on her belly where their child grew. Wishing to have nothing between them, she wriggled out of her skirt then set her sights on stripping him of his breeches. He was willing to help her from her moccasins as their clothing littered the ground around them. His hands cupped her swollen breasts, holding them as if weighing. His eyes feasted on her.

With loving reverence in his gaze, he caressed them. "You are fuller, heavier. More sensitive I believe." He bent to torment one hardened tip with his lips. He laved then nipped before he sucked one deep into the hot moistness of his mouth. When he looked up, the nipple shimmered with the moisture his kiss left behind. Her body vibrated with each sweet caress. "Yes. More sensitive."

He sucked again, sucked harder, bringing as much of her breast into his mouth as he could.

"More sensitive," she murmured sighing with the pleasure he aroused. She pushed against him. "Fuller too. You say? There is more of me than just a mouthful?"

Running his hands along her toros he seemed to examine her. "Oh yes...your belly is still flat. Soon, I'll be able to see the bump that will confirm my child's existences. I want to be at your family's ranch before the babe is born. Either that or in London." He gave his ardent attention to her other breast then nipped kisses down her torso to her most secret places. "Open for me, love."

"Not so fast."

"Ah, Chauncey, this is sheer torture."

Chauncey was curious, her mind agile. She wanted to know everything she would be facing. "When we are in England will you have a lodge as Kane does? Lyssa told me how they spent nights in his furs. They drank wine and played together. I find the thought of having you in your lodge when there are no longer fears tormenting us to sound much more enjoyable. Also...I would love the wine."

"Yes, to both your questions." He pulled back to study her. "What are you up to?"

She ran her tongue across her lips. "I believe you will appreciate what I've planned."

She slipped lower, taking over the seduction of their bodies. Placing tender kisses on his hard belly she inched farther down his torso. When she touched his sex with her lips, he jerked. His fingers wound into her unbound hair, tightening.

She wasn't finished with her questions. Wished to prolong these moments, liking the way his eyes darkened, the way his lips were pulled back from his teeth as he strained with his pleasure. "Can we have wine there? I miss having a glass at dinner. I would dribble the wine along your erection then suck it off with my lips and tongue." She continued with her descriptions. "Miss having that extra glass when sleep eludes me. Miss not smelling wood smoke while we are in the lodge. Though I doubt if wine is good for the babe. We'll have to figure that out once we return. In any case, what little I could suck off you would not hurt the child growing inside me."

"Already have one on my property...a lodge...filled with furs along with a cook fire."

It seemed he was having trouble speaking. Chauncey delighted in the fact she could touch him, arouse him. "Good," she murmured then licked again, touched the velvet tip of his shaft with her mouth.

He sipped air when her mouth enclosed him. Just as he sucked on her breasts she did so on the length of his swollen sex, milking him. "There is firewood aplenty for cold winter nights. Will you stay with me in my lodge? We can speak about our time here. We can talk about the wagon train and how you boldly claimed me as your husband so you wouldn't find yourself kicked off before you could get into more trouble than any woman I know."

When she started to speak, he placed a finger on her lips. "Only the good times," he told her. "The times with mother when the two of you laughed so hard I thought you might pee yourself. The times when I made love to you in this lodge. The moments when you surprised me by taking me into your mouth. Like now."

"There are good times. You are right." She gasped when he pulled her up his body then sucked her breast into his mouth while fondling the other one. She had not finished her explorations of him. She needed to finish, to bring him to such a point he wouldn't be able to put a coherent sentence or thought together.

"Not yet..." He seemed to read her mind. "Not until I've pleasured you at least once, seen to your needs. I've no control now. If you draw me into the warmth of your hot little mouth again. I might truly explode."

"Detonate?" She laughed as she tilted her head back giving him ample space to spend his sweet kisses there.

"Explode...detonate...ignite, you've got the right words."

They did make love. She did ply him with her mouth until he pulled her away to bury himself deep inside her. The night was spent in bliss. When the morning light filled the lodge, she was still terrified of what was yet to come. Chauncey tried not to think about the fears wedged in her head.

Stephen was right about the snow. The silvery white flakes fell for three days. Snow accumulated to well over two feet. After the blizzard stopped, sun blazed out of a brilliant blue sky. When she stepped outside the lodge to feel the fresh air on her face, she was blinded for a second by the sun's reflection off the snow. She blinked a few times before her eyes adjusted.

The men left to hunt game. Once Stephen disappeared from sight, Chauncey quickly strode to his mother's lodge. While he was gone, she spent the day with Stephen's mother, making baskets idling away the hours with various chores. They cooked dinner in anticipation of his return. The two women didn't speak of her leaving. The time for their departure was now only three weeks away.

Pearl did not return to the village. Some asked about her. No one knew anything. That fact didn't surprise the people of the village who knew her. Chauncey stayed with his mother. Stephen warned her many times not to do anything alone. Time passed. She was both eager to leave as well as remorseful. When the topic was brought up, Little Flower would retire inside herself. Moisture would cloud her beautiful eyes.

Chauncey understood Little Flower was not pleased her son would leave her again.

It was on one of those days, when the world was dark and gloomy that Chauncey decided she would proceed with her plan. She hoped Stephen would be pleased with her idea. She approached his mother. "Would you come with us? When we leave?" Chauncey asked Little Flower one afternoon while they were preparing the evening meal. "There is no one here for you. Wouldn't you like to be able to hold and pamper your grandchildren?" Chauncey placed her hand on her belly. She thought if Stephen's mother came with them, it was the perfect solution. From what Stephen told her about his home, there would be more than enough room. In her golden years, she would have more comforts than here. There would be physicians to tend to any illness. Food would be plentiful. She would never be cold again. She wouldn't need to fear the white soldiers.

A tear slid down Little Flower's cheek. With the back of her hand, she brushed the moisture away. She looked so wistful. Chauncey felt certain that Little Flower would agree with the proposition. When she looked up from stirring the pot of stew, she spoke her words with hesitation. "I'm too old to change my ways. Too old to travel. What if I took sick on the trail? Still Water Runs Deep would have to stop to take care of me. I would not want to be a burden or slow him down."

Chauncey didn't want to think of those words as a refusal. His mother would never become a burden to either of them. "Bah..." She slashed her hand in the air, furious the woman would think so little of herself. "You are not too old to do anything that would make your heart warm. If you don't travel with us, you will never see this grandchild or the ones that follow. I want Stephen's children to know his mother! Their grandmother." She found that her anger grew with each word Little Flower spoke.

"You make me want to say yes," she spoke again her eyes sparking. "Everything you say is true about me wanting to be with the people I love." Little Flower placed her hand on Chauncey's belly. "I do want to hold my grandchild."

Certain her words were getting through to her husband's mother.

"What do you have here that is worth staying for? Make a list of everything you would be heartbroken to leave behind. After that make a list of everything that would break your heart when we leave you here."

She hoped Little Flower would not be able to say anything negative. Hoped that all her thoughts would send her with them. The woman had no other family.

"I've spent my entire life here, in the mountains as well as the prairie. It would be hard to say goodbye. What do I know about living in your world? Nothing." Little Flower paced around the cooking fire, her back stiff with the apprehension she must feel. "Life would be so very different."

Chauncey didn't wish to lie to her or make anything out to be different than it would be. "Very different. At first living in my world might be difficult for you. I'm certain you will learn. In his home, though, you would have us. You would not be dependent on anyone other than family. From what I understand, Kane lives close. He will have children you can also pamper. Isn't Kane like family? Another son to you? More grandchildren to spoil with your abundant love?"

She rocked. Her arms crossed in front of her. "Black Thunder is family. I will think on this strange notion of yours. You are right though. There is little for me here. I've no one, yet the tribe always takes care of each other. I was terribly lonely before you and Still Water Runs Deep visited. I will be lonelier when you are gone."

"Still Water Runs Deep will be happy if you decide to come with us, as will I. Promise me you will think hard about all I've said. About all you will have."

Chauncey felt certain she put something into Little Flower's head that would please her as well as her son if she accepted.

Over the next two weeks they talked of her traveling with them. Spoke of all the good times they would have over the years. Chauncey told her more about the life she could live if she wished. The freedoms she would have to explore other interests. Made certain that Little Flower understood she could keep to her traditions if that was what she wanted. This was perfect. Chauncey wanted to clap her hands together with happiness when Little Flower began to sway in her direction.

At the end of the second week, she sat with Stephen in their lodge. He pulled her between his legs, her back pressed against his hard chest. Chauncey didn't say anything to him until she was positive Little Flower had made up her mind. Just this morning, his mother told her she would leave with them. Stephen held her breasts in his hands, touching upon the hardened tips, rubbing his thumbs across them until she whimpered with her pleasure.

They would make love soon. She needed to speak of this plan with him while she could still talk.

"Stephen?" Chauncey turned to look up at him.

"Hmm..." He nuzzled her neck with his lips, found the sensitive spot behind her ear then trailed kisses down her neck.

She coiled within, feeling the heat he generated, the magic. Her body melted, turning to liquid fire. Hesitating, yet understanding the topic had to be broached, she began, "What would you think if I told you your mother was going to come with us when we left?"

"That you are crazy...a mad woman." He bit the tip of her ear then soothed the tiny mark with his tongue. "She will never leave her people to go over the great ocean to live in a foreign country.

She jerked with the pleasure. Between her legs, she ached. He ran his hands along her legs. Closing her eyes, she leaned into him, begging with her body for more. As the embers in the fire popped in front of them, she needed to resist the tempest, the storm and fierce passion he orchestrated with so much ease. "Stop it. You have to understand."

"What I understand is that I want my woman now. Not when she finishes weaving fairytales."

Placing her hand on either side of his face, she willed him to look at her, to listen openly. "I planted the seed of adventure in your mother's head two weeks ago. She's been thinking about the idea since. Today, she told me she would come with us. Once we leave, there is nothing left for her here."

"You did what?" He bolted back holding her wrists in his hands. His eyes were wild, alight with what appeared to be furious displeasure.

Shocked by his apparent anger, she moved away turning toward him so she could better see his eyes. They were dark in his anger. Tilting her head trying to understand, she stared at him with concern. He couldn't be against this plan. There was no reason for that. What would she tell Little Flower? Chauncey didn't apprehend. Stephen should be pleased his mother would live with them, would grow old knowing she was loved. Would be near her grandchildren Little Flower was still young. She might find happiness in this new land. Might find another man to love her.

"You cannot be angry."

"Shocked. In disbelief," he countered, cupping the back of her head with his hand. "Time is what I need to grow accustomed to this notion of my mother's."

Before she could reply she sipped in a couple of breaths of air, storing the oxygen briefly within her lungs. She touched his lips with a fingertip, smiling as if that would cause the frown lines on his forehead to vanish. "I talked her into traveling with us. It is my fault. If you are to be angry, be angry with me." When he slanted her a look that told her he meant to argue, she shook her head. "No, wait. She understands all the problems she might have. This is her choice. Life will be different, true. She will encounter things she has never seen or heard of before. Your mother wants to know her grandchildren, Black Thunder's as well. Without you, your mother has nothing here." She sat back, holding him at a slight distance, her hands pressed on his chest, studying his rigid countenance. "She has no one she cares about in this encampment. Anyone to love. Would you have her spend her last years alone weeping for everything she lost?"

She smoothed the lines around his eyes. Sent a shudder vibrating in his large body when she ran her thumb along his damp lips.

"I would have my mother happy. Did you tell her everything? All the pitfalls? There will be many who scorn her because of her heritage."

Sensing the win, "What, pray tell, is everything? I did not down play anything that would happen on this journey east to a distant land if that is what you're asking. Most likely she will encounter a few people who will scorn or belittle her. She will be living with us, close to Kane's residence. The people she will know will love her as we do."

"You told her about sailing on the ocean?" He brushed his

knuckles across her collarbone then lower.

"Yes."

He would come around. Already, he was moving onto a different direction.

"You told her about the bathtubs along with the different type of clothing she would have to wear?"

His thumb traced across her bottom lip.

"Yes, and no. Told her she could wear anything she felt comfortable wearing. Told her she could take her baths in the stream behind your home or in the hot water inside your house. She much prefers the thought of hot water and a tub where no one might come along to invade her privacy."

"I don't have a stream behind my home."

"Oh...a small matter to correct."

"What else did you tell her?"

"I answered every question she asked with all honesty."

Chauncey flung her arms around his neck, placed a gentle sweet kiss on his open mouth. Sent her tongue deep inside the heat he offered when he invited her inside. "She wants to be part of our lives." She pressed his hands on her belly. "As well as our children's lives. Don't say she can't come. Please don't. You would disappoint her as well as me."

He laughed, the sound vibrating around the small enclosure. "Tell my mother she couldn't be part of my life? Never. I was sad that this would be the last time I saw her. Now, I'm pleased. You've made me a very happy man. I would have never thought she would wish to travel half a world away from here."

"I did believe she would refuse. For many days she hovered on the edge. When she finally agreed..."

"Are you content?"

"Yes, nonetheless, I thought you were furious with me. You quite confused me, Stephen. It was not well done of you to make me wonder."

"Come, wife, make love to me. Show me how satisfied you are that I agreed to this mad scheme of yours. Spread your legs for me."

After removing her clothing, she nestled against him. Touched and caressed all of him. They made love beneath the furs eager now to have the journey east begin. There were no tears to cry at leaving this place behind. Expectations for their new life together blossomed.

As it happened, two days before they were to depart, the weather changed. Clouds covered the once blue skies. While no snow fell, torrents of rain pushed down from the clouds to soak the land. The ground became a muddied mess. Traveling would be difficult until the earth dried.

While the sky continued to shed its moisture, Chauncey despaired that they would never be able to depart. They were ready. The horses were corralled and prepared. Little Flower packed all her important possessions.

So close to leaving, forgetting the precautions taken for the last month, Chauncey walked to the stream to say a last goodbye to the land where Stephen grew to adulthood. Rain fell but she was clothed in a sturdy cape the water seemed to sluice from. Little Flower made it for her with the long trip in mind. With the hood of her cloak up, she stared out on the landscape that had become familiar as well as hated. This was where the women drug her that long ago day. Where they thrashed her until she bled, until she couldn't walk. Where she lost her child. They stripped her not only of her clothing but also her pride. The women meant to humiliate her.

The air she breathed into her lungs seemed hard and stuffy, smelling of wet earth. Oxygen seemed to catch in her throat. Shaking her head, she turned away from her imaginings, trying to concentrate on the more pleasant future that awaited her. Soon they would leave this fear of hers behind. Soon the sun would warm the earth. They would be home by the first of summer. If she was well, they would sail for England as soon as possible.

Lost in thought she walked along the bank. A startled frog leapt into the water. Out in a deeper part of the river, a fish jumped. She would miss none of this because much could be found in England. The memories she harbored in this land were too harsh. Her life would change again. Thoughts of seeing her father and mother gave her heart a jolt of pure pleasure. More thoughts of traveling to London made her smile with enjoyment. She would see her cousins as well as her host of aunts and uncles. This would signal a new beginning for her, for the both of them. She would never be far from family.

She settled her hands on her belly. She didn't know how far along she was. She was still flat. Stephen was positive she carried a boy. She didn't know but she argued just for the sake of challenging him that she carried a girl. It was too soon to know for certain. Ah, but she did have a few fears about the babe. She knew nothing about children. She was the youngest of the siblings as well as her nearby cousins.

An eagle soared high in the sky. Above her a squirrel scolded her as if she encroached on his territory. A deer drank from the water up river. All of this would remain the same even though so much would change in her life. She didn't have a crystal ball to see into the future. Most thought the lives of these people would change in the worst sort of ways. The future was not bright for the tribes. People, white people, moved west at alarming rates. Soldiers came to defend the whites. Buffalo were slaughtered for sport, not food.

Stopping to sip air, she felt a presence behind her. The hair on the nape of her neck prickled. She whirled, thinking Stephen was there, following her as he always did. He was not.

"Pearl!"

~ * ~

From behind her, a large hand covered her mouth. She struggled, her fingers tugging on her assailant's. She wanted to scream. Could not. She clawed at his hand then his face, feeling the skin tear. Hearing the curse.

"No..." she whispered.

A low sob tore from deep inside her, a scream of forsaken desolation. Panic raced through her. Thoughts of Stephen riddled her brain. He would not find her soon enough. They would do as they pleased. There was no hope, no hope at all. She would kill herself first.

"Hold still, you little hell cat!" the man yelled as he pulled her taunt against his large body. His arm circled her waist holding her tight beside him. "Curse you. If you don't, I'll knock you out. A sharp blow to your chin should do the trick."

Chauncey wasn't about to give into threats. She tried to ram her head against his face. She hit his nose. His hand tightened on her mouth, pushing her lips against her teeth. Breath trickled into her lungs. Blood filled her mouth.

"Hold. You can't get away from me. If you keep this up, you'll only hurt yourself." He shook her. "Behave!"

Greeley stepped in front of her, his smile stretching across his face. "Got you at last! Witch!"

The man holding her stuffed a nasty tasting cloth into her mouth then finished gagging her with another cloth. His voice was terrifying. Calm. "You're not going anywhere. Just settle down and it won't be so bad for you. You'll get used to us. Might even like us better than the savage."

Chauncey pushed on the fabric with her tongue. Nothing budged. She kicked back with her heels but connected with nothing. Frantic now, she squirmed trying to dislodge the hold the man had on her. She had to get away. They would tie her. She would be helpless. After what the women did to her, she never wanted to be helpless again. Stephen told her he would protect her. He couldn't keep her safe from her mistakes.

He was strong. His fingers tightened on her shoulders. Wrenching one hand behind her then the other he tied her wrists together. He toppled her to the ground. She landed hard on her stomach, her face in the moss and pine needles. *The baby...* The scent of dirt assailed her. The stench of the man filled her with hatred. With more leather thongs he bound her feet. Using her long braid, he hauled her to her feet then bent a shoulder so she landed stomach down on top of him.

This was her fault. She did it to herself, walked alone. Disobeyed another firm rule laid down to her by Still Water Runs Deep. He told her he didn't spout rules for his enjoyment or her discomfort. Told her everything he did and said was for her benefit to keep her safe. If she flaunted the directions, she would live to regret her actions. His commands were guidelines to save her life. She didn't listen or heed his words.

"Hurry," the big man told the others. "We've got to get out of here before Wilkes discovers his wife missing. Don't want to be close when the man's fury erupts. Get on your horses. We ride hard. We ride until we can't ride any longer. Distance from here is what we need. We know injuns are tireless."

Pearl was clapping her hands, jumping up and down delighted by Chauncey's capture. "You've got her. You've really got her! I never thought you could do it!" she cried out as if she never thought that would happen. "It will be my turn to torment her. I want to watch when you have your way with her. Take her now! Jackson, take her now. Stick it into her! Want to hear her scream."

"Yeah, she made a mistake. The little bitch has never been left alone, not since the snows stopped," Jackson spoke as if he admired her. "We got her now. They won't find her unless we tarry here. I've got a hankerin' to see how she tastes but there are times when a man's got to be patient to save his life. This is one of those times. We've got to put distance between us and this place by nightfall lest we lose our scalps."

Stephen would find her. She knew he would. Soon, he would come to the stream wondering where she was. Little Flower would miss her. Slade would come looking for her so he could tease her. Jess would be with him. Red Feather liked to joke with her. White Pony wanted to hear all about England. Someone would miss her. She hoped the missing of her presence wouldn't come too late.

The man tossed her over the horse. She landed stomach down, her head hanging perilously close to the pounding hooves. Jackson mounted from behind his hand on the small of her back. "Hold still, little fire. You'll do just fine. Don't move."

As the horse began to pick up speed, she struggled, nearly fell beneath the stallion. His hand on her back pressed her down. She caught the sob in the back of her throat then tried to cling to whatever she could find. Ending her days beneath the sharp stinging of hooves was not to her liking. She had time. All she needed was patience. Stephen would come for her. She had to live for the child she carried.

The others followed suit. They were riding now, hard and fast. Branches swiped across her, slashed on her bared arms. The cloak billowed out around her until he brought the fabric to her back. Wind stung. Cold air bit deep. The thought of what the men intended speared her to the core.

Bounced around, she thought she would be sick. Time passed. She closed her eyes as well as her mind to the physical as well as the mental pain. Chauncey tried to find a mythical place where her head could wander. She needed to minimize the pain as well as the anguish of the uncertain future looking ahead of her. She remembered what Beth told her about her mind wandering to pleasant places when Greely raped her.

The sun's shadows cast a gloom through the forest. The pace slowed for a few minutes. She thought she might be able to breathe again. Just when she thought her stomach would stop rolling, they raced the mounts. For hours the pace continued in the same vein.

The chill of the night settled into her bones. She was hungry, cold, as well as exhausted. They would need to stop soon. The horses could run at this grueling pace only so long. Stephen would have more than one horse at his side when he raced after her. He could move faster as well as longer.

"When are we going to stop?" Greeley complained. "My head is throbbing. Need a good drink and some food in my belly. After that I've a need to satisfy myself with the lady you got head down in front of you."

"No time for that," Jackson said. "You're not going to have the woman until I've had her. "That's only when we're so far away from the village, I feel safe. Don't need no war party coming down on us. Like to keep my scalp intact. Since we stole her, we race for our lives."

"War party? No one cares enough about the girl to follow us except Still Water Runs Deep. He won't come for her. Let alone no war party. He'll be happy the bitch is gone," Pearl cooed in broken Sioux and English her seeming delight at Chauncey's fate. "Let him have her tonight. 'bout time she stopped flaunting her arrogance."

From somewhere behind her she heard the woman's voice. Once she found an opening, she would fight these men. Until then she would save her strength. They wouldn't keep her bound hand and foot forever. That thought terrified her more than any other. When they planned to force her, it would be right after they untied her. That wasn't going to be tonight, thank God. A ray of hope filled her.

When they stopped for the night, the moon was high in the cloud littered sky. A stiff breeze flowed from the mountains chilling everything. During the ride they continually climbed to higher elevations. Breath caught in her lungs, burning, searing. Chauncy gasped to fill herself with oxygen.

The man, Jackson, she discovered was his name carried her. He set her down on the ground near a tree. "Pearl, fetch firewood. Make certain its dry. Want a smokeless fire. Not that I expect anyone to catch up to us tonight."

Jackson was wrong. Chauncey could feel Still Water Runs Deep's thoughts every time she closed her eyes. She heard him chanting to her. *Stay brave, love. Stay strong. I'm on my way. Don't fear.*

He turned to speak, his voice harsh. "Greeley, get the beans out of my saddlebag. That's all we'll have tonight."

Jackson sat on his haunches staring at her. His knuckles ran along her cheek then down her neck. She flinched away. Her eyes smoldered. "Feisty little thing aren't you now. I can tell why Greeley wanted you. Why the injun' married you. What I can't quite understand is why Pearl wished you harm. What did you do to her? Hmm..." He laughed at her. "I'll have you first. When I'm done, if it suits me, I'll give you to Greeley. If you're real nice, maybe I'll keep you for myself. Would be better than the old man. Don't you think? You could warm my bed during the long cold winters. I'd be real nice to you. Not like the old man. He abuses women."

With the gag in her mouth, she couldn't speak. He would know that. She was shaking her head no. Even though anyone would be better than Greeley. He was toying with her while he taunted her with what was going to happen. Not tonight but tomorrow or the next night. Jackson ran his finger across her collarbone then the tips of her breasts. She jerked. He chuckled then continued the motion. She thought she would die. Wanted to strike out at him.

"Your eyes are flashin' all pretty like. All that fury in one tiny little woman. Wonder what it will be like to plow your belly. Nice and hot would be my guess. I'll tame you, sweetheart, tame you to ride me. If you buck me off, I'll climb right back on for more. Do your worst. You won't be gettin' away from me."

Shaking her head, she whimpered, scooting further against the tree at her back. She couldn't get away from him. He could touch her anyway he pleased. *No! no...no...no...!* Her body quivered with fear.

At least when Pearl and the women tormented her, they weren't forcing her. She couldn't imagine this man inside her or touching her the way Stephen did. Tears filled her eyes, slipped down her cheeks. A sob broke from the back of her throat. She didn't want to cry.

He caught a tear with the tip of a finger. "I won't treat you bad...ah, but honey, don't need to worry about tonight. Not letting Greeley near you or myself for that matter, not until we're safe and sound and I know that injun husband of yours isn't following us. Don't want to be caught with my pants down." He tasted the tear he collected on his finger. "If I had you for my woman, I'd follow you to hell to get you back. Imagine your man will be hot on our tail. Can't allow him to catch up to us. If he does, I'll shoot him as soon as I see him. Pray he doesn't find us."

Sitting back, he seemed to study her. He touched her belly, dipped his hand lower. "You need to relieve yourself?"

Of course, she did. She nodded thinking he might get careless. In the dark she could escape him. He would have to untie her. He would give her privacy. No, he wouldn't. He would stand by and watch.

The leather thongs binding her feet, he unfastened then fashioned a noose that he slipped around her neck. He tightened it until the leather bit into her flesh then secured a long strip of leather to the noose. After that he tied her hands again so they were bound in front of her. She tried to wiggle her numb feet to pump blood back into them.

"Let me at her!" Pearl screamed, shaking her fist at them. "Scratch her eyes out I will if you won't take her now. You're bein' too nice."

Chauncey heard Jackson curse. Pearl was screaming, her voice filling the air with shrieks of anger.

He ignored the woman. "Come," Jackson said. He jerked on her leash once then a second time. "If you waste time, I'll let you go right here."

As the leather tightened around her neck, she stood, following behind him, stumbling. Her feet were numb with no feeling. She tripped again landing on her hands and knees, her nose hitting the dirt. The leather around her neck bit into her flesh. She felt the slow glide of blood. He waited while she stood.

"Don't waste my time, woman. Over here. There's a nice spot. Don't take too much time." He nodded toward a row of bushes.

She cringed understanding this was all the privacy she would get. Pearl was still shrieking. She finished, adjusted her dress then meekly followed him back to camp. Once she was sitting again, he bound her feet with a new piece of leather. The leash and noose he kept on her, tying the leash to a high branch. Even if somehow she could get her hands free, she would never be able to reach the knot.

"Food will be along shortly. Best you get sleep while you can. We'll be up early." He left her alone. She breathed in a silent breath of relief understanding he meant what he told her about tonight.

Leaning back against the tree she closed her eyes, imagining other, more beautiful times. She recalled when Stephen made her listen to the night sounds. He taught her different bird calls. Told her to remember how they sounded. During those tender moments when she was listening to the bird calls, she didn't understand his purpose. Now, she realized he was teaching her to recognize his voice if she ever needed him. Tonight, with her mind whirling, she heard nothing except Pearl. Where was he? Was Pearl right?

He would come for her.

He had to.

The body fell against her. She jerked awake, knowing Pearl was defying Jackson again. Her eyes flew open. Pearl was trussed up in much the same fashion. She lay face down beside her whimpering through the gag one of them tied.

Jackson stood over her, his feet braced apart, his hands on his hips. "You will do as I say, woman." his voice was harsh. "You've no more rights here than this one."

He pointed at Pearl then at her, fury in his dark gray eyes. "I should let Greeley have you tonight. This time there won't be anything in it for you. Keep your mouth shut!" Jackson's anger was obvious.

"Greeley, go to sleep. I'll keep guard for the first shift. I'll wake you when it's time for you to keep watch."

Chapter Eleven

Stephen strode through the flaps of his mother's lodge, ready to pull Chauncey into his arms. After that, welcome her more thoroughly with a deep hard kiss that would create a firestorm of desire. He saw only his mother who looked up then smiled at him.

Expecting Chauncey to be there, he was confused. He stepped forward, "Where is my wife?"

Stephen didn't understand why the sick feeling rolling in his belly left him sweating. Something was very wrong. A cold wave stabbed up his spine. His instincts kicking in, he suddenly feared for Chauncey' life. It was as if he heard her crying out to him. The voice calling to him in his imagination was Chauncey's. She was supposed to be with his mother. Going anywhere by herself was forbidden. She understood that. On this last day, did she once more break the rules that were meant to keep her alive?

A look of stark horror swept across Little Flower's face. She paled, her hands shaking, she lifted one to implore. "I thought she was with you. I would not have left the lodge had I thought she was somewhere else. Where would she go?"

Stephen didn't have an answer for his mother. He didn't know. Though he could make a few guesses. He cleared his throat as he began to think of all possibilities. His mind scrambled for ideas. This was not yet the time to think of trouble. She could be just about anywhere. He had to think. "I believed she was here with her mother-in-law."

It was useless for Stephen to ask questions. As it was clear his mother had no ideas where his wife was and was growing more fearful with each passing second. Chauncey wasn't going to miss the village. She didn't like life here. Why would she step outside? He didn't have an answer.

"She will be here for dinner," Little Flower murmured though the stricken look on her face told him she didn't believe what she told him. "Your woman just went to relieve herself."

His woman wasn't even supposed to do that by herself. "Can you think of anything she might have said to you?" He peered out the door of the lodge as if he thought he would see her delicious hips swaying as she walked toward him. There was nothing to see except one of the dogs, toying with a huge bone. "Does she have anyone she would wish to visit? To say her goodbyes to?"

Stephen could think of no one that wasn't traveling with them on the morrow she would wish to speak with. Perhaps Buffalo Stalker, though to his mind Chauncey never forgave the man for allowing the women to punish her in the manner they chose.

His mother looked up from the pot where she was stirring their dinner. Her face was lined with tears. "No, she was very quiet. The last time I saw her was when you were still here." Tips of her fingers traced the tears sliding along her cheeks, drying them. "I left to say goodbye to some of my old friends. When I returned a few minutes ago, neither of you were here. I thought that you went to your lodge to...to..." she broke off, her face flushing with color.

No, he'd not taken her to the lodge to make love to her. Though the thought was a nice one. With angry strides he stalked through the village, his gaze searching, finding nothing that would clue him in on her whereabouts. The only place she ever went was to the river. He looked at the spot where she sat on the boulder the other day. Where he teased her with heated caresses. Where he seduced her until she cried out her pleasure.

Nothing.

He strode along the bank looking for signs that she walked this same path earlier today. He saw moccasin prints all too big for her tiny feet. He saw booted marks on the bank where the soil was muddy. His gut clenched. All too well, he understood a white man stood here, watched his wife. His mind flashed to Greeley, the sniveling coward. These prints were too big for Greeley to have left them.

Boots.

He continued, haunting all the spots that had been part of her life these last months the enjoyable parts as well as the terrifying parts. When he walked to the place where she told him the women left her naked and beaten, he paused. Stephen closed his eyes, sensing the wind, listening to its call. When he opened his eyes, his trained gaze touched on all he saw. All types of tracks were left there.

Tracks left from the moccasins of two small women. Tracks left from boots of two large men. "Pearl..." he swore beneath his breath.

His heart raced. These men had at least two hours head start. They would not have time to hide their trail. He could gain on them with little effort but would it be too late? What would they have done to Chauncey. They wouldn't dare take the time to force her until they were certain there was enough distance covered. If the men were smart, they would wait until they were far, far away from the village.

His eyes squeezed shut. Chauncey, he thought with quiet desperation. So saucy, so sweet, she was everything his dreams had ever pictured for him...Chauncey! He screamed her name in silent anguish. Pain ripped through him. He felt as if a sword had been drawn through him from throat to groin. He saw the twinkle of her eyes when she teased, saw the rims darken with the rush of passion when he touched her. Saw her fear when she thought Greeley might force her. The compassion when she walked with Beth while she tried to stop her friend from walking forever, until she could not put one foot in front of the other.

He had to get control of his thoughts along with his actions. The air he brought into his lungs tumbled out in a rush of fear. This was no time for idle memories.

She needed him now.

He wanted to start after her this instant. Wanted to ride until he could strangle the men who dared capture his woman. Torture would be too good for those men. Their scalps would hang in his lodge. While he clenched his fists tight, holding his breath, the red haze of rage dimmed. With ardent concentration, his nerves relaxed. Amid excruciating agony, he tamped down the need to kill. Turning his attention to the moment at hand, an instant where there was no time to dally, he turned back toward the village. He found both Jess along with Slade in the lodge with Red

Feather and White Pony speaking of the departure scheduled for the next day. They were laughing, chatting about the fifty-five horses they would escort to the east coast. Jess reminded them about his father's reaction when he witnessed Black Thunder leading the horses while he was dressed only in his breechclout, his war cry splintering the peace of the summer day.

When they looked at him, the laughter as well as the chatter stopped. Deathly silence clung to the small room that only a few minutes heard the soft sound of people anticipating a journey.

The air reeked of fear. Stephen's fear. He could smell the terror, taste the distress as his body thrummed with shock. Darkness settled around him, ate at his soul.

Stephen broke the horrible silence with a few words, "He has Chauncey."

Who exactly he was talking about Stephen wasn't certain. They heard rumors about Greeley with a trapper named Jackson. There were two sets of prints. Two men. Greeley would have never been able to achieve this alone.

"Greeley? Pearl is part of this too?" Slade questioned as he set the knife, he'd been sharpening into the sheathe.

"The exact part she plays leaves much to think about?" Jess asked standing while grabbing his coat. The other men did the same. "Rest assured, nothing will happen to Chauncey that you can't fix with your love."

"Pearl brought these men with her with the intent to harm. The omens are all bad."

He gritted his teeth refusing to compromise this further with words. Stephen was heading to the door. He didn't need to ask if his friends would go with him. Slade would want his sister back. Jess would expect his cousin to be returned with no harm done to her.

"I will tell Little Flower that we follow your wife then I'll catch up," Red Feather spoke, his voice tempered. "I ride fast...like a strong wind."

He was out the door.

In no more than a few minutes the men were surveying the signs, finding where the horses had been tethered a mile from the river. The men made no effort to cover their tracks. To Stephen it was clear that Chauncey rode on the same horse with Jackson. It also became apparent the men did not plan on stopping soon. They would ride until nightfall or until they could ride no longer or push the horses further.

Stephen didn't believe they would catch them before dawn unless they rode through the night. Later, when dawn would only be a few hours away they would bed down. Two hours would have to be enough sleep. On many occasions they got by on less. He wasn't certain how Jess and Slade would fare. They alternated riding different horses, changing every hour. The men continued. The signs left by the three horses were evident, even in the dark. They all understood tonight or the morning they needed to take care of this.

The men would be taught a lesson. Pearl would be brought back to camp for her punishment. Before he left, Stephen would have Buffalo Stalker's word that the woman would be punished to the full extent of the Sioux law. Pearl deserved whatever was doled out to her and more.

Sometime around four o'clock in the morning they stopped. Stephen pulled out the pouch of dried berries and nuts, some dried meat too that his mother handed Red Feather as he was leaving. He gave Jess and Slade a pouch. They ate.

Red Feather scouted ahead.

Leaning against a fallen tree trunk, Stephen closed his eyes. As he fell into a deep sleep, he saw visions of Chauncey, bound hand and foot. As if he was beside her, he saw the noose around her neck, the long leash tied high above her to a tree branch. She was captive to two men who would take her with no care.

His nerves stretched taut. He counted the minutes until he had the men in his control. They would rue the day they attacked Chauncey. Greeley had been warned. Jackson deserved a warning too. He wasn't going to get one.

Red Feather woke him with the coming of light. A soft haze of gold appeared above the mountain tops. Mist fell from the sky, swirled around the fire. It would feel like a cold day in hell to the men who abducted his wife. The others were roused, quietly taking care of their needs. Without words they mounted.

"They are only ten minutes from here. We need to get there before they rise. The element of surprise is always nice," Red Feather said, grinning as if he anticipated the meeting. "The women are tied. The men will find themselves..." Red Feather left off when Stephen slanted him a hard stare.

"We won't kill them or take scalps. I've something else in mind." Stephen urged his horse forward, eager to see this to its ultimate finish.

They dismounted then walked with no noise to the camp. Crouching in the bushes near Chauncey, he called to her with the hoot of an owl, hoping she recalled the night he taught her bird sounds. When she stiffened then looked around a silent smile creased his mouth. She remembered. She would know he was here for her. Once he got her alone, he would chastise her for leaving the sanctuary of the village without protection. For these minutes before he got her back, he had only one thought...

Good girl.

You remembered. Raising his hands to his mouth, he created the sound of the owl once more. Her back still against the tree, she nodded. His heart in his throat he waited until he saw that Red Feather and White Pony secured the trapper. He turned his focus on Slade and Jess. Greeley was now bound and gagged in the same manner. Neither made a sound. Both men had been knocked out as well as muzzled.

To his immense pleasure, they would awaken soon. The two men would understand their fate, their destiny.

Stephen's smile was grim. The men would not like their new position. With haste eager to set her free, he was beside Chauncey, untying her, swearing as he saw the welts caused by the leather when he saw the dried blood around her neck. When her hands were unbound, she threw her arms around his neck, sobbing. Her head was buried in his chest. He felt the heart-wrenching sounds of her pain.

He stroked her back; slow, measured soothing strokes, "Hush, love. It's all over now. Wait until you see my surprise for you." With tender care, he kissed her lips, a light touch, nothing more. "After you see, it will be up to you what happens next."

He didn't want to give away too much. Needed to see some pleasure etched in her face when she set her eyes upon the men.

"Do I want to see? I'm afraid. Did you kill them? Did you stake them out naked? What did you do with Pearl?" She was breathless from her questions.

His grin widened as he touched his hand to her heart. A heart that was thundering. "No, though if you wish it, they are dead men. They might well be dead before they can extricate themselves from the position they've been placed in. We will see. Now, do you wish to see our handiwork?"

"Stephen?" she asked, her eyes questioning. Her fear still evident in the sheen of her eyes. "What about Pearl? What will you do with her?" She looked at the woman who sat next to her, eyes wide with fear. The noose was still around her neck. She was still bound and gagged.

"What about her?" he gritted out wishing he could leave the woman here with the two men. Given time, Jackson would get out of the leather binding. Whether he would help Greeley was a matter of conjecture, nothing more. "What happens to Pearl is up to you...you alone. It is your decision."

"You can't leave her here, trussed up. As much as I wish it so, you cannot. I don't want her to die. I don't wish for those men to die either." She was rubbing her wrists, stamping her feet. It seemed after hours of confinement; she had no feeling in her feet or hands.

"No, you're right. I cannot. Buffalo Stalker has agreed to punish her. We will take her back to the village with us. Though I believe she will be a slave for the rest of her life. There are men in the village who would use her for their needs. She will be given no choice. I'm not certain she will care."

"I'm not certain I condone that." Her face was pale, her eyes soft with compassion her words uttered with a force that surprised him. "I would not want her hurt, just punished in some way she would understand."

"No, it is the way of the People. You will have to forget and accept what Buffalo Stalker decides. We will not be there to see what happens. We leave in the morning after our return."

Massaging her hands and feet, alternating between the two, he waited until she could rise of her own accord. They would make their way back to the village. Their departure would have to wait for the following day. One more time his plans were thwarted.

"Would Buffalo Stalker listen to me if I voiced my opinion?" It seemed she would not give up on this. "I would tell him what I believe to be true."

"She would not learn a lesson if he listened and did as you asked. Your heart is too kind. Pearl, if given the opportunity, would do the same to any other woman she thought wronged her." He lifted his shoulders though, pleased with his woman, pleased that she didn't hold a grudge. "Can you stand on your own?"

She nodded, moistening her lips. He held out his hand to help her to her feet. She blinked looking down for a moment before meeting his gaze. "I can with help. You are going to show me my captors now?" She smiled at him. "Is this something I might enjoy? Did you tie them? I would that they understand they will not escape."

They would understand. No way in hell would he allow them to escape. In their condition they might not want to. "Come..." Stephen helped her to her feet. His hand held lightly on her elbow he helped her along. He thanked all the gods he ever prayed to that he found Chauncey before they could harm her. Another night or two and it would have been too late for that promise.

Startled by the sight in front of her she gasped. When he looked at her expression, his heart turned over. This was right as well as just. After that she began to laugh. The giggles came through her teeth, slow at first then long and deep soon turning into desperate sobs. She turned into him. Her face pressed against his chest. He held her close, listening to her, feeling her small frame shudder against him. He tightened his arms.

"It is what they deserve," she murmured as she gazed into his eyes. "How will they survive? They cannot be left here to die. I don't want them murdered. It is what it will be if you don't give them a chance to live."

"Not my problem," he told her, his body stiff, lifting her chin so he could watch the shimmering of her eyes. "These men brought this upon themselves. They deserve to die. If they live, they deserve to live."

"No, I suppose it isn't anyone's problem but theirs. You will leave them without a horse too? No clothing, no food, no way to travel except on bare feet, it is a death sentence you dole out."

Her voice was hoarse as she recounted her feelings. What she wished for more than anything was to forget. "I cannot be party to this, Stephen. Murder is not right."

Her words disturbed him. Stephen was pleased with the sight of the two men, now straining against the bounds that were remarkably like the ones they placed on the women. In his mind they deserved death. He heaved a long sigh as he tried to come to terms with Chauncey's statement. Red Feather, for he was certain it was his idea, carried his direction farther than he mentioned. He didn't understand Chauncey's objection to leaving them this way. He would discuss it further with her. If she had another idea, he would listen.

The man, Jackson, while he stood at attention, his eyes blazed fire. He appeared so angry he'd like to spit nails. In his condition, that wasn't possible. He would have heard Chauncey's opinion of the punishment. Jackson might even now be thinking he would leave here a free man. He would not. Perhaps as he was leaving the punishment of Pearl, he would leave the punishment of these two men up to Buffalo Stalker and the tribe. If he did so, they would be slaves for life. Slaves rarely fared well. That was also a death sentence.

He would run this by Chauncey.

By the steel glint in his eyes, Jackson wanted to fight. He could not. With the tiniest twitch, the leather around his neck tightened. Ultimately, he would be able to cut the thongs binding his wrists. Red Feather purposefully put his hands behind his back. The bark of the tree was rough-edged. If left to their own strategies, they might not die. Whether they lived or passed on with no one to mourn them, might well depend on the weather. If it snowed again...

Each man wore a noose along with a leash that was tied high on a branch, just as they had done to Chauncey. There feet and hands were bound securely. They were both gagged. Stephen soaked in the sight.

However, there were differences. The men's pants were cut from their bodies. All that was left were narrow strips of fabric, hanging from their hips, covering nothing. Their male parts were exposed, vulnerable. Greeley's head lolled to the side. He'd not yet woke from the blow to the head. Jackson woke within minutes after being bound.

"They are half naked," Chauncey giggled again as she stared at the men, at the limp part they would have used to abuse her. She turned to touch Stephen's cheek. "Thank you. I would that they understand the vulnerability. I'm hoping they feel the humiliation of their naked state to the roots of their hair."

"True, they are half...naked. Would you like the rest of their clothing stripped from their bodies? Anything you wish? It would not be a difficult task to render them completely naked."

"What..." Chauncey looked to the circle of friends along with her family who gathered around them. "What will they do now? When Greeley wakes?" She held onto his arms. "Truly we cannot leave them like this. As much as I relish the thought of these two men suffering..."

"There is enough left of their clothing to fashion a breechclout," Stephen said, lending his laughter to her giggles. "If we take them with us instead of leaving them here defenseless, we will not fashion clothing for them. They will march through the forest just as they are. They will not be able to cover themselves with their hands."

"If they are careful not to tear anything too much," White Pony said smoothly, his male hoot of laughter joined with the others. "What is this? Take them with us? Back to the village? We're not leaving them here?"

"Yes, Chauncey doesn't want them to die. She feels this is murder. Should we allow our chief to administer the punishment to the captives?" Stephen asked them.

He focused on each man there as well as his wife.

"If they are walking, they will slow us down," Jess said while he circled the tree where they were bound. "Yet, I understand what she is talking about. I don't condone murder either. What would happen at the village? What would be their sentence?"

"They would be made slaves. First, we would give them to the women," White Pony said. "That is never pretty. Most times though it is captive females who are given to the women. Sometimes their hands and feet are burned. Maybe we should allow these two men to decide what will happen to them."

"I believe we've made up our minds."

He turned, "Chauncey?"

"Taking them back with us would be fine," she said. "They would have a chance at life. The kind of life not so much..."

"They might die either way," White Pony pointed out.

Stephen straightened his shoulders. It was time to proceed. Greeley was beginning to wake. He moaned. It would not be long before he was aware of his predicament. The captives would not be fed this morning. They would walk barefoot at the pace they set or find themselves dragged.

"Shall we eat? Wait for Greeley to wake up so we can see his eyes when he fully understands the predicament they are in? No one steals my wife. He was warned," Stephen said as he looked at Jackson knowing full well Greeley would not have accomplished the feat without the trappers help.

Jackson was wide awake. He ceased fighting his bonds. Impatient to leave, Red Feather tossed water in Greeley's face. The man jerked awake. Surprised, he fought the bonds until the leather around his neck tightened.

"All they have are beans," Slade said as he set the pot on the fire to simmer. "Think these are left over from last night."

"Found coffee," Jess said as he was searching through Jackson's saddle bag. "Not much else. Food was not a priority."

"How long before we leave," Chauncey asked, rubbing her still swollen wrists. "Want to depart this place as soon as possible. Don't like looking at it or remembering."

"As soon as we finish eating. Look," Stephen said his voice soft. "White Pony and Red Feather are starting." Each one held a leash. They sat their horses while Greeley and Jackson stumbled along behind.

"Can we ride ahead of them. Don't want to watch." She touched her hand to her neck.

"Yes, as soon as you eat, we'll be on our way."

~ * ~

With Stephen by her side, they crested the hill that looked down on the ranch where she spent her life. A host of emotions rambled through her. She realized she'd been hungry to see her home again. The thirst for adventure was gone. Now all she wished for was the peace and quiet of sheltered life. Wildflowers blossomed along the hills. The scent of violets redolent in the late spring air wafted to her. She knew the spring near the ranch house would gurgle merrily, casting its enchantment on the surrounding world.

She would visit. Her home was now with Stephen.

High above, on air currents an eagle soared. Chauncey breathed in deep the air around her. All of this would be memories cast into her mind. She needed to forget the sight of Jackson and Greeley surrounded by the women in the village. Within seconds they lost the clothing they'd been wearing. The next few minutes passed while she tried to close her ears from the sounds of their screams. Perhaps it would have been more humane to have left them to their own skills. When they left the next morning, there were no more screams. Pearl was also given over to the women. Chauncey shook off the images.

"Are you alright? You've that look in your eyes again. Put the thoughts into your past. They have no place in the present or our future," Stephen spoke with a softness she'd never heard before.

He watched her at night when the dreams took her to the pits of hell. Through those long nights he held her, comforted her, soothed her fears.

She pointed down the hill, not wishing to speak about the dreams or the men who tormented her. "We will ride fast and true. I can hardly wait to see the expression on my father's face. You are ready?"

Stephen turned to look for the horses. Both Slade and Jess held up hands to signal him. White Pony and Red Feather did the same waiting for the gesture from Stephen.

The time was here.

This was the only home she'd known. They would leave in two weeks for Baltimore where they would book passage to London. Just as Still Water Runs Deep left his past behind him, she would also. Little Flower clucked over her because of her pregnancy. She now rode up beside them, grinning, seeming more than pleased to be here. Chauncey always hoped his mother would not harbor regrets. So far, it seemed her wishes were true.

"This is my home, or was my home," Chauncey spread her arms wide. "I've always loved my life here. Suppose Still Water Runs Deep felt much the same about his land. Seems we all grow up then move on to something else. It is a large ranch. Slade is supposed to inherit. He wants to go west. What will happen?"

"There will be children who might wish to work this land. Our children might hope to return here," Stephen said. He grinned at her, his green eyes flashing his excitement. He tossed a wink her way. "I won't be out done by Black Thunder."

"No, I didn't imagine you would. We picked up twenty more horses on our way here. What will father do with them? He will own seventy-five horses."

"Your bride price. Do you think he will..." Stephen broke off because he sensed movement behind him.

"He knows we are coming. Slade rode ahead to tell him to get the coral ready. Told him it needed to be larger. Looks as if they worked the night through."

She pointed, "There he is now, coming to help herd the horses. I doubt if they were able to make the corral large enough,"

She was laughing, couldn't help herself. They spoke last night about what they would do with the horses that wouldn't fit. The animals could be left on the open range. That wasn't acceptable to Stephen. Jess suggested they take the majority to the Andrew's ranch until a larger stable could be built. What happened to the horses would not be her problem or Stephen's. He was eager to begin the new life that beckoned to them. He wanted his child born on solid ground. That earth would be England because he wasn't planning to stay through the summer then into the fall. Didn't want to cross the Atlantic that late in the season.

Her hand on her belly, she smiled. She was just beginning to show. Her stomach was no longer flat. Stephen liked to caress her belly, eager to watch her body change. Throughout the pregnancy she'd not been sick, only a small amount of nausea that a tiny bit of food cured. Little Flower was always helpful. Knew herbs that would ease any sickness.

"Are you riding with me? Down the hill or would you like to go on ahead?" he asked as he brought her hand to his lips. He kissed each knuckle. Held her hand tight within his.

She nodded wishing she could ride side by side with her husband. When she asked him, he nixed that idea before she could finish the statement. He didn't wish to take any chances. One slip could be dangerous...deadly. Riding with the horse's was man's work. She imagined she would have to get used to his foolish notions though in this case she agreed at the head of seventy-five stampeding horse was no place for a pregnant woman. "I'll stay in the rear and off to the side. Don't want to miss anything."

He was shaking his head, telling her no. To her surprise, he changed his mind, "I want my Woman Who Breaks Rules to ride next to me."

"You told me..."

"Hush, a man can change his mind. Nothing will happen if you heed me. If you will allow this man to become...to become less of a tyrant, I would listen to more of your outlandish ideas."

Chauncey couldn't help but bristle at his use of the word outlandish. She had to give credit where credit was due. He was becoming less stubborn where she was concerned. Less protective as well as less autocratic.

White Feather dubbed her that name on the ride back to the village the day after she was abducted. She vigorously protested. Nonetheless, the name stuck. Chauncey thought the name should be Woman Who Thinks On Her Own. It wasn't so much that she broke rules, it was that she possessed a mind of her own. An agile mind, a mind that didn't think because she was female, she should have a separate set of rules to follow in her life. Her parents never treated her different from

Slade. Well, not that different. They all lived by the same set of guidelines. The chores were different as they grew older. She did have to admit to that fact.

For several seconds her gaze roamed over his body. The solid wall of his chest, the strong muscled legs. All but the most masculine part of him was naked for the world to see. His dark green eyes blazed with fierce possession as he stared at her. His black hair was braided. Stephen was a warrior proud and tall. He was so handsome, so virile. She thanked God every day that he was so competent. If he wasn't, she might have perished several times.

"You like what you see," he asked, his words soft as well as smooth, his finger touching beneath her chin.

"Very much," she murmured.

"When I look at you, I do like what I see. Are you ready?" he asked as he held up his hand in a salute.

At the bottom of the hill, ranch hands gathered. The gates were swung open.

She nodded breathing in a long draught of air. He cupped the back of her head with one large hand. Brought her mouth to his for a long hard kiss. He swept the inside of her mouth with his tongue. She played with his. Instantly, she felt the inferno build.

When he pulled away her lips were damp with the contact.

"Now!" He waved his hand forward.

Together they raced the wind. Her heart clamored as the whirlwind of life stampeded behind her. She raced forward.

"Ai—ye—ai ye, ai ye..." His cry reverberated, echoed between the hills surrounding the valley. Horses thundered behind them. Dust rose. Over the top of the hill the horses crested, wild manes flying, tails flashing, Slade and Jess flanking the horses. She looked back but for one moment. The sight was magnificent.

Still Water Runs Deep cried out again and again. The war cry reverberated above the sound of the horses as well as the pounding of her blood through her head. His voice was followed by the other men, Jess and Slade lending their war cries to the cacophony of sound. Her skirt was pulled up around her thighs, her bare legs held onto her mare as they thundered toward the ranch. Terrifying excitement flowed through her. She'd never experienced anything such as this.

They flew past her father and mother as the animals were herded into the new corral that was hastily built for the offered bride price. It would hold if not all the horses most of them. Unlike the race horses Kane brought the Andrews, these would be good work horses. They could be bred and sold for tidy profits.

Sitting off to the side, Stephen held her hand as the horses milled one after the other into the corral. Her father was beside her, his hands on her waist lifting her. Once her feet hit the ground, he hugged her.

"You ran off without telling anyone."

He stared at Stephen. His brows furrowed together.

She understood he was asking if they were wed. Chauncey looked to her husband. "We are..." Stephen placed his hand on her shoulder a gesture meant to silence her.

Stephen stood straight and tall beside her, his hand now possessively resting on the small of her back. "Mr. Lakeland," he began his voice commanding attention.

Her father grinned. Her mother stepped up beside him. Aric wrapped an arm across her shoulder. "Stephen," Ravyn spoke as she watched her daughter with an intense gaze, silently questioning.

"Will you accept the bride price I'm offering? There are seventy-five of the finest horses the other side of the Mississippi. We've traveled with them from the Rocky Mountains," Stephen asked, his voice both stern and strangely hesitant.

Chauncey wondered what her husband would do if her father refused. Her imagination ran rampant with various thoughts. She also wondered if her father would guess how Stephen acquired most of them.

"My daughter is worth a lot of horses," Aric said straight faced. He paused for the longest time. Chauncey thought her nerves would unravel. "Don't know if this enough to show her worth."

"Father!" she gasped outraged that her father would dare spout such outlandish words. "How dare you?"

"If you need more then I will find them. To me your daughter is priceless. Just as you must feel the same about her." Stephen spoke slowly, with great confidence. Nonetheless, Chauncey didn't miss the anger in his tone.

She liked the way that sounded. Priceless. She would remember that word until she stuck her spoon in the wall. "Seventy-five horses are more than enough for me. It is twenty-five more than Black Thunder paid for Lyssa."

Chauncey was both indignant as well as irritated with her father that he would dare to haggle. Her annoyance grew tenfold. "Don't be ridiculous." She stepped toward him, growing more furious with each passing second. "Stephen did not need to bring you anything. We are wed. She held up her hand to show him the slim gold band that Stephen bought at the trading post. He doesn't need your permission and neither do I. I am old enough to make decisions for myself."

She knew by the darkening of her father's features she should not have been so blatant. She also understood by the way Stephens fingers tightened where they rested, he was not pleased with her interference.

With a chuckle that annoyed Chauncey, her brother decided to put his thoughts into the conversation. "Woman Who Breaks Rules should learn to keep her lips sealed when the most important men in her life haggle over her. The bride price is between the father of the bride and the groom. Say nothing more," Slade said with smooth finesse as he walked up to stand on the other side of his sister.

The snort of derision coming from her mother shocked her. "Such foolishness coming from my son. Thought I raised you smarter than that. Of course, there are enough horses. We are pleased, speaking for Aric as well as myself. We don't know what to do with this many. More would be overwhelming. Seventy-five are overwhelming."

Aric stroked his chin, his eyes laughing. "Woman Who Breaks Rules? Now, I wonder how our Chauncey got that name." He hooted with his laughter before looking at his wife with a glint in his eyes. "Ravyn is correct. This is more than enough. I'm pleased by the gift of horses. Pleased that you thought to honor my daughter in the way of your People."

"There will be a wedding tomorrow," Ravyn said, expectation ripe in her voice. "Don't argue." Holding up her hands, she went on. "A real wedding with all your family and friends to witness the joining of two loving couples. Tira and Jamie are on their way from Baltimore. They will be here later this afternoon. Of course, Lyssa won't be here but the rest of the Andrews will attend."

"Reverend Brown?" Chauncey asked thrilled that her mother would arrange the wedding. "I was hoping to have this second wedding. Stephen has been agreeable since he was witness to his friend's third wedding here at the ranch."

"Yes, didn't have to do anything but mention your arrival with Still Water Runs Deep and the good woman set the wildfire in motion. Everything will be ready by two tomorrow."

Little Flower dismounted. She was winded from the quick ride down the hill but she was smiling. The journey, at times, had been difficult for her. All would be easier now. Chauncey pulled her mother-in-law close, holding her hand, winding their fingers together in a show of unity. "Mother, this is Little Flower, Stephen's mother. Little Flower, this is my mother, Ravyn. Little Flower is coming with us to London. We decided to call her Lily...Lilly Wilkes. She agreed."

"So nice to meet you," Ravyn said, her smile brilliant. "You are traveling all the way to London? Come tell me all about your journey so far. You can rest while I finish dinner. If I traveled that far, I'd be exhausted."

"I can help," Lilly was quick to offer her assistance.

"No, no, sit down. Rest. You are a guest. I won't have you working. You can sip on a glass of sherry while we talk. I want to know everything."

They disappeared into the house. Chauncey didn't want her mother to know everything. She wasn't about to tell her about Greeley or Jackson. She prayed Lilly would not mention the men. They were a part of her life she would rather forget.

"That went well. Don't you think?" Stephen asked with a bland voice as he waited for further negotiations of the bride price.

"You will not ask for more," Chauncey said indignantly directing a pointed finger at her father. What she wanted was to poke her father in the chest, Stephen as well for continuing this travesty. "We want to be on our way, not out searching the range for more horses just to suit your ego. When we started, we had only fifty-five. You need to learn to be satisfied," she said angrily.

Once again, she was afraid someone would chastise her for putting her thoughts into the conversation that seemed to be presented as a male only discussion.

"Tonight, the two of you will sleep alone." Aric tried to look stern. It didn't seem he had the heart to pursue the statement.

Chauncey snorted. "Not likely," she told him. Her hands resting on her belly, "I'm more than three months gone with your first grandchild, father. We've been wed two times. Just as Lyssa protested this stupid rule, I do too. After all, I'm Woman Who Breaks Rules."

Stephen squeezed her shoulder, appearing pleased with her statement. Even though she felt certain, in privacy, he would tell her he should have been the one addressing her father. "That you are. This day I'm certainly appreciative of your penchant of breaking rules."

She understood he would not wish to argue with his father-in-law. "I didn't think father would put up much of a fight." She laughed as he pulled her into his arms, his lips finding and molding his to hers. His tongue swept deep. In his arms she moaned softly a small purr of delight.

"What would you like now?" he asked once he lifted his head to stare into her eyes. "I know what I would like."

His shoulder was the target of her punch. "A bath. Want nothing more than to settle into heated water in the tub. Come," she held out her hand.

Together they walked to the guest house where she decided they would stay for the next two weeks. Lilly would find her bed in the main house if she wished. Red Feather and White Pony decided they would sleep in the bunkhouse if the men were acceptable to sharing their quarters with Sioux warriors. If not, they would find a sheltered spot somewhere on the land.

~ * ~

Amidst all the fanfare Reverend Brown's wife could muster, they were wed the next day. The feast contained all her favorite foods. Just as with Lyssa's wedding the congregation came together to make the day special. She saw all her old friends and school mates. The end of the wedding was bittersweet even though she promised one and all she would visit, telling her best girlfriends they were welcome to see her in England.

Chauncey wore the only nice dress that still fit her. It was a light blue muslin with lace trimming the hem as well as the corsage, belted just below her breasts with a dark blue ribbon. Ravyn gifted her with a sapphire pendant the original duchess gave her before she left London for her new home. Lilly wove a band of wildflowers into a circlet that she wore on her head.

After telling her how beautiful she was, Stephen was quick to disrobe her that night. They made love reveling in the soft mattress and equally soft pillows. Closing her eyes, she ran her hands over the covers. Though she did enjoy the furs in his lodge, these covers were nicer. He told her they would have a lodge they could visit for the night any time he was homesick.

"I need clothes," she told him the next morning as they lay in bed sated from their lovemaking. "I've outgrown everything. My belly seems to get larger with each breath I inhale."

His hand settled on her stomach, his touch light, stroking the small bulge that could barely be seen. After he finished caressing her there, he cupped a swollen, sensitive breast in his large hand. Chauncey felt the calluses. Loved the feel of his large hands against her skin.

Laughing, he addressed her problem. "Suppose you are asking for money. Are you going to be a greedy wench?" he chortled when she punched him in the chest.

"Would you rather I went naked," she tossed out the words understanding that as long as he was the only one seeing her, that was exactly what he would like.

"Yes..." He laughed and she was sure his amusement was at the look of indignations she tossed his way. "You are splendid with nothing on. This man's dream come true."

"We will be on a ship. I will not remain in the cabin for the entirety. Your mother needs clothing too. I know I told her she could wear whatever she wished but..."

"Do not believe mother would be receptive to wearing a corset. Nonetheless, a few modern dresses that would fit her with comfort might be appreciated. I doubt if she will wish for anything too complicated.

"We will take her to the little shop in the village. The seamstress there is sweet as well as very talented with a needle. The store has yards and yards of fabric to choose from. Mother will come with us. After watching the two of them today, I believe my mother likes your mother. That is always a good thing."

Closing her eyes, exhilarating in the breadth as well as the texture of his broad chest, she ran her hands along the smoothness of his body, delighting in the rippling of his muscles.

His eyes narrowed as she ventured lower then lower still with her questing fingers. She thought he would stop her. He did not. The breath he sucked in when she reached her goal, gave her reason to smile. She loved to touch him, tease him to full arousal. Enjoyed running her fingers along the velvet hardness when he was swollen and needy. Always liked to learn what gave him pleasure.

"You play with fire, Woman Who Breaks Rules." His nostrils flared as she wrapped her fingers around his solid length. "If you continue," he told her the sound rough, broken, "If you persist, you will not be ready to go to the dress makers when the mothers knock on our door. Instead, you will be embarrassed to the tips of your tasty little toes."

Ignoring his words, she sucked him deep into her mouth. He groaned, pulled her up then settled her on top of him. "Ride me."

"Yes."

The knock did come before she could finish what she began with him. A shattered sound caught in her throat. Stephen called out, "She'll be ready in a few minutes."

While there was chatter behind the closed door, she couldn't tell what was said. She closed her eyes, breathing in deep the scent of her husband. "I will never regret chasing after you, Stephen. You fill me, make me whole. I want to always be a part of you."

Three weeks later they were on board one of Jamie Lundin's

clippers heading to London. Lilly stood at the side of the ship watching the land disappear. As the ship moved from the harbor and picked up speed, her knuckles that closed around the railing were snow white. The wind blew her long dark hair. When she turned to cast Chauncey a hesitant smile, Chauncey understood Lilly would be just fine.

It was only a few weeks later having made exceptional time when they watched London come into view.

"This is where we will live?" Lilly asked as they stood on deck waiting for the gangplank to lower.

"No," Stephen said. "My home is to the east of here. Tonight, we will stay in the city. Tomorrow, we will travel to my home. It's about two hours from here. Kane lives about ten minutes away from me."

Epilogue

Stephen leaned back on his elbows watching his wife and daughter play on the mossy spot in front of his lodge. Love wedged in his throat, beat a hard and fast cadence. She flirted with him, her dress rising and falling around her slim ankles while she dodged this way and that to avoid the toddler.

Their shrieks of pleasure filled him with wonder, the giggles made him grin besotted with his two girls. The baby was always a miracle to him. That cold night when she was born, fear tore at his heart. The labor took so much from Chauncey. She was so weak. He was afraid to have another child. Chauncey wanted one. He didn't like to see her in pain. He didn't want the fear.

"Join us!" she called out as she grabbed the little girl then whirled her around in the air.

Her lovely smile stole his heart time and again.

"Papa! Come here," his little sweetheart called out sternly then pointed to the spot where she wanted him. "Here! Now!"

He hooted with laughter and did exactly what his little girl wanted. She was so much like her mama. With his arms outstretched he grabbed his daughter. He placed a kiss on her cheek then the tip of her tiny nose. Between her small hands she held his face. Kissed him back, a sloppy wet kiss on his mouth.

Sitting down he pulled Chauncey to the grass. He set his girls between his legs as he held them close.

"What do you think? Should we call Lilly to take her granddaughter back to the house. I'm thinking I'd like to ride with her mother."

He was thinking about riding, yes. She would straddle him when he sat atop his stallion. He would come deep inside her then he would set the horse to a hard gallop. He groaned recalling the erotic pleasure they both experienced when he made love to her in that manner.

The way she relaxed against him told him she was thinking along the same lines. He ran his hands along her arms. Then higher so his knuckles brushed enticingly along her neck.

"You've wicked thoughts, Mr. Wilkes."

"I want another child." Realizing that was true, he nuzzled her neck, teasing, drawing forth small noises from his wife. "What do you say? Shall we ride together and see what happens?"

"I say...oh..." she swallowed. "I say we should wait...I don't know..."

"You're ready. We've all the help we need to have a baby."

Despite the presence of his baby daughter, he cupped her breast, ran his thumb across the tip, delighted when the nipple hardened.

"I," she sighed softly leaning into him.

"You are wicked. You've nothing on beneath the gown. If you...I would think you want me to have my way with you. I won't withdraw this time. We will have another child." He knew he shouldn't put it that way. Also, understood the birth had been difficult for her. "There is nothing to fear."

"Easy for you to say," she shot back to him.

The hint of laughter in her voice surprised him, pleased him too. "You're right." The words as well as the thoughts were easy for him. "Still...there is no reason to believe the next birth will be hard. I've read a great deal on the subject as has Kane. We both are aware of how to deal with a multitude of issues that might arise. Lilly has attended many births."

"We both know it was Lilly who saved me."

"Please," he grinned at her scowl.

"I also want another child. You understand mother and father will be here in a week or less. We..."

"We need to take this opportunity. Finding time to be alone might be difficult when they are living under our roof." He wasn't complaining but he loved having his wife all to himself. Lilly now lived in a small cottage next to the larger home.

"They will stay with Aunt Ella some of the time."

"The Duchess?" he cocked an eyebrow. "When will she have her next charge."

"Christel's daughter, Tara, is coming here. She has her first ball next week. I believe we are all expected to attend," Chauncey whispered as his fingers found their way beneath her corsage.

"She's asleep," Chauncey whispered.

"Good, we have time to play." He scooped the toddler into his arms then strode to the lodge. The cradle he fashioned for the baby sat next to their furs. This afternoon they would make love outside.

When he was with her again, he pulled her into his arms. "If I leave, will you chase after me again. I would chase Woman Who Breaks Rules and I would have her chase me."

"Yes, you know I would. If he were ever to leave me, I will always chase after Still Water Runs Deep."

"I love that you chased me to the land of my people. Showed me how much you love me. Though you were a bit hesitant those first days. Yes, chasing Still Water is always good."

Coming Soon
by the author at
Rogue Phoenix Press

Tara's Reckless Heart
Naughty Book Five

Chapter One

London 1840

Tara MacLaren swayed in time to the music, tapping her toes, satisfied to watch the ball progress. Her spot behind the potted palm gave her the opportunity to observe without being seen. While she enjoyed the music, she didn't wish to be here. Longed for the security of her home.

She was in London with a ferocious protest. Staying at the castle on the other side of the island was her preference. Her older half-brother called her a loner. She was. The other male sibling simply told her she was feeling sorry for herself and should snap out of the snit then get on with her life. She told him she wasn't in a snit nor was she pouting. The drama of a London season was more than she was up to.

In London everyone excepted her to be looking for a husband. As a debutante at twenty years of age she was already on the shelf, though she admitted easily she wasn't horse-faced. Aunt Ella was her chaperone. Though The Duchess, as she was beginning to be called by family as well as friends, played more the role of matchmaker than chaperone. When she thought one of her charges had an eye for a certain man, she found a means to put them in a direct line that could never be avoided.

Aunt Ella took on the role of chaperone to the family females after the original duchess, Charlotte, passed on a few years back. Neither duchess seemed to be able to control their charges once the female in question decided on the man she wanted. Tara didn't think for one moment that either Charlotte or Ella cared about that little *faux pas*. Ella put Lyssa in a compromising situation with her now husband though she didn't realize Nickie ran off with the McInnis. Drake and Ella along with others chased after them to demand a wedding after she was compromised.

Tara didn't want a man. A wave of pain at the memory shook her to the core. In the past the horrid memories would have sent her to her knees. Now, she somehow learned to look inside herself when the past overtook her. Looking around the room, she caught the eye of Liam, her half-brother. He nodded then set off in her direction with Jeremy, one of his best friends, in tow. Her brother would be determined to make her laugh. Laughter was a hard commodity for her to come by, particularly so close to the anniversary that changed the course of her life forever.

After they reached her, Liam kissed her on the cheek while Jeremy picked her up then whirled her around in gigantic circles several times before he set her on her feet. Once her feet touched the ground, she swayed slightly, closing her eyes and shaking her head to get rid of the dizziness. Jeremy supported her for the minute it took her to recover. She leaned her head on his broad chest catching the spicey scent he favored. Tara wished she could feel more for Jeremy. She couldn't. Never would. Jeremy was a good friend. That was all.

"You're beautiful. More beautiful than I recall." He kissed her cheek. "Dance with me, Sprite. I know you want to whirl around the room. Make a few of the dandies want to hold you in their arms. They will be jealous of me."

"Of course, for you anything," she told him smiling shyly as he twirled her into the crush of people on the dance floor. It was then she saw a man, tall and darkly handsome. He was the most beautiful man she'd ever seen. Her heart lurched to her throat. His eyes narrowed as if he scorned her as he watched them dance away into the crowd. Why would he look at her in that manner? He seemed to accuse her of something.

"Who is that man?" Tara asked while she looked over her

shoulder to get another glimpse of the man who had just caught her attention.

"Who? Has someone taken my place in your affections?" Jeremy searched the room for the object of Tara's question.

Tara tried to see the man. He disappeared. "I don't know. He's not there any longer." She was thoroughly disappointed. Knowing the man's name seemed important.

"Is your dance card full?" Jeremy asked, looking down at her while she tilted her head up to see into his eyes. "It is if you dance with me for the rest of the ball. Otherwise, it's empty. Don't care to have men I don't know or want to know maul me. I'm not a debutante with a wealthy dowry. I'm not looking for a title. None are going to want me save for one purpose. I'm not willing to give any of them what they are after." It would take a very special man for her to want to spend time with. She didn't believe one existed for her.

Jeremy's crack of laughter surprised her. "Maul you?" he asked still laughing. "With Lady Ella hovering over you, doubt if any man here would dare do such a thing as man-handle you. Besides isn't that what big brothers are for, protecting little sisters? Liam is here not to find a debutante but to help Ella protect your good name."

"I wouldn't know. Liam is out having fun and playing at being the lord while Kenzie is chasing sunrises just as father used to do…still does. Now he does it with mother on his arm. I'm not at all certain why Liam showed up here." Maybe he was looking out for her best interest. Liam was closer to her than her brother. He understood her whims, her depressions. Always tried to lighten her day.

"You've been alone for far too long. Are you feeling sorry for yourself? You need to get over the grief. When that happens, you can start to live again. Lord knows you deserve that. You're a beautiful young woman who should be out having fun."

Tara gasped a bit startled by his callousness. "No…yes well…maybe a little. It's almost been two years. In a couple of days…" her voice trailed off while she felt sadness collide within the part of her that needed healing. Her heart ached for what she would never have.

"Sorry, I didn't mean to remind you," Jeremy said his soft-spoken voice holding a wealth of regret. "Would you like some fresh air?

We could go for a walk in the gardens or stand on the balcony. Whatever you would like."

"Appreciate your concern. What I would like would be to go home. Nonetheless, Aunt Ella won't let me. Mother and father aren't there. One would think a twenty-year-old woman would be allotted some independence. I'm most certainly capable of taking care of myself," she said in a strangled huff that almost turned to tears. Tara fought them back, pushed them away with all the strength she could muster from deep inside. She turned all her thoughts inward, searching for an inner peace before she unraveled in front of this large crowd of people.

"Is that a nod to the fresh air or a nod to staying here with no one on your dance card?" he asked with the persistence she was coming to associate with her beloved Jeremy. If she could have another brother, she would pick him. At one time he wanted more. She didn't have more to give.

"Liam will dance with me as soon as he can pry himself away from all the young ladies who are hoping to become a countess." Her laughter caused Jeremy to grin. She touched his lips with the tip of her finger. "What about you?" She needed to direct the conversation away from her and to something more suitable. "You should find a young debutante to dance with. You're not getting younger."

"We both understand, Liam is not looking for a wife as yet. Neither am I. Unless of course, I could somehow convince you I'm a good catch." His voice was wistful. His smile charming. It was too bad she felt nothing except friendship.

Her soft sigh didn't go unnoticed by the man dancing with her. She understood a relationship with this wonderful man would never be. "Would hate to ruin our friendship. You understand you will never be any more than a very good friend." Tara knew Jeremy wanted more than friendship. It just wasn't the same as before. "In every way except by birth, you are a brother to me."

"Much to my chagrin, I understand." Once again, he picked up the pace as the music moved from a slow waltz to one with a bit more stamina to it.

She laughed, clinging to him as her cheeks heated with the exuberance of the dance. Perhaps she needed that fresh air to cool her flaming face. Walking out onto the terrace with Jeremy would set tongues wagging. Tomorrow, the *on dit* would be that they were a couple. She wouldn't allow that to happen. Wouldn't hurt him in that way. She owed him part of her sanity. He and Liam helped her through the darkest times. Though Jeremy would just laugh and tell her people could believe whatever they want to think. He didn't care what people thought of him. However, she did need to guard her reputation.

Jeremy leaned close to her. The scent of his breath was mint when he whispered, "Would you like some punch. I'm certain it's spiked." His voice was a bit husky.

"Because you and Liam spiked it?" she was quick to ask; another tiny bubble of laughter was generated. They would do exactly as they pleased. They both had a bit of wicked inside them.

"I would never confess even to you, sweet sister."

The laughter sparkling up from deep inside couldn't be helped. The amusement healed the ever-present ache that seemed to be part of her soul. "I would like some. Just don't fill the glass to the brim. Don't want Uncle Drake to have to carry me out of here. Nor do I wish to make a complete fool of myself."

"Whatever you would like, my little Sprite. Come with me." He led the way moving between people. With deft precision, he guided her, keeping her hand in his so she'd stay close.

They ended up at the table with the punch along with the food. He poured them both glasses then he filled a plate they could share. She should eat something, anything if she was going to imbibe the spiked punch. She was hungry. When had she eaten last? She didn't remember. Food was never important to her, held no appeal until she was too weak to remain standing.

Together they wandered to the balcony then found a table. She leaned back staring at this man who helped her with so much of her grief. He held her hand when all she could do was weep for something that would never be. Sometimes he walked with her through the gardens at the Maclaren keep just to ease her wounded spirit.

"You are a wonder. You know that don't you? Some lucky lady will find you then you will be glad I turned you down."

Jeremy coughed, clearing his throat. "Not a wonder…not enough to be more than a friend to you." He waved his hand in the air to silence the retort that was on her lips. "No, don't say anything else. If all I can ever be is a friend, that is what I want for us. Drink your punch. Eat the food. You'll feel better after you do. I know you must be starving. After that, I'll see if I can fill your dance card with a few suitable names. Have you seen that man you asked me about earlier? If you would like a dance with him, I can see what he will say."

"No, no! No, don't ask him if you find him. Don't search for the man. I was only curious. There was something dark as well as brooding about him. Gave me shivers." Tara was more than curious. On first glance she thought him the most handsome man she'd ever seen. His face chiseled, his lips firm. His eyes though, his eyes blazed and simmered when he looked at her. With his broad shoulders and lean hips, he cut a dashing figure. She wanted to understand what he was thinking at that moment, when their gazes met then held for seconds. She felt somehow connected to him.

"Anyone else catch your fancy?" Jeremy asked.

"No, though Liam will dance with me. Since he's my half-brother he can have more than one or two twirls around the dance floor. I don't care to dance with anyone else." She lied. There was the man who caught her attention. He stared at her through veiled dark eyes, menacing eyes. The man was someone who was used to keeping to himself, shuttering his thoughts from everyone. For that brief moment that he looked at her, she felt as if he saw into her soul. She touched a finger to her lips, wondering how his lips would feel against hers. After that she shook the insanity from her head.

"As will your cousin, Ashcroft. Do you have any other relatives among the guests here?" Jeremy asked.

Tara didn't understand why that solitary man caught her attention. Somehow, he intrigued her like no one had ever done before…except… except the man she once called her fiancé. That time was long ago. She could never call it back though she wished she could.

"Tara? Where are you? You haven't said a word in the last five minutes. Is the punch getting too you?"

Tara snapped back to attention. "Oh, yes, there is Colby. I suppose Steven and Kane might also attend. I could dance with Colby.

He'll be around for a little while longer. Aunt Ella wanted everyone to be here for a short time to lend me a bit of moral support. Aunty understands this is the last place I'd like to be. Colby is not interested in debutantes as yet."

"Your dance card will now be filled with relatives. The Duchess will never understand what you are about. You shouldn't sulk or give that impression. If it can't be me, there is a man out there for you somewhere."

"She understands. Aunt Ella just doesn't agree. There he is. Don't look at him that way. He'll know what you are about." The man stared at her, his eyes still dark, still brooding. She felt as if there was a subtle threat issued. He nodded as if he understood she was attracted. It wouldn't do for her to show too much interest.

What did a nod of his head mean? He acted as if he understood what she was thinking. He didn't. Couldn't. Tara looked away her heart in her throat feeling uncomfortable with the situation. The breath she stole from the air singed her lungs burned when she exhaled.

"Care to dance?" The deep voice startled her out of her reverie.

Her breath caught then hitched. When she looked into his eyes, relief washed over her. She felt as if she could breathe again. "Ash! Yes. Of course, yes. You surprised me. Caught me unaware. I..." she held her bottom lip with her teeth. "It seems I was lost in thought."

"You were staring at a dangerous man. You would be well advised not to make his acquaintance. He has a reputation you wouldn't wish to be associated with," Ash told her. "Rumor has it he frequents the shadier parts of the city. Has been seen with some of my father's associates. He's shady. The man is a bounty hunter."

The order put her back up. "You're father's associates are either in the parliament or they are spies. Besides, the *on dit* about you puts you in many of the same places. Are you also a spy? Following in your father's footsteps?" she retorted. "You've no idea what you've just started by your words. You've issued me a challenge I mean to accept. What is his name?" Tara didn't understand why she decided then and there she would discover as much about this man as was possible.

"Case Ferguson," Ash spoke his words soft and low while he turned to look at the other man. "Dance? I'd rather not get into an argument here."

With as much haste as decorum would allow, she stood, smiling at one of her favorite cousins, tilting her head as she meant to flirt. "Thought you would never ask. Need Liam to come around for a dance too." Tara set her hand on his shoulder. "Case Ferguson, you say. Nice name."

"Tara, best you listen to me." He tried to argue again. "You could be getting in over your head. He steals women's hearts then leaves them with the shattered pieces. That's the last thing you need is your heart shattered."

"Heard you do the same."

Ash bent down to kiss her on the cheek. A few seconds later they waltzed around the room to a romantic ballad Tara loved. She hummed as they moved around the floor. Ash smiled down at her. "You need to…" he cleared his throat. "Suppose a man can wait longer than a woman to wed. We are of the same age. No one is insisting I attend galas to find a wife. Everyone understands a man of twenty isn't ready."

She bristled at his careless words. "I'm not going to marry. Not ever. No one." No, would never settle for second best though she would like to find someone she could share her hopes along with her dreams.

"Enough of that." His boyish grin made her smile in return. "I'm only here at the ball for you. Got a lot of life to live before I set my sights on a debutante. Hope to get as lucky as father did when he found my mother." Ashcroft whirled her in a tight circle dancing her through the throng of people.

Tara inhaled, a deep breath of air filling her lungs. She allowed him to lead. Ash was good. He'd been trained well. He was the heir apparent to the dukedom. By the time they finished and he brought her back to her favorite potted palm, her breath was heaving. Aunt Ella wasn't there. When Ash left she would be alone. Tara slid a deep breath of air into her lungs.

"Mother is dancing with father," Ashcroft nodded into the crowd of colorful swirling gowns. "Will you be alright if I leave you?"

"I won't swoon or do something else that might be construed as foolish. This palm and I are the best of friends," she spouted but she just might seek Mr. Ferguson. A challenge was a challenge. Tara would see what would happen if Mr. Ferguson did approach.

"No, I didn't think you would. I'm off to find some interesting entertainment for the evening."

"In other words, you're going to gamble and drink with your friends then…if the right woman comes along, you'll spend the rest of the night in her bed."

"You know me so well." He tapped her on the nose. "See that you don't get into troubled while I'm not around to bail you out."

"You know I won't," She was watching her aunt and uncle. "He seems to love her as much today as he did last time I was here." Thoughts of her lost love pummeled her. She sucked in a long draught of air that always seemed to have a calming effect on her.

"Would you like me to wait here until mother returns?" Ash was looking toward the door as if he needed to escape as soon as possible. Brent, one of Ash's friends waved to him before motioning with his arm. "Think I'm being summoned. As I told you, we've a night planned out on the town. You take care. Heed what I said about Case. Don't want you to get so far in over your head you drown. He has moves that will leave you breathless as well as at his whim. Despite your advanced age, you're an innocent still. He's an experienced man. He could eat you for breakfast then spit you out just as fast."

"You go on. Have fun." She rose on her toes to give him a quick hug then kiss. "I'll manage just fine. Maybe I can take the carriage home sooner than later. I'm through with this affair. The only ones I haven't danced with are Liam and Colby. They both seem to have disappeared."

"You would have to gain permission from The Duchess to leave so soon," Ash laughed when he used the name others were giving to his mother. "We both understand she won't give that approval until the wee hours of the morn." He looked at his watch. "It's only one o'clock now. You've got hours to go before permission will be granted."

Aunt Ella along with Uncle Drake were acquiring quite the reputation. They knew so much about every member of the ton, the thought boggled the mind. They knew who cheated on their spouse. Knew who owed money and those who committed fraud. The list went on. Drake was involved with the government. Once, he was a notorious spy in the Secret Intelligence Service. Uncle Drake always called it SIS if he mentioned it, foregoing the long words. Though most of what he knew was top secret. Now, he was in charge of recruiting new spies. Even though the men weren't called spies. They were more often called agents. What was a bounty hunter?

While Tara watched him leave with Brent, she fingered the amber necklace. The man who gave it to her told her it was the exact color of her eyes. The day still vivid in her mind, she clung to the images as if her life depended on doing so. She held on to the past. Jeremy was right in his assessment. Sometime she would need to put that past behind her.

The hour was growing late. Way past the witching hour. Tara felt as if she'd done her duty. She meant to find Aunt Ella then tell her she would retire for the night, take the carriage home. Waiting for consent went against the grain. She would send it back for her and Uncle Drake. Tomorrow's sunrise beckoned to her. She needed to get home so she could change her clothes into something suitable to ride. Rushing out to watch a sunrise was too much like her father for her to feel comfort. When she watched the sun begin a new day, it was one of her ways to remain calm. She didn't seek adventure. Tiny, her Irish wolfhound, would go with her for protection though the huge dog was too friendly by far. He loved everyone to the point where they would have to push him away.

He slobbered.

"What? No one to dance with?" The hard-edged voice surprised her. Her heart jumped to attention as the man she watched earlier stood in front of her. He was here… "Thought your dance card would be full."

"It's not," she said, surprised the man would approach her though earlier he did stare at her. She thought about Ash's words. He did look dangerous. Was he the challenge she needed to help her through each day? Tara supposed she should discover the truth. She needed to learn more about this man who beckoned her with his ominous dark eyes. He held secrets no one except him knew about.

"Wasn't the last one a bit young for you?" he asked sending her a look that covered her from the top of her head to the tips of her toes then back. "You're too old for him."

"He's my age." Tara's back was up, felt the fine hair on the nape of her neck bristling. The interrogation was not to her liking. He had no right to judge her or her cousin. She'd dance with Ash anytime she liked. What did his age have to do with anything. Why was this man she didn't know concerned about who she danced with?

"Young," he said succinctly his threatening stare boring into her. "Can't you handle a man? Boys are easy. Suppose some women need to be in control. That won't happen with us. You won't control me."

What the devil was that supposed to mean? She let the air she'd been holding since her first gasp of surprise go out is a slow stream as she tried to process this new information he shoveled at her. Everyone knew that Ash was her cousin just as Colby was, "What do you want?"

"A dance, that's all," he said his voice filled with sarcasm. "What you've been giving othes." The dark edge intrigued her enough to encourage her to take the bait he offered. "Just the same as your suitors. Want to understand why you…" Seeming to think better of what he was about to say, he swept his hand across his chin. It didn't seem he wanted to say anything more.

Tara held the distinct impression that wasn't all. She wanted to know what he didn't finish saying. Didn't Ash just tell her the man was treacherous. Knowing him might be hazardous to her wellbeing. A spark of something went through her as if it was a lightning strike. Heat roared to life. "I don't know. Suppose I could make room on my card for one more dance. Though I was looking for The Duchess to tell her I was going home." Until Case approached her the air had become stagnant. The room boring. Monotonous.

The slow smile creeping across his lips sent another wave of fire surging. He spoke, his voice low, as if he knew exactly what she would do. Understood she would fall into his plans. The challenge was on.

"I'll take you home after the dance. No need to concern The Duchess." He held out his hand in silent invitation. The deep blue of his eyes sparkled with fire and heat. She hesitated, knowing this step might very well be irrevocable.

Another challenge. Was he testing her? For what possible reason? No single young woman would accept that blatant invitation. He overstepped. "Can't. That wouldn't be appropriate," she murmured wondering what the *on dit* would be if she accepted the brazen request. The ton would have her wed to this man before she could breathe. Uncle

Drake would make certain he wed her just as he did Nickie and Colin.

"From what I've seen, you don't seem to care about your reputation. You flirt with anyone wearing pants. So, what would a ride home with me matter. Nothing would change."

The words unsaid did more to catch her attention than the ones he enunciated with a clear even voice. He didn't know anything. Nothing she did tonight would create a scandal. "You…you have no idea what you are speaking about. You don't know me."

"Am I right?" His question challenged again. He crossed his arms over the width of his chest waiting with what seemed to be never-ending patience for her to answer. "Would like to know you much better. Interested in all of you." His languid gaze raked over her body.

She caught the underlying thought. "I don't even know your name and you are insulting me as if we've known each other for years." The lie caught in the back of her throat. She held out her hand thinking she would like an introduction of sorts. The introduction would have been better coming from Ash as he seemed to know this man. Despite his attitude or perhaps because of it, she did want to get to know him better. "I'm Tara MacLaren and you?"

He brought her hand to his lips, kissed the back before turning it over to place a damp kiss on the heart of her palm. One more time she jumped startled from the unexpected contact, her body vibrating with a need she never felt before. The one kiss packed a wallop. She swallowed down a lump in her throat. Wished she dared fan her face which she knew heated to a raging point. Last minute thinking caused her to tug on her hand. He let it go with a deep masculine chuckle.

"Case Ferguson. About that dance you owe me? Shall we?" he queried as he pulled her toward him, tugged until her body was flush against his. She set her hand on the hard plane of his chest to steady herself. Far too close to be appropriate. He wasn't allowing distance between them. When he looked down at her, she felt his breath wash over her, caught the scent of spearmint as well as man…dangerous man…spicey as well as arrogant.

Hazardous!

The devil, she needed to know what the man was thinking. *He's a danger to me. Ash told me to beware of this man. What do I owe him?*

A dance? I don't think so.

"A dance, you owe me a dance," he repeated, his voice deepening, huskier than before.

Why? Tara found herself held within his hot embrace. With singlehanded purpose, he wove a spell around her. This was not like the other dances she shared with her friend as well as her cousins. He held her too close. He was too imposing, too male. Intimidating. Handsome. His hand that was now settled on the small of her back heated her through the thin layer of fabric that lay between them.

He moved with ease around the floor. Her feet flew. At times she felt as if they didn't touch the dance floor. "Tell me about…" Her heart caught in her throat.

Tara stumbled as he moved too fast. She was awkward. Her other dance partners took that into consideration. Case wouldn't understand. He caught her in his strong arms. Brought her up against his hard muscled chest. She closed her eyes then lied again. "I'm sorry. Don't usually have two left feet." Two left feet was her middle name.

"Nothing to be sorry about," he replied with smooth calm continuing as if nothing happened. He stopped in front of Aunt Ella. "Duchess," he nodded politely at her aunt as if he knew her. "Tara says she would like to leave. With your permission, I'm taking her home."

"That would be nice," Drake cut in looking amused at this new development. "See that the two of you behave."

To say she was startled again would be an understatement. Her breath caught in the back of her throat. "But…" She reached out as if asking for a different answer only to find herself whisked away again. His hand rested on the small of her back, guiding her with ease across the dance floor to the entrance. She felt as if he couldn't get out of there soon enough.

"You changed your mind?" Case asked as he led her to the coatroom. "You do have a wrap? Right?" One of his dark eyebrows lifted skyward.

"No…yes… I wish to leave here. It's just that…" She swiped her tongue across her parched lips. "It's just that…" Tara still couldn't get the words out that she was thinking. Her brain and her mouth didn't want to cooperate.

"Did you have too much of the spiked punch? Or…you didn't expect The Duke and Duchess to give me the opportunity to be alone with you?" He paused for a few seconds as if he expected her to talk. "I work for the duke. If anything happened to you on my watch, he'd skin me alive. You're safe with me."

"Oh."

She found her shawl.

He draped the fabric around her shoulders, touching her. His fingers brushed against the tops of her breasts. She sipped in air, the caress mercuric.

~ * ~

Case wasn't at all certain what to make of Tara MacLaren. By all standards he recognized she was an enigma. In time he would get to the bottom or the top of what made Tara so reclusive yet at the same time appealing. When he looked into her eyes, they seemed haunted by something intangible.

She was acting.

Had to be

There was no other explanation. No woman could lie with that much conviction. By watching her this evening, he understood he would be last in line for her affections. Not for long though. He intended to have her then let her go. Sassy little flirts like Tara were good for a fun romp in bed. She would be good in that capacity. That's all he wanted, a good lay. A way to spend the time. Most any woman would do. Though he liked the ones that would pose the greatest challenge. Tara would be a challenge to him.

In the coach she sat opposite him. Played with the fabric of her satin ballgown. Stared at him as if she was trying to delve beneath his skin. He needed conversation if he was going to begin to understand her. "Tell me something about yourself."

"Not much to tell," she murmured as she seemed to focus on a point outside the carriage. The definite feminine lift of her shoulders, the slight sway of her breasts appealed to all his masculine senses.

"I'm certain that's not true. The way you look at men tells me you've experience." Crossing his legs, he stretched out. Case let his leg rest against hers. She moved away, giving him more room. He thought about pursuing this avenue. Changed his mind. Physically, it might be prudent to move slower. At times, she seemed to be a flighty little thing.

"What's Jeremy to you?" He wanted to ask if she slept with him. If the man was her lover. In time he would know. The question was abrupt. He wasn't surprised when she flashed him a deep dark scowl.

Her eyes darkened as she seemed to search for a polite or maybe not so polite reply to his impertinent question. "You overstep."

Yes, where she was concerned, he meant to exceed all polite boundaries. Until he found a way to take her to his bed, he would continue to test her, to challenge. She would be his delight for a few months or for however long they were mutually suited for each other. He believed it would be a while before she bored him. "Perhaps," he hedged not wishing to give away his plans.

"Why did you wish to bring me home?" she asked for the first time, her voice sparked of curiosity. "We mean nothing to each other. Why?"

He drummed his fingers on his leg, wondering how much truth he dared tell her. "The Duchess suggested we get to know each other better. Told me you planned on riding out to see the sunrise this morning. Seems she thought you should have a protector along for the morning ride. Since I'm good at that type of thing, she approved." He smiled at the glower she returned. Wondered if the way her anger was building, her passion, when he finally made love to her would be as intense.

"I've Tiny to protect me. Don't need a protector...or a man. I stand alone."

"Another of your lovers?" he asked wishing she wasn't quite so promiscuous. Curbing wayward proclivities to be with one man at a time would be his mission. He knew Ashcroft warned her away from him. The young pup told him he would do that. Told him to stay away from her and that Tara wasn't for him to play with. The boy protected her. Ah, she said they were the same age. He wondered how old she was.

Sitting back, he watched her with more intensity. While she didn't deny she had lovers, she didn't confirm his thoughts either.

"Why of course, I have so many," she murmured, her face turning dreamy while she did corroborate his thoughts. "Would you like me to list them? I've only about ten at this time…give or take. I will need to think."

Case heard the sarcasm in her voice, he didn't read too much into the tone. During the following silence, Tara played with her gown. The ball gown was lovely, the ice blue complimenting as well as enhancing her features. When he touched her, the tops of her full breasts, the flesh was silken. Her waist was narrow. He was positive her hips would flare with enough provocation to arouse him. Hell, he was stimulated looking at her dressed. How would he feel when he saw her naked? Her golden hair was swept into a knot while strategically placed tendrils framed her small oval face. Her nose was pert, tipping a *wee bit* at the end. It was her lips that drew him. He needed to taste and savor, leave a dewy trail of moisture on their fullness. He wanted to nibble on her top lip. While he listened to the soft sighs of pleasure he created. Needed to see what lay beneath the fabric. In time he would.

"We are here. I don't want a companion this morning. Don't need protection. Need to be alone with my thoughts," she told him as he helped her from the carriage. "You cannot go with me."

"Promised The Duchess. I wouldn't want to hear her scalding words when she discovered I didn't accompany you. That I was derelict in my duty." Case set the steps by the carriage door. Held out his hand to guide her downward.

"Why? Why is she acting this way?"

Because The Duchess formed plans of her own. If he didn't miss his first guess, and he rarely did, the woman was playing matchmaker. In this case, she waisted her time. If she hoped to marry off her wayward niece to him, her plans would fail. Nonetheless, he would enjoy the adventure along with this beautiful woman.

"You will have to ask The Duchess. I'm certain she has a reason for everything. Since you are one of her charges, she will do what she thinks best. What are you to her?"

"You don't know?" she asked as he held her elbow escorting her to the front steps of the large townhouse the duke and duchess owned in London though they didn't spend a great deal of time in the city.

The question surprised him. "Should I?" It didn't appear she meant to tell him or give him a clue.

"If you did your homework, you would know the answer. I'm going to change my clothes. If you still want to ride with me, meet me in the stable. Don't be late. Punctuality is important." She flounced away from him, her skirts swaying as she strode through the hall then up the stairs. The devil, he'd like to know her thoughts.

What she didn't know was that he occupied one of the guest rooms on the second floor. Once she disappeared, he raced up the steps to his room. Just as she was a guest of the Montgomeries, so was he. With a hurried pace, he changed to buckskins and a white shirt. Instead of boots, he pulled on a pair of knee-high moccasins. It wasn't his intent to be late. He figured he would beat her to the horses. His clothing was so much easier to take on and off than hers. Just so he wouldn't seem too eager, he poured a small snifter of brandy. Once he finished, he strode to the stable.

Inside, the large room filled with numerous horses was lit by a lantern. With muffled steps, he strode down the length. Listening. Watching intensely. It smelled of leather and liniment. The scent of horses wafted through his nostrils. The murmuring two stalls down caught his attention.

"Why, you big oaf, I'm rubbing behind your ears just the way you like. Isn't it enough that I give you the bulk of my attention. You still want more. Always more. What else I can do to please you?"

Another lover she's brought to ride out to see the sunrise. Anger simmered deep in his gut. The lady would have to learn that while he was seeing her there would never be anyone else. Second thoughts hit him in the gut. He knew exactly what she could do to please him. He would make certain she understood sharing pleasure was important to a relationship.

"You're drooling, big guy. Can't you ever control that slobber? No, I suppose you cannot," she giggled, her laughter sending a wave of heat to his belly. The sound was so pure and delightful. "You're supposed to protect me not drown me." Once more, her laughter was light and airy, filling the confines of the stable.

Case liked the way her voice trilled, liked most everything about the woman except her penchant for men. Ah, but that would also work in his favor. She was an experienced little jade. Wooing her into his arms wouldn't be hard. Experienced in his own right, he would seduce until she panted, until she wanted no other man in her bed. They would both give and receive pleasure. Then and only then would he walk away.

Whoever this lover was, he meant to rid himself of the man before they left to watch the sunrise. He wouldn't be going with them on this first jaunt as he was never a fan of threesomes. His anger simmered only skin deep. He swung open the gate to the stall where the two lovers were trysting, murmuring sweet nonsense.

His jaw dropped. He rubbed his chin speculating why he thought she was speaking with a man, a lover.

In the corner of the stall, he gazed at the largest dog he'd ever seen. His paws were on her shoulders. He was licking her face. She was laughing so hard her face was a rosy glow. Tara pushed at him. The dog was immovable.

"Tiny, stop that. Get down, you big oaf!" She was still laughing, to no avail trying to push the animal from her. It seemed the animal was an immovable force. Amused, Case leaned against the fencing. He watched. Delighted with the ensuing event.

Tiny's head was above hers. The dog could kill her with one blow or one bite. Case moved forward, deciding it was time for the dog to behave. "Down, Tiny!"

The dog dropped. On all fours, he stood eye-level to her breasts. Tiny looked at him with clear brown eyes, his tail wagging as if he hadn't just been disciplined. Tiny barked a greeting then sat as if waiting for another order.

She was breathless as she spoke as if she had been rolling around in the hay with her lover. "When did you come in?" Tara asked brushing wayward locks of golden hair from her eyes. "I didn't hear you."

Case grunted. She was too occupied entertaining her huge dog to hear anything. "You were too busy talking nonsense to that big hound of yours." He wasn't about to tell her he thought she was entertaining another lover. Though a tryst with her in the hay would be fun. As long as he thought of her as his, he would never allow her to be with another man.

"Well, are you ready?" She sauntered past him to another stall where a horse was saddled and waiting for her. The mare was a russet color. Pretty as her owner but in a different way. "Come along, Sunrise. We're going to see your namesake. In the meantime, we have to let this man keep us company."

Not giving her a chance to mount by herself, he grabbed her by her slender waist before tossing her on the horse. "Glad to see you're not riding sidesaddle." A woman could kill herself riding that way. He didn't understand why more females didn't opt for a safer and more comfortable means of riding.

She nodded in the direction of another stall. "I had your horse saddled. The big black stallion you ride is waiting."

Bloody eyes, he'd been so busy listening to her banter with her dog, he forgot about having Black readied. He was pleased though that she accepted his company. Time spent with her could be enjoyable. He would see into her jaded soul.

After he mounted, "Lead the way."

For the first few minutes, he elected to follow. Tiny ran along beside them, barking then chasing after whatever seemed to appeal to him. Case enjoyed watching her back, the way she rode with ease. If anything, she was an accomplished horse woman, at home on her mount, her movements fluid yet feminine too. The britches she wore, fit nicely to the curves of her hips and her delectable fanny. There was so much more of her he was going to see. He could wait. Patience was the name of this game he played. He needed her to want him as much as he wanted her.

By the time they left the city, he was abreast of her. "Where to? Where is this beautiful sunrise you're taking me to view?" Curious, he was interested in the destination. Tiny seemed to have lost interest in chasing butterflies as well as bees. Now he trotted beside them, his tongue lolling from his massive jaw. The dog was too friendly. Would never do his job of protecting his mistress unless he drowned someone in his drool or jumped on the person to get his ears rubbed.

Tara flashed him a beautiful smile. He could get used to seeing that smile. She didn't do it often. "Into the country. Are you familiar with the Montgomerie's country estate?" she asked, sugar coating her words, her eyes looking through him as if concentrating on something only she understood.

After he shook his head, "No. Can't say that I am." Bloody eyes, he wished he could see into her pretty head. One moment she was smiling the next she was sad. He needed to understand why she looked haunted as if she was in constant pain, as if a ghost disturbed her. Needed to see inside her soul. Needed to discover her falsehoods as well as her truths.

"Just this side of the drive we'll veer off and go overland. A few miles into the countryside there is a lake that spreads out across the rolling land. That's where I mean to watch the sun's rebirth. There is a boulder that has my name on it."

The sun's rebirth.

"This isn't the first time you've watched the sun rise over the lake? Is it?" he asked becoming more curious about this fetching woman. She had many facets to her. It would take time to learn what she hid from view.

"Nope."

Case mulled all her words over in his mind, liking the sound of them. In many ways Tara was different from the other women of his acquaintance. Not that very different though. She was a better actress. Could hide her true feelings. All women were after what they could get from a man, wealth as well as a title. Women needed to feel secure as they aged. This woman could no longer claim to be a debutante yet she did. While he didn't have a title, he had more money than he knew what to do with. He could never spend it all unless he started gambling. Something he would never do. Tara wouldn't know about his wealth unless The Duchess told her. Case held the distinct impression The Duchess told her charge next to nothing about him. She didn't even know his name when he walked up to her at the ball. After thinking about it, he would have expected Ashcroft to fill her in on his name as well as profession. Ashcroft would warn her to stay away. Since he rode with her this morning, the man didn't tell her. Either that or she didn't appreciate being told what to do.

As far as he knew, the MacLaren clan were not titled though they did own a castle on the east coast bordering the highlands. That was about all he was able to learn at the ball. The Duchess didn't tell him anything more about her. Discovering all the intriguing facets of this lady would be amusing.

This lady's agenda with a man could be anything. Maybe all she wanted from a male was good sex. Perhaps she wasn't looking for marriage. He sure as hell wasn't going to go down that path. He could give her good sex as soon as she asked. Once he learned about all the men in her life, he decided she would have to beg. Given time she would. The problem for him was keeping his hands to himself until she did plead.

They crested a hill. At the glorious sight, he sucked in his breath. The sky was just beginning to glow with golds and oranges as well as various shades of pink on the horizon. When the sun rose even higher, the site to greet them would be spectacular. Tara chose the place well. She did say she'd been here before.

She stopped. For a few seconds, she stared at the beauty in front of her. A smile grew on oh so kissable lips. Tiny ran for the pond. In one great leap coupled with a bark of pleasure, he landed about four feet away from the beach making a splash as big as if a cannon ball landed in the water. Her laughter rippled around her. The sound so pleasant, he felt something in his mind change. During those moments watching, listening to her, he thought she was different than what he expected. Tara certainly took pleasure from the simpler things in life.

Still laughing at her big dog, she spoke through giggles. "He's such a big oaf. I love him so much." Her words held sadness within them. When she pulled in a ragged breath of air her small frame shuddered. The haunting of her breath terrified him. It was as if she lost her soul in that moment.

Case saw that same sorrow at the ball when she spoke with Jeremy. The man knew something about her that seemed to be a secret between them. Her eyes haunted with pain, she remained very still as if she savored this moment. It seemed she thought of some other time or place. Perhaps a moment with another man.

To find a place inside her head would be nice. Case didn't think she would enlighten him as to her private thoughts. A time would come when she would confide in him. Wondered what it would feel like to be loved by her.

The thought that she was burrowing into his head disturbed him, would waylay his plans until he could control his baser drives. He reminded himself, she was just like every other female, out to get what she could from a man. His mind traveled back ten years ago to the woman he thought to love for the rest of his life.

To the betrayal.

He dismounted then helped her down. When she slipped into his arms, he brought her close enough so he could feel the softness of her breasts pushed against his chest. The sensation wasn't the same as when they danced. She wore nothing beneath her shirt, not even a chemise. An invitation he meant to ignore for the time being. If she was truly that needy, she would have to wait to find her pleasure. Tara was a brazen little thing, displaying herself this way. If The Duchess didn't know about her charge's proclivities, he wasn't going to be the man to explain things to Ella.

Tara didn't seem to notice the bulge pressing against her belly while he still held her, his hands cupped around the lushly feminine curves of her bottom to steady her. Either that or she didn't mean to give his need for her credence. When she turned her face so she looked at him, she was flushed with a rosy glow. Mayhap, she did notice.

Case set her away from him. She moved with a few awkward steps toward the boulder as if she was in pain. After she seemed to get her feet beneath her, she relaxed.

"Any special place you watch this spectacle from?" His hands rested behind his back while he rocked on his heels, studying every subtle nuance that was Tara MacLaren. She was the perfect study of innocence coupled with sensuality. Her passion would rock him until he couldn't breathe or think. He wasn't positive how he knew this.

He just did.

Tara pointed, "Over there, by the boulder. I usually sit on top until the show is over. After that I appreciate the solitude as long as I dare before I go back to the estate. Never want The Duchess to send out a search party."

"How often do you come here?" Case followed Tara to the boulder. She moved with fluid liquid grace. Her hips the perfect size for her frame. Sometime during the ride, she had unbuttoned the top two buttons of her shirt. He wanted to look at her more closely, so he could see what he could see. The slight swell of her breasts would be evident.

If he had his wishes, she would go for one more button.

"Whenever I visit the duke and duchess." Her long fingers pushed at her hair away from the small perfect oval of her face. "That's not often though. I like home too much."

"You're hear for the season?" he asked expecting a round of lies. She was too old to have a season. The lords searching for a wife were looking at younger women, malleable women. Tara wouldn't be easily swayed by any man. Case didn't want to change her in any way, just wanted to experience her company. Needed her to grace his bed for as long as they both wanted each other.

He helped her navigate the boulder then jumped up beside her.

"No, not here to find a husband or to parade for the men who are searching. Don't want a husband." She leaned back, her hands supporting her, the view provocative, challenging him to keep his hands to himself.

Case believed her even though the sigh following her words held a bit wistfulness in them. There might have been a time she felt different. "Why ever not?" Seemed she never failed to surprise him. "All women want a husband." A bit of his jaded self-came out in the tone of his voice.

"Don't believe there is a man out there I can fall in love with. Have to be in love to marry." She let out another breathy sigh that brought more questions to Case's mind. "Won't marry for any reason except love." She turned to him searching out his features. Her gaze locked with his. "What about you?"

A dark shadow swept through him as he thought about the woman he once thought he loved. She killed love for him. Taught him love wasn't real. He learned women betrayed men to get what they wanted or needed. He pointed to the sun rise as he spoke. "Love doesn't exist. Don't want a wife. Guess we're a matched pair in that respect."

When she turned to look at him, the concern in her eyes shocked him. He didn't recall knowing a woman who was ever concerned about anyone except themselves. A slight tilt to her head coupled with vertical crease between her brows, she asked, "What happened? Who hurt you so terribly you lost all hope for love?"

The question hit him as hard as if she swung a sledge hammer into his gut. This conversation was at an end. He wasn't about to talk about his past when the future would prove to be more gratifying. "Suppose we should enjoy the rebirth of the sun as you put it a few minutes ago." Revealing a past to any woman was a mistake he wasn't going to make. He wasn't stupid. Doing so would give the female an advantage. Case wasn't a man to allow himself to become vulnerable.

"That bad?" Tara leaned back again, her hands behind her. Once more in that provocative pose he enjoyed. She'd crossed her legs so she sat Indian style. Her breast pushed forward against the fabric of her shirt. Nipples hard and tight showed against the tiny barrier she called a shirt.

Case appreciated the view. While her breasts were not large, they would fit in his hands. She was more beautiful than the sunrise that now splashed color across the horizon. More intriguing. If he could paint, he would paint the sunrise with Tara's face part of the parade of colors. In his mind, he imagined the portrait.

When she turned abruptly, she caught him staring at her. He wasn't about to answer her question. What he experienced was more than bad. The encounter changed his life forever. No one needed to know. Everyone who did either left him or had passed on. Ella Montgomerie knew part of the story as did Drake. No one except Case Ferguson knew it in its entirety.

When he joined the SIS, he'd had to enumerate a few of his reasons. Drake Montgomerie had been privy to those reasons. Ella, well Ella was a different story. She had this way about her. Somehow and for reasons he didn't understand, he confided in her. The Duchess promised not to tell anyone, not even the duke. Husbands, especially, Drake at his finest interrogation had a way of drawing unwilling truths from people. If the devious pair put the information they knew about him together, they would know everything.

"What happened is in the past. Doesn't need a recounting of details." Case supposed that much of what he read in Tara's haunted and sad eyes revolved around the past. She wasn't recounting details either.

"Is that your way of telling me it's none of my business?"

"Yes."

They both held secrets close to their hearts.

To his surprise, she leaned into him. The gesture was almost as if she wished for comfort. He wrapped his arm around her, pulling her close. Her head on his chest, he heard a throaty little sigh of contentment.

Lost in thought, he barely noticed she'd fallen asleep. Minutes passed. His arm was growing numb. He didn't want to wake her. From some of the gossip he heard last night, she arrived at the Montgomerie's with just enough time to prepare for the ball. She hadn't slept last night. He decided it wasn't the company that put her to sleep.

As carefully as possible, he lifted her into his arms. At the base of the huge rock, they'd been sitting on, he sat down. His back against the boulder, he relaxed. She smelled of lilies coupled with sunshine. To his surprise, she snuggled in his arms, her hand set on his belly. His gut tightened. Heat spiraled straight to his loins. He held tight to control while her small body was cradled against his.

Case wanted to chuckle when he heard the little snore. If he confronted her with that fact, she would deny she snored. He closed his eyes, content to hold her for as long as she slept. Maybe not as long as she slept. The Duchess knew where they were. Would expect them at the country house at a respectable time. If they didn't show up, there wasn't a single doubt in his head that Ella would send someone after them.

The brilliant colors in the sky faded, turning to a brilliant summer blue. A few clouds dotted the horizon as the sun inched its way upward. The breeze was slight. Leaves in the trees above them rustled to the stimulant. She burrowed into him, running her cheek across his chest. He flamed from the insignificant contact. If this was any indication of how they would do together, she would heat his bed to an inferno. He should wake her soon. Didn't know her well enough to know how to go about doing so.

"Grant…" she whispered, her hand roaming, exploring across his belly.

Grant?

Case tightened, jealousy surging ahead. Who the devil was Grant? The man had to be another one of her lovers. He would have to discover who this man was as well as what he meant to her so he could let him know that Tara was hands off until they no longer wanted each other. That time would come.

When he looked down her sleepy-lidded eyes, slightly dazed, she whispered again. "Kiss me. It's been so long."

Case fought the urge consuming him until he could no longer control the impulse. The man must be in her past. "If that's what you want, baby, then who am I to deny you your carnal pleasures. Your sensuality is why we are together. This might be the first kiss but it won't be the last."

His lips feathered across Tara's mouth, light butterfly caresses, teasing nips, flirting sultry touches. His tongue to her mouth urging her to give more of herself. Her fingers wound into his shirt pulling him closer. She sighed. He placed undemanding kisses on the corners of the sweet curve of her mouth. With his teeth he nibbled on her top lip until she opened more fully for his attention. Even in her sleep she knew what she wanted. She gave all that he asked then a *wee* bit more.

A broken sound then a soft mewl was his reward for the tender attention. His body hardened with need as well as restraint while he steeled himself to seduce not respond. With this little vixen he found that feat impossible.

As the day progressed, she'd unfastened buttons on her shirt. Now the sight of the rounded swell of her breasts were visible between the two sides of her shirt. Touching and tasting were in the forefront of his mind. That could wait. One thing at a time.

"Oh, Grant..." she sighed again, running her hand across the expanse of his chest. "I've missed you."

There it was again. Tara needed to learn it wasn't Grant who was kissing her, who was giving her pleasure. He deepened the kiss, smoothing his tongue over hers as she opened for him giving him easy accesses. Inside her mouth she was hot, a sultry inferno that begged for discovery. He touched all of her, tugged on her bottom lip, caressed her teeth then delved deeper into the inferno that grew with each passing second.

When she was arching toward him, her hands winding into his hair while she accepted the intimacy he offered, he pulled away, the movement slow. Case was watching her eyes. Needed to see the moment she realized he wasn't Grant. He was so close to her. His wishes confirmed. Knew the exact moment she opened her eyes. Her hand touched feather light on his cheek. She stared, confused for the moment. Eyes widening, she sat up, her head hitting his chin.

"You're not Grant!"

No…he wasn't.

"Who is Grant?"

~ * ~

Ella paced the sundeck where they were eating a late breakfast. She continued to stare in the direction of the lake, worried about Tara. Case was notorious for his womanizing. She'd put them together for a solid reason. Drake agreed with her. That thought didn't make her feel better. Acting as matchmakers could be disastrous. Ella understood why Tara shied away from men. Knew also why Case didn't want a solid relationship with a woman. The two of them both needed healing. They were perfect for each other. Perfect unless Case seduced her before she was ready.

"She is in good hands," Drake told her as if he meant to encourage. "Case is a good man."

Ella understood her instincts in this affair were right. Still, doubts whirled in her head. While Case might never allow himself to be hurt by a woman, Tara was vulnerable. "That's what I'm afraid of…his hands," Ella retorted as she continued the frenzied walking from one end of the patio to the other.

Drake tossed his head back, barking with the laughter that she knew all too well. "He won't hurt her. Won't take her virginity, at least not yet. When the time is right for both of them, if the pair continue to see each other, they will come together. Tara needs to wake up to the fact Grant is no longer alive. We both understand she needs to move on with her life. Who better to do that for her than a notorious rake?" He lifted his broad shoulders in a very male shrug accepting the inevitable without feeling a moment's guilt.

"I know. I agreed with you because Tara believes her life ended with Grant's life. It very nearly did. We are all thankful she is still alive. Something or someone has to shock her into living again," Ella said, though she knew Tara had come a long way in doing so on her own. The girl did agree to come for a season even though Ella knew full well that Tara would have been happier wandering the trails around her ancestral home and hunting. Since her fiancé's death she'd become such a loner.

"When the right woman comes along, every man falls," Drake mused seeming to think of how he fell for his wife.

"I just hope that she doesn't have to give up her innocence before the wedding." Drake was so positive there would be a marriage. Ella wasn't so certain. There were things she knew about Case that she didn't think her husband had learned or if he did, being male he wouldn't understand.

"You gave up yours," he said blandly as he patted his thighs, an invitation to her to come to him.

"You didn't give me much of a choice," she retorted ignoring the invitation.

"No, with good reason. In Paris they will have company of sorts. Ashcroft has left for the city. He will have things prepared for them when they arrive in a day or two. How long do you think it will take Tara to ready herself."

"Bah! Our son will be no chaperone to that pair. He will be out to whatever party he can find, testing his manhood in every feasible way. What makes you think Tara will agree to go?"

"I don't know. What does she have here except a broken heart? Case offers a warm heart. Companionship. She needs both."

"More likely a warm bed is what he is extending to her."

"I saw the way he looked at her. Yes, the man wants her in the most basic way. Our Tara won't give herself so easily into his hands. He will have to work to get her into his bed. By then he will have fallen in love."

"I know." Ella gave in and sat down on Drake's lap. "I hope they will heal each other."

"Kiss me."

Nick's Tender Rogue
Naughty book One

Once a McClellan lass

Beautiful, naughty and audaciously daring, young Nickie Gray is a McClellan princess through and through—as wild and reckless as the most incorrigible of her male cousins. Now that she has reached a marriageable age, Nickie has set her amorous sights on a most unsuitable male—the notorious rake and womanizer known to all mamas on the debutante scene in London as dangerous. When her chaperone tells her all rakes are off limits, she finds the challenge one she sets her mind to.

Always a McInnis rake

Not expecting to find a ravishing woman throwing herself at him yet blatantly willing to accept whatever overtures she makes, handsome Collin McInnis is thrilled by the brazen escapades of this naïve creature and is willing to experience her high-spirited advances with no expectations of commitment. On the high seas, he is bested by a vivacious beauty whose love of freedom and adventure rivals his own...and by an inescapable tidal wave of passion that threatens to engulf them both.

Dream About Lyssa
Naughty book Two

When Lyssa Andrews sees the earl sitting behind his desk scowling, she knows she will someday put a smile on his face. The handsome brooding earl isn't playing the same game. He resists her outrageous comments and questions until she is ready to give up. Lyssa didn't come to London with the intent to find a man. Now, though, she is willing to chance love with the stodgy earl of Blackmore.

Raised by the Sioux when his father sought adventure then fell in love with a Sioux maiden, Kane has been betrayed once by a white woman. He isn't about to give his heart to another, especially one who is as white as newly fallen snow. Despite his best efforts, he can't deny Lyssa's intoxicating effect on him. Now Kane will risk his very life to protect the innocent beauty who has seduced him with her tender love.

Deke's Magic Kiss
Naughty book Three

She would risk everything to become a practicing doctor

Annie Lundin's dream of practicing medicine and a life of dignity and self-sufficiency vanishes in the small Kansas Territory town of Denver City. When the men of the town refuse to become her patients, all she has left to fight for is her practice. She is thwarted from every direction. She didn't mean to fall for the dark, handsome sheriff. Didn't mean to ask for his help. Annie needs Deke Sullivan to protect her from the dark secrets that follow her from Boston. In return she offers all she has—herself.

He would stop at nothing to win her love and trust

Raised by the Cheyenne, Deke Sullivan was churlish, overconfident, and dangerously handsome. His life changed when his Irish grandfather discovered him. He was sent to West Point, fought the

Seminole in Florida as well as some on the planes where his loyalty was divided. A woman is the last thing in the world he needs. Especially a woman who belongs in Boston, not the rugged Rocky Mountains. He has commitments that don't include a woman. The moment he sees Annie her intoxicating beauty changed him forever. Love has a way of changing the rules.